A TRAITOR'S
FATE

DEREK BIRKS

DEREK BIRKS

This is a work of fiction. Names, characters, places and incidents
are either the product of the author's imagination or are used
fictitiously, and any resemblance to any persons, living or dead, is
entirely coincidental.

Derek Birks asserts the moral right to be identified as
the author of this book

To Janet, who does not write the words but without whom the words would not be written

ACKNOWLEDGMENTS

I would like to acknowledge the debt owed to Rob, for editing the book and in particular for his constructive suggestions and astute observations and also to Katie, for her invaluable help, both technical and creative, with the cover design.

DEREK BIRKS

CONTENTS

DEREK BIRKS

PART ONE: REBELS

DEREK BIRKS

1

13th April 1464 before dawn, outside Bamburgh Castle in Northumberland

Why was he awake? He had neither a warm bed nor wife beside him so at the very least he needed rest. What Ned did not need was to be woken from his precious, fragile sleep before he was good and ready. He half-opened one eye; it was still dark. He lay still and listened but all he could hear was the east wind rattling the roof timbers again. Now he would never get back to sleep.

Something sharp came to rest against his neck and he lifted his hand to give it a rub.

"Lie still or my blade might slip." The gravel voice was thick with a Border accent.

Now Ned was fully awake. "Who are you?" he demanded.

The knife pressed against his throat and the voice growled again. "Never mind who I am. Are you Ned Elder?"

Ned said nothing, his body tensed. If he was given even the smallest chance, he would take it.

The knife pressed harder. "Ned Elder or no?"

"What if I am? Are you going to kill me?" He winced as the blade nicked his skin.

"Might do, if you carry on blathering…"

"I've a hundred men outside in the dunes," said Ned, wondering how his assailant had got past them.

"You've got one youth outside – and he's fast asleep."

"But one shout from me and a dozen men at arms will be in here."

"Aye... if you can shout with my blade in your gullet."

"So be it! I'm Lord Elder - Ned Elder - it's hardly a secret! So if you're going to do it, get on with it!"

He held his breath but the pressure of the blade against his neck eased and then the weapon was abruptly pulled away. He raised himself up cautiously onto his elbows but it was too dark to see more than his visitor's outline.

"How did you get in here?" he asked.

The stranger squatted on the floor opposite him. "I could've got a score of men in," he said.

Ned sat up, making a mental note to do something about that later.

"Well, since you're not here to kill me, what do you want?"

"I'm Rob Hall and my family hold some sway here in the borders."

"I've never heard of the Halls."

"Well, my grandfather was a bastard of the Hall family - but a Hall nonetheless!"

"Good, I'm overjoyed, but I've never heard of you, him or any other Halls - nor do I want to! Now, since you've bothered to wake me up, you must want something - what is it?"

Ned was still irked at how easily the man had found his way past his supposedly alert sentries not to mention his own personal servant and bodyguard, Hal.

"I've brought a message for you from Crag Tower."

"Never heard of Crag Tower either," said Ned, "but you've a damned strange way of delivering a message."

"It had to be done ... privily."

"This is about as privy as it gets around here."

Their voices had risen above a whisper and the sound must have eventually woken Hal for Ned could hear him scrabbling around in the darkness outside, no doubt searching for his tinder box.

Ned shrugged. "Where is it then - this message?"

"It's not written down."

"Why not?"

"I never write anything down!"

"Why not?"

"Why d'you think?"

Ned gave a weary sigh. It was going to be a long, slow morning and it wasn't even dawn yet. He shouldn't be surprised - of course the fellow couldn't write but he had rather assumed his master could.

A torch flared outside and threw its wavering light on Hal as he poked his head through the decayed timbers of the doorway. The young lad started when he saw the stranger and threw a nervous look at Ned. "My lord?"

"Yes Hal, thank you for your concern. As you can see, I'm still alive! Now you can piss off again - oh, but leave us a torch."

"They're damp," muttered Hal as he lit another torch from the first and then shuffled out awkwardly.

Damp? Everything here's damp, thought Ned, as he got his first look at his visitor who now leant casually against the wall. He was probably about his own age though with more hair which had a reddish brown hue in the amber glow of the torchlight. He looked as if he had slept in a ditch but probably no more so than most of his own men.

"I'd be careful leaning against that wall if I were you," he warned.

The 'house' he had commandeered for his base during the siege was the ideal choice because it happened to be the only building left standing in the dunes; but it was only barely standing. The dripping roof timbers were rotten from constant exposure to the cold, wet winds of the north east. A few more months would finish the place off.

Ned pulled up the only two stools in the room and ushered the other man to sit down.

"Well then," he said, "the message?"

The stranger appraised Ned silently for a few moments.

When he did gabble a response Ned turned away in despair.

"For God's sake, slow down! Your speech is hard to follow." He could do without this at the start of his day.

Rob glared at him and then spoke with exaggerated slowness. "Not... where... I... come... from."

"Tell me what news you have that's important enough to wake me before the sun - and at knife point."

Rob took a deep breath and spoke slowly: "I've ridden from the east march -"

"We're in the east march," interrupted Ned.

Rob shook his head. "Will you listen? I've come from the borderlands to the southwest of here and my message comes from Lady Maighread Elder."

Ned began to pay the messenger a little more attention. "I'm guessing the Lady Maighread claims to be related to me in some way?"

The border man nodded, "Aye, she's your cousin... no, well, I think she's your aunt...but by marriage."

Ned didn't know he had an aunt and the suggestion that he did raised a host of questions but he let them lie. "You don't seem too sure. Very well, what's the message, then?"

"I've had to learn it." Rob grinned and launched into a rehearsed speech. "My dear Lord Edward, if you're hearing this then the bearer will have taken many risks to get it to you – please reward his bravery."

Ned groaned aloud. "Spare me the begging and get to the meat of it!"

With another sly grin, Rob continued: "You won't know me: I am Maighread, widow to your father's older brother, Will. I doubt you even know your grandfather, Sir Thomas, but when I learned you were in the north, it was too good a chance to spurn."

Hearing the words of the message recited by the gruff young man, Ned found it almost impossible to call up an image of the woman who had sent it.

"Stop," he said, "I'm already lost. It's too early in the day for riddles."

Rob's cheerful expression changed once more to a resentful glare and Ned relented.

"Come - start again."

Rob sighed and began his speech all over again. Ned listened more carefully this time but soon interrupted once more.

"Sir Thomas Elder, you say? Are you remembering this or just making it up?"

Rob looked aggrieved. "I've no cause to make anything up! It's what she told me to tell you! Well, it's much as she said it ... Do you want me to carry on or not?"

"Yes, yes, in God's name, go on. Let's get it over with!"

"You've cut me off now; I'll need to collect myself again."

Ned reached for his cloak and threw it round his shoulders whilst he waited for Rob to continue his version of Maighread's message.

"Two years ago Sir Thomas took Henry into our household at Crag Tower. Henry's a young man full of malice but Sir Thomas can see no ill in him. I don't trust Henry and I fear for Sir Thomas ... for us all. Your grandfather's a good man; he needs your help. I beg you to come."

Rob came to an abrupt halt.

"Is that it, or have you forgotten the rest?" asked Ned.

"Isn't that enough, then? I had to remember all that!"

Ned studied Rob's face: the young man looked weary now. Ned guessed that taking messages of any kind was not his strength.

"Hal!" he shouted, though he could have whispered and Hal would have heard for he must have been close by the door. He hurried in. "My lord?"

"Find this man some bread and ale... and some cheese - if there's some that still looks like cheese. He's done good service to his mistress."

"She's not my mistress," said Rob gruffly, "she's my sister!"

"Indeed?" said Ned, unable to hide his surprise. Well, it explained why she would trust him with such a personal plea.

"Well Rob Hall, I'm not sure what your sister wants of me," he said. "You say she has fears – but surely, nothing has actually happened."

"Not yet, but you're here now – close by. Henry's a worthless shit. She wants you to stop something happening! You'll be no help once men have died."

Ned was silent for a moment. "Your sister's right about one thing: I know nothing of a grandfather. My father never spoke a word about his family – we assumed they were all dead - and you've told me nothing yet to persuade me different."

"Did you never ask your father? Did you never want to know?" asked Rob.

Ned tried to imagine asking his father such a question - he couldn't. You didn't ask Sir John Elder many questions and now he was no longer there to be asked.

"Where is this Crag Tower?" asked Ned.

"It's in the north Tyne valley - some way south of here."

"Mmm, sounds too far," murmured Ned, "and why all the damned secrecy?"

Rob looked uncomfortable. "Like to keep things close, you know."

Ned nodded but he was unconvinced. It was too early in the day and he needed to clear his head.

"Close, eh? Is there something else I should know?" he asked. "Wait, how did she know I was even here?"

Rob shook his head. "I've just told you what Maighread told me to tell you."

"Well it's not enough - not near enough to make me leave here. I've a siege to keep an eye on."

Rob pulled a face. "You'd better keep a damned close eye then."

Ned glanced up sharply. "What's that supposed to mean?"

"Just what I said … but I'm sure you're already keeping a close eye without me telling you."

Hal walked in with a small wooden platter of food and handed it to Rob.

8

Ned stared at his visitor for a moment and then stood up. "I need some air - or what passes for air in these dunes," he said. "Make sure you're still here when I come back."

He wrapped his cloak more tightly around him and walked out of the house. His legs were still cold and stiff as he set off onto the dunes to see the first light of dawn creep across the northern shore. It usually gave him fresh hope but not this morning.

He looked out to sea where the Farne islands were black specks against the dawn light. Then he turned his gaze north across the dunes towards Bamburgh Castle. It was a brute; there was not a chance they could storm those walls - not without cannon. His esteemed commander, Richard Neville, Earl of Warwick, must have reached the same conclusion for he taken the main army north to the border. That had been a week ago and he'd not seen Warwick since. There had been rumours of a Scottish invasion – but then there were always such rumours and Ned had learned to ignore them. He was still at Bamburgh because Warwick had left him there.

"Go to Northumberland, Ned," King Edward had told him in February, "hunt down these last few dogs of the House of Lancaster for me: Somerset, Ralph Percy. Root them all out."

So he had abandoned his young wife Amelie as she awaited the birth of their first child. He had ridden north with most of his retained men, leaving her, his castle and estates in Yorkshire in the care of a handful of young boys, women and old men.

It was spring in Northumberland but it did not feel much like it for the cold winds and incessant rain had made their lives utterly miserable. His camp was wedged between the sea and the rough track south. To the west, beyond the track, there was a narrow band of trees and more beyond the village to the north. He had started with close to four score fighting men at arms and archers and now they were scattered around him in the pockets of long grass between the sand bars. Clinging doggedly to each of them were the whores and other wretched hangers on that his company had somehow acquired. The result was a sprawling, disease-ridden camp where in a few weeks his disciplined fighting force had been reduced to an unruly band of mud-caked, pus-dripping, shit-squirting cripples.

Yet for all the unrelieved misery of his situation, he knew he could not leave Bamburgh. Even if he accepted that Maighread Elder's call for aid was genuine and that he did have a grandfather still alive, he dared not abandon his post. To provoke the most powerful man in the land would be foolhardy in the extreme. The Earl already detested him, which is why he had left Ned squatting outside Bamburgh to rot to death among the dunes. For Ned's part the loathing was mutual and he could not forgive all that Warwick had done. But besides all that, he already had a family: a wife, two sisters and their young sons and when he left Bamburgh it would be to them that he would go first, not some distant, prospective relative.

He would give the bluff messenger, Rob, a swift response but something else the ruffian had said was starting to gnaw away at him: why had he said: 'keep a damned close eye' on the castle? What did he know? What could he know? He had been on the road - had he seen something?

Ned peered at the castle again; the light had improved a little but he could see nothing new. It looked just as it had done every morning: the flag of the old king, Henry, fluttered above its grey walls and the Percies' banner too and though he could not make out the colours he knew well enough what they were.

Below in the dunes Sir Stephen trudged slowly towards him. He'd grown fond of Stephen since they had first met in the chaos and slaughter of St. Albans. He was steady and reliable, though not afraid to speak his mind – a good man to have beside you if you were in trouble - and trouble seemed to follow Ned around.

"Good morning, my lord," Stephen greeted him breathlessly as he reached the crest of the dune.

"Aye, Stephen, by God's Grace, I truly hope so," replied Ned, "though it's not begun very well."

They stood side by side and Ned told him about Maighread Elder's message. He tried to gauge Stephen's reaction but the knight's expression rarely revealed his thoughts.

"Will you go?" asked Stephen.

"No, of course I won't," replied Ned, "and there's something about that messenger I don't trust."

"Do you think he was warning you?"

"About what: Somerset? The Scots? If it was a warning, it wasn't a very helpful one! We've heard a different story every week and we've yet to find any trace of Somerset, the Scots or anyone else."

"They may be nearer than we thought," said Stephen quietly.

Something in his tone made Ned look up.

"Look!" said Stephen, pointing to the northwest.

Ned stared to the left of the great fortress and the sheer rock upon which it stood. He focussed on the track winding up the gentle rise to the small village of Bamburgh and then scanned the hillside beyond it. His throat suddenly felt very dry and he could feel the hairs on the back of his neck stirring. A pale shaft of sunlight bathed the hillside and glinted on a forest of helmets.

"Could it be Warwick returning?" asked Stephen.

"It could be… but it isn't," said Ned. "They're not riding in, they're charging in. How many men do we have up in the village?"

"About a dozen," said Stephen.

"Well, let's hope St Michael's watching over them!"

"I'll get the men up to the rampart."

"No!" said Ned. At once he was on the move, struggling across the dunes with Stephen close behind him. The sand sucked at every footstep as they tried in vain to run.

"The rampart's as rotten as shit," said Ned. "and they'll ride straight through it. We can't defend this camp against so many; we'll have to make a run for it! Rouse the men at arms and take them out through the sea gate. I'll get the archers to the north side and cover your retreat."

Ned realised that his scouts must have fled the village for a call to arms was already sounding throughout the camp. All about them was the clamour of men being woken in alarm and the shrieks of women thrown roughly aside as the men strove to dress and arm themselves.

"Stop their gabbling and get them mounted!" Ned shouted to Stephen, "Take them along the shore to the south! Don't wait for me. I'll pick a few to stay with me and protect the archers."

"But they'll trap us on the beach!" protested Stephen.

"I doubt it. They must have ridden for an hour or two to get to us so early. You'll have fresh horses; they won't. The tide's out and the sand's firm! Ride hard; then when you've lost them cut across to the old road south. Meet me at the Devil's Burn."

"Where in God's name's that?"

"We camped there on our way here – you must remember: the deep burn by the small wood!"

"That was five weeks ago! We must have crossed a score of burns! Only God knows whether I can find that one!"

"Just go!" urged Ned.

"What about you?"

"I'll take the archers west and meet you later at the burn. Now, for Christ's sake, go!"

Ned left Stephen and dashed into the house. Of Rob Hall there was no sign. He should have foreseen that a man who delivers a message under the cloak of darkness would hardly linger much after dawn - especially if he had an idea what was coming.

He quickly donned his leather jerkin and snatched up his sword. There was no time to arm himself properly.

"Hal!" he bellowed.

Hal appeared at once at the door, an ill-fitting helmet covered most of his fair hair.

"Horsemen on the ridge, lord - and they're not ours!"

"I know. I've seen them and they're well past the ridge. If we don't go now, we won't be going at all!"

Hal tossed him a battered breastplate. "Your horse is saddled, lord!"

"Good! Come on, then!"

Outside, the men at arms were hastily mounting their horses, the beasts neighing and snorting at the abrupt start to their day. Ned swung up into his saddle and stole a glance northwards. The road from the village was choked with riders.

"To horse!" he bellowed at them. "Leave everything - take only your weapons!"

"But what about the women, lord?" asked Hal.

"Leave them," Ned said savagely, "we've no horses for them. They shouldn't be here anyway. I dare say they'll find new friends within the hour. Now, get me Bear, Wulf and the three Johns. Bring them to the north gate – and hurry!"

"But -," Hal was about to protest but the look on Ned's face silenced him and he hurried off.

"Archers to the north gate!" shouted Ned. "Take your mounts - you'll need them soon enough!"

He rode to the gate ahead of them and was horrified to see the enemy horsemen hurtling along the track towards the castle. He'd said that he could not leave Bamburgh; well, he'd be leaving it soon enough now.

A reassuring figure drew calmly alongside him: Bear, an ex-mercenary and a giant of a man who always seemed to have full armour on and carried enough weapons for ten men. Ned had never known his real name but 'Bear' always seemed appropriate enough. With him was Wulf, one of Ned's most promising young swordsmen.

"Hal's on his way, lord," said Wulf, as Ned waited for the archers to form up in a disorderly line in front of them.

"Make haste! Make haste!" he urged them, "every man - three arrows!"

At once they let fly a ragged shower of arrows. Hal arrived

at a canter and Ned was relieved to see the Johns with him, for the three cousins were the most dogged fighters he had in his company.

A second flight of arrows flew into the bright morning sky towards the oncoming riders but Ned saw there would be no time for a third volley; the gap was closing too fast.

"Mount! To horse!" he bellowed but his archers needed no telling for they could see for themselves and many had already unstrung their bows. A wave of helmeted men at arms swept past the bridge to the castle and thundered on towards them down through the low trees that bordered the dunes. This was the archer's worst nightmare: a hasty retreat before a mass of horsemen. Ned stared at the oncoming riders weaving their way through the scrubland that marked the northern edge of his camp. He could pick out clearly the pennants of Percy but also several for Beaufort. So, at last, the Duke of Somerset had come to Bamburgh.

"Ride!" he cried. "Ride for your lives!"

And they did. Ned led them west over the grassy banks of sand, across the track that ran parallel to the shore and on into the fields beyond. The track would be too dangerous; they must escape across country. There was no sign of Stephen or the rest of the men at arms and he prayed that they were already pounding their way south along the beach.

They passed several fleeing whores who screeched at them to stop but Ned swept on past them, his face set hard as stone.

"Don't stop, Hal," he growled, seeing the youth glance back. "All you'll do is get them killed as well as you." He had trodden that path himself at Hal's age, believing that he could always protect the innocent, but now he knew better.

They sped on across the fields. He risked a look back: the enemy horsemen were about a hundred yards behind but they were strung out in a long disordered column. If he could get his archers into some cover, they might be able to do a little damage. To his right a small herd of cattle, survivors of the winter, sheered away at the sudden intrusion to their bare pasture. In front of him lay a string of low hills and at the highest point there was a rocky outcrop. That would have to do.

"Hal!" he shouted, "Take the archers into the rocks on that summit. I want them to slow our friends down a bit!"

Hal flashed past him and took the lead. Ned slowed a little and drew his men at arms closer to him.

"Another hundred yards, lads," he urged, "let's draw them on! Ride on!"

The archers reached the high ground and dismounted to string their bows. Ned prayed they would move fast but Hal was a bright lad and he timed his intervention perfectly, scattering the chasing horsemen when Ned and the others were only thirty yards from the rocks. A volley of arrows swept low over Ned's head and despite himself he ducked then grinned at his folly. The tactic had worked though for the Lancastrian riders were hit hard and soon they sheered away to withdraw out of range. It was a small victory and he knew that would not be the end of it but it bought them a breathing space.

The archers knew their business and were already remounting when Ned's men at arms reached them.

"Good work, lads!" Ned shouted to them. "Now, ride on! Ride on!"

They made good distance and managed to leave the pursuing Lancastrians far behind them but Ned knew they would not give up that easily. They would regroup and come after them. There was band of trees ahead of them and he hoped that the ford he was looking for lay just the other side of the strip of woodland. It seemed to take forever to cover the distance to the tree line and he could feel his horse tiring under him – the poor beast must think it had already worked hard enough.

When they reached the safety of the trees, Ned dismounted and set about deploying his small force. There was no sign of Sir Stephen's main company but it was far too soon yet. He was relieved to find the burn close by as he had hoped. Now they must secure the ford and wait.

"Hal," he ordered, "send a couple of men into the woods and several across the ford to scout ahead - just in case... Then draw up the rest of the archers on the tree line."

Hal wore a pained expression.

"What?" asked Ned. "What is it?"

"We're low on arrows, lord... we left our wagons, supplies, everything," said Hal.

"Aye, of course we did. Well, you'll just have to make every one count, won't you?"

He clapped Hal on the shoulder but he could not ignore their perilous situation. His score of archers were strung out on one side of the long band of trees which ran parallel to the burn behind it. He could cross at the nearby ford whenever he liked and they might even defend it but then Stephen's men at arms, if they had made good their escape along the coast, would not be able to reach him without fighting their way across.

It occurred to him then that if they were outflanked by an attack through the trees he had no defence at all. At that moment, as if he had willed it, one of the scouts ran up. The man was breathless which was not encouraging.

"You've not been gone long!" said Ned. "What is it?"

"There's mounted men at the north end of the woods, lord," the man said.

"Shit!" said Ned to no-one in particular. It was to be expected; the horsemen would not be keen to risk attacking his archers again from the front. "Hal, I'm taking the men at arms into the forest. Hold the line here."

Hal looked at him bleakly. For a moment Ned hesitated, but then he remounted his tired horse.

"Take care, Hal," he murmured and rode off at a trot through the trees.

These were the occasions when he missed Bagot's advice and cursed himself for leaving him at Yoredale. Yet he knew the old soldier's ravaged leg would not have coped with the cold and damp of Bamburgh, let alone the exertions of the day. At least he had the comfort of knowing that Bagot would be keeping Amelie and the others safe. He pictured her, heavily pregnant and glowing with life; but if he knew her at all, she would also be increasingly irritable as the days passed and her confinement edged closer. She had seen both of his sisters through childbirth and now it was her turn. He must do all he could to get back to her before the birth.

Bear reached across and touched his arm and he realised with a jolt that he had let his mind wander, not noticing that the forest track was about to split into several pathways. He could ill afford to divide his few fighting men but he called up the cousins John.

"Follow a trail each," he whispered. "We'll wait here – and be careful."

"We know, lord," affirmed Black quickly. He was named for his shock of black hair, but Ned thought "blunt" would have been more apt since he could not remember him uttering a word that was less than surly.

Ned dismounted and the others followed his lead. John Black set off on foot flanked by his elder cousin, Grey, and his younger cousin, Green. Ned knew that Black had three more cousins named John on the Elder estates but he was relieved that they were still too young to bear arms. The three men soon melted into the light green of the forest, its tight young leaves the tiny harbingers of spring.

Ned had grown up in the forest of Yoredale and he drew meaning from every woodland sound he heard. His three scouts trod with precision yet he heard the rustle of old leaves at their feet and the alarm calls of birds as they passed. Beside him the vast bulk of Bear stood impassively, so still he might have been carved from the forest itself. Beyond Bear, young Wulf fidgeted; he was always fiddling with his sword, his breastplate straps or his short mail coat. When he began tapping his leather scabbard with his hand, Bear shot out a great paw and seized his wrist. He glared at him and then gently released the hand, which Wulf examined ruefully before sensibly keeping it away from his scabbard.

Every now and then there was muffled crack from the forest, but whether it was his own men or others he could not tell. Waiting was shredding his nerves but then a more worrying thought stole into his head and when it did, his blood ran cold. What if the enemy weren't coming through the forest at all? What if they had already passed through or round the forest? What if they were even now circling behind them alongside the burn to cut them off from the ford and trap them in the trees?

He was still brooding on the possibilities when sounds of urgent pursuit came from the forest and the three Johns burst through the trees at speed.

"They're right behind us!" shouted Black. He snatched his reins from Bear and prepared to mount.

Ned seized Black's reins. "How many?"

"We should fall back, lord!" urged Black.

"How many?" repeated Ned.

"At least a dozen - and mounted!" snapped Black.

Ned could hear the thunder of hoof beats through the woods and he let fall the reins.

"Mount up!" he ordered. "We can't face that many here!"

Several drew their swords as they set off. "Sheathe your swords!" he shouted. "Just ride!"

In one swift movement he swung himself up on to his horse and a squeeze of his knees sent the mare plunging back along the forest path after the others. He looked back to see a knot of riders crash through the trees behind them. Black had been wrong: there were more than a dozen, in fact there were more than two dozen - more than enough to rip his six men apart if they caught them and he had little doubt they would be caught.

Horsemen hemmed them in to right and left as they fled back through the trees. The lead riders hastened to cut them off but Bear rode in front swatting aside opponents as if they were no more than annoying flies. Even the most powerful sheered away from him but not before he had casually impaled one of them in the neck with a gentle swing of his poleaxe.

Yet, Ned knew, and they all knew, that only Bear was keeping them alive and even he could not do so for much longer. Nor could they ride much further through the forest or they would bring the Lancastrian horsemen down upon Hal and his lightly armed archers who would be cut to shreds before they could loose a single shaft in anger. No, they had to give the archers a chance, but which way to go?

He could make for the ford but he could not defend the ford without his archers. He needed those damned archers but he was running out of forest and he judged he must only be a mile or so from Hal's position. If Bagot were there he would already be in his ear – do this, lord or do that, lord. But what would the old veteran advise now? He would say what he always said: keep them guessing, do something different. The thought flew into his head and he shouted the command at once.

"Bear! Turn east - out of the trees!"

Bear looked around in surprise, for he knew that in the open faster horses would cut them off all too easily.

"Just do it!" Ned shouted. Communication with the Flemish Bear was always at a simple level and he had no time to explain further. He was relieved when Bear nodded and without pause dragged his sturdy mount to the left. Ned and the others plunged after him packed as close together as they could, branches of hazel and birch whipping at their faces as they galloped through the swathes of bracken.

"Ride on!" he yelled, "ride on! If you pull up, you're dead!"

They burst out of the trees like storm water from a gutter spout and leapt an earth bank to land in the open fields. Ned led them beside the forest edge and they fanned out into a broad line. He risked a quick glance behind and wished he hadn't for there must have been thirty or forty following. He had only a few seconds to work out how to play his hand – and it was a very weak hand.

"Green!" he bellowed.

19

"Lord?" The youth's voice was strained and fearful.

Ned didn't blame him, but he knew Green's horse was the fleetest of them all. "Ride ahead!" he ordered.

"On my own, lord?" the youth cried.

"Yes! Get on ahead! As fast as you can!" repeated Ned. He hoped he would be giving Hal enough time. He turned to the others: "Be ready to turn and fight!"

He was grateful of Bear's firm nod and grin for the others avoided his eyes, their uncertain faces fixed on the ground ahead of them. Their mounts were eating up the yards but they were being steadily caught. Ned desperately sought to get his bearings: surely Hal and the archers must now be close. Green was thirty yards ahead of them now but their opponents were barely ten yards behind. Then he knew where he was: he was certain this was where they had first entered the forest. He prayed that Hal was alert.

Sure enough he heard a shout from amongst the trees ahead. He tried to keep his voice firm and steady. "On my call," he shouted, "wheel to the left and stand against them!"

Then they were there, passing the first of the long drawn out row of archers at the forest's edge.

"An Elder! An Elder!" cried Ned and turned his startled mount around to come to a dead stop facing the oncoming riders. The sudden manoeuvre caused their enemies to hesitate and, before they could resume their charge, arrows thudded into their flank. At such close range, Hal's men could hardly miss for Ned had halted the enemy horsemen right in front of them.

Panic gripped the riders who, having been in full pursuit, now twisted and turned to escape the carnage being wrought by the archers. Ned, desperate to press home his advantage, drew his sword and rode at the nearest group.

"Time to earn your keep, you idle bastards!" he bellowed. "On me, Ned Elder! On me!"

Bear shouted nothing but savaged his way through the front riders with a poleaxe in one hand and a sword in the other. His horse seemed to move wherever he willed and where the colossus rode his opponents backed away in panic. Behind him Wulf and the Johns forced their way through the faltering soldiers and hurled them backwards. Several horses were down, bucking and bleeding. Ned wheeled back to regroup his men and once again the formidable wedge of steel surged into the Lancastrians.

Ned clubbed the nearest rider on the helm and knocked him from the saddle. Then he turned right, gathered pace and punched back through the bewildered pursuers again, weaving through the growing melee of horsemen. Ned was mightily relieved when the core of the enemy company surged away across the fields leaving behind a dozen or so of their dead. The skirmish was over and he hastily took his few men at arms into the trees for he could see at a glance that one or two had taken wounds.

There was a cheer from the archers when Ned rode in and Hal waited with a broad grin on his face.

"Not caught out then?" said Ned cheerfully.

Hal shook his head. "No lord, we heard the horses coming and seeing young John, we knew it was you."

"You did well, Hal," said Ned as he dismounted.

"Aye, but we've not a shaft left between us," he replied.

"Well you'd better go and pick up the ones out in the field," said Ned, "then we'll pull back across the ford. No fires – we've enemies all around us. Leave a few men here to keep watch. Sir Stephen and the others will surely be here soon."

§§§§

But Stephen did not come soon. He did not arrive as night fell nor during the damp hours of darkness and by dawn the following day there was still no sign of him. Ned did not sleep at all. His chilled and weary mind spent all night agonising over the bleak choice that he now faced: should he stay where he was or go in search of his men at arms? Perhaps they were already dead – hacked to pieces on the broad sandy beach south of Bamburgh. Yet…what if they were trapped and needed his help to break out? His force was weak: a score of archers with few arrows and half a dozen men at arms - could they provide enough support to make any difference? He doubted it.

Hal brought him a crust of iron-hard bread. He tried to bite into it but gave up and tossed it back to his squire. "Where did you find that?" he asked.

"Threw it in my bag with a few other things before we left the dunes," replied Hal.

"You could hammer a sword straight with that! Pity you didn't pack a few more men at arms in your bag…"

"Yes, lord." Hal paused uncertainly. "Do you think they're taken?" he asked.

"No, they won't be taken; they'll either be safe or dead. Somerset and Ralph Percy don't have the men to guard prisoners. They'll have to take out every man King Edward sends north to have any chance at all. You know how it was at Towton, Hal. It's just the same now: not much quarter given – not by them, or us."

"What'll we do now, lord?"

"We'll wait a bit longer, Hal. Sir Stephen will do all he can to get to us. We must give him at least another day. Tell the archers – they must defend the ford today. How about arrows?"

"Not enough; barely two per man, lord."

They were camped in a stand of trees beside the ford and to the south of them lay an irregular pattern of open fields and woodland. To the east, the fields looked larger and the cover more sparse. He felt cut adrift in a foreign land: every local man would be for Ralph Percy. He reckoned they must be barely a few miles south of Wooler. The local road south, if he could find it, would offer them the best chance of escaping quickly but it also provided the best chance of discovery.

He badly needed reinforcements but where was the Earl of Warwick, who had left him at Bamburgh in the first place? For all he knew, Warwick was back in Newcastle – but what about his brother, John Neville, Lord Montagu? He was probably even further south at York with his feet up. No, that was unfair: John Neville at least would not rest until he had killed every Percy in the north. He shuddered: what a bitter mess it all was.

It was a stinking wet day and the dripping trees, barely in their spring growth, gave little shelter to his miserable archers. He watched them getting colder and more irritable as they waited in the sodden undergrowth. He could see it in their aggrieved looks and hear it in their low, grumbling voices. Many eyes were downcast, many faces grim. Some had brothers or cousins - and all had friends - amongst the missing men at arms.

So Ned waited for Stephen throughout another day but by nightfall he still had not come. It was Sunday and several times during the evening Ned heard men muttering prayers for their safe deliverance. Whilst his men endured another damp, unhappy night by the ford, he spent it worrying about what he would do next.

At first light many of his men were already awake.

"Will we wait another day, lord?" asked Hal.

"Aye," replied Ned, "one more day and then, whatever happens, we'll leave just before nightfall. We'll aim to travel across some of the open fields through the night and hide out in the forest by day. We've been lucky so far but we daren't wait any longer: we'll have to move on tonight."

"Can we not give them more time?" persisted Hal.

"No, Hal! Understand this: every house we pass, every hamlet, village and town is thick with our enemies. No man here will lift a hand to help us."

Hal nodded; his usually cheerful face was bleak with worry.

So they spent a final anxious day, watching the treeline beyond the ford and listening for sounds of movement. There was a splash in the stream and a dozen men scattered for cover only to re-emerge sheepishly a few moments later when Hal pointed out the dead branch floating by. By mid-afternoon every nerve was taut and ready to snap.

"Lord Elder!" The shout of alarm rang through the trees. Ned looked up to see one of his scouts splashing across the ford towards him. He met him at the water's edge.

"What is it, man?" he demanded.

"Riders coming through the trees where we fought yesterday, lord!" reported the breathless archer.

"Could it be Sir Stephen?" Ned enquired in hope, though he knew the answer.

The archer shook his head.

Ned cursed his weakness: he should have left a few hours earlier. Now they would be forced to defend the ford when the day was almost done. His delay had probably condemned them all.

"Lord?" prompted Hal.

"To arms!" cried Ned. "Hal! Go to each archer. Make sure they know to join the fight when they've spent their arrows."

"They already know, lord," said Hal quietly, but he went anyway.

Ned gathered his few men at arms around him: John Black had been wounded in the thigh and would struggle to defend the ford on foot. Young Wulf seemed eager for the fight – perhaps too eager – how would he cope when blood was spilled all around him? Bear, thank God for Bear, who simply looked ready – as always.

"When the arrows run out we must fill that ford with our bodies," he told them "Black and Grey, you'll be mounted: if any man gets past us you must cut him down."

The two Johns acknowledged their role with a solemn nod and for once John Black had nothing to add, for which Ned was grateful.

"The rest of us will hold the ford on foot: Bear and I in the centre, Wulf, you take the left flank and you, Green, the right. The archers will join us but we must give them a brave lead."

He picked up his worn old breastplate and Bear removed

his gauntlets to help him secure the straps. When he'd fought at Towton he'd worn a full set of plate armour but he had not done so since. Now it was just a short old fashioned mail coat, breastplate and helmet - no man would have thought him a lord.

He watched Black and Grey mount their horses; they moved silently, their faces set in grim resignation.

"Keep out of sight until we know we must fight," he ordered.

The archers crouched low in the bracken; no doubt they could all hear the horsemen now on the other side of the burn. Ned went down on one knee in the damp grass beside Hal and put an arm on his shoulder as the riders approached the crossing point. The archers waited, their grimy faces traced with sweat despite the cold.

"Steady, lads," he breathed. "Wait for them to start across."

The approaching riders seemed in no hurry to cross, stopping at the water's edge to allow their horses to drink. It was then Ned realised that these were not the same men they had fought the day before. These men were clearly unaware of their presence and were probably just intent on camping for the night at the end of a day's ride. All the same, their badges showed they were Percy men. He sighed; it was simply ill fortune that had brought them to the crossing point. He gave a silent prayer that they would water their horses and move on without crossing.

He could feel the tension amongst the archers near him: they had half drawn back their bows ready to shoot and now they were straining to hold their weapons still. The longer the horsemen delayed, the more nervous the archers became.

Ned's prayer went unanswered and finally a few riders began to make their way slowly into the ford. The burn was not very broad and the leading riders were soon halfway across whilst others arrived behind them and waited on the bank. Ned almost groaned out loud for he needed more of them in the water or the ambush would have little effect.

Nevertheless, he could not wait much longer: he patted Hal's shoulder and the youth fired his arrow, which punched through the neck of the first horseman. The man was so close the shaft almost passed right through him, the force of the impact throwing him back over the rump of his horse.

Shouts of alarm rang out as the men crossing tried to turn and warn their fellows. The rest of the bowmen let fly and several other riders were unhorsed or wounded. One of the horses was struck in the side and veered away into the deeper water where his rider wrestled to get him back to the bank. The shallow water of the ford was churned up as riderless horses panicked and hampered others trying to escape from the arrows. Three more men at arms fell but several of the wounded managed to reach the relative safety of the bank.

Ned waited until Hal fired his last arrow and then rose to his feet and drew out his sword.

"Meet them in the middle, lads!" he roared and jumped into the water, knowing that Bear would be by his side. He ran forward and stabbed up at one of the mounted knights; his lunge was fortunate and it caught the man in the groin. The knight screamed knowing the wound would be fatal and blood splashed down onto Ned's helm. He blinked away several spots of blood that had evaded his visor and dragged the wounded man off his mount.

More of the enemy were starting to cross, spurred on by the sight of Ned's few men at arms on foot before them. Bear hacked at one of the riders with his great poleaxe, missed and cut deeply into the horse's neck. Blood spurted from the wound and the animal collapsed to its knees with a shriek, tipping the rider over its head. The dying horse thrashed its hind legs helplessly and its screams unnerved the other horses. The fallen man lay stunned in the cloudy water at Bear's feet and without pause he brought the point of his axe down onto his head, killing him stone dead.

Some men at arms slid from their saddles to lead their mounts away from the bloody frenzy of men and horses; others rode back to the bank to dismount and re-enter the ford on foot. Ned looked to young Wulf on his left: the youth was skilled with a sword for his age. His quick hands reminded Ned of his friend Will, the way he moved with such lightning speed and apparently so little effort. Beyond Bear on the right, John Green was being forced back by one of the few men still mounted. Green looked anything but confident and was barely holding his own.

Ned continued to hack his way forward using his strength to thrust men aside into the deeper water if he could not wound them. A number of the Percy men were down, but more and more men were charging into the ford towards them. His archers cast aside their bows and drew their swords to join the fight with raucous shouts. This was the only moment, Ned knew, when they might break their opponents' nerve for the struggle. Little by little the sky was darkening and if they could push them back and hold the ford until the light failed, they might yet win through.

The narrow ford was filling with men and there were already two horses down, one still thrashing its legs in agony. In the close-quarter melee the combatants struggled to keep to their feet in the writhing chaos. Falling was half way to dying; Ned knew it well for he had fallen before. If he fell now, he and his men would be cut to pieces. So he stabbed and chopped his way forward, intent on keeping his balance. A sword thrust slid across his breastplate but he seized his assailant's arm and sent him reeling back with repeated blows to the face with the hilt of his sword. Then he drew his heavy blade across the man's shoulder knocking him down into the murky stream, but there was no time to stand still.

Seeing his archers as easy meat, some of the men at arms had started to wade through the deeper water on the margins of the ford to outflank them. They must have been cold for his own legs were growing numb even in the shallow ford. All he could do was hope that the archers could hold their ground. He could not help them for the press of men against him was still growing as more men reached the ford.

In that moment he realised with a dull pain in the pit of

his stomach that it was hopeless. They could not defend the ford against so many even till darkness fell; their thin line was buckling against the sheer weight of numbers. Bear and Wulf were still either side of him but he could no longer see young John Green on his right flank. Bear was left to stem the tide almost single handed but even with his strength he could not do so for long. Ned struggled to deflect blow after blow; a sword glanced harmlessly off his helm but it rocked him back. With more room his archers might have darted in to stab at unprotected legs and arms, but in the congested ford it was impossible. He took a pace back and in his heart he knew it would not be the last.

He scarcely had a moment to see what was unfolding around him but to his left John Grey's mount slipped from the ford into the deeper burn where he was surrounded by several men at arms up to their armpits in the water desperately stabbing and thrusting at his legs and torso. He won't last long, thought Ned, as he took another step back. He moved closer to Bear but Wulf beside him was struck on the shoulder and fell into the shallow water. Ned lurched unsteadily towards him and took his arm to raise him up.

"Bear!" he cried and the giant warrior's head turned sharply towards him. At once he abandoned his axe buried in the man before him and snatched from his back a halberd. It was not unlike the poleaxe but the longer handle and broader blade gave him greater reach. He planted his immense boots in the centre of the ford and held the enemy at bay simply by swinging the weapon from side to side with ferocious speed and power. Ned lifted up the wounded Wulf, whose shoulder was bleeding profusely.

"Get back and get that wound bound up!" he ordered, pushing the youth towards the bank. Then he turned breathlessly to help Bear, who had cut such a bloody swathe through their opponents that they now stood off him, no-one wanting to be the next to take him on.

There were just the two of them with Hal and a dozen or so of the archers behind them. If they surrendered the ford now the opposing men at arms would cross, fan out along the bank and encircle them. Ned looked in desperation at the gloomy sky but still night refused to come.

Several of their opponents had found longer weapons with which they now prodded at Bear in the hope of forcing him back. Don't bait the Bear, warned a voice in Ned's head and sure enough Bear took an angry step forward and the press of men ranged against him were forced to give ground or be cut by the halberd. Ned did not blame them as he too had to step aside to evade the lethal sweep of Bear's blade. Even so, it seemed hopeless.

His sword felt heavy in his hand but every nerve in his body urged him to attack. It was who he was, how he was made. At twenty three years of age he was a veteran of King Edward's campaign to win the throne. He acknowledged few peers in battle but who was left now who could join him in the charge? He glanced back at the archers behind him; there was no-one, save for Bear.

He turned to Hal. "Get your archers back across the ford! Head south!"

"No!" shouted Hal.

"If you love your lord, Hal, take the archers away," said Ned.

Bear suddenly thrust his halberd forward into the midriff of the nearest man at arms and in a swift movement let go of the weapon and drew out his heavy battle sword from its worn leather scabbard. Ned stepped forward to stand alongside him and then he launched himself forward, crashing into the first man and chopping his sword down through neck and shoulder.

Now he was in a different place, where there was only blood to spill and bone to shatter. He shut out every thought save one: to wreak havoc before he fell. The ferocious Bear matched him stride for bloody stride and they pressed on relentlessly across the ford, ankle deep in the reddish brown water. They struck at any man they could reach, stepping over the fallen and carelessly crushing flesh and bone beneath their boots. Before Ned knew it he had reached the far side of the ford and the retreating men at arms scrambled back up on to the bank to escape the brutal onslaught. At the bank Ned stopped and watched them run.

Bear slapped his back. "We fought them, lord!" he roared. "We fought them!"

Ned surveyed the bloody carnage they had wrought: he had killed three men and another crawled slowly onto the bank a few yards away. With bitter fascination he watched as the wounded man heaved himself to his knees, leaving a small pool of blood on the muddy grass, and then took a few steps towards the safety of the trees. For no reason he could make sense of, Ned was willing him to get there, but he stumbled and fell. He lay coughing up blood until his pitiful retching ceased and he was still.

A giant hand suddenly gripped his arm. "Lord!" warned Bear, staring ahead.

Coming out of the trees in front of them were a score or so more men at arms and in their midst was a mounted knight. He could not make out the rider's colours but it mattered little who he was now. Their opponents had not been retreating in disorder, they had been reforming and soon they would advance once more and finish off what remained of his small company. He was spent and even the mighty Bear was breathing hard. Hal and the other archers were still in the middle of the ford. Hal ran forward.

"We weren't going to leave you alone, lord," said Hal

Ned shook his head. "Well, we're all dead men now." There was more movement on the edge of the forest ahead. "What do you see Hal?" he asked wearily, for the youth's keen eyes were always sharper than his.

Hal stepped up alongside him and searched the treeline for a moment and then his chin dropped onto his chest. "Oh shit," he said.

"What?" demanded Ned, but he did not need an answer for at that moment the sun, which had been absent all day, made a late appearance low in the western sky. A handful of weak rays fell upon the trees, illuminating a line of at least a dozen archers. Shit, indeed. He looked along the line and his eyes rested again upon the mounted knight.

"Flee, lord!" entreated Hal, seizing his arm.

The knight rapped out a command Ned could not quite make out and then raised his right arm. Bear and Hal were trying to drag him away but he could not tear his gaze from the tall rider. As he stood and watched, the man let fall his arm.

Too late, Ned turned to run. His legs were stiff and numb from the cold water and he had not covered two yards when the arrows struck. One grazed his helmet, another plucked at the bottom of his mail coat. Bear took a shaft in his arm and snapped it off while Hal was hit in the thigh. Ned saw several of his archers go down; their padded jacks unable to stop an arrow at such short range. Silhouetted against the yellow glow of the setting sun they were easy targets for the enemy archers.

They tried to help each other back across the ford as another volley of arrows thudded into them and more of his men were hurled into the water. He felt a blow in the shoulder which knocked him off balance and he rolled down onto one knee. They were helpless he realised: almost every man was hit. He staggered angrily to his feet and turned to face the enemy.

"If Ned Elder must fall," he cried out, "then he's going to fall with arrows in his chest not his back!"

Hal looked on in shock as Ned began walking unsteadily back towards the enemy. Bear glanced down briefly at the three broken shafts that protruded from his arm and legs then he nodded and set off to walk with Ned. Together they raised their swords and embraced death.

DEREK BIRKS

2

11th April morning, on the moorland
above the North Tyne Valley

Henry of Shrewsbury scanned the hillside ahead: a movement caught his eye just below the crest of the hill, black against the snow. The old man was slowing up, not surprising given the trail of blood he was leaving behind him. Damn him - how much more blood could he lose? Why didn't he just give up? He must know he was finished, must feel it by now. Sooner or later he would bleed to death or fall off his horse - either would do.

Henry climbed on after him traversing the snow-covered slope. His horse slipped and slithered with every step – how the wretched beast didn't fall he did not know. When he finally reached the crown of the hill and looked down into the valley on the other side, he saw what he wanted to see: the old man had stopped and dismounted. He grinned then with satisfaction and, sure now of his prey, took his time going down to him. When he faced the old warrior though, he felt a trace of admiration for this man, thirty years older than he, who stood tall despite the fearful leg wound.

He was tempted to stay mounted and simply ride Thomas down but he had waited too long for this moment to let it pass so swiftly. Instead he dropped from his horse in front of Thomas and unsheathed his sword. He could see the strain in the old man's face and already there was blood on the ground, mingled with the powdery snow.

At first the knight regarded him in stony silence and Henry found his stare unnerving.

"Good morning, Sir Thomas," he said.

"I took you in," said Sir Thomas, his voice tired and bitter. "I employed you – no-one else would have you!" He shook his head sadly. "I fed you, treated you as one of my own."

"One of your own?" repeated Henry with a trace of a smile. "More true than you imagine, old man, because I'm closer to you than you think."

"You think I care where your miserable carcass came from?"

"You should do - I'm your grandson."

Thomas laughed at that. "My sons are all dead – long dead, fighting in God-forsaken France, for a God-forsaken king and the only grandson I have is lost to me."

Henry smiled. "You're wrong old man; you've got another grandson: me."

"What, a bastard then? No kin of mine would take up arms against their own. And God knows you've already shared what I have - what more do you want from me?"

"What do I want?" Henry asked softly, "I don't want a share; I want all you've got."

"All I've got?" Thomas laughed again. "All I've got is little enough. Take a look around you – do you see rich fields for planting, or lush pasture? No. Do you see even a lime-washed cottage? No! The hovels round here are built of shit and straw. And where are my folk? Gone - mostly. Oh, you'll find a few but they've been beaten into the ground by border raids and bad harvests. All I have is barren land and a handful of tired souls, Henry. Kill me and that's all you'll get."

Henry smiled again. "Well, it'll serve for now."

"Words, no more of your damned words," said Sir Thomas.

Henry could see that the injured knight was trembling just

with the effort of standing. He'd no more strength to fight.

"There is one fine jewel you have got," said Henry.

"I'll play no more games with you!" retorted Thomas. "Just get on with it."

"Your pretty young granddaughter, my cousin Joan… I've wanted her since the first day I saw her."

Sir Thomas growled in response and raised his sword but Henry's was already fizzing through the air. Thomas tried to parry the blow but he was too slow and Henry's long blade struck his shoulder, knocking him to the ground. He half-raised himself up but another strike followed and the heavy steel slid across his breastplate, cutting into his neck, severing the muscle and slicing through the artery. His body dropped to the ground, blood pumping out onto the snow. A final ripple of life shuddered through him and then he lay still.

Henry frowned. He stood for a while, staring down at the man who had been his master for two years. He supposed he ought to feel elated but he didn't. He lifted up the corpse and thrust it over the saddle on the old knight's horse. A dribble of blood ran down the animal's hindquarter. Henry wiped it away and then he rode back with the body to where Mordeur had finished off the rest of Sir Thomas's household retainers.

"Take the horses, strip the men and leave them," he ordered, "I'm told there are still a few wolves left up here in the Marches – the poor beasts must be hungry. We'll take his body back though – we don't want any doubters."

It must have been twenty miles or more back down the north Tyne valley to Crag Tower and it was almost dark when they reached it. The gates were opened and Henry rode in.

"Reivers!" He shouted loud enough to ensure that all heard him. He expected few would doubt that the usual enemy were to blame. He dismounted in the courtyard and carried the body of Sir Thomas Elder into the Hall. There he laid him out on the long trestle table. The household stared at the corpse in disbelief and then the wailing and weeping began.

§§§§

If the occupants of Crag Tower were in any doubt that night about what would happen in the wake of their old lord's death, they were clear enough the following morning when more of Henry's men arrived and with them a small band of clerks and scribes.

Now, thought Henry, he could begin the real work. He sought out Sir Thomas's widow, Lady Margaret Elder. The old woman received him in her private chamber attended by her daughter-in-law, Lady Maighread, and her granddaughter, Joan. All were suitably attired for mourning and he decided that black made the fifteen year old object of his desire no less alluring. He was a little surprised when, despite the circumstances, Joan favoured him with a smile. He noted Maighread's disapproving frown and grinned to himself: the more she condemned him, the more Joan fell for him. It was perfect; she would only need the slightest encouragement and she would be his.

"My dear Lady Margaret," he began solicitously, "how are you bearing this awful tragedy?"

"She'd bear it better without you!" spat out Maighread.

"Gently, daughter," said Margaret quietly, "there's nothing to reproach Henry for."

But Maighread stood unbending, arms folded firmly across her breast, facing him down. "Murderer," she muttered.

For an instant he lost his temper and took a pace towards her, daring her to challenge him.

"Do you have a question, my lady?" he asked.

"I don't believe it was reivers," she said flatly.

"Well, Sir Thomas is dead," he said, "and now I am your lord."

Maighread stared at him stony-faced. "I don't know what you are, but you're not - and never will be - my lord."

He slapped her face with the back of his gauntlet. It was

so sudden she cried out and stumbled backwards, clutching at the wall-hanging behind her. She put a hand up to her torn face.

Lady Margaret gasped to see the blood well up where slivers of skin had been gouged out but he noticed that Joan was staring in fascination at Maighread's bleeding face.

"Henry?" said Margaret. The old woman was slowly working it all out, he could see.

"New times, new ways, my lady," he replied, "there'll be a few … changes. My Norman friend, Mordeur, is even now … reorganising your household – don't get in his way, please."

He took his cousin's hand. "Joan," he said, "go to your chamber and wait for me there."

Joan looked disappointed but she acquiesced, leaving her grandmother open-mouthed.

"Take more care, Lady Maighread," said Henry, "if you want to keep the rest of your head."

He walked out, leaving them to their shocked outrage. How he would have liked to while away several hours with Joan but that pleasure would have to wait. There was still much to be done if he was to carry through his plans.

What Mordeur's 'reorganisation' meant was that some of the existing incumbents of the household were pushed outside the castle gates to fend for themselves – except for the castle steward whose rash indignation so offended the Frenchman that he threw him off the northwest wall. There was a sheer drop of about fifty feet to the rocky outcrop below upon which Crag Tower stood looking out over the north Tyne valley. Soon only Margaret and Maighread remained and they were imprisoned in the old cells under the castle keep.

Henry awaited Mordeur in what had, until recently, been Sir Thomas's privy chamber.

"Is it done?" he asked.

The Frenchman nodded. "The widow was … unhappy."

"She's a minor nuisance," mused Henry.

"Do you want her to join her steward?"

"No, Mordeur! You are a barbarian at times! We're not animals. It's one thing to blame the husband's death on the border Scots but quite another to hurl his widow from the castle battlements. Anyway, we need to keep her alive – at least until we're secure here. We have her locked up for now – later we'll let the steward have the key."

Mordeur nodded approval. Then it was firmly to business and Henry ushered in two clerks for documents had to be written and letters sent.

"First, and most important," said Henry, "is the letter to Queen Margaret pledging my undying loyalty to King Henry, my offer of help in the rebellion, and so on - stressing my poverty and the need for aid from his hopeful majesty's coffers. I'm also asking for a Commission of Array so that I can raise more men. Second - and this is more delicate so a letter will not do - you will go to Ralph Percy at Bamburgh and offer him my support."

"And what shall I offer – since we have nothing?" asked Mordeur.

"We're simply offering him our support. Sir Thomas Elder was already a Percy client; we're just going to be a little more active. The Scots are still in the game too, Mordeur. There's still much to play for. Just tell him I need money to raise more men."

"You think he'll give you money?" said Mordeur.

"No, not him but you can be sure he's in touch with the Queen too and he may add enough weight to our own plea to persuade her to part with some of the contents of her war chest. When you've done all that, I want you to go south, recruit some more men and take care of that other matter we spoke of."

"What am I promising the recruits?" demanded Mordeur. "We can scarce feed those we do have!"

"Promise of pay, the chance to kill a few Scots and tell them they get to keep all they steal - that usually works. We'll have to shed a little more blood – that'll bring in a profit.

You'd better leave at once. And now, I'm going to pay my long overdue visit to Lady Joan."

"Do you want to see the widow first?" asked Mordeur. "She's been asking to see you."

"Touching," said Henry. "Oh, very well then, I dare say Joan can wait a few minutes more."

Henry left the privy chamber and from the Great Hall descended the steps into the dark void hewn out of the rock beneath. The cells, built during earlier years of border warfare, had not been in use for a generation or more. The whole area smelt foul and the only light was provided by a flickering torch half way along the passage. Water dripped slowly down the green walls and the air was foetid with damp and decay. Henry lifted up the torch from the rusted wall bracket and held it to a door grill illuminating the filthy interior of the cell.

Margaret Elder, still dressed in black, sat with quiet dignity on the rough stool provided for her. She showed little immediate reaction to the sudden flare of light but slowly turned her head in his direction.

"Why have you imprisoned me?" she asked him, her eyes cold. She had a voice like pitted iron. He had forgotten how hard she could be.

"We took you into our household. I was like a mother to you. We trusted you and my lord husband heaped honours upon you."

Henry shrugged. "Not exactly 'heaped' I think – but it wasn't enough. I wanted more and with your poor husband falling prey to reivers… "

She fired him a withering look. "Don't think you can fool me so easily: he wasn't killed by reivers," she said quietly. "I know his blood's on your hands! I can smell the guilt on you. And now I suppose you'll kill this old bird too."

"Let's leave your life in God's mischievous hands, shall we?" said Henry, pulling the torch away and plunging her into darkness once more. Mordeur was right, he thought; she would have to go - deserved to go really. He turned to the cell on the right and waved the torch slowly across the grill. A gobbet of spittle flew out onto his cheek. The indignity stung him and he angrily wiped his face with the back of his hand. Then he slammed the flaming head of the torch onto the grill.

"I had hope for you at first, Maighread, but you're worse than she is!"

Maighread rested her face against the grill, oblivious to the heat from the torch. The dried blood from the blow he had dealt her earlier showed black in the glare.

"You're just a little boy," she said, her voice soft but tight with anger, "too weak to rape me and too scared to kill me."

"Rape you, you dirty Scottish bitch – I wouldn't rape you with a long pike!"

"Then kill me."

"You're going to rot down here for the rest of your days," he said with quiet satisfaction.

"I've sent for Ned Elder!" she spat out.

He was surprised but then, after a moment's thought, unconcerned; the reckoning with Ned would come soon enough whatever Maighread had done.

"'Tis no matter to me, lady, for you won't see him until the pair of you meet in the fires of hell," he said. That was a phrase he hadn't used for a while - his mother had used it to him all too frequently, as he recalled. He turned to go and replaced the torch on the wall.

"You'll both rot down here!" he yelled, as he made his way back along the passage. "You'll hear the door slam behind me and you'll never hear it open again!"

His footsteps echoed along the stone passage and he shut the door before continuing back up the steps into the Great Hall. Then he mounted the stairs to the chamber which Maighread had once shared with his young cousin Joan.

He could scarcely believe that this would be the first time he had ever been alone with her – the bitch Maighread had been with her it seemed every hour, asleep or awake. Yet he had lusted after the girl ever since he had first ridden into

Crag Tower for she had been the first one of his new relatives he had seen. Then she was a girl of thirteen but so achingly beautiful and now, at fifteen, she was ripe fruit and more than ready to be picked. He did not hesitate on the landing but opened the door and strode in.

She was not dressed, or at least she wore only a short linen shift and her feet were bare. She stood by the narrow window opening and a light breeze rippled across the linen. Her hair was long, reaching down almost to the small of her back, a swathe of dark brown against the white linen. She looked at him without emotion, her face pale and round, her red lips slightly parted. The sight of her stole his voice and all he could do was stare. A suspicion of a smile then teased across her lips and she turned her back on him to face the window.

"Did you want something, my lord?" she asked distantly.

Still tongue-tied, he blurted out: "You're not dressed."

It was not at all what he intended to say but something about her manner, let alone her lack of clothing, unnerved him.

"Well, how was I to know you were going to burst in on me, my lord?" she mused.

He shook his head to clear it.

"Do you want something?" she repeated. "Because I don't think it's proper for us to be alone – especially since, as you've said, I'm not dressed. Don't you think Lady Maighread should be here?"

The mention of Maighread's name was like a slap to his face and he swiftly recovered his composure.

"No I don't!" he said, "You can forget your aunt. You won't be seeing her again, so why don't you take off what few clothes you've got on?"

Joan stood very still and then glanced at her bed. Then she turned and looked him in the eye. "And what exactly do I get for that?" she asked.

"You get your life – and my continued good favour," Henry replied tersely.

41

Joan smiled. Somehow, it unsettled him: it was a thin, hard smile, he thought.

"You may or may not be Sir Thomas' grandson, Henry, but I am most certainly his granddaughter. I would have thought that my…legitimacy and your ambition might just be the perfect alliance."

"I could have you whipped to death for speaking to me like that," replied Henry.

"You could, but then I wouldn't be much use to you – either as an ally or a … wife."

He was being forced to reconsider his opinion of his young cousin. Clearly she was not the innocent cipher he had imagined. What's more, she was right: if he married her he would undoubtedly strengthen his claim to the Elder lands.

"Do we have an accord?" she asked.

He reached across and took her hand.

"Yes, I think we do," he replied smoothly.

She nodded, smiled that barely perceptible smile and took his hand to lead him to her bed.

§§§§

He spent less time with Joan than he would have liked over the next few days. She could be infuriatingly aloof at times and his visits to her chamber were all too few. Thus the time passed slowly until, after three days, a letter arrived from Ralph Percy. It told him much and not all of it was welcome. Later the same day Mordeur returned bringing a score more men and a purse of money – but they both knew that it would not be enough.

"Well Mordeur, it seems Ralph Percy and the Duke of Somerset have somehow managed to put an army together. According to Percy they've taken several castles as far south as Hexham but they're desperate for aid. They want to press on to Newcastle but they daren't; they're not sure of the Scots at their back and I don't blame them."

"But the Scots are surely good allies of the old king?" said

Mordeur.

"The Scots, like the rest of us, are just trying to come out of this chaos better off. They've already got a truce with King Edward and it's my guess they'd be glad to see the back of the old King Henry. Edward has sent an escort to take some Scottish envoys to York to talk about a formal peace."

Mordeur shook his head. "Without Scottish help, the Percies are doomed, my lord. Their resources are already meagre. Are you sure you want to take their part?"

"Exactly my thought," said Henry, "which is why we also need a Commission of Array from Edward of York."

Mordeur scoffed. "So you raise your men and wait to decide whether they will fight for York or Lancaster? That will take some doing."

"As long as they've the hope of pay they'll fight for either," said Henry, "but sadly we can't wait that long. Our friend Ralph Percy wants us to do something for the money he's given us."

"What?"

"Ambush York's escort before it gets to the Scots," he replied.

Mordeur grinned. "Ambush - now that makes my Norman heart sing but you can hardly claim to be a loyal supporter of King Edward after such an act."

"Ah, but that will depend on who knows what we've done. We must move fast. Send some reliable men south to track the escort. If we can find it, I might squeeze a few more men out of Percy or Somerset. Now, so much for that - what about the other errand? Did you get to see him?"

"No, he's been up here for weeks but I found someone in Yoredale who might be able – and willing – to help you."

"Who?" demanded Henry.

"Durston…"

"Oswald Durston? Durston's a fool!"

"Yes, Durston's so foolish that while we were being cut to pieces at Towton in '61 he was back at Yoredale with the serving girls keeping him warm!"

Henry grimaced. "How much did you tell him?"

"A little … but I did not mention your name. I said only that you were an enemy of the Elders and I explained what you wanted."

"Hmm. And what did Durston, the great strategist, advise?" inquired Henry with heavy irony.

"He said he could do it."

"Did he? And you believed him?"

"I believe so," Mordeur growled in response. "I only had but a few hours to arrange it. It was the best I could do and my best is usually good enough."

Henry doubted whether Durston was up to the task. He remembered him as a devious and unreliable slob but perhaps such qualities might serve him well.

"Very well, we'll have to wait and see," he said for there were more immediate plans to make.

"I'll send men out to find the escort," said Mordeur.

"Wait." Henry was only now beginning to think through his next moves. "We'll need to take them by surprise."

"Of course, as you said, an ambush."

"Ambush alone won't do. We need some ruse or deception: if I'm to play both hands then we must mask our involvement."

"Yes. Leave it with me, my lord," said Mordeur. "I have some ideas."

Henry nodded and Mordeur hurried out. He is almost purring, thought Henry. The Norman irritated him at times but perhaps it was better not to know exactly what the man had in mind. If he was to gain the prize he wanted he would need every ounce of ruthless devilment that Mordeur could give him.

3

14th April, in Yoredale in Yorkshire

Eleanor Elder stood naked on the ledge staring down at her reflection in the still waters of the pool below. Thank God for a place she could be alone, just herself – well, almost alone. She was twenty years old, unmarried and the mother of a two year old son. For a lady of gentle birth, this should have meant misery but Eleanor cared nothing for such matters. What did cause her some concern was what she saw in the stark reflection: thick, flabby thighs and a slack belly - how far was she now from the lithe, sleek girl she had been only a few years before? She forced herself to look down at her breasts, scarred forever by the slash of a Radcliffe sword. There were other wounds too, any one of which might have killed her, yet here she was, still alive.

Beside her a beck poured its bubbling contents down over a short fall into the pool. It was a bright morning but the air was cool and she had goose pimples all over her. She shivered, took a breath and dived into the pool; it was deep and ice cold. She thrust her way to the surface, lungs gulping for air and gasping from the chill of the water. There was great splash beside her as Becky plunged in and quickly resurfaced.

"It's too cold!" she squealed.

"Child!" retorted Eleanor and reached out a hand to push her head under. Becky struggled free, bobbed up and screeched as she tried to retaliate. They wrestled in the water, giggling and screaming until they stopped, breathless but a little warmer, by the sheer edge of the pool. There they could just reach the stony bottom with their toes. Eleanor suddenly let go of the rock and embraced her servant, laying her forehead against her breast.

"I would have died without you," she said, kissing Becky's cheek, stroking her hair and letting her hands rest on her shoulders.

"When we were twelve, you told me we'd always be together," said Becky.

"I thought so then; but I also thought men were wonderful."

"You had a wonderful man," murmured Becky.

Eleanor cupped Becky's face in her hands. "I did but I don't want another one."

"Just me, your little slave," said Becky with a grin.

"Slave? I don't think so!" protested Eleanor. She kissed Becky lightly on the cheek and hugged her; then she lifted herself up onto the rock, its surface smoothed by her frequent visits. Becky looked up at her smiling, but slowly the smile froze into a puzzled expression. She raised a hand to her mouth, her eyes fixed on the craggy slope behind Eleanor. When Eleanor turned to look she caught only a glimpse of the retreating figure. Then he was gone and if she saw him in a moment's time she would not know him. Becky stood still in the pool, shivering and not just from the cold.

Eleanor reached down and took her hands to lift her out. She wrapped the woollen blanket they had brought around her as she stood on the flat rock. Still naked, she walked up the slope a few yards, feeling the sharp rock graze the soles of her feet. From there she could see the crags that lay around the pool but there was no-one in sight. She returned to the ledge and sat down with Becky, stretching the wool around them both. She supposed the observer must have seen enough of them to whet his appetite.

"Is there nowhere on this estate that we can have peace?" she ground the words out angrily. "Did you see who it was?"

Becky looked at her blankly.

"Becky?" she repeated softly, "did you see him?"

"Oh yes, I saw him; and I thought, I prayed, never to see him again."

"You know him? Who? Who was it?"

"Oswald Durston."

"Who's Oswald Durston?"

"He's a shit, a real shit! He was the Radcliffe's castle bailiff ... in the worst days."

"Ah, I remember and I remember what you told me about him." She recalled her tearful reunion with Becky amid the ashes and rubble of Elder Hall. It had been a bleak time, a bleak and brutal time for both of them. Now she could feel Becky trembling beside her and held her tightly.

"He hurt you, you... and the girls," she said softly.

"Hurt? Aye, he hurt us all, one by one, whenever he pleased – poor Jane and Sarah. When the Radcliffes fell, he fled that night and I didn't think he'd ever dare come back."

Eleanor stared at the water in front of her. "But, if he's a Radcliffe man, why is he back now? The Radcliffes are all dead."

Becky shrugged, but Eleanor could still see the fear in her eyes.

"Come on," she said, "let's get back."

§§§§

They rode back to Yoredale Castle in silence. Eleanor dared not share her thoughts for they were growing darker by the moment, fuelled by a question to which she could find no answer. What would cause a faithful servant of the Radcliffes to return to Yoredale three years after his masters had been killed. As she had told Becky, the Radcliffes were all dead – even Edwina, except... there might be one, one she had glimpsed for the first time in the dark shadows of the nunnery where Edwina had held sway. One who was neither Radcliffe nor Elder, and yet was both. But surely he perished at Towton.

When they reached the castle, the gates were wide open

and the small courtyard beyond was crammed with horses, their riders at ease but harnessed for war nonetheless. They had clearly just ridden in for the castle grooms and stable hands were busy feeding the horses and rubbing them down. It took Eleanor a few moments to recognise the livery worn by the men at arms, but when she saw the yellow lion she was relieved if a little surprised. What, she wondered, was William Hastings, the king's Lord Chamberlain, doing here? Surely he must have known that his friend, her brother Ned, was already in the king's service further north? She thought it unlikely that he had ridden out of his way to enjoy the company of two young mothers and Ned's pregnant wife.

"Are you alright?" she asked Becky.

Becky smiled ruefully. "You know I am. It was just a shock is all."

Eleanor nodded and they dismounted. Becky held out her hand and Eleanor squeezed it gently as she handed over her reins. Becky grinned and led the mounts off to the stables.

Eleanor expected that Hastings would be in the Great Chamber on the first floor with her sister Emma and Ned's wife, Amelie. She glanced down at her clothes: under her cloak she had worn a simple linen smock for ease of undressing at the pool – not really what was required to greet such an illustrious visitor. It was bad enough being ogled surreptitiously by the clutch of men at arms outside. She dashed up the steps into the Hall and then on up to her chamber high in the north east tower. There she changed her clothes and then hurried back down one flight of steps to stand outside the Chamber. She was out of breath and, if she was honest, a little apprehensive. She adjusted her coif so that a little more of her blood-red hair spilled out then she took a deep breath, put on her most extravagant smile and threw the doors open.

Emma and Amelie were sitting together on the long oak bench – she was mildly amused that neither had chosen to occupy, in Ned's absence, the tall French chair in the centre of the room. Will Hastings, standing in front of the

Burgundian tapestries, broke off in mid-sentence and stared at her open-mouthed. She had that effect upon men.

She noted Emma's disapproving frown and her smile broadened even further but one glance at Amelie's drawn face gave her reason enough to be serious.

"It's a pity you weren't here to greet our guest when he arrived," said Emma. And where were you anyway, her cold stare demanded.

"Do you bring news then, my lord?" enquired Eleanor.

Emma answered for him. "Lord Hastings tells us that the Cliffords have retaken their castle at Skipton!"

"Then the Cliffords have more nerve than I thought," said Eleanor.

"And they have no love for the Elders," said Emma, "young Clifford hates us – he believes Ned had a hand in his father's death!"

"Which he most likely did," said Eleanor, with a wry grin.

"It's not amusing, Ellie. Skipton's not far south of here! It's a threat to us!"

"Now I didn't say that, my lady," protested Hastings, "and I didn't say that because it's not true. I'm sure you're not in any real danger. This isn't an uprising; it's just one family seizing back what they've lost."

It was Amelie then who looked him in the eye.

"But my lord, if we are not in danger then why did you ride fifteen miles out of your way to tell us that Skipton had fallen?"

Hastings remained silent and looked in turn at the three young women.

"Ladies, you live in a fortress here and behind these walls you need fear no-one but outside… Well, I would suggest prudence, that's all."

Amelie nodded. "We understand, my lord, and we are grateful for your warning."

"Lady Elder, I must stay no longer," said Hastings. "I've been too long already for I am expected at Middleham before nightfall."

49

"Will you see Ned in the north?" she asked.

"No, I'll be heading south again soon. I sought only to give you a gentle warning but I fear I've made you all uneasy for no good reason."

"Don't reproach yourself, my lord," said Eleanor, "we're accustomed enough to receiving unwelcome news."

"I wish you a safe journey, my lord," said Amelie.

He went to the door but a sudden thought seemed to stop him on the threshold.

"Ladies, you have a powerful friend close by. I know that Ned has fallen out with the Earl of Warwick in the past, but if there is any local trouble, you should send to Middleham. There are men there."

They thanked him warmly, but Eleanor knew they all shared the same thought: Ned would expect them to seek help from the devil himself before they turned to Richard Neville, Earl of Warwick.

Hastings wasted no more time in taking his leave and strode out into the small courtyard, where his escort awaited him impatiently in the freezing cold.

"So, what's to be done?" asked Emma as they watched the column of riders trot out through the gateway.

Eleanor had been in her sister's company for only a few minutes but already Emma had begun to irritate her.

"There's nothing to be done because nothing needs to be done," she said, "but I'll warn the guards to be vigilant in the coming weeks."

She left the others in the Great Hall and went at once in search of Bagot and Gruffydd. In Ned's absence the pair of curmudgeonly old warriors had been left in joint charge of the castle garrison, a generous description of the motley collection of male specimens upon whom their security now depended.

As was often the case, Bagot was elusive, but she eventually found him down in the brew house with Gruffydd, where they seemed to be fulfilling an entirely supervisory role. When she came in Bagot stood up too quickly and teetered a little. Gruffydd chuckled at his comrade's expense.

"Bagot, are you alright?" she asked.

"Oh yes, my Lady, of course. It's just the same old leg complaint," he replied, darting an aggrieved look at Gruffydd.

She knew the dreadful leg injury was genuine, but could not help wondering whether he was unsteady for another reason which was more closely related to the contents of the brew house.

"Can we be of service, my lady?" Gruffydd asked.

Good question, she thought, because, though it pained her to see it, neither of them was getting any younger. Bagot was no longer the battle-scarred lion of several years earlier. His hair was now a straggling grey mane, streaked with a few darker threads and he had become a little stouter since the days when he had saved her brother's life countless times during the feud with the Radcliffes.

And Gruffydd? He had been her own personal hero, her saviour, pulling her from the jaws of death when she was far beyond hope. But now he was an untidy hulk of a man, ravaged by the aches and pains of old age and the unrelenting consumption of ale.

She begrudged neither of them some respite in their twilight years but she wondered whether either would cope if anything serious came of Hastings' concerns. Nevertheless she flashed a confident smile at them for the two men were all they had to rely on if trouble came.

"We've had some news," she said and then explained the reason for Hastings' visit and told them about the reappearance of Oswald Durston.

"Two unconnected events?" asked Bagot.

"Do you think so?" she asked.

"No, I don't," he replied bluntly, "and I never liked or trusted the Cliffords."

"But nothing connects the Cliffords with Durston," said Eleanor.

"Both served the old King Henry," observed Bagot, "though I'll grant you, my lady, it's a bit thin."

Something in Gruffydd's expression led Eleanor to study him more closely, though the light in the brew house was dim. "Is there something else?" she asked them.

The two men exchanged a glance of resignation.

"Wait here if you please, my lady," said Bagot and he went out of the brew house.

She turned to Gruffydd. "Well?" she asked.

"Just something we found yesterday, my lady - didn't think it was worth mentioning then."

Bagot reappeared with a small sack in his hand. It had a dark ugly stain upon it.

"This isn't very pretty, my lady, but I think you'd best see it," said Bagot.

He opened the sack and drew out the body of a small lamb, much of its sparse woollen coat covered with dried blood. Eleanor pulled a face.

"It was found just outside the main gate," said Bagot.

"It's hardly uncommon to find a dead lamb at this time of year," said Eleanor.

Bagot brought the lamb closer for her to see the wound on its neck. "It's had its throat cut," he pointed out.

"So, a sickly lamb has been despatched," she said.

"It looks healthy enough to me," said Gruffydd, "and there's a family dinner under that wool. Why leave it at our gate?"

Eleanor understood what they were implying but she could see nothing to link it to Durston and certainly not the Cliffords.

"We have nothing here," she said, "though I'm glad to see you're already vigilant. We must all be on our guard, especially outside these walls. I want to know at once if you find out anything else. Oh, and Gruffydd… "

"Yes, my lady?"

She hesitated briefly but then her resolve hardened. "Come to me in the late afternoon, in the east gallery by my chamber."

"Lady?" said Gruffydd puzzled by the request.

"And bring your sword; you're going to need it."

She left them without waiting for his response and went back up to her chamber. She slumped down onto her bed gratefully; she was weary, too weary from just running up a few stairs. Young Will toddled in and leant against her, clasping her legs in a warm embrace. She smiled down at him and then bent down to pick him up. He was growing fast, the one fine outcome of the bitter feud and without him she would have surrendered to despair long ago. The boy was a remembrance of her lost love and she lived now for him. His father had never seen him, would never see him.

Sarah ran in breathlessly and sighed with relief when she saw Will in his mother's arms.

"Oh, thank God," she said, "the little one got away from me, lady! Now that he's walking he's getting too quick by half. I turned around and he was gone in a blink!"

Eleanor didn't blame Becky's young cousin, for Will had given her the slip too on more than one occasion.

"Well, we'll all have to watch him more carefully, Sarah," she said and the words suddenly carried more meaning than they would have done a few hours before. "I want you to watch him very carefully," she added.

"Of course, my lady. I'm always careful with him."

"I know, Sarah. I know," she reassured her. Sarah looked a little chastened though she still appeared to be in very high spirits. Eleanor was pleased to see her happy for both she, and her cousin Jane, had suffered more than any children should. If the pair of them could squeeze some small pleasure from their humdrum lives, they richly deserved it.

"You're cheerful today," she said.

She noted the sudden flush in Sarah's cheeks and smiled knowingly. She had forgotten that it was not only young Will who was growing. Sarah and Jane were now in their teens and she remembered enough about her own misspent youth to make a shrewd guess what Sarah's glowing cheeks signified. She made a mental note to discuss it with Becky later. Well, at least someone was free from care, she thought.

§§§§

When Gruffydd duly arrived outside her chamber it was nearly evening and the east gallery was a gloomy place. He looked concerned and she realised with a pang of regret that the poor man had been worried since she left him but when he saw how she was dressed he could not hide a sly smile.

"Do you remember this Lady Eleanor?" she teased him. She wore leather breeches, a long linen shirt and a leather jerkin; her full red hair was uncovered and tied back behind her neck and her feet were bare. In her right hand she gripped the jewelled hilt of a long narrow blade.

Gruffydd shook his head. "Your feet'll get cold, lady," he said.

"Do you see how tight these clothes are on me?" she asked and then grinned, realising that he did not know quite how to reply.

"I've grown fat, Gruffydd," she explained. "Fat, soft and weak. I want you to spar with me … help me get back my sharpness."

"That was a long time ago," the Welshman said, "are you sure, lady?"

"Yes, of course I'm sure – do you ever remember me not being sure!"

"If it's your wish," he conceded reluctantly, "but careful you don't stab me. That blade looks dangerous!"

"It was Will's – one of a pair my father gave him." She felt the tears form unbidden in her eyes. She forced them back angrily and hastened to take her guard with the sword held out in front of her and the point aimed at Gruffydd's chest.

"Are you ready, lady?"

"Yes!" she retorted impatiently. "Can we get started?"

Swiftly he tapped his sword against hers and knocked it from her grasp.

"Gruffydd! You might give me some time!" she snarled at him.

"You said you were ready…"

She snatched up the fallen blade and then leant on it, looking up at him.

"I just want to be able to defend my son… if need be, that's all," she told him in a small voice.

He smiled at her but his eyes were moist. "And so you shall, lady, but before we … spar any more I think we should first relearn what we once knew very well but may have forgotten."

She nodded, took a deep breath and raised her sword.

"Let's look at that guard first – your grip must be a lot firmer."

They spent the next hour rehearsing all the moves that she had learned long before from Will and Ned when they were all a good deal younger and had not a care in the world. It was almost dark when they finished and what she had learned was that she was a long way from where she had been three years before.

After the feud she had been broken in body and spirit but she embraced motherhood and her fierce love for her son saved her. It restored her strength of spirit, her faith in herself but motherhood did nothing to repair her body, torn and ravaged by the scars of the Radcliffe feud. Now she needed her body to be strong for she knew that her love alone would not keep Will alive.

DEREK BIRKS

4

16th April late afternoon, south of

Wooler in Northumberland

Ned forced one aching foot in front of the other, waiting for the end, waiting for the last hail of arrows he would ever see; but no arrows came. They had him cold. Why didn't they finish it? He reached the far bank. Still no arrows came. Then he heard the first cries of anger and alarm and prepared once more for death. He peered into the shadows at the tree line ahead. Was there a tangle of horses and men there? What were the fools doing? Suddenly one of the horsemen rode straight at him. He tensed, ready to throw all he had left into one final blow but the rider pulled up short and dismounted before Ned had the chance to strike.

"You two look dreadful," said Stephen with a grim smile.

Ned let his sword fall and dropped to his knees. At once Stephen bent down beside him.

"You … took your time," slurred Ned as he fell forward into Stephen's arms. Soon a host of willing hands raised him up and more of Stephen's men hurried to help the rest of their wounded comrades who were still in the ford.

Ned shook his head. "What happened?" he asked.

"We hit them hard," said Stephen, "and they've gone - at least for now."

"And their archers?"

"We cut them down. I'm afraid not many will ever pull a bow again." Stephen's voice carried a genuine regret, for he had never been a warrior by nature.

"Did you see who led them?" demanded Ned, remembering the mounted knight.

"I can't be sure but I think it was the Duke," replied Stephen. "I've never seen him so I'm only going by his livery – the portcullis is pretty well known."

"Somerset? Shit, I couldn't see his colours in the trees."

"Yes, the blue and white, but you were hardly in a position to do anything about it," said Stephen gently.

"Aye, he can wait for now," muttered Ned, "because we need to get moving."

§§§§

It was black as pitch by the time Stephen's men had patched up the wounded and buried the dead. Ned thought their losses catastrophic: half his archers slain and the rest could barely stand. Among his small group of men at arms all had sustained wounds and for two, they had been fatal. Green had been cut down and killed at the ford and his cousin Grey had succumbed to his many wounds soon after the fighting ended. Ned made light of his own shoulder wound but took their deaths to heart.

"Young Green's mother has lost all her sons now," he said bitterly. "Two fell with their father at Towton, and the youngest of a fever last winter. Now she has three young daughters and no-one to work the land."

"Yes, but given the way we were caught at Bamburgh, this is a better outcome than we dared hope," said Stephen, "it could have been much worse!"

"Not for her," said Ned. "I gave the archers the harder task. I wanted you to get the men at arms out and you did. There had to be a price…and we paid it."

"But you were right," Stephen insisted, "Somerset's mounts were already tired – they must have ridden for hours to surprise us Bamburgh. We outran them along the sands though they pursued us south for the whole day. By evening our own horses were spent and we had to rest. In the morning there was no sign of them and now we know why: they'd gone north after you. Trouble was by then we were utterly lost. It's taken us two days to find you. If only I'd reached you sooner, we could have saved some lives."

"Whether I was right or wrong won't make any difference to Widow Green, Stephen. Come on, we'd better move for they may come at us again."

"Ned, we're all exhausted, with so many men wounded. We must rest, at least tonight."

Ned shrugged wearily. "I suppose a few more hours will help. We'll leave at dawn then."

They did not leave at dawn; in fact the sun was high in the sky before they set off. They followed the burn south for a mile or two until it forked, then headed west along the bank of the smaller stream. Ned had no local men serving with him and any course he chose might get them hopelessly lost deep in Percy territory. All he knew was that the further south and west he could get, the nearer to his allies he would be. Here in the Percy heartland from Bamburgh in the north to the great castle of Alnwick in the south he would meet hostile forces at every turn. He had to find Warwick – not that he was keen to – but Warwick was the king's commander in the north and Ned knew he had no option but to work with him. The knowledge that the Duke of Somerset, a key ally of the old king, was nearby did little to ease his fears.

They made slow progress, keeping to forested tracks where they could, anxious not to draw any attention as they passed near small villages. In such territory even a labourer in the fields might report their presence to his lord. Towards the end of the day, thick, low cloud rolled in from the west, drawing a dark shroud over the whole landscape. As the cloud dropped lower and formed a light mist around them, all they could do was ride on blindly beside the meandering stream they had followed most of the day. At least, Ned thought, it would cloak their movement from local eyes.

"The men are hungry," said Stephen, riding beside him.

Ned sighed. "I know. They're hungry, hurting and sodding annoyed with life. So am I!"

"We should find somewhere to rest for the night."

"I know that too," Ned snapped and immediately regretted his sharp response. Stephen did not deserve it.

"At least this fog is a shield for us," said Stephen, "with God's help it'll still be here in the morning."

Ned forced a smile. "You've a touching faith in the Lord's willingness to help," he murmured. He turned behind and found Hal, as always, watching his back.

"How's the leg, Hal?" he asked.

"Fine, lord," replied Hal, straightening his back to sit more upright in the saddle. The youth looked chilled and exhausted but so were they all.

"Good," said Ned. "You can ride ahead then, ahead of the scouts; see if you can find somewhere we can camp for a few hours."

Hal nodded and pushed his mount past them.

"And Hal," Ned added, as the young archer disappeared into the mist ahead.

"Yes, lord?"

"Don't get lost – and don't fall into the stream!"

Hal was already out of sight but his words crept back to them: "I'll do my best, lord."

"Somerset and Percy will never find us in this," remarked Stephen.

"Thank God one of us can see good tidings in any of this," said Ned. The cold seemed to make his wounds ache more but he knew that his were nothing compared to those suffered by some of the others. He glanced behind at Bear and began to wonder if he had imagined the big man's injuries for he showed no sign of discomfort at all.

Hal emerged suddenly from the damp mist ahead and he was not alone.

"You've only just gone!" protested Ned. "And who's that

with you?" But he knew even before the question was out. Rob Hall urged his horse towards Ned.

"You? Take his sword, Hal!"

"I came to you willingly!" protested Rob.

"Take his sword!"

Rob drew out his weapon and handed it hilt first to Hal. Ned's anger burst upon his prisoner. "You left us to be slaughtered at Bamburgh! You let your traitorous friends fall upon us! Bind his hands, Hal."

"I did no such thing!" retorted Rob, as Hal tied his hands. "I gave you a warning - I told you to keep a sharp eye!"

"Aye, when there was no time to heed it! You could have told me sooner!"

Rob looked away. "I've ridden with some of those men – some are kin! I couldn't just betray them."

"Well I trust I've despatched a few of them!" declared Ned. "I should kill you now, here."

Rob dropped his head. "Just now," he said, "it might be a mercy."

Ned stared at him thoughtfully: he looked dreadful. Had he been involved in the skirmishes at the ford?

"I ought to kill you," repeated Ned, but they both knew he would not.

"How did you find us? Did you track us?"

Rob gave him a rueful smile. "Track you? I wasn't even looking for you."

"You expect me to believe that - from a man who crossed the county to find me at Bamburgh?"

"Just now, I don't care whether you believe me or not."

Ned was perplexed by the change in Rob. The brash self-confidence had gone; the lad seemed only weary now.

"Lord," said Stephen, "we should keep moving."

"There's a village ahead, lord," said Hal. "I was about to return to tell you when he rode up."

"How far?" Ned asked, at once alert.

"Half a mile at most, we're almost there. I didn't notice till I passed the mill."

"God's mercy!" breathed Ned. His first thought was to make a hasty retreat but to do so meant simply retracing their path along the stream – and then what? They would be heading back towards the Lancastrians who had attacked them earlier.

"If you want my advice -" began Rob.

"I don't!" said Ned.

"- I'd ride on, as far from that village as you can."

Ned ignored him. "Is it quiet?" he asked Hal.

"As a graveyard, lord."

Not a very encouraging comparison, thought Ned.

"I'm giving you enough warning this time," growled Rob.

Ned hesitated. It made sense to avoid contact with Percy tenants if he could. If the village was sleeping peacefully they might continue through it with little disturbance. If they did wake anyone, they should be gone before folk took any notice of who they were.

"Pass the word, Hal: no noise," he ordered.

"You're making a mistake," murmured Rob.

Ned glared at him and rode on. "Keep a close eye on our slippery friend, Stephen."

He hoped they might ghost by the village on the riverbank but there was a near impenetrable thicket down to the water's edge which forced them to head into the village itself. He found he was holding his breath as they reached the small green heart of the settlement, expecting dogs to bark or perhaps geese to raise a strident alarm but there was nothing. They walked their horses past the village church and something struck him as odd but he could not think what. All was quiet across the village – could it be too quiet? He had survived this long by following his instincts but perhaps he was losing his grip. Still, it didn't feel quite right.

On the far edge of the green there was a large single storey building that seemed to have been converted into a tavern of some sort. It was not unusual and he had seen it at Bamburgh village too where the locals aimed to profit from the large numbers of soldiers traipsing past their homes. He was surprised though to find a tavern in such a small village. He came to a halt outside thinking of his tired and hungry men; there would be food and ale inside. But could they defend the tavern if they were trapped there? He suspected not but they had to stop somewhere - and soon.

Rob suddenly rode up alongside him. "Lord Elder," he pleaded, "ride on. Don't go in there."

Ned pushed him away. "Hold your lying tongue!"

"Stephen, tell the men to stay mounted – and silent!" he ordered. "Then find me four reliable men and join me at the tavern door."

He dismounted and threw his reins to Hal. He was surprised they had not disturbed a soul so far. Even though they had tried to be quiet, it was impossible with so many of them. The horses alone always made some noise yet it seemed the village was content to sleep on.

Stephen came up with several men at arms.

"You're going to search the village," Ned told them softly. "Pair yourselves up: one pair goes to the east end and the other to the west end. Move quietly and don't get lost. And don't touch anything. Just look and listen. I want to know how many cottages there are... and don't open any doors, however tempting. I don't want villagers running about in panic. Is that clear?"

"Aye, lord," they said as one.

"Good. Come back to me here." He watched them set off stealthily into the night.

"Cottages?" Stephen queried.

"I want to know roughly how many men there might be here."

"Lord ..."

"What?" asked Ned.

"Perhaps Rob's right. We should just ride on. I don't like the feel of the place - and we've enough troubles of our own."

"You'd better say a prayer then, Stephen," he muttered, "for I don't like the feel of it either. I'm not sure what I'm doing but we're going to take a look at this tavern. It's a strange tavern that throws out no noise and very little light, don't you think?"

The tavern was hardly worthy of the name: a large rambling cottage with a simple sign outside which proclaimed only that it sold ale. Ned sent one of his men at arms around the back and waited.

"No way out there," the man reported when he returned.

"Very well, let's take a look," said Ned.

Carefully he tried the latch that held the door shut. It was a standard round handled drop latch but, when he turned it, he was surprised that the door opened. He expected it to be barred from the inside – but it wasn't. One of its hinges must have been rusty for it screeched as he swung it slowly open. He winced and held it half open, standing motionless and waiting for some reaction from within. There was only silence but at once the smell struck him. The last time he'd encountered the sickly stench had been several years before amid a sea of butchered bodies on the field of Towton. It brought back bitter, unwelcome memories.

He paused on the threshold and drew out his long dagger.

"Stephen, come with me – the rest of you wait here," he whispered.

He pushed the door fully open and took a step inside. It was not completely dark. There were a few guttering tallow stubs which gave several troubled pools of light in the large chamber. He stood for a while, eyes adjusting to the darkness whilst he struggled to make sense of what little he could see.

"There's some blood been spilled in here, Stephen," he said, his voice a whisper.

They stared about them in disbelief. There must have been fifteen to twenty bodies: several were women, but a dozen or more were men at arms. They began to walk from one to another, looking for signs of life.

"What have we walked into?" said Ned.

"A tavern brawl?" suggested Stephen, bending to pick up a fallen stool.

"Leave it where it is!" snapped Ned.

"Sorry, lord," mumbled Stephen.

"Spend your time looking at how these folk died," said Ned. "This was no brawl."

They were no strangers to the most brutal, pitiless wounds of battle, but this was different: it was cold and clinical. The first man he examined had a broad puncture wound ripped in his neck and must have quickly bled to death without moving a muscle. He noticed at once that hardly any man seemed to have tried to defend himself. They must have been taken very swiftly, for these men were no green recruits; they had the look of seasoned veterans. A few had defensive wounds, their hands raised in a vain attempt to protect themselves; others had been struck in the back. There were few knife or club wounds, which would have been commonplace in a brawl; instead, almost every wound was from a heavy battlefield weapon - sword and poleaxe mostly. These men had been slaughtered - and not too long ago.

"In the name of God…" breathed Stephen.

"This was an execution," said Ned, "and I doubt it was carried out in God's name."

"We should just walk out and shut the door on it," whispered Stephen, "I told you: whatever happened here has got nothing to do with us."

Ned stood staring grimly at the bloody tableau.

Stephen let out a long sigh. "But we're not going to, are we?" he said.

"No, we're not. I want a closer look at this."

"But it's not our concern!" persisted Stephen.

"Isn't it?" asked Ned. "A bloody massacre in a Percy village? Whoever did it must be on our side and I don't much like that."

"Yes, it's bloody and you know I abhor it more than any man but will you risk all of your men to find out more?"

"I saw enough of this mindless butchery after Towton," said Ned, "and, at the very least, Stephen, I want to know who did this. Besides, the men need to rest somewhere and it may as well be here. If there's a morsel of food to be found, it's as likely to be here as anywhere."

Stephen shrugged. Ned could see he didn't like it, but he could not leave it. He had to know. He made his way outside and looked up at Rob, still mounted.

"You knew," said Ned.

Rob shook his head. "I don't know exactly what you've found, but I've an idea."

Two of Ned's scouts returned. "Well?" he demanded briskly.

"We went to the west end of the village, my lord," began one of them.

"I know where I sent you. What did you find?"

"Two dead dogs, my lord."

"How dead?"

"One skewered by an arrow and another with its throat cut," the man explained.

"And what else?" asked Ned.

"Well, nothing else; it was a bit odd. There was nobody around, not even in the cottage."

Ned stared at them wearily for a moment. "I told you not to open any doors."

"But the door was already open, lord," replied the man hastily. "Wide open!"

"And the house was empty?"

"Aye, lord."

"Signs of trouble?"

"No, lord."

"Very well." A sudden thought occurred to him. "Was there any bread there or other vittles'?"

The two men exchanged a swift glance. "There might have been," said one awkwardly.

Ned frowned. "Take Hal with you – if he can still walk – and gather up what you can, if you've left any that is…"

The men at arms he had sent to the east of the village told him a similar story of abandoned cottages. At once he told the rest of his men to dismount and make camp on the village green; then he posted men on watch at the outskirts of the village to warn him of any approach.

"Be at ease," he told them, "but watchful. Remember where we are."

"Not that we know where we are..." observed Stephen quietly.

Ned tried to suppress a grim smile and failed. "Only too true," he admitted.

"The village is called Alnham," said Rob.

Ned looked at him with cold eyes. "I'll get to you shortly - then you can tell me what you know about this."

The low cloud still pressed in on them and the damp air covered everything with fine droplets of water. They needed to dry out. They would need to be careful but in the heart of a village they could get a fire going and any smoke would not attract curiosity from outside.

"Stephen, no-one's to go into that tavern - except to look for some food. In the morning we'll take another look."

"If we must, lord," said Stephen.

One of those he had sent to watch the track from the east ran up.

"What is it? Are there men on their way?" demanded Ned.

"No, lord," said the man, "It's just something odd."

"What is it, man?"

"There's some noise from the church, lord."

"What sort of noise?"

"Sounds like ...voices, lord."

Ned suddenly felt a knot in the pit of his stomach. Something about that church had drawn his fleeting attention as they had ridden past.

"Stephen, stay here. Keep your eyes open - and watch him," he said, pointing to Rob. "Bear, come with me - and you," he barked at the messenger. "Someone light me a torch - there's candles still lit in the tavern!"

The church was only a hundred yards away, just off the green. Ned heard the voices long before he reached it.

"People are praying in there, you fool!" he said. "That

explains where everyone is - and I'm not surprised, having seen the tavern…"

The west end of the church had only a narrow rounded window between its two buttresses and nothing could be seen within. When they reached the church Hal brought up a torch and they found to their surprise that the door was barred in makeshift fashion from the outside: two great timbers had been hammered across it.

"This gets worse," said Ned. "Get it open, Bear."

At the sound of his voice, the noise from within quickly subsided. Bear tried to prise off the timbers but even he could not shift them. Then he reached over his shoulder and took out his pole axe. Using it as a lever he managed to inch one of the timbers slowly off the door. Then he tackled the other and tossed it casually aside. Whilst he had been working, there had been not a sound from inside the church. But when he stopped, the prayers began again and Ned threw the door wide open.

"Light, Hal - if you please!" Hal held the flaming torch aloft.

Crammed inside the nave there must have been thirty people, mostly women and children, though there were a few older men too. Many sat on the floor, huddled together before the altar, under the great round arch of the chancel. At first they blinked at the light then looked at Ned with relief. Several stood up and started to move towards the open door, but then they faltered and shrank back again.

A young woman at the front carried a babe in arms. Her eyes blazed at Ned, she stabbed her finger at him and spat at his feet. "Murderer!" she screamed.

But one of the older women pushed her aside and cried "Mercy, lord!"

Several others took up the cry, "Mercy, lord! Have pity on us! Let us go to our homes!"

Ned was utterly bewildered by their reaction.

"But… you are free to go to your homes!" he shouted. This was greeted by sullen silence and he knew mistrust when he saw it on so many troubled faces.

"I am Lord Elder - you've nothing to fear from me," he said.

"We know what you are and we know what you've done," a grey-haired old man ground out the words. "We know your badge well enough now, even if we didn't before - and none here will ever forget it!"

"My badge is my father's badge and I wear it with honour," declared Ned, "and I don't make war on women and children."

"It was your men who did their bloody work at the tavern and locked us up to start with!" declared the young woman angrily.

"I - and my men - have only just arrived here," he replied stiffly, "and we could have ridden on but - and only God knows why - I decided to stop. We found the men slaughtered in your tavern, dogs with their throats cut and now all of you trapped in here. That's all I know about what's happened here. Now either go to your homes or help me discover what has been done."

They looked shocked and confused: a few stared at him with hope in their eyes, for them perhaps his words had rung true but others remained suspicious and angry.

"If you don't trust me, then stay. It's your church. Either way you'll come to no harm from my men. If anyone wants to tell me what happened, I'll be at the tavern."

He turned on his heel and left them. As he returned to the other end of the green, he cast a glance behind him and saw shadowy figures leaving the church and scurrying back to their homes in the dark.

Outside the tavern his men had made camp and the smoke of their cook fire mingled with the mist stinging his eyes. He found Stephen standing alone, awaiting his return.

"You found something worth eating then," Ned observed.

"Some bread – not too stale – quite a lot of cheese and a great deal of salt! The lads are trying to cook up a potage with what little else they've found. But what happened at the church?"

"We found the villagers…"

"And were they were pleased to see you?"

"No, they weren't."

Most of the villagers had disappeared into the night but the grey-haired man and his elderly wife came to find Ned.

"Do you know what happened?" he asked them.

"Aye, some," the man replied. "The men who lie in the tavern came two days ago. They told us they were just passing through and if we gave them some bread, cheese and ale they would do us no harm. They slept in the tavern."

"Do you know who they were?" asked Ned.

"No. And we didn't ask. Folk come through here on the old salters' track. It's usually merchants going north or drovers coming south; but not companies of armed men - at least it didn't use to be…"

"But these men were not merchants or drovers," said Ned.

"No, they were men at arms but they wore black and red so at first most of us thought they were Percy men."

"But they weren't?" prompted Ned.

"No, they weren't. They weren't wearing Percy badges."

"So… Neville men?"

The old man nodded. "Aye, ragged staff and bear."

"Warwick," breathed Ned.

"So I believe."

In the last few moments things had just taken a turn for the worse: Warwick's men, it would be Warwick. It had to be his men. What were they doing in Alnham? Perhaps a scouting party…

The old man seemed to sense his disquiet.

"Carry on," urged Ned. "Did they keep their word?"

"Aye, they did but they decided to stay another day. Tom at the tavern was licking his lips but his profit was short-lived, God rest him."

"So, what happened?" asked Ned.

"Late this afternoon," said the old man, "it happened before we knew it. It might have been afternoon but it was cold and dark. Bess and I were just thinking about an early supper, a bit of bread and cheese – not that there was much left – when a couple of rogues burst into the cottage. Their swords were drawn and they bade us keep quiet."

"And?" Ned's tiredness made him impatient.

"We kept quiet!"

"Aye, but what then?"

"One of them stayed with us and the other went into the tavern with a host of others. The cries were terrible ... I've lived in this place all my life and, dear Lord, I've not seen or heard the like here."

"Do you know who they were?"

The old man paused and put an arm around his wife's shoulders before continuing.

"When they came out, their swords and axes were bright with blood and not a sound came from Tom's tavern. They all wore badges." He pointed to Ned's pale blue badge. "They all wore that badge…"

At first Ned was too shocked to reply but at least it explained the reaction at the church.

He had already heard more than he wanted but he had to know all.

"What then?" he asked.

"I don't think they knew what to do with us – if we'd been fewer, they'd have killed us straight. So they gathered us all in the church - but you know that."

"Did they say they'd come back?"

The man looked Ned in the eye. "They weren't coming back."

"And you're sure they all wore my badge; you could have been mistaken," said Ned.

The old man seemed to consider for a moment before replying.

"When I was a lad, I served for a time in the stables at Alnwick Castle. I saw all sorts of folk come and go – saw quite a few liveries, surcoats, badges and all sorts. Saw a lot of black and red, most of the Percy badges I should say and a few of the Nevilles – I've forgotten what all the emblems on them meant, deer, boars, and so on. I didn't often see Tom Elder's men but I can recall their badge because it was a different colour - pale blue, just like yours. You said your name was Elder but you're too young to be his son, aren't you?"

"This is Lord Elder, man," interrupted Stephen sharply with the emphasis on Ned's title.

"I meant no offence, my lord," said the old man but when Ned met his eyes he did not look away. Ned smiled. "You've no fear of speaking what's on your mind, have you?" he said.

"At my age? I've seen enough to speak my mind. Anyway, you told us you'd do us no harm, my lord."

"So I did," replied Ned, "and I meant it. My name is Elder, but I know little or nothing about Sir Thomas. I didn't even know our badges were similar."

"They're not similar, they're the same. I didn't remember the badge till we were in the church and I had time to think about it. I seem to recall folk thought well of Sir Thomas. Of course he was a Percy man and the dead men were Nevilles, but even so…You're not a Percy man are you?" said the old man.

"No," admitted Ned.

"And you've fought Percy men?"

"I have," agreed Ned.

"I am a Percy man and our young men are serving now with the Percy Earl of Northumberland… but I thank you, my lord, for setting us free."

Ned looked at the couple thoughtfully. "Can I trust you not to send word to Northumberland that I'm here?" he asked

The old man hesitated.

"All I want to do," said Ned, "is go south without losing any more lives."

"Good enough, my lord," replied the old man and he

took his wife's arm to lead her back to their cottage.

"What do you think we should do next?" asked Stephen.

"Stephen, my shoulder aches, I'm dog tired and I must get some rest before I do anything else. There's as much mist inside my head as out! Check the sentries and wake me if anything happens."

He trudged off to lie down outside the tavern where many of his men had settled to rest their weary legs and wounds. Hal limped up to him and handed him a thick woollen blanket.

"From the tavern, lord," he said, "there's no blood on this one…"

Ned smiled at him and took it willingly. He did not expect to get much sleep. He expected to lie awake fretting but when he lay down and wrapped the blanket around him, he fell asleep at once.

§§§§

He was roughly shaken awake and rolled unsteadily onto his knees.

"What?" he mumbled, half asleep. "Give me a chance to sleep, damn you!"

"Lord," said Hal gently, "you've slept all morning."

Ned regarded his servant suspiciously for a moment and then finally came to and made sense of what Hal had said.

"All morning? Why didn't you wake me sooner?" he demanded crossly, tossing his blanket at Hal. He'd woken with a stiff neck and it did not improve his humour. The air was still damp and if anything the mist was thicker. It must be past noon he thought but there was only a dull glow where the sun should have been.

"Stephen!" he shouted and the knight hurried to his side.

"Time we had a closer look in the tavern," he said, "but first let's have the bodies out."

They brought out the corpses one by one and laid them in two neat rows on the grass beside the tavern. There were more than he had realised: sixteen men, of whom all but two appeared to be men at arms, and five women.

Ned walked slowly along the rows with Stephen.

"This one must be the tavern keeper," said Stephen, "judging by his clothes, and the other fellow's a labourer – look at his hands."

"What do you notice about the men at arms?" asked Ned.

"You mean apart from the obvious?"

"Aye, apart from the large holes in them," said Ned.

"No weapons? No plate? No helms?"

"And? Look more carefully."

"Ah," said Stephen, shaking his head, "no badges…they've been ripped off."

"You can see here some threads of red still remain." Ned pointed to one of the padded jacks. "We know they're Warwick's men."

"The women look as if they were serving girls," said Stephen. "The owner's wife perhaps and four others – that seems too many for such a small place."

"By the look of them I doubt they were just serving bread and ale," said Ned, "but this isn't getting us very far."

"Master Hall says we're in Alnham, but where the hell is Alnham?" asked Stephen.

"God only knows," said Ned, shaking his head, "but we do know it's on the old salters' route from the coast."

"Does that help us?"

"No, not really - at least not at the moment. Christ, what a mess!"

"This is none of our doing," Stephen reminded him.

"If you were the Earl of Warwick and you heard that men wearing my badge slaughtered your men, what would you think?"

"Oh…"

"Exactly. Get them covered - some linen if you can find some - and get the priest. They need a decent burial. Time I had a long talk with Rob. I'll take him into the tavern."

Stephen looked doubtful. "Are you sure?"

Ned made no reply, but just waved him off and leant

against the tavern wall. His mind was so befuddled with conflicting thoughts he did not know what to think. He stared again at the line of bodies and then moved slowly into the tavern. They had opened the shutters and the deathly odour had dissipated a little but a trace of it was enough to remind him what they had found there. It was dark inside and he reckoned more mist came through the window than daylight.

He chose a table and swept the debris off it with one swipe of his hand. Then he found two stools and sat down on one. Stephen escorted Rob in and Ned pointed their prisoner to the other stool. Before he sat down the border man cast his eyes around the room, there was still dried blood everywhere. He looked sufficiently shocked, thought Ned.

"Wait outside please, Stephen," Ned ordered. Stephen looked put out and stalked away without another word.

"What were you doing here?" he asked. "And don't tell me you were bringing me another message."

"No, there'll be no more messages," said Rob. "It's too late for that now."

"Why too late?"

"What do you care?" asked Rob. "You didn't seem much interested before."

"Go on. Spit it out," said Ned.

Rob met his stare with dark, troubled eyes.

"It's too late because Henry's already made his move: old Sir Thomas is dead, his castle taken and, for all I know, my sister's dead too."

"When?"

"Soon after I left her. I was a poor messenger. I took too long. If I'd moved faster, been less distracted, we might have saved them."

"It would have made no difference," said Ned.

"It might have!" Rob thumped the table in frustration. "It might have."

"No, it wouldn't, because I still wouldn't have gone there," stated Ned flatly.

"But Sir Thomas was your grandfather…"

"So you keep telling me but in case you haven't noticed I've had a few other matters to attend to. Anyway, if it's too late, why did you come here?"

Rob waved a lazy arm around him. "I came here because of you. I just came through…"

"Why did you warn me off?"

"I'd an idea what you might find," replied Rob.

Ned looked at him in disbelief. "How could you have any idea what we'd find unless… You knew about all this, these butchered men and women, the villagers trapped in the church?"

"No, no. I didn't know what had happened – and I'd no idea about the villagers. I swear! Or I'd have come back sooner."

"Come back?" Ned was hungry for answers and he knew now that Rob had some of them.

"Well, listen and I'll tell you what I know," said Rob. "As soon as I left you at Bamburgh I headed back to Crag Tower."

"Crag Tower?" interrupted Ned.

"You remember: Crag Tower is – was - Sir Thomas's castle. The moment I got there I knew I was too late: the village was in mourning and the castle gate was heavily guarded. No-one was getting in unless Henry said so. And I wasn't going to tell him I was there – he hated Maighread but he had to put up with her. Me, he could shit on if he wanted. He made it pretty clear what he'd do to me if he got the chance."

"So you didn't get in?"

"I didn't dare try! There were too many and I knew what would be waiting for me inside. There's a girl I know - a girl who was still inside the castle. I know her pretty well… They let her out once and I managed to see her; she was scared as shit. She hadn't seen either Maighread or Lady Margaret, Sir Thomas's widow. If they're still alive, they're locked up fast. She said she could get me in the postern but I'd be no match for them on my own."

"And so instead you chanced to come here?" said Ned with heavy irony.

"There was no chance about it but I wasn't following you. I was tracking some of Henry's men from Crag Tower."

"Now, why would you do that?" asked Ned.

"Wanted to get a look at some of them, see if I could hook up with them. I thought I might find out about Maighread. You know, have a drink with them…in a tavern …somewhere…" He paused and looked around him.

"This tavern?"

"Wait. Yesterday I followed them all day. They rode all over the place, as if they were searching. They covered a lot of miles but sometime after noon they met a couple of riders on the north road. They spoke for a while and then they made straight for here. I followed them but it was over open ground and I had to give them some distance. So by the time I got here, they were already in the village. I saw there were lights in the tavern but it was quiet, which was odd. I stopped outside. I felt really pleased. I thought how clever I'd been because now I could talk to them.

"I opened the door as the first man cried out. A young girl was facing me in the doorway. I remember her mouth was wide open and, as I stared at her, I saw her head and shoulders split from behind by an axe. I'll never forget that face. I shot out of there fast. I didn't know whether they'd seen me or not but I wasn't risking it. I just leapt on my horse and fled."

"So you only saw the start of it," said Ned.

Rob nodded. "The start was enough! They were butchers… I rode along the stream and hid for a while by the mill. Later on I heard your horses and I thought it was them coming back. It was only when I saw your man, Hal, that I knew it was you. I couldn't believe it."

"So you've no idea who the victims are laid outside?" said Ned.

"No, I only know where the bastards who killed them

came from."

"They slaughtered them – and afterwards they ripped off their badges," said Ned, "and you're saying Sir Thomas' retainers did this?"

"No! I'm not!" declared Rob. "They came from Crag Tower but they were never Sir Thomas's men. They're from the south. My lass told me that none of Sir Thomas's own men have been seen since he was killed."

"How did he die?" asked Ned, and as he posed the question he found to his surprise that his voice was husky and his throat felt dry.

"Henry claimed it was reivers but it wasn't."

"Reivers?"

"Border men."

"How can you be sure it wasn't?" asked Ned.

"Because I am a reiver; I live in the borderlands and I fight ten skirmishes a month with rival families. But mostly it's thieving with violence, not murder. I'll grant you there are feuds but there was no feud with Sir Thomas: Maighread's marriage years ago was the price of peace between Sir Thomas and the other border men. No man beholden to my father's family would dare attack Sir Thomas."

"Honourable folk then, your kin," said Ned doubtfully.

Rob jumped up from his stool and made to draw his long knife until he remembered that Stephen had taken it from him earlier. He sat back down, but with a fierce expression he pronounced slowly: "The honour of my family is not in doubt."

"To me, everything about you is in doubt," said Ned.

They sat in silence for some time. Ned tried to make sense of what had happened now that Rob had added a few more stones to the wall. The men from Crag Tower, Henry's men, had slaughtered over a dozen of Warwick's men and stolen their badges but he was still no wiser as to why they had done it. He suddenly looked at Rob.

"You're a self-confessed thief; why would you steal a badge?"

"I wouldn't. It's not worth a pisspot to me," replied Rob easily.

"Aye and there lies our answer," said Ned, "who would want, even need, the ragged staff badges those men wore?"

Rob simply shrugged.

"If you met a man wearing a badge what would it tell you?" asked Ned.

"Well… it'd tell me who he served... Oh shit!" exclaimed Rob. "Henry's men killed them for the badges - but why?"

"This Henry - is he for Neville or Percy?" asked Ned.

"Sir Thomas was always a Percy man - though he was no man's slave. Henry went with him a time or two when he met the Earl of Northumberland and others. But Henry would support either if he thought it would serve his purpose."

"But even if he wanted to join Warwick and forsake the Percies, he wouldn't need badges to do that. It makes no sense," said Ned.

"Aye, but you don't steal Warwick badges to be Warwick men… you take them to pretend to be Warwick men."

Ned shook his head. "Well, that may be but it gets us no further. If a deception is planned we don't know why or where or how soon."

"We should go to Crag Tower and find out what Henry's doing," said Rob.

"Aye, you'd like that wouldn't you?" replied Ned thoughtfully. "Stephen!" he called and the knight almost fell through the door of the tavern in his haste to get inside. Ned managed a grim smile for the first time that day. "Steady, Stephen; there's no danger."

"What about him?" asked Stephen.

"Aye, what about me?" echoed Rob.

"For now, just untie his hands," said Ned. He strode out through the door with Stephen and Rob in his wake.

"What are you going to do?" asked Stephen.

Ned paused midstride. "I'm going to find Warwick … but not today. Night will be upon us soon enough." He noticed that all the bodies had been moved.

"The men are burying them now under the watchful eye of the priest," said Stephen.

Ned shrugged and immediately felt a twinge in his shoulder. He rubbed it gently which seemed to make it worse. Bear had applied a foul smelling poultice earlier and promised him it would soon be "better." He wasn't sure though what Bear meant by "soon" or, for that matter, "better".

"We'll sleep in watches," he told Stephen, "I'll take the second one so wake me up this time!"

He returned to where he had left his blanket and noted that it had been neatly folded. He lay down gingerly, swathed once more in the warm wool.

"Oh, for a night's uninterrupted sleep," he muttered.

He didn't get it for the dead men preyed upon his mind and he knew that when Warwick heard what had happened, he would assume the worst and hunt him down. He must find Warwick and tell him before he heard from someone else.

5

19th April dawn, at Alnham in

Northumberland

"What do you mean: missing?" Ned demanded. Stephen had woken him early for his watch and he had barely slept at all. Hearing that two of the men on middle watch had disappeared was a very bad start to the day.

"They're gone," said Stephen, "no trace of the pair of them."

"I suppose you've searched?"

"We've done what we can in the dark."

"Who were they?"

"Good men. Ned Longdale and his son," replied Stephen. "They won't have just wandered off."

"No. His son was barely fifteen…"

Ned closed his eyes for a moment and conjured up an image of Longdale's wife and the young children he had left behind.

Ned had intended to leave Alnham at first light but they spent two hours scouring the fields and forest around the village. They finally found Longdale and his son in a ditch more than three furlongs from the green. The two men had not died peaceful deaths. Longdale's tongue had been cut out and his son badly carved about before he died.

"Someone badly wanted to know who we were,"

observed Stephen.

"Well, we must assume that now they know," said Ned, "and may they rot with their knowledge!"

They buried the pair with the tavern victims. When they finally moved off, the mist still lay heavy around them and the mood was subdued.

"The sooner I get to Warwick, the better," said Ned.

Rob guided them on to the old salters' road to the south and they made good time.

"Where does this trail meet the coast?" Ned asked him.

"My hands are still raw from my bonds," grumbled Rob.

"Just stop whining and tell me!" said Ned.

"Newcastle."

"Newcastle?"

"Aye, Newcastle! Of course, Newcastle, where else would it go? Southerners! When we get to Newcastle you should keep on going south!"

They reached Newcastle just before dusk and Ned was impressed by the sheer scale of its defences. The height of its walls must have surpassed every town save London, he thought - not that he had seen many towns.

"Well, I've got you here," said Rob, "now will you let me go?"

He seemed distinctly nervous.

"Have you been into the town before?" asked Ned, ignoring his plea.

"Aye, once – but I was a young lad, I wouldn't know it now any better than you," said Rob. "I'm no more use to you."

"Why were you there – if you were just a boy?"

"Some family business…"

"Aren't I family, then?" Ned grinned. He could see that the border man was not keen to venture inside for he slowed his horse to a walk as they neared the town gate.

"No, you're not family – not if you don't let me go!"

Ned rode on, pleased that they had reached the town before nightfall. It had been a long day's ride but they passed through the north gate without incident. Ned was mightily relieved to have escaped from Percy territory without further casualties but he was not looking forward to attending on the Earl of Warwick to tell him his news. And the news could not wait until morning.

"My father took me," Rob muttered.

Ned looked at him, waiting for further explanation.

Rob sighed. "Two of my uncles were to be hanged. My father thought I should see it. This town has only bad memories for me."

"We've all got bad memories," said Ned, trying not to call them up, "I want you to stay with me until I've discovered what Alnham was all about."

"Are you saying you'll let me go after?"

Ned gave a curt nod.

"Do you give me your word?"

"Aye," agreed Ned. He had intended to release Rob in any case.

"Right then, where do you want to go?"

"I thought you didn't know the town," said Ned.

Rob looked sheepish. "I might remember a few places..."

Just as well, thought Ned, for the town was crowded and a good many fighting men were in evidence. The road south from the gate was broad but splintered in several places where it had to cross a network of narrow streams that wove their way down to a river. In the late afternoon a mist was creeping up the hill towards them. It seemed he had spent every day in Northumberland either in mist or driving rain. Despite his king's assurances, he had yet to find anything in the shire that he liked and he longed to go back to his beloved dales.

He stared down the hill towards the large river which he knew must run through the heart of the town. Ahead of him a great church soared skywards through the gloom, its squat central tower clad with wooden scaffolding poles. The glow of torches illuminated the tower and the small turrets that seemed to sprout from it. He glanced at his reluctant guide.

"St. Nicholas," said Rob. "Big, isn't it?"

"And getting taller by the looks of it," observed Ned, eying the construction work. Beyond the church he saw the outline of a stone keep. "The castle," he breathed, "if Warwick's here, that's where he'll be."

"Well as you can see, if you keep on this road you'll reach it or you'll pitch yourself into the River Tyne," said Rob.

Ned wasn't thinking about how to get there; he was recalling his previous meetings with the Earl. All had gone badly. He must make a decision: how many men did he take with him? Too few and he put himself at Warwick's mercy; too many and he risked offending the Earl before he had said a word. How far could he trust Warwick? Not enough to leave himself no way out.

"Bear! Pick a dozen fit men. Hal, find two archers and come with me."

He put a hand on Stephen's shoulder. "Take Rob with you. Find somewhere to feed the men and water the horses. They both deserve some rest but keep them ready. And make sure you're by the river, close to a gate – just in case."

"In case?"

"In case it doesn't go well with Warwick," said Ned quietly.

He turned to survey the escort jostling into an untidy column behind him. He could see that Bear had chosen his men well – he only hoped they would not be needed.

He gave Stephen a weary wave of the hand and set off through the town, skirting the church and working his way down to the large barbican which gave entrance to the castle keep.

The keep towered above the other buildings nearby and, though the light was fading, he could make out the banner fluttering above the gatehouse: the bear and ragged staff. So Warwick was certainly in residence.

As they arrived the gate opened and a horseman rode past them at speed, so close his leg brushed Ned's and they all but collided. The rider was cloaked and Ned was so busy taking evasive action that he had no chance to see the man's face. Yet his anger dissipated swiftly for he had more important matters to worry about and in any case the horseman soon disappeared into the town.

He talked his way through the two gates easily enough but in the courtyard beyond he was forced to leave most of his men.

"Bear – come with me," he ordered. He then turned to Hal and lowered his voice. "Do nothing without my word but make sure you're able to secure the gates if you have to."

Hal nodded.

This was not Warwick's castle but he expected that many of the men on guard would be his. However, the efficient and respectful knight who was in command of the barbican did not wear the Earl's livery. Warwick was not his master but he was certainly a formidable resident.

"I need you to take me to the Earl," Ned said.

The man hesitated, clearly weighing up the risks Ned might pose.

Ned was aching from the day's ride and anxious just to get the meeting over with. It had already been a long day.

"Very well, my lord," the knight agreed, "but you'll have to give me your sword."

"Is the king with him?" Ned snapped.

"No, my lord," stuttered the startled knight, "but … the Earl has ordered it."

Ned knew he was too weary for this and he made bad decisions when he was tired.

"I've urgent news for him – news he'll want to hear. So when I stop talking to you I'm going to find him - with my good friend here. He's called Bear…" He pointed to the bulky figure beside him. "But it would be easier if you took us."

"But…" the knight started to protest but Ned cut him short.

"If Bear sets about you with his axe there won't be enough of you left to make a rush light."

Bear laid a large hand on the handle of his axe. The knight shook his head but capitulated. and led them across the courtyard up the steep flight of steps on the outside of the keep. It was, Ned realised, the only way into the heart of the fortress. They followed into a modest Hall with a high ceiling; there was a gallery looking down upon them and several doors off the Hall. The knight paused.

"You were taking us to the Earl," Ned reminded him. He glanced through a door on his left which led to a spiral stair. Opposite him was another short stair.

"He's in Privy Chamber," said their guide, "but, I warn you, he's not going to be happy."

"No," agreed Ned, "he's not. Who was it that was leaving in such a hurry when I arrived?"

"I couldn't say, my lord," replied the knight.

"No, I dare say you couldn't. Well he can't be that important then, can he?" said Ned.

The knight stopped outside a chamber door.

"I should go in first, my lord…"

"Aye perhaps you should, but you're not going to. Wait for me outside, Bear - if I need you, I'll shout." Bear nodded, showing not a flicker of emotion and Ned gave a wry smile.

He entered the chamber which was small and narrow - not exactly what Warwick was used to, he supposed. As he expected, the Earl was displeased to see him and yet did not seem particularly surprised.

"I told you to stay at Bamburgh," Warwick said before Ned uttered a word. He spoke coldly but with the easy confidence of a man who expected to be regarded as the superior of almost any man in Christendom.

"The camp at Bamburgh's lost, my lord," said Ned.

"Lost!? How is that possible?"

"We were overrun," said Ned. He had expected more reaction from Warwick, more anger.

"You run a deal too easily – and too often," said Warwick. "I haven't forgotten Ferrybridge!"

Ned bristled at the reminder. "I doubt either of us has

forgotten what's passed between us, my lord. But we shouldn't waste valuable time on old scores for there's much amiss in the north."

"I don't need you to tell me that. So why are you here?"

Ned was still puzzled by Warwick's reaction: there was no bluster, no fiery outburst.

"Somerset pursued us south from Bamburgh. We fought him off but he's still at large with Ralph Percy."

"Hardly news!" Warwick scoffed. "We knew the Duke would turn up after he left here but surely they have few men even between them. My brother John is coming north with an escort for the Scottish envoys - but I'm sure you know that. Then we'll see how the Queen's revolt fares without Scots' help!"

"There's more, my lord…" Ned had been dreading this moment. However well the Earl had taken what he had related so far, Ned had no doubt how he would react to the bloodshed at Alnham.

"Well?" asked Warwick.

"We found some of your men at a village - a small place called Alnham - they had been killed and their badges ripped off."

Ned watched Warwick's eyes carefully as he described in detail what he had found. The Earl certainly looked more interested and pressed him for clarity on several points. But Ned began to worry: where was the anger and outrage he expected? He worried even more when Warwick spoke.

"Who do you think, Ned Elder, in all England holds the greatest grudge against me? Who is there that holds me in such low esteem that he would carve up my men for his amusement?"

Ned was tempted to brush aside the question until he realised what the answer was.

Warwick continued. "You've hidden behind the king before but this time you've gone too far. This time even he won't save your head."

Suddenly Ned made sense of it all: it had to be the rider

who had passed them at the gate. That was why Warwick was in such a relaxed mood in the face of such appalling news.

"You knew about all this, didn't you," said Ned.

"A good commander doesn't just rely on one source of information," said Warwick.

Ned heaved a great sigh. "You can't possibly believe that it was me!"

"I'll admit I didn't expect such a thing- even from you… yet I'm reliably informed it was you. A witness saw the Elder badges that you wear."

Surely, Ned thought, no-one from the village could have betrayed him so quickly.

"What witness?" he demanded. "I saw plenty of witnesses and they can attest that I did them no harm – I released them!" Ned felt the anger rising in him. They were discussing the wrong issue!

"But," said Warwick, "can your witnesses attest that you did not murder my men?"

Ned hesitated for he was not sure they could, or indeed would, if they were asked. The Earl clearly took his silence as an admission of guilt and moved on. He stood up swiftly.

"I arrest you now on a charge of treason and murder. I'll take you to York but you'll see your men hanged in the morning."

"But this is madness! I came here myself to tell you about it! Our hostility is hardly a secret but I wouldn't slaughter your men on a whim! It wasn't me – or my men! We buried them for you! What's more there's a reason for the theft of the badges-"

"Indeed there is," interrupted Warwick, "and my informant has told me the reason: you intend to ambush my brother as he comes to Newcastle! Oh, I have it all - every chapter, every verse!"

"My lord, you can't seriously suspect me of treason?"

"Now there you are on very shaky ground, Ned Elder." Warwick gave a wry smile. "I've always suspected you of treachery: remember St. Albans … and Ferrybridge - there was already a pattern there. But it will end here tonight. You'll not leave this castle to strike at my brother."

Ned took a pace back. "Your informant knew a great deal about this crime, about where I've been and what I'm supposed to have done. But he's not only a liar, he's a fool: why the devil would I steal your badges? My men could ride up to your brother wearing their own badges and he'd suspect nothing! Who is this informant? I'd like to meet my accuser."

Slowly, deliberately, Warwick drew out his sword. "I am your accuser. I'll also be your judge, but since you've no intention of surrendering your sword, we'll make an end of it now!"

Ned was slow to draw his sword and only just managed to parry aside Warwick's first blow.

"Bear!" he shouted. But Bear had heard the clash of swords and burst through the door like a wild boar on the charge. Warwick drew back in surprise and in one movement Bear slipped out the axe from his belt and swung it against Warwick's sword sending it spinning across the room. It clattered on the floor and Bear raised his axe to strike.

"No!" shouted Ned. The axe blade stopped an inch from Warwick's neck.

"You'd better kill me now," snarled the Earl, "for if you don't I'll hunt you down!"

"I probably should," admitted Ned, "but I'm not going to – just as I didn't kill your men or steal your badges!"

Before Warwick could reply Bear tapped him on the side of the head with the flat of the axe head. "Better to kill him," he said.

"No, it's not," groaned Ned. "But what the fuck do I do now?"

"Go?" suggested Bear.

Sometimes the man's command of the language was perfectly adequate, thought Ned. "Aye," he breathed, "Go."

They ran out of the chamber into the Hall. Several men at arms had already come up from the floor below. "Is something wrong, my lord?" asked one.

"Upstairs!" Ned ordered, "the Earl's been attacked! The villains have fled up the steps!"

The men hurried on up the steps and Ned went outside and down the exterior stair to the courtyard. He saw at a glance that Hal and the others were prepared for trouble but trouble was the last thing he wanted: if men died here it would just make his guilt appear more certain. He tried to look unhurried. "Mount up, we're leaving. Open the gate!"

The portcullis had not yet been lowered for the evening and the two wooden gates were still ajar so he waved to the men at the gate to pull them wider. There was a shout from the keep. The gatekeepers could not tell what was being said but they recognised a cry of alarm when they heard one. For a moment they stared in confusion at Ned and then began to push the gates shut again. Ned moved towards the gate and an arrow thudded into the wooden shuttering behind him. Several crossbow bolts flew down from the battlements as his men attempted to mount. It was all unravelling faster than he could think. He had expected a hostile reception but not this catastrophe.

A horse went down shrieking, its hind leg smashed by a bolt. The rider scrambled to his feet and Ned seized his hand to pull him up onto his own horse. He was a big man and Ned feared the horse might buckle under their weight.

"No mortal wounds!" he shouted.

No mortal wounds? What the hell did he mean by that? Bear clearly did not know either, for he ignored the command and rode down the men at the gate, crushing one under his horse and striking the other with a deadly blow of his axe. Single-handed, he prised open one of the large gates and Ned's men began to pass through.

Hal and the other archers kept heads down on the ramparts as they made their escape through the barbican. The portcullis at the far end began to growl into life but they ducked under before it could be lowered more than a foot or so. Ned led them blindly through the narrow murky lanes until he was utterly lost; then he slowed to a walking pace. They would be followed, of that he was certain. They must leave the town now for Warwick would close it up tight as soon as he could. The Earl would never forgive this.

He put it from his mind - he'd have time to reflect upon the consequences if he escaped but at the moment that was by no means certain. Dusk had come and gone. All the town gates would be closed. Their headlong flight had taken them along the docks by the riverside. There were no gates here - not even a wall, just warehouses and row upon row of shambling hovels. Each seemed to lean upon the next for support and a strong gust of the north wind would surely blow them into the Tyne.

Ned had told Stephen to camp near one of the southern gates but if there was no wall here, there could be no gate. He expected that his sixty or so men would be easy to find but he hadn't reckoned with the sheer numbers of men at arms choking the town. The dockside was more crowded than anywhere for it offered men the prospect of cheap food and an easy night's pleasure. He forced a path through the crowds of men at arms and the whores, tinkers and other sellers displaying their wares. There were angry looks from some but Ned urged his heavily laden horse on through the milling mass of people. A dozen mounted men armed to the teeth could not pass by unnoticed.

He turned to Hal who followed close behind him.

"Hal," he shouted, "I'm looking for a gate or a bridge – well, both. Get closer to the water's edge – there'll be a bridge to the west."

By now Warwick would have despatched a pack of chasers after them. Good Christ, what had he got them all into? Stephen had warned him: he should have let it go at Alnham. His curiosity was going to kill them all.

"Lord!" It was a shout of triumph from Hal.

Along by the shore a low town wall started to appear, now draped with soldiers and the wenches that clung to them. Further along, the wall grew taller and fifty yards ahead Ned could just make out the bridge. There was little light to guide them along the street as night closed in but soon the gatehouse loomed in front of them and Ned cast about trying to pick out his own men from the rest.

There was a shout from his right, away from the river. Stephen's voice guided him and he made his way down a narrow lane towards a dimly lit tavern. There Stephen was waiting for him outside with a broad grin on his face.

"It's a relief to see you," said Stephen. "The men are well provisioned – though it's taken most of your coin!"

"Well get them outside and mounted!" Ned ordered.

"What?"

In three years it was the first time Ned could recall even a hint of insubordination from his friend. He ignored it.

"Now!" he shouted. His voice was harsher than he intended but Stephen needed to grasp the urgency. "We must ride now, my friend! And send me Rob."

Stephen turned on his heel and hurried into the tavern.

Those who had followed Ned down the lane filled up the confined space.

"Bear, Hal. Go back to the top of the street. Keep a watch – and keep the way clear!"

He could hear Stephen cajoling the rest of the men. They left the tavern in ones and twos and scattered to find and saddle their horses. They were weary and cursing, reluctant to leave the welcome respite they felt they had earned.

"Hold your tongues!" ordered Stephen.

"Fuck off!" answered an aggrieved voice in the dark. Ned couldn't blame them; he would have felt the same.

Rob sidled his horse alongside. "You're good at bloody chaos. I'll give you that, my lord."

"Can you get us out?" demanded Ned.

"Are we in haste by any chance?"

"Can you get us out?" repeated Ned. Why did he always have to tell Rob twice?

"I can get you out of the town if you don't mind breaking most of the town ordinances; but what you do then, is up to you."

"Leave me to worry about that," replied Ned quietly.

"Oh, I will, my lord, I will." Rob chuckled.

Hal came up. "There are horses coming along the road, lord!"

"Come on!" cried Ned, "move out!"

They trotted up the lane in a long straggling line and crossed the street to the gate. There were only two watchmen at the gate and Ned bade them open it. They looked like experienced men and having glanced at Ned's heavily armed retinue, they complied without a word. The gate led them onto a great bridge where ramshackle buildings clung uncertainly to the stonework. They hurried across the bridge and out of the gate on the south bank of the River Tyne.

"Take the road south," ordered Ned.

Rob looked at him in surprise. "A bit obvious, isn't it?" he said, "if they're coming after us."

"We'll just have to ride faster," said Ned but he knew that however fast they rode, Warwick's reach stretched across all England and perhaps even beyond."

6

19th April, in Yoredale Forest in Yorkshire

Emma enjoyed her rare visits to the Abbey at Coverham for they reminded her of the old days when she had visited the canons often. Canon Reedman especially had enjoyed passing on his vast knowledge of how to provision a household to a young and willing pupil. The White Canons at Coverham were different from other monks: they did not hide themselves away in their abbey cloisters but played their part in the lives of the parishes nearby. She was so young when she first met Reedman, just thirteen. How old Reedman was she had no idea; he was already greying then but he cut an impressive figure in his pristine white habit and cap.

They first met in the village of Aysgarth when he struck up a conversation with her in a way she had not expected from a monk and there was an immediate empathy between them. He was complaining of the lack of eels in the river that year and, as cellarer at Coverham Abbey, it was a subject of much concern to him. Over several years Reedman had been the nearest thing she had to a friend. She had learned a great deal from him and much that helped her to cope with her position. Her knowledge of herbs and remedies had all come from him.

She often wondered what benefit he took from their meetings but he told her once that God had sent a daughter to him since he could not have one of his own blood. She had been so innocent then. Now, 22 years old, a mother and twice widowed, she knew more of the world and liked less of it. She cared for her young son only because he was her son but she could not bring herself to love him. Eleanor, of course, had breezed through pregnancy, birth and motherhood as if it was all a trifle but then her child, Will, was a child of love - unlike her own. She had given birth to Edmund Radcliffe's son and now all she could do was to try to ensure that as he grew he did not become his father.

The Radcliffes had done them all much harm, but Eleanor and Amelie had braved their way through the unspeakable things done to them. Her wounds, on the other hand, had never healed; or at least she did not feel that they had. Her spirit was mortally scarred, so these visits to the abbey were for her alone, to help her wash clean her soul. The visits had become a welcome ritual - a crutch perhaps, but there could surely be no disgrace in seeking strength from the hand of God. She no longer asked herself what Reedman got from her visits for she no longer cared. He never touched her or asked any more of her than her company and conversation; she could think of few other men who could claim that.

Amelie always insisted that Emma take several men at arms with her. To start with Bagot had accompanied her, but with his leg she knew he hated riding and he hardly fitted in well in the abbey environment. So in recent weeks he had given her three of the younger men as an escort. She admitted, but only to herself, that she much preferred their company for they were bubbling with youthful hope and exuberance. She was glad of that. After only a little encouragement they would talk freely to her about their families and where they lived, feeding her little morsels about their lives on the estate and sometimes even asking her opinion on the girls they had eyes for.

This was the third time these three, Garth, Robin and Guy, had been with her and they now knew the route through the forest better than she did. Garth had become a special favourite with her. He was a youth of sixteen, tall and strong with an unruly head of hair so fair it was almost white.

He seemed to enjoy regaling her with stories of his exploits with the village girls and she glowed unashamedly to hear them. He became fiercely protective of her, always insisting on leading her through the thickest parts of the forest as if a wild boar might rush out at her at any moment.

"We're too near the castle for wild beasts, Garth," she would declare, smiling. "They were hunted down a long time ago." Yet she enjoyed his attention and whenever he turned to her and grinned, something stirred in her that she had not felt for a very long time, perhaps not ever.

They were picking their way through the woodland on the journey back from the abbey, when Garth pulled up in a tiny clearing and motioned them all to stop.

"Keep quiet," he said softly. He was listening; Emma listened too but she had never taken much interest in the forest so she had no idea what she was listening for.

Garth seemed satisfied though. "False alarm," he said with a grin. Then his grin froze and he coughed and Emma laughed until she noticed a small patch of crimson high on his chest. She frowned uncertainly and then to her horror he slid from his saddle and rolled down into the dead leaves.

"Garth!" she screamed

"Crossbow!" yelled Guy and seized her bridle to pull her away. She brushed off his hand and would not move. She stared down at Garth who was struggling to get up. Robin leapt from his horse to help. There was a dribble of blood on Garth's jerkin. He tried to speak as Robin lifted him to his feet and leant him against the flank of his horse.

"Come, Lady! For God's sake, we must go!" Guy beseeched her. Abruptly he fell silent and Emma turned to see him slumped forward with a quarrel protruding from his back.

"Flee, lady!" Robin shouted, "I'll look after Garth. Ride, before it's too late!"

A dark figure broke from the trees on foot and made for the two youths. She wanted to ride away but could not move. Instead she watched transfixed as the hauntingly familiar man plunged a knife into Robin's slender back.

"No!" she screeched. The attack had lasted barely the beat of a swallow's wing and yet all her sweet boys had been cut down. She tried to dismount but caught her clothing on the saddle and fell to the ground, winding herself.

Garth looked down at her in despair and with a last great effort drew out his sword but, before he could even raise it to strike, their assailant felled him with a blow to the side of the head. Then he stepped with easy confidence over to the prostrate Robin, who was holding out a long knife in his trembling hand. He kicked the hand sending the blade spinning into the trees. Then he knelt down and sliced his own knife through the youth's throat.

Emma scrambled to her feet and ran at him screaming. He caught her effortlessly and struck her hard across the face, stopping her in her tracks. Only then did she recognise him. She closed her eyes and waited for the next blow.

It didn't come; instead Durston threw her onto the ground. She opened her eyes and saw Garth lying still nearby. There were brown leaves caught in the curls of his hair and she wanted to take them out; she wanted to ease his pain. Beside him lay Robin, eyes fixed and devoid of life. She shivered: it was happening to her once more.

Durston crouched down next to her and laid the point of his dagger on the pale skin of her neck. She trembled at the touch of the cold blade and watched as he carefully wiped Robin's blood onto her cloak. He lifted the knife and teased out the necklace she wore.

"A pretty piece," he said, "the jewels, not you." He chuckled to himself and ripped the necklace from her throat. He indicated her three guards. "Didn't do very well, did they," he observed, "three of them against only me – and my little friend." He stood up and retrieved his crossbow, slinging it over his shoulder.

"Come on," he said, offering her his hand.

"Where?" she demanded, struggling to her feet without his aid.

"Why, back to your castle, my lady; we wouldn't want any harm to come to you, would we?"

She stood still, unnerved by his smile.

"It's not far, as you know," he said cheerfully, "but on the way we're going to have a little talk."

"What do you want?" she asked absently, staring at the bodies of her men at arms.

"Nothing," he said, "just to talk, as I said." He scattered the horses and led her into the woods on foot. He talked to her as she stumbled in front of him along the track towards Yoredale castle.

"I want you Elders to know I'm back and I can do whatever I like to any of you. No-one's safe if I choose to hurt them."

"You'd not be so lively if my brother Ned was here. But the Radcliffes are all dead," she told him. "What do you hope to get from us?"

"Are you sure, Lady, that the Radcliffes are all dead? Not quite all, there's your son, Richard – he's a Radcliffe, isn't he? He's not an Elder."

Emma started at the mention of Richard.

"Oh, don't worry, he's safe; but the rest of you... you're already dead, as dead as those young boys we left back there in the forest. I serve someone who has no love for your family - a man who would have the Elders out of Yoredale Castle. A man who would pursue the feud you all thought was over. So take this as a warning: he's coming and you'll feel his angry breath upon your face, soon enough."

Emma paled for his words struck her to the core: these three years of respite, it seemed were only that: respite. If Durston was to be believed, the bitter feud had begun again.

"Until then, I'll be watching... always," he said, "and you'll be hearing from me... soon."

He left her at the edge of the forest and for a while she stood still, doubting he had really gone. Then she scrambled up the muddy track and stumbled into the guard at the main gate.

Her arrival caused uproar in the castle but it took her many minutes to control herself enough to explain to Bagot a little of what had happened. At once he took out half the garrison to pursue Durston and find the young men who had fallen but he found no trace of Durston.

§§§§

Eleanor slammed her sword hard against the wall and screamed in frustration: the sound rang around the castle like an alarm call. She threw the weapon aside and it clattered down onto the boards of the gallery floor.

Bagot limped in with his sword drawn. He stood in the doorway breathing heavily and stared at Gruffydd in confusion.

"'Tis alright," said Gruffydd wearily, "we were just … sparring." He picked up Eleanor's sword and handed it to her hilt first.

She snatched it from him and waved Bagot away. "Again!" she told Gruffydd.

"Perhaps we should…" the Welshman began.

"Again!" The single word crackled like lightning and he knew better than to argue.

Eleanor had a face like a storm about to break for he had just beaten the sword from her hand for the third time. He prepared to take guard once more but she thrust at him so fast he couldn't parry her blade. She pulled back at the last minute but not before the point had punched a small hole in his thick gambeson. He looked down at it and frowned.

"You're getting slow, old man," she snapped, but her fury vanished in a moment when she saw his wounded pride. She lowered her weapon and laid a hand gently on his arm, leaning her head in against his large shoulder.

"I'm sorry. What would I do without my great Welsh man of war?" she asked. "You know I'm not angry with you – just my weak body. Are you hurt?"

He moved a respectful distance from her and took her

hand to kiss it. "No, but I'm getting too old for this," he conceded.

"Never!" she replied fiercely, "you'll outlive us all!"

"Do you want to continue, lady?"

"Yes, if you will. After what happened today, I think I must."

"You're getting better, moving quicker," he said.

She patted his arm and smiled at his words of encouragement, even though she knew he was lying. "Come. Once more," she said.

§§§§

In Ned's privy chamber below them on the first floor Bagot was in earnest discussion with Lady Amelie.

"We must lock this place up tight, my lady," urged Bagot, "Durston served here for years, remember; he knows this place better than we do."

"We cannot be prisoners in our own castle," said Amelie.

"Just until Lord Elder returns, my lady," insisted Bagot, "then he can take care of Durston - but we can't."

"Are we to lie cowering in our beds because of one man?"

"We're doing what we must do, my lady," replied Bagot. "Remember how distraught Lady Emma was only a few hours ago; and there are the children to think of …"

Amelie frowned in irritation. "You do not need to remind me about the children," she said, "but I've stood up to such men, and worse, before – you know that! And I am still here!" Her French accent rang around the chamber as she flung her arms wide in annoyance.

"But you weren't with child then, my lady," said Bagot quietly.

She saw his tears then and her own eyes filled up. "I'm sorry, Bagot. I know you want only to protect us."

"Ned would never forgive me if you were harmed, my lady – nor would I forgive myself."

She gave a sigh. "Very well, it shall be as you say, Bagot. We shall lock ourselves up tight until my Ned returns."

"No visits beyond the walls then," he said, "even the Lady Eleanor…"

She smiled. "That lady, I fear, is outside my control - but I will ask her."

Bagot bowed and left her alone in the chamber. At once she sat down for she was feeling more and more tired as each day of her pregnancy came and slowly went. Now the worry caused by Durston's return had made her feel even worse. Emma seemed to become more fragile by the hour and Eleanor was intent on waging a one woman war against… well, who knew what demons Eleanor was fighting?

The way she saw it, neither of her husband's sisters were much help to her. When Ned had left, Emma had agreed to manage the day to day running of the household but as the weeks went by she had become increasing reclusive, only venturing out to visit her precious monks. Now on top of everything came this violence by Durston. It was all a great trial for her. After so long she was finally bearing Ned's child and now she faced all these complications - as if childbirth wasn't enough of a hazard in itself.

§§§§

Upstairs, Eleanor had finished working with Gruffydd and was in her chamber with Becky and young Will.

"He's going to be just like his father," said Becky, ruffling the boy's auburn hair.

"Do you think so?" said Eleanor uncertainly. "I pray for it to be so."

"And when did you last pray, my lady?" Becky scoffed.

"You don't know everything I do," said Eleanor, but Becky held her eyes for several moments before she conceded: "Alright, perhaps you do… and you're right: I haven't prayed for three years. Why would I? I prayed my life away in the nunnery – but it didn't save Will, did it?"

"Those times are past," said Becky.

"Are they? What about Durston?"

"Oh, Durston's all talk -"

"I thought that too but he isn't is he? He's attacked our young men at arms and driven my sister near out of her wits. We can't take him lightly, Becky."

"Aye, I know, of course," she soothed. "I know better than anyone what Durston's like."

"Make sure Sarah and Jane understand that. They mustn't leave the castle on their own - even together – and they must always have your permission - and have men with them."

"Lady Emma had men with her…" said Becky.

"Yes, I know…"

"I'll make sure they know, but they've no reason to leave the castle."

Eleanor met her eyes. "Are you sure? Sarah seems a little…"

"Distracted? I know. She can't keep much from me: there's some lad she's fallen in with. You know what it's like when you're fifteen."

"It was usually like a hayloft when we were fifteen, as I recall!" retorted Eleanor. "The girl has a future here. She must be careful."

Becky gave her a knowing look.

"No, I mean it," said Eleanor. "More careful than we were!"

"It's alright, I've told her what's what and she's agreed she won't see him anymore."

"And you believe her?"

"Aye, I do. She's a good girl is Sarah."

"When I was fifteen I told a lie every time I went to meet a lover," said Eleanor, "and so did you."

Becky sighed. "Aye… that would've been a lot of lies then, between us."

7

20th April evening, on the road south of Newcastle

"God's blood! It's not much of a road," observed Rob.

They were crossing a swathe of open moorland and in the dark they had just lost the road for the third time. It took some searching on foot before they could locate the worn track once more. Ned was keen to keep to the road despite the risk of pursuit, for it was the quickest means of putting some distance between himself and Warwick - or at least it would have been if they didn't keep losing their way. Added to which, it was the most likely route for Warwick's brother, John Neville, to take and Ned believed that warning Lord Montagu was the best hope he had of showing his innocence and escaping Warwick's wrath.

He reckoned they must have ridden at least ten miles already and, despite the delays, they had seen no sign of a chasing force in their wake.

Abruptly Rob came to a halt.

"What is it?" asked Ned. "The road's clear enough here."

"Right enough, my lord," agreed Rob, "so you don't need me any longer. Anyway, I don't know the lie of the land from here on any better than you do. Just keep heading south on this road and you'll get to Durham."

Ned was reluctant to lose the border man but he had given his word twice and already broken it once. He could not deny that Rob had done all he had asked of him.

"Very well," he said. "I suppose you'll make for Crag

Tower?"

"Aye. I need to find out if Maighread's still alive - at least you seem to be able to remember what the place is called now..."

"If matters were different, I'd go with you," said Ned. "I pray Lady Maighread is safe."

He meant what he said but his words seemed empty. How many times had others said similar words to him in his long search for his sisters three years ago? Three years... it seemed barely three weeks. He should have enjoyed the peace while he still had it.

He nodded to Rob and gripped his arm in a brief parting gesture. Then without a backward look he dug in his heels and his weary horse started forward again.

"How far do you intend to ride, lord?" enquired Stephen, "Only the men -"

"Yes, I know. The men are tired and hungry and so on," replied Ned.

"Yes, lord, they are," said Stephen.

"Well perhaps the men should thank the Lord they're still alive... but even so: you're right. Durham's too far. We can't ride all night. We'll stop as soon as we can find some cover near the road."

But it was several leagues further on before they reached the sanctuary of a forested valley which sloped up to the west away from the road.

"This should suit us well enough, lord," said Stephen, clearly relieved.

Ned thought at first sight that it was as secure a spot as they were likely to find. Then it occurred to him that it was also an ideal place to ambush Lord Montagu with ample tree cover close to the road. They would have to be on their guard.

"No fires!" ordered Ned, as he halted the column to make camp. "Just get some rest."

Grumbling men at arms dismounted and slid the saddles from their horses. They made themselves as comfortable as they could. Some removed their breastplates or items of mail, most did not bother but merely found a carpet of dead bracken fronds to lie on and rested their heads on their saddles. One or two had small blankets or cloaks which they wrapped around them. It was spring, not midwinter, but it was cold enough.

Ned posted men to north and south to watch the road. Warwick had said his brother was on his way north but Ned doubted Montagu would be on the road with his commissioners in the middle of the night. Still, others might be. If Warwick had despatched men to warn his brother, they would certainly use the same road and, unlike Ned's company, they would have fresh horses.

What concerned him most were those who really did intend to carry out the ambush. He knew next to nothing about them. How many were there? How would he know them? He assumed that a dozen or so would wear the stolen badges of Warwick; others might have Elder badges similar to his own … or neither. His ignorance could bring chaos. Rob was right: he was good at chaos.

He dared not stop for long; they must find Lord Montagu before any of the others did. He was dog tired but could not sleep. Instead he paced through the woods for an hour or more. He considered prayer; most would have found solace there but he had long ago tried the Lord's patience beyond any forbearance. He and those he loved had survived the feud with the Radcliffes; he could ask no more favours of God.

He wandered through the woodland west of their camp until he came upon a narrow stream running north to south. He sat down on a fallen tree beside the water and listened. For a while he dozed but started awake when he heard someone approaching. His hand moved instinctively to the hilt of his sword and then he saw Stephen and relaxed.

"You make a lot of noise," he remarked. "What is it? Is there someone on the road?"

"Sorry, lord; it's nothing. Just that … I couldn't find you."

Ned's face softened and he smiled. "You'll not lose me that easily, Stephen."

He was one of only a few men Ned might call a friend but, since Alnham, Stephen had been more distant, and addressed him formally. Where there had once only been trust Ned could see there was now doubt.

"You want to say something," he said gently.

Stephen shrugged awkwardly and sat on the dead trunk beside him.

"Go on - out with it," said Ned.

"Why did you place so much trust in Master Hall?" Stephen blurted out. "I always thought you valued my counsel above others..."

"Do you know, Stephen, I really have no idea but my trust in you has never wavered. With Rob Hall, well … there's something about him. I don't know what. I suppose because he may be a link to my grandfather, to my father's family."

"But surely he was telling you lies," protested Stephen.

Ned smiled. "I'm not so sure now," he said wistfully. "You may be right but we'll probably never know. All the same, don't forget that without him we'd still be wandering around the Percy estates north of Newcastle."

"I suppose so," conceded Stephen. "You did the right thing to let him go. He earned that much."

Somewhere in the woods a twig snapped. They both turned instinctively towards the sound, beyond the stream to the west. In the dead hours of the early morning it sounded like an axe splitting a branch. Ned half expected to see one of his men appear through the trees but there was no-one in sight. They exchanged a swift glance and slowly crouched down behind the fallen trunk - not an easy task since neither had relinquished their breastplate. The tree cover ahead of them was sparse - a few spindly saplings had forced their way up through the rusty bracken - and if any man was out there they should be able to see him. They waited in silence but heard nothing more.

"I used to love the forest," whispered Ned, "but not

anymore. I used to discover a new wonder every day but now the trees hold all my bitterest memories. I find it a wretched place."

Ned got up slowly, his legs stiff and aching.

"There's probably nothing out there but take a walk around the south side of the camp anyway. Find the men on watch and make sure they're all there ... and see they're all awake too! I'll do the same to the north."

Stephen nodded and rose awkwardly to his feet, shaking the stiffness form his own chilled limbs. Then he walked off and Ned stared beyond the stream a moment or two longer. The ground rose up to a low ridge in the distance. Was there movement in the tree line? He drew out his long knife from its scabbard.

"Lord knows who I'm going to stab," he mumbled to himself, "I shan't know friend from foe."

And yet, as he moved off silently and thought about it, all became clear. He realised that he would know the perpetrators of the ambush very easily because they would be moving in stealth - like his own company – wary of any unexpected contact which might forestall their attack.

He found all the sentries in place and awake - though he might not have described them as alert. Then he re-joined Stephen in the camp. "Well?" he asked.

"All present," confirmed Stephen. "It must have been an animal."

"No, I've got a feeling there's someone out there."

"A woodsman perhaps?"

"It's a little early, even for a man of the forest. And it's not Warwick's men or John Neville's commissioners. None of them would be creeping around in the forest."

"So?"

"So, if there is anyone there - apart from your woodsman - they're up to no good. We can't take the risk of being caught ourselves. Get the men up - quietly!"

"But they've can't have had more than a couple of hours, lord. And we've seen nothing, nothing."

Ned glanced at his comrade. He understood Stephen's reaction and years before he would have felt the same; but he had learned and, whilst he learned, men died.

"Aye, alright then, Stephen. Give every man a choice: he can get up now or sleep on and have his throat cut where he lies! Remember who we're dealing with. Have you forgotten their handiwork? These men slaughtered some of Warwick's best. They'll give us no quarter so we'll take no chances. Now, get the men up and I want every one armed with all he's got!"

Stephen met his eyes and then looked away. "It'll be as you say, lord."

Ned stood facing the forest to the west. One by one his men joined him. He could feel their resentment but they were not fools. Archers strung their bows or smoothed the goose feathers on their arrows. Men at arms eased swords from scabbards and hastily strapped on pieces of armour. Soon they were milling about in a great wedge behind him.

"Spread out," he ordered and they fanned out into a long straggling line.

"Hal?" Ned called. Hal was beside him at once .

"Archers at the front, lord?"

"No, archers to the flanks and out of sight until I give you a shout."

"Lord?" Hal looked at Ned doubtfully.

"Just make sure it happens – and Hal?"

"Yes, lord?"

"You'll need to hit what you aim at first time…"

Hal nodded and took the archers with him. There were only about nine of them left, Ned reflected with sadness. They had at least acquired more arrows in Newcastle but they still had precious few.

He took a long, deep breath and then stepped a pace forward and then another, and another. Behind him he heard the soft tramp of boots on bracken as his men at arms kept station with him. He darted glances to left and right: the line was spread across a sixty yard front. The stream was no more than twenty yards ahead. It was shallow enough to walk straight through but the moment they splashed across the narrow strip of water the enemy would know they were there – if they did not already. In a few more paces he reached the stream. He took one step into it and stopped, watching the dark water wash over his boots. Then he moved forward again and the sound of three score men crossing the stream seemed impossibly loud in the silent forest.

On the distant ridge ahead of them the trees seemed closer together. A low mist was drifting towards them on a light westerly breeze but in the east he noticed the first stirrings of dawn. He could make out the green leaf shoots of spring on the branches. He pushed aside a thin birch sapling as he passed; not many young buds there, he thought, but birch was ever late.

He led them up the shallow incline, taking his time, his eyes eager for a sight of the enemy. He scanned the ridge with care - perhaps he had been mistaken before and there was no-one up there. Yet, it was spring and where was the bird song of dawn? There had been no birds fluttering to safety, startled by their approach. Had they already been driven from this part of the woods? He eased out his sword and behind him he heard the hiss of other blades sliding out, steel against leather.

Then he saw them, below the ridge ahead, a line of shadowy figures emerging like wraiths from the mist. Many, like his own men, had sword or axe in hand. He scanned the line anxiously for archers but saw none. The two lines were soon a mere fifty feet apart and drawing ever closer. Without warning several of his men at arms were thrown back from the line as iron bolts punched into mail, plate and flesh. Crossbows! He counted three men down, so four or five crossbows at most. Now they would have to reload but they would have time for another volley before the lines met.

He marched on, judging where the two lines would collide, focussing on the clutch of men in front of him. More bolts! Another three fell - not many but it might yet be enough. Through the trees each man could see his opponent but the only sound was the bracken being crushed underfoot. In every encounter he had ever fought men had shouted until their lungs almost burst as they closed upon their adversaries. They would scream the worst obscenities to ease their own frayed nerves. But this time neither side uttered a word. It was eerie, unnatural, but his mouth felt too dry to raise a shout. Ned had Bear to his left but it was Wulf to his right that he was worried about. The youth's wound was healing well but it would be sorely tested now. He never worried about Bear.

He stared at the oncoming men, now less than twenty paces away; their faces were set hard and their expressions were grim. His shoulder still ached from the skirmish at the ford; somehow it seemed to ache more now. There was no convenient clearing here; they would have to hack at each other amongst the scattered hazel and birch. It will be bloody, he thought, as he focussed on the advancing line.

At the last moment an awful thought struck him: could these men be Warwick's own, sent to track him down? Hastily he tried to pick out their badges - there were a handful of ragged staffs among them but there were others too and the man that came towards him bore the same blue badge as his own men. Thank God and St Michael! He had found the murderers he sought.

As if by some prearranged pact, the two ranks broke into a run over the last ten yards before they crashed into each other. Men at arms on both sides grunted with the effort of throwing all their energy into the first blow. In the cramped space between the trees no-one could give a full-blooded swing of their weapon, so they bludgeoned and stabbed at their opponents. Bear growled as two men took him on at once. He charged, like a raging bull, using the head of his great axe to punch both opponents back in turn, buffeting them onto their backs and crashing the heavy blade down with grim precision to finish them.

Ned had learned years ago to shut out all thoughts in

battle bar one: kill or be killed. It was always the same: he would start sluggishly and struggle to parry the first blows, barely deflecting them aside. Then he would adjust to the pace and rhythm of mortal combat and then his enemies would fear him. His first opponent was tall and rangy; he was well harnessed too but Ned spotted a gap between breastplate and helm. He lunged forward, driving his sword straight through the exposed neck. The stricken man crumpled silently but a comrade in a jack and sallet stepped over him and swung a bill at Ned's chest. It slid to the side of Ned's breastplate and caught for an instant on the lip. In trying to pull it back, his opponent only drew Ned closer - too close for either sword or halberd. They grappled fiercely, face to face. Ned butted his steel helm into his opponent's chin. The blow knocked him back and Ned saw another faded blue badge on the chest of the dazed man's jacket. Ned snatched out his long dagger and before the man could raise his halberd again, Ned stabbed him through the badge. The jack did its job well enough but Ned's blade was razor sharp and he forced it home.

The dying man let the halberd fall and for a moment he was held in Ned's arms. His sallet had no visor and Ned was forced to look as the lustre of life left his eyes. No quarter, thought Ned; this is what it means. Bagot had often said to him: if you're going to kill a man you should be prepared to look him in the eyes as you do it. Ned threw aside the halberd and left his knife stuck fast in the body. He stole a look around him: the forest echoed with the clash of steel on steel and voices now raised in agony and anger. There were many fallen but the lines had moved neither forward nor back: they just fought, man against man.

Another came at him and chopped down two ferocious blows with a poleaxe - the shorter weapons worked better in the confined space, Ned decided. Behind his opponent, he was alarmed to see several more men coming down from beyond the ridge. He ducked to avoid another swingeing blow and looked again: fifty paces away were the three crossbowmen. They had moved forward so that they could pick their targets more carefully. Any man fighting well could expect to be hit. Ned forced his opponent back, hoping he would shield him from a crossbow bolt.

He raised his visor. "Hal! Crossbows!" he bellowed, hoping his voice could be heard above the clamour. He need not have worried for suddenly each of the crossbowmen was struck by a brace of yard-long shafts. Ned grimaced with relief until the pole axe struck him a glancing blow on the side of his helm. Pay attention, you bloody fool! It felt as if an ox had kicked him.

He stepped back and shook his head. At once he wished he hadn't as dizziness threatened to engulf him. Instinctively he reached out to a tree branch for support. The pole axe was swung again but this time spent most of its force on the branch and barely grazed his arm. Slowly his vision began to clear but it was still blurred when he brought his blade down on his opponent's outstretched arm. There was a sickening crack, a yelp of pain and the man released his hold on the axe handle. Ned chopped his sword down on the shoulder joint and the crippled man dropped to his knees. Ned, still unsteady, hesitated; then he remembered Alnham.

"No quarter!" he shouted, his voice hoarse, and drove his sword down through neck and chest. Blood poured from the wound but he struggled to drag out the blade. Now he was vulnerable and he looked up, expecting a man to be upon him in an instant but no-one was. He realised that a change had occurred and the reason soon became clear: beside him, Bear had killed every man who had come at him and now they had stopped coming. They had edged along the line to fight elsewhere which meant that their line was broken in two with a gap in the middle.

Bear did not stop; he never stopped. He attacked them from the flank and the break in the line became a gaping hole. A few were already beginning to fall back towards the ridge. When Hal's archers let fly at the retreating line, half a dozen arrows thudded into their targets and the line disintegrated.

"Hold your lines!" Ned shouted, concerned that some would break out too quickly in pursuit. The fleeing men ran up to the ridge and then disappeared from sight. His eyes followed them and he wondered what dangers lay beyond the ridge. Then he blinked and looked again. He swallowed hard; the blow to his head must have done more damage than he thought. It could not be! The light was not good; perhaps he was mistaken. He seized Bear's arm.

"Look! On the ridge - do you see? In the black armour."

Bear stared impassively at the figure until it turned away and passed beyond the ridge. "Well?" demanded Ned.

Bear nodded. "Mordeur," he pronounced solemnly.

Ned stood still in disbelief.

"We go?" asked Bear.

"Yes, yes; come on!" yelled Ned and they hurried after the routed men at arms. By the time they crested the rise their enemies were already making their escape across some open grazing land for the trees ended at the ridge. Some were on foot but many were mounted.

"Hal, Mordeur's there! See his armour! Take him down!" roared Ned.

Hal followed where Ned pointed but made no attempt to loose an arrow.

"Hurry, lad!" urged Ned.

"We've no more arrows, lord."

In the light of the gloomy dawn they watched Mordeur and the others make their escape. Finally Ned tore his gaze away; he must decide what to do next.

"Very well, lad," he said, "you used your arrows well. Are your boys alright?"

"Aye," said Hal, "for once..."

"Good," said Ned. "That's good. Well done."

The rest of the men had collapsed, exhausted, at the tree line, grateful that there was to be no pursuit. Ned did not need to look too closely to see that they had been badly mauled in the encounter. He too sat down and leant his back against a tree but all he could think of was Mordeur. He realised now that it was the Norman he had seen coming out of the castle barbican at Newcastle. He had only glimpsed him at the time. He had assumed the brutal servant of the Radcliffes was long dead. What in God's name was Mordeur's involvement in all this? He found himself trembling at the very thought of the man. He must not be distracted! Mordeur's presence explained the ruthless efficiency of their enemies but it changed nothing.

"Hal, since your archers are so fresh, you can take them back to where we camped and keep a watch on the road. If anything moves on that road, I want to know at once!"

"Aye, lord."

"And mind you stay out of sight!"

Hal picked up his bow and gathered his archer comrades around him. They did not look pleased and set off with exaggerated slowness. Ned frowned. He had never seen the lively Hal so subdued. Only then, in that moment, did he realise that he was driving these habitually loyal men harder than he had any right to do. They had endured much already and with only muted complaints. He must take care.

Stephen sat down beside him. "God's blood! We survived again then, my lord. By Christ, you keep trying to finish us off and we keep breathing - just to spite you!"

Ned met his forced humour with a grim expression. Stephen's words were only too close to the truth - and by no means all his men were still breathing.

He sighed and said quietly: "Mordeur was there."

"What? Are you sure?"

"Bear saw him too - or I'd have put it down to my imagination."

"But..."

"Exactly right: but," said Ned. Somehow he was too exhausted to move. "We should see to the wounded - and the others..."

"It's already being done, lord," said Stephen. "Stay here awhile. Dawn's upon us and you've not slept yet."

§§§§

Stephen woke him a few hours later when Hal returned.

"There's a small column of riders on the road, lord," reported Hal, "heading north."

Ned leapt to his feet. "Come on then - they must see us coming clearly. It won't look very friendly if we're chasing after them, will it? Get every man on his feet and back to the horses."

"The wounded have already been taken there, my lord," said Stephen.

Ned clapped him on the shoulder by way of thanks and together they made their way back down the wooded slope, picking their way past the bodies. Ned paused only to retrieve his long knife.

"I've counted the badges on the dead," said Stephen, "eight wore Warwick's badge and none of them were sewn on: I'd wager a great deal these men were at Alnham."

"I suppose it's some comfort to know we haven't killed the wrong men, then," said Ned.

He sheathed his knife and they continued across the stream to their camp where their horses were already saddled and waiting.

"Hal, keep everyone under cover in the trees for the moment," ordered Ned, as he mounted. "We must not appear to be a threat."

He rode out with Stephen to meet the oncoming riders and only just intercepted them before they swept on northwards. Ned could not have been more relieved when he recognised Lord Montagu at the head of the small column. Montagu, though, was more than surprised to see him.

"Ned Elder, eh? I wasn't expecting to see you here. I thought you were at Bamburgh annoying my good brother, Richard!"

"No, the Earl awaits you in Newcastle. There was a risk of a Percy ambush so I came to warn you."

Ned did not engage in any lengthy explanation for he

knew from experience that Montagu would not welcome it. Once he heard the word Percy his curiosity was satisfied. His feud with the Percies went back many years. It was personal and because of it he would be content to kill Percies till the day he died.

"I know this country as well as any," said Montagu, "we'll take another route across the moor to the east. Will you come with us to Newcastle?"

"No, it's best we keep a watch to the west in case there are any stragglers from the force we've just routed. And…well, let's just say your brother and I have fallen out again."

Ned told him of his recent run in with the Earl. Their quarrel was well known by the men who served the cause of York. It made them all a little uneasy. Ned was a renowned warrior and many had witnessed his brave exploits on behalf of their young king but Warwick was … well, Warwick - a knight feted throughout Christendom. A quarrel between the two was unthinkable and Ned knew that many had tried to build bridges between them, but to no avail.

"He'll want your head this time, Ned," said Montagu, "and the king might just agree with him."

Ned feared as much himself.

"Still, I've seen your mettle several times and I'll need every man I can get when I head out of Newcastle."

"I could skirt the town and join you later," suggested Ned.

"Hmm. Morpeth," said Montagu. "Join me there in … two days. That should give me enough time to gather a force to match the Percies and Somerset."

Ned watched the small escort leave the road and head off to the east.

He turned his horse back to their camp. "Come on, Stephen; now we can rest for a while."

8

23rd April morning, at Morpeth in

Northumberland

Ned was growing more uneasy by the hour: two days had passed and still no sign of Lord Montagu. They had made good time to Morpeth, riding in a wide arc northwards around Newcastle and its outlying villages. In the lands to the west of the town they found only isolated crofts or shielings for the shepherds on the upland pastures. Their main obstacle northwards was the River Tyne but they forded it on a moonless night and, once across, they rode through the green, undulating land to Morpeth, approaching the town from the southwest.

They passed close by a great abbey on the heavily wooded southern bank of the river to avoid riding too near Morpeth Castle. When he reached the sturdy stone bridge across the river Ned was in two minds: most of the town seemed to occupy the north bank but he dared not risk being trapped there – most of all, he feared a trap. So he remained on the south bank and set up camp in the cover of the trees.

Though Ned had rested his men after the skirmish with Mordeur, they needed more. Some of their wounds were slow to heal and, if one or two were to fight again, he feared for their chances. Yet, for all that, their mood was cheerful for the first time in weeks and he knew why. The cause of their good humour was full bellies. Stephen had told him that many were fishing the river but he turned a blind eye to it.

Someone no doubt would be more than aggrieved when they found out but he had little coin left to buy food and they had eaten nothing but scraps and forage for days.

"You'd better be on your guard for angry monks," advised Stephen, grinning. He sat beside Ned as they enjoyed the fruits of the fishermen's labours. Ned had noticed that the inmates of the abbey were Cistercians for he had seen some working in the nearby fields, distinctive by their white habits and black scapulars.

"If only angry monks were all we had to worry about," he said. "What if Warwick persuades Montagu to surrender me? In the end, blood outweighs all."

He had drawn his sword against the Earl. It would matter little that Warwick had drawn his first or that Ned was merely defending himself. The Earl had sworn to have his head and the Earl was never forsworn – all of Christendom knew that.

Stephen shook his head. "I don't see why you would doubt Lord Montagu. He's been steadfast before-"

"The Earl's his brother and the Earl's a hard man to refuse. In the field I'd trust Montagu with my life, but here … I'm not so sure."

"He needs us if he's going after Somerset and the Percies," observed Stephen, "and I'm sure he knows that."

"Mmm, perhaps, but at the price of bringing his brother's wrath down upon him? Oh, did you put men out to watch the road from Newcastle?"

"You know full well I did – and you asked me again last night."

"Aye, of course. Hal!" he shouted.

As always, Hal was there almost before his name was called. "Yes, lord."

"Go and see that our men on the south road are alright – better take them some fish."

Hal grinned. "At once, lord," he replied and ran off.

"What would you do if you didn't have your young shadow to fling orders at?" asked Stephen.

"I'd fling a lot more in your direction," said Ned, smiling.

The day passed slowly but in the evening Hal brought news that a large host had arrived at Morpeth.

"Montagu?" Ned asked.

"Yes, lord, many wore the red and black of Lord Montagu," said Hal.

"Not the livery of Warwick?" Ned pressed him.

"In the dark, lord… the red of Warwick could be muddled with Lord Montagu's but I saw no ragged staff badges."

"And you're sure it's not Ralph Percy? His livery is red and black too."

"No, lord," Hal replied patiently, "I know their badges; they would've been very different."

"And where are they camped?"

"I watched the lords ride straight to the castle here on the south bank but the men are still crossing the river - there's hundreds of them. They must be making their camp to the north of the town."

"I hope there are more than just hundreds!" said Ned. "Well, I'd better go and see Montagu. Stephen, you have command. Hal, find Bear and Black and meet me by the track to the castle."

Stephen put a restraining arm on his shoulder as he moved. "Lord, perhaps it would be wiser to take a few more men."

"If I take too many it will hardly encourage Montagu to trust me, will it?" said Ned.

§§§§

At Morpeth Castle, Ned was expected but the guards would not permit his armed men to enter with him. After some haggling they agreed that Hal could accompany him and Bear and Black would wait inside the main gates. Ned was in no position to argue. He was escorted to a privy chamber on the first floor where he found Lord Montagu settling himself in.

"You got here in one piece then, Ned." His voice was gruff; he sounded tired but it was more than that. Montagu was a direct man and he did not wait long before telling Ned the bad tidings. He held out a piece of parchment and tossed it across the table to Ned.

Ned unrolled the document and scanned it quickly; its contents made unhappy reading.

"It's a warrant for my arrest," he said.

"Indeed it is," agreed Montagu, "not very helpful to our cause, but a legal document nonetheless."

"What do you intend to do with it?"

"I've said: it's a legal warrant. It will receive ... due process. I shall put it into the hands of the Sheriff at the earliest opportunity. We shall march at noon tomorrow and I shall deliver it to the sheriff on the way." He paused. "You, however, will ride out of the town at dawn."

Ned sighed with relief. "Thank you, my lord."

Bu Montagu had not finished.

"Ned, before you offer me any more thanks, you should know that this is but a brief stay of the warrant. After the fighting's done - if you're still alive - the warrant will still be there too. For a man of your status there'll be no shortage of folk to tell my brother where you are. Understand this: whatever the rights or wrongs of your quarrel, I'll not stand against my brother – not for you, perhaps not even for the king. The Earl wants you dead and there's nothing I can do to stop him. After we've dealt with Somerset, you must go to King Edward. He's the only one who can save you now."

"Do you think he will?" asked Ned.

Montagu looked at him. "I neither know nor care, Ned. In my view you've brought all this upon yourself. But for now, we'll put it aside."

Easy for Montagu to say, thought Ned.

"Now," Montagu continued, "as I said, I want you off early tomorrow to scout the route ahead. I'll give you some local men. I've learned that Somerset was at the Percy stronghold of Alnwick until yesterday. Now he seems to have gone north again. Find him for me. I still have the Scots envoys to pick up from Norham Castle and I don't want Somerset up my backside when I do!"

"Very well, my lord. I'll pick out some trusted men to keep you in touch."

"Good. When you've found him, get an idea of his strength. His welcome up here must be wearing thin by now. I should think he must be bleeding every last Percy boy from these lands. This treason has gone on long enough. I want it done, ended."

"Aye, my lord," said Ned but when he took his leave of Montagu his thoughts were not of Warwick, Somerset or the Percies but of Amelie and the child she was carrying. This business with Warwick would put everything he had at risk - including his loved ones. He cursed Warwick. He might have returned to Yoredale once the men of Lancaster were subdued, but now he would have to go to the king to beg for his support. And no-one loves a beggar.

§§§§

The following dawn the air was cool and the sky grey. Ned watched his camp being roused by Sir Stephen, Hal and others. The men had slept well but they moved sluggishly and it seemed to take a long time before the company was ready to move off. The horses were a constant problem; just providing enough fodder for the poor beasts was difficult enough but now lameness had already accounted for several of them. All the same, he had never regretted for an instant his decision to take only mounted men. Without their horses they would have perished at Bamburgh – and several times since. Yet the cost had been great: though most of his knights provided their own, there were many others to provide for, not least the archers.

Montagu's scouts seemed anxious to be on the move and they looked relieved when at last Ned's column of horsemen moved off. They crossed the river by the low stone bridge close to the abbey and passed a mill on the north bank as they entered the streets of Morpeth. Despite the early hour the town was far from asleep. The arrival of Lord Montagu's army had made outrageous demands on the small community: the bakers' ovens were working overtime and in every workshop throughout the town smiths, farriers and armourers could be heard at work.

"Where are we?" he asked one of the local scouts.

"This is Newgate, my lord. We're heading north as you commanded."

"Good," he acknowledged. And the sooner we're out of here the better, he said to himself.

§§§§

They caught up with the army of Lancaster by midday and from then on they played a long and tedious game of watch and move as they endeavoured to keep pace with the enemy host. Within two hours his scouts had explored the northern limits of Somerset's army and reported their estimate of its strength.

"Well?" Ned was impatient for news. "Give me the bare bones."

"My lord, the Duke has a host of perhaps four or five thousand with him; no cannon, only a few hundred archers and a score or so of crossbowmen."

"How many horse?"

"Could be as many as two thousand horse, my lord."

"He's moving very slowly – is he waiting for more men to come in?" asked Ned.

The scout shrugged. "If he can squeeze any more men out of this poor country, I'll be surprised."

"I don't care if you're surprised," retorted Ned, "but I don't want to be!"

"Sorry, my lord; there are still men coming in but their numbers are few."

Ned continued to track Somerset's force as it moved

slowly north but in the early afternoon the enemy stopped and made camp. Ned withdrew south, well out of contact distance.

It was late afternoon before Montagu's main army arrived and Ned was able to brief his commander.

"So," said Montagu cheerfully, "our foe has set up his standard and he means to block our passage to Norham - well, he means to try at least. In the morning we'll see if he's up to it. I want you in the centre with me tomorrow, Ned."

"In case I try to escape?"

"No, because I value your company in the field! It'll be an honour."

Ned shrugged. "We'll do our best, my lord, as always." Montagu was clearly looking forward to the imminent battle more than he was but he did seem to sense Ned's apprehension.

"Do I sound too eager, Ned? Does that trouble you?"

"I'm keen to see an end to all this too," said Ned bitterly. "I just want to get back to my wife – a child is due soon. I want to take my men back to their wives and mothers too, before I lose any more of them."

"You had some trouble before, didn't you - with the Radcliffes?"

Trouble? Ned reined in his indignation. "A little more than just trouble, I'd say, my lord."

"Aye, Ned. So would I. The Percies are my Radcliffes and I'll not rest until I've utterly broken their power."

Ned gave a curt nod. "Very well, my lord. Let's pray God favours us tomorrow."

§§§§

When the following day dawned they could neither see nor hear the enemy but they knew the Lancastrian host was there, to the north of them, on the moorland plateau. Montagu's scouts, or prickers as he called them, had reported that the Duke of Somerset had laid out his army across their path. Somerset clearly did not mean to let them pass to Norham for if the Scots made a peace with King Edward, the cause of Lancaster would be dead.

In the past Ned had found that in the calm before the storm of battle he preferred idle banter to silence. Some men did remain silent; others muttered familiar prayers or oaths whilst a few concentrated solely on retaining the contents of their bowels.

"Come on, Stephen," said Ned and he began to walk through the ranks of his men. He had first noticed other captains do it at St Albans and he had done it himself for the first time on a bloody Palm Sunday at Towton. He had no idea whether it helped his men to face what was coming but he knew it helped him. He spared a word of encouragement for some who needed it and a nod of respect to those who didn't. He remembered how King Edward, no older than he, had ridden along the battle lines at Towton and the surge of belief his presence had given them all. It was not enough for him to speak to the men; they had to believe that their best chance of surviving the day was to fight alongside him.

As he looked for the steel in their eyes, a succession of commands rang out in the still morning air. Hal looked towards him and Ned gave a nod of assent. Hal took Ned's few remaining archers and trotted forward to join others in the front ranks as the army began to advance. Ned led the men at arms on foot up the gentle slope ahead and when they reached the crest they saw the rebel army arrayed before them, perhaps a hundred paces away, perhaps nearer. Soon the archers of both sides would let fly – this was the moment Ned hated most, feared most: winged death falling upon them from the sky.

"Keep your heads down!" he bellowed but he knew that somewhere on the field there would be some keen lad, clad in the most expensive plate armour his family could buy, who would lift his head and raise his visor. He would see death coming, but too late.

Now the assault began – it mattered little which side

advanced first for in the end the two battle lines would shudder together and the grind of combat would take its bloody course. He expected it to be an even, blood-sapping contest. It might last all day and many would die but perhaps it would be the last battle, the very last. But then he always hoped the next battle would be the last.

He tramped down the slope onto the level ground with Bear, as always, walking slightly behind him on his left hand. Near him were some of his youngest men at arms. Wulf was there, and Green ... no, Green of course was not there: Green had fallen at the ford. Ten paces to his right was Stephen, his plate armour dulled and dented by struggle.

The Lancastrian archers let fly as soon as they saw them and within seconds the arrows began to fall and the men around him faltered. Ned was surrounded by loyal men, yet he wished Bagot could have been there. Not the worn out Bagot of now but the Bagot he had first met. The bad tempered, oath-blasting knight who had dragged him away from his first bloody combat, the man whose strength and dogged loyalty had kept him alive when he was shitting himself with fear. But that man was gone, reduced by his service to a ghost of what he had been.

Ned walked on though comrades crumpled alongside him. An arrow flew past him and he heard it thud into a padded jack behind him but he did not stop. He did not even glance behind even though he knew one of his own must have fallen. Instead he strode on across the moor towards the ranks of men advancing towards him.

He knew how the battle would play out. Blore Heath, Mortimer's Cross, Towton - they had all followed the same pattern: the two battle lines would meet with a shudder and a crescendo of noise from voices and steel. He waited for the first blow, for the first scream of agony and for the first man to cry out for his God or his mother. He lowered his visor and charged the opposing line. All he could see ahead of him were armoured breastplates and steel-clad limbs wielding axes, bills and swords. All he could hear was his own

breathing until the moment of impact when his head rang
with the chaos of a hundred blows. A long-handled poleaxe
swung past him, missing him by inches and split a man's
shoulder apart. Bear had entered the fray. Ned swayed back
to avoid the tip of a sword and braced his feet to keep his
balance as he thrust his own sword forward. In a matter of
moments the front lines of the two opposing armies were
fully engaged just as he had anticipated – but then something
happened that he wasn't expecting.

Encased in his helm, Ned saw nothing out of the ordinary
at first: men were trying to bludgeon each other to death all
around him. Yet even as he battled forward he thought he
could hear cheering - not where he was in the centre, but
somewhere else on the field. And he knew others had heard it
too for it changed the way the men of both sides fought. Men
who are distracted in battle, die. Yet it mattered to all of them
who was cheering and why. Ned stepped back a pace until he
was alongside Bear and then he lifted his visor and scanned
the field.

He saw at once what the cheering was about: the right
flank of Somerset's army was fleeing back across the moor,
their banners streaming out behind them as they ran. He was
astonished: who would come to battle and turn away after
only a few minutes? It was soon clear to all and some of his
own men became over eager and sallied into the opposing
ranks expecting them to fold. But they did not and the men
paid a full price for their folly.

"Hold your lines, damn you!" Ned bellowed and struck an
angry blow at an opponent. The Lancastrian centre was still
pressing forward, the colours of Percy in the van. There was
a mounted knight just behind the front ranks, urging his men
on. Ned could hear his words ringing out across the field:
"Forward!" he shouted. "Forward for Percy and King
Harry!"

The knight must have seen his right flank crumble, must
have feared the worst but he drove on. Commands and
counter commands were screamed in vain across the field but

then the blue and white banners of Henry Beaufort, Duke of Somerset, began to fall back. The Lancastrian commander, who held the centre of his army, turned and retreated, following the others already fleeing back across the moor.

"Good Christ! It's a rout!" cried Ned, hearing the shouts of jubilation echo across the field.

But the knight who led the vanguard did not seem to share his commander's faint heart and he cajoled his men at arms forward, pushing his armoured destrier into the line to give them spirit. In the face of this sudden advance Ned's men were hurled back, as were Montagu's, close by him on the right. Ned lowered his visor once again for he realised that his immediate opponents would not be fleeing with their comrades.

"A Percy! A Percy!" roared the knight and the cries were taken up by those all around him as he bullied them forward still further, pushing Ned's line back to the crest of the rise. All the while Ned knew that these men could not win for closing around them already were the flanks of Montagu's army. They might make some ground but they would surely be surrounded and the end was inevitable. Yet Percy's vanguard was still pressing him back. He and Bear hacked at the horseman's legs from either side. Ned could see that they had drawn blood but quickly they were driven aside by Percy's dogged men at arms on foot.

And so it went on, Percy's vanguard forcing them back down the slope they had marched up earlier. Percy was hemmed in now on all sides and his rear ranks were obliged to fight the men of York hounding them from behind. It's madness, thought Ned. This must be Sir Ralph Percy and they can only be his household men – nothing else would explain such diehard loyalty.

"You are all dead men!" he shouted at them but with every step they took forward the name Percy rang out. He tried to stab at Percy's horse but could only strike down a spearman before he was driven back once again.

"Someone kill that horse!" Ned cried out. But his cries

were to no avail for both horse and rider seemed invulnerable.

Even so, Percy's strength was dwindling and he must have known it. Ned almost wanted him to escape but suddenly Percy stopped and a gap opened up as Ned's line continued to retreat. Percy raised his visor and cast a look about him.

"Surrender Sir Ralph!" cried Ned, "You've done all you could. Now, yield!"

Sir Ralph nodded to himself, as if somehow satisfied. Then he lowered his visor once more and dug his spurs into the horse's flanks. The great beast surged forward and took a running leap to land in the midst of Ned's front ranks. Its hooves stove in men and metal as it screamed in agony. It had landed on a halberd which sliced through its belly. Sir Ralph Percy fell forward into a group of men at arms but got swiftly to his feet and swept several aside with a few well-judged blows. Around the stricken horse the rest of his bloodied followers gathered, fighting back to back with weapons falling upon them from all sides.

Ned carved a path towards the beleaguered knight. Sir Ralph was strong but he would not prevail and he must have known it.

"Yield, man!" shouted Ned. "In the name of God, yield!"

Sir Ralph fought his way to him and raised his visor. "Why would I do that?" His voice was hoarse from encouraging his men.

"You can do nothing more!" yelled Ned.

"I can die," replied the knight calmly and he took a step forward. For once Ned hesitated but those around him did not: Bear's axe struck Percy in the neck, loosening his breastplate and a sword thrust found its way across his chest. Two men hacked at his legs and Bear's second stroke knocked Sir Ralph's helm from his head. He dropped his sword and fell to his knees, blood running down his face and chest.

"Hold!" roared Ned. "No more! He's my prisoner. Finish the others if they will not yield!"

A few looked at him aghast. Here before them was a traitor, an oath breaker and a man who had caused the deaths of many of their comrades. They had heard the cry of "no quarter" often enough in the past and they did not see why it didn't apply now. They were seething but they accepted Ned's command and vented their anger upon Sir Ralph's retainers.

Sir Ralph lay on his side but raised his head to look at Ned.

"I rode towards you - saw old Tom Elder's pennant." His eyes clouded.

Ned knelt down on the ground beside him.

"Who are you, boy?" the knight mumbled. A trickle of his blood ran from scalp to chin.

"I'm Tom Elder's grandson, Ned." It was the first time he had said so to any man.

For a moment the bloodied face looked confused then he nodded slightly. "John Elder's son - a young eagle returned to the nest, eh?"

"It was my father that flew the nest," said Ned, "he was the eagle, not me; I'm a bird of a different sort."

"A different bird..." muttered Percy, closing his eyes.

The fighting was done and Ned looked up to see that a cluster of his men had gathered around the pair of them. Across the field he saw Lord Montagu striding towards them. Sir Ralph choked and blood spluttered from his mouth as he tried to speak again.

"I was a different bird too, Ned. I should never have taken that damned oath to Edward of York..."

"No?" said Ned.

The old knight's bloodied hand suddenly gripped Ned's wrist tightly, "Let it be known," he said.

"Let what be known?" breathed Ned.

"Let it be known," repeated Sir Ralph, "that I've saved the bird in my bosom..."

"You'll be remembered with honour, Sir Ralph," said Ned, but the knight already lay still.

"He died a brave death," said Stephen, kneeling down to join him beside the corpse.

"He died a needless death," said Ned quietly, "but I don't want his body mistreated. He's dead, so let's hope Montagu won't still want to take his head.

His friend nodded. "I'll do my best."

Ned took Stephen's arm. "We need to talk," he said and drew him aside.

"Lord?"

"Now the battle's won, my life's not worth a splintered lance," said Ned.

"You think Warwick will come for you with his warrant?"

"If not the Earl, then one of his lackeys. I need to get to the king - only he can overrule Warwick."

"Then you must go at once."

"Yes, I'm afraid I must. I'll take Hal and young Wulf with me but you'll need Bear and the other older hands. Montagu told me that once the battle was done he'd release the men under your command. I think he'll keep his word."

"What if the war continues?" asked Stephen.

"Who can say what turn the war will take up here? I trust you, Stephen. Whatever you decide will be good enough for me. You know what must be done."

"I suppose I do. Where shall we meet you then?" asked Stephen. "We're still strangers here and there are few places either of us could find our way to."

Ned had no answer. He hadn't even considered the problem.

"The further south the better," he said. "Let's assume the fighting's all but over, we don't want to be any further away from Yoredale than we have to. That's what matters - getting back home."

"But where then?"

"Do you remember when we first came north, all those weeks ago? We passed through a large village - Corbridge was it? We forded the Tyne there - the first time. We could meet there - the men can camp on the south bank near the ford."

"Was there not a tavern some of the lads found? Hal will know it: the Golden something."

"Cock, if I remember," said Ned, "I'll meet you there if I don't see your camp."

"How long do you think you'll be?" asked Stephen.

"Hard to say; it'll take at least a week - unless the king's in the north. It could be longer…"

Stephen looked him in the eye. "I suppose what I'm asking, Ned, is how long do we wait?"

"Aye, my friend, and it's a fair question."

Ned wiped his hand across his brow and was slightly disconcerted to find a smear of blood. He stared at it for a moment before continuing.

"If we're not back in two weeks, head home for Yoredale," he said. He felt suddenly very weary, the exertions of the battle catching up with him. Yet now he had a long journey ahead.

"Let's hope by then the king has intervened and the warrant is annulled," said Stephen. "Once Lord Montagu releases us, I'll be at the Golden Cock in Corbridge at sunset each day until you come."

Ned put an arm on Stephen's shoulder. "If I'm not there in a couple of weeks, I probably won't be coming. Get the men back home for me, to their wives and families."

"I will," said Stephen. "God speed, Ned."

9

26th April morning, at Crag Tower in the North Tyne Valley

Henry sat in the privy chamber at Crag Tower slumped in his grandfather's large oak chair. Strange, he thought, how he still thought of it as his grandfather's - but it was not just the chair. It was the room. It was every room. It was every stair, every tapestry that clothed the walls. He could sit in Crag Tower for all his days but it would still not be his, for every stone was etched with memories of Thomas Elder.

"So much for Ralph Percy," he said bitterly.

"He died like a fool," said Mordeur, "but Somerset still has an army, even without Ralph Percy."

Mordeur was awaiting for him to make a decision. Henry had never liked Mordeur much when he rode with Edmund Radcliffe and he liked the Norman knight even less now that he had come to rely on him so much. Mordeur - 'the one who bites'- well he had had his fill of Mordeur's biting and sniping at him. For the moment Henry needed him but he would not always need him.

"Somerset and his friends fled at the first sight of Montagu!" Henry could not disguise his contempt. "Well, Somerset can do what he likes now but I'll not be following his banner. There's another road I can take to get my birthright."

"Are you sure?" said Mordeur, "Perhaps the Earl of Warwick is aware that you were among his foes at Hedgeley Moor - although, of course, you were not so…obvious."

"Oh, he'll still be very eager for my help, have no doubt about that," he said with a confidence he did not quite feel. "I already have his Commission of Array."

"You had a Commission of Array from Somerset too," said Mordeur, "but it is worthless to us now. The House of Lancaster is lost."

Henry knew he was right: he might as well wipe his arse with Somerset's Commission; his only hope now was Warwick.

"We must act quickly," he said. "I want you to go to Warwick. It had better be now, today, for he won't be in the north much longer. He's got too many other pies to poke his noble fingers into. This time I want more than a Commission to raise men - men are thin on the ground. I want him to give me some of his own."

"Oh?" said the Frenchman, clearly doubtful, "and why would he do that?"

"Ned Elder's banner flew on Hedgeley Moor. I didn't see him but I know he was there."

"You weren't there long enough to see anyone," muttered Mordeur.

Henry ignored the insolence. "It tells us that Ned Elder is not yet under arrest, despite the Earl of Warwick's great desire to see it done."

"But we want Elder arrested," said Mordeur, "so how does it help us?"

Henry noted the use of the word 'us'. Mordeur was getting above himself but this was not the time to tell him that.

"The all-powerful Earl is having trouble getting his hands on Ned Elder. I have something to offer him because I can deliver Ned to him."

"That will not be so easy, you know," said the Frenchman. "You've never fought him - I have."

"Yes, remind me how many times you've run from him?"

Henry saw the flush of anger in Mordeur's face where his dark beard reached the high cheek bones.

"I was not the only one who fled after Towton," he growled, "I only say it will not be easy - Ned Elder is not some wounded old man to be hacked down with ease."

Henry stood up and faced the Frenchman. Mordeur needed to feel his resolve.

"I know well enough that if I fought Ned Elder a hundred times he would kill me every time. But there are other ways... I've thought of little else these past few years and I've no doubt I can find the bait to bring Ned Elder to his knees but to do it I need more men at arms. So, you go to Warwick: offer him Ned Elder, or Ned Elder's head - whichever he pleases - but get me fifty more men!"

Mordeur shrugged. "Very well," he said and turned to go.

"Wait!" said Henry for a sudden thought had occurred to him.

"When you went to Warwick - at Newcastle - did Ned Elder see you?" he asked. Mordeur hesitated and that worried him. "Did he see -"

"I heard," said Mordeur. He spread his arms wide. "I don't know... it's possible."

"Do I need to ask you again?" enquired Henry coldly.

"However many times you ask, I will still not be certain," said Mordeur. "What does it matter?"

"Because if he knows you're involved he may start to ask himself why."

Mordeur shook his head. "In truth, it matters little if he saw me in Newcastle, because I'm certain he saw me later when we tried to ambush Lord Montagu."

Henry cursed. "You should've told me! Now he'll be wondering how you are involved - he won't know yet but he'll be thinking about it and the less he knows about me, the better."

"He knows nothing of you at all - only me."

"And how do you know that? It's better if he doesn't know about any of us - not until it's too late. The Elders always come back," he murmured, "even when you think they're dead and gone. Edmund made that mistake and so did my mother - but I'm not going to."

Mordeur grinned, baring his ugly teeth, several of which were black with decay.

"If that's all, my lord, I'll take my leave."

"Yes, yes. Go."

Henry looked after him thoughtfully; he would need to watch Mordeur. To his own certain knowledge the Frenchman had already abandoned two lords to their fate - Henry did not want to be a third.

He made his way down the narrow spiral steps - Crag Tower was a far cry indeed from Yoredale Castle. He crossed the Great Hall and ascended another stair to Joan's chamber. As usual he did not bother to knock but simply walked in, perhaps because he knew it irritated her. Joan had two servant girls in attendance and she did not look pleased at the interruption. One was combing out her long hair and the other was preparing an elaborate headdress. He nodded with approval. Around the castle she revealed more of her wanton mass of hair than was seemly for a married woman; it was good to see her showing better judgement. She wore a thin linen shift untied at the neck and the sight of the curve of her breasts stirred him. He stood for a moment mesmerised by the rhythmic movement of the comb through the hair.

"Lord?" she said, "how may we poor ladies help you?" He noted how much more submissive she appeared when the servants were present.

"I must speak with you, my lady," he said but he wanted to touch her, tease out those breasts. They had been married for two weeks and for several nights she had come to his bed willingly but since then she had rebuffed him every night.

Joan favoured him with her sweetest smile. "But my lord, we are engaged in important business here - can't it wait?"

He was furious. She was deliberately toying with him but it only served to increase his desire. "It must be now, lady!"

Her smile faded. "I have said, my lord, that it isn't convenient now."

"Hang your convenience - the master doesn't wait for his

horse to be groomed!"

He turned to the two girls who were nervously fiddling with comb and wimple.

"Get out!" he ordered. They glanced at Joan, who gave the slightest nod of assent.

He must make a real stand with Joan, he decided. Like Mordeur, she was getting too full of herself. But when the servant girls had gone Joan spoke first, her voice as cold as stone.

"Don't do that again, Henry. I am not your trinket!"

"But you are exactly that. You're my wife, you're mine." He rested his hands on her slim waist. "As your body is mine."

He slid his hands up to her breasts and felt her tense at his touch. "You're bound to me and you'll do my bidding as a good wife should."

His fingers found her nipples and he could smell her sex but, even when he touched her intimately, Joan's icy stare did not waver.

"I may be your wife but I'm not just any wife. We're equal players in this game - you and I -because I'm a wife with a legitimate claim to every part of the Elder inheritance you crave - unlike you. You need me - and, as long as you do, you will enjoy my body only when it pleases me to let you."

"My claim will be confirmed soon enough!" he snapped, pulling away from her. Damn her, she always seemed able to rile him.

"Confirmed? You put your trust in Somerset but he has ...run away. Now you must rely on Warwick's aid."

"Somerset's finished - whatever he does next, he'll end up on the block but Warwick is a different matter." He had explained it all to her before and he was damned if he would justify himself to her. "Leave such matters to me."

Joan walked towards him until her face was only inches from his. Her stern countenance crushed his resolve and he took an involuntary step back.

"You can't trust a man as powerful as the Earl of

Warwick. He has the king's power behind him - why should he care what we want? We're nothing to him."

He shivered as her eyes bore into him, reaching into his heart and gripping his soul. She lifted her hand and he gasped, thinking she was going to hit him but instead she touched her hand gently against his cheek.

"I know you, Henry. I know you very well. You would kill a man with no regrets - if only you had the will…but, most of the time, you don't." Her voice was soft but her words cut him like a steel blade. "But I have enough will for both of us," she murmured softly. "You just need to remember that."

She pulled his face towards hers and kissed him hard on the lips. As he started to respond she pulled away with a smile - but there was no humour in it. She walked back over to the narrow window.

"Now, was it just my breasts you wanted or was there something really important?"

Henry could not think clearly - she'd caught him off guard. He was torn between wanting to drag her to the bed and wanting to knock her stupid little head from those slender shoulders. In the end he did neither, for she was right about one thing: he needed her legitimacy - for the moment. But when he no longer needed her, he would treat her as Edmund had treated his women. He'd never understood it before - but now he did. She would play her part in their great enterprise and then he would toss her aside. Then she would feel the strength of his will.

He could still feel her eyes upon him as the silence lengthened between them.

"Did you find out whether Maighread's brother is still hanging about?" he asked.

"I was trying to when you interrupted me," she said, her voice flat and hard.

"You were being pampered by your maid servants as I recall."

"Maighread would not even speak to me and she'd hardly

hear anything in that filthy tomb you have her in. But one of my girls - that you so helpfully sent away - is my eyes in the village."

"And?"

She gave him a smug look. "Maighread's brother is back."

"Can you trust this girl?"

"Aliena's been with me since we were girls and she hates Rob - I know that for certain."

Joan was still a girl, thought Henry. "How well does she know him?" he asked.

Joan gave him a wicked grin. "I'd say she knows every last inch of him."

He grimaced. "I can imagine... but she's hardly likely to betray him, is she?"

"She tells me he forces her," said Joan. "Can you imagine such a thing, Henry? I think betraying him might be her pleasure. I'll put it to her."

"Good, the last thing we need is Maighread's kin poking their noses in."

"Now, don't you have a sword to sharpen - or a breastplate to polish?" she said.

He sighed. "You need to ..."

"Yes?" she enquired. He said nothing as he opened the door and went out.

He descended the stair to the Great Hall and in the courtyard outside he found Mordeur preparing to leave with some of the men. He studied them closely: they were hard men - he could see that at a glance - hard and pitiless. Mordeur had chosen well for they would need such men if they were to survive the next few months and they would need a lot more of them.

"I want you back here by tomorrow night at the latest," he told the Frenchman quietly.

"Why... lord?"

"Because the Duke of Somerset commands our presence at a new muster near Alnwick. We've to be there by nightfall on the day after next and it'll take us the best part of a day to get there."

"But I thought you were not going to ride with the Duke?"

"I'm not but I can't afford to ignore his summons until you get me Warwick's men. Then we can abandon this shithole and head south."

He left Mordeur and retired back up to his chamber, calling for some wine. When it came he spent the evening drinking a great deal of it, his head spinning with images of the rout at Hedgeley Moor: Somerset fleeing the field, Ralph Percy hurtling forward to certain and pointless death - and his own men, everyone a mercenary, running for their horses and mounting before he had even given the order to go. Mordeur would not stand; he knew that much from past experience.

Amidst all this weakness and treachery, whom could he trust? It should have been Joan but she was a cold, cold bitch - not much succour there. He drained the contents of a wine jug and tossed it across the room where it smashed against the foot of the wall sending shards of pottery spinning across the floor. He picked up another full pot from the chest by the window and carried on drinking. Joan had rebuffed him earlier. He couldn't allow that. She thought him weak; he must disabuse her of that. He belched noisily.

"I shall visit my wife's chamber," he said aloud. There were none there to hear him but he carried on nevertheless. "Visit her chamber indeed!" He chuckled. "I'll give her chamber a healthy thrust or two! And a very ripe chamber, it is," he sniggered.

"Mustn't waste my seed," he muttered as he stumbled along the narrow passage to her room. The hasty marriage had been Joan's idea but it had seemed in his interest too - now he was not so sure. He walked in and found Joan already abed. The room was brightly lit - there must have been at least a dozen candles, he thought. Did she think he was already a great lord to countenance such waste?

"What do you want?" demanded Joan. She's not pleased, he thought.

"I am here to visit your chamber," he announced, leering at her unsteadily.

"You're drunk and you're going to get out of my chamber now!" said Joan, raising her voice.

He guffawed noisily, grinning from ear to ear. "But I've not got into it yet!" He lurched forward onto the bed. "I've come to pick the fruits of the marital bed again, my dear," he said, still grinning.

"You've already picked the fruit, Henry and it'll be a while longer before you pick any more!"

He laughed and put his hand on a small firm breast, sliding his thumb roughly across her nipple.

She looked at him stony faced. "Stop pawing at me, Henry," she snapped.

He stared at her in disbelief. "Now that we're married you might fulfil your obligations! We've lain together but once or twice."

"Thrice, I believe, but now that we're married you can stop treating me like a whore!" she said. "Think on that!"

"Your job is to give me a son! And I will have you whenever I fucking please!" he said, seizing her by the shoulders. "So think on that, lady!"

She laid her hand upon his and slowly tightened her grip. Her nails dug hard into his palm as she prised his hand away.

"When you've delivered what you promised: lands and titles - then there might be some point in giving you a son."

It was all words to Henry, words that he didn't even listen to. She was his wife. She must submit to him. He examined his palm: her nails had drawn a trace of blood.

"Bitch!" he said.

She moved then faster than he could ever have imagined, twisting from his grasp and drawing out a small blade from under her pillows. Before he could react she somehow had the knife at his groin and he felt the keen point.

She moved her face until it was close to him and her next

words chilled him: "I may be your wife but you'll not bed me again until you have Ned Elder's inheritance firmly in your grasp. Your bastard's claim is worth nothing yet. Now you think on that!"

The blade remained against him and he feared she was just angry enough to use it. For a moment he dared not move.

"As you please," he said hoarsely. Joan withdrew the knife but kept it in her hand. Their eyes met and he looked away.

"Have your sport," he said, "sooner or later, I'll have mine."

He drew back from the bed and stumbled out of the room. "Bitch," he muttered but her cold rejection had not dampened his desire or eased the ache in his loins. He made his way back to his chamber to find some more wine but at the door a sudden thought struck him: there was at least one woman in the castle who could not refuse him - a woman he had never had.

He went down to the Hall and looked outside into the courtyard. The night was warm for April. It was not completely dark for several torches shed flickering pools of yellow light around the walls where steps rose up to the ramparts. He made his way on down to the cells below the Hall. He had told Maighread he would not rape her with a long pike. Well, perhaps he had been too hasty in his judgement; she was still a fair looking woman, after all.

PART TWO: OUTLAW

10

30th April late evening, at Stony Stratford in Buckinghamshire

Go to York, they had told Ned, you'll find the king there; but King Edward had not reached York. At York they said he'll be in Nottingham, he's sure to have got that far; but the king was not to be found in Nottingham either and there they told him his grace had lately been at Coventry. Ned had already been four days on the road but he went on to Coventry for he dared not waste a day. There, to his dismay, he found that the king had already left the town for Stony Stratford. So, late on the evening of the fifth day of his journey south, Ned trotted wearily into Stony Stratford followed by Hal and Wulf.

It took almost no time to discover that the king was there for the town was alive with the hangers on that followed him wherever he went. All the inns were full but it mattered little to Ned for he had long since used the last of his coin. His name had earned him a meal and a bed in York but since then the three of them had slept rough. When he saw some of the courtiers in all their expensive finery he was acutely aware that he did not have the look of a lord. He could not shake the dust from his clothes for it was sealed on with a layer of grime and filth.

It was late so he knew the king would already be abed with some wench he had spied in whichever hostelry he had favoured with his royal presence. In any case Ned was too tired to speak let alone think. If he was to persuade Edward of the justice of his cause then he must sleep the night and see his grace in the morning. With luck, his good friend Will Hastings would be close by the king and could procure him a speedy audience.

Though he was desperate for the king's help, he was also aware that every day he was away from his men the more likely it was that they would perish in some pointless Neville skirmish. He had left Stephen in command but their fate would not be in Stephen's hands as long as the company was still at the disposal of Lord Montagu. Moreover, he was worried about Amelie. He had already been away too long and he knew the birth could not be far off. He had promised her that he would return before she was closeted away with the women. So, haste was imperative.

§§§§

They slept the night in a makeshift stable with the horses and to find even such luxury they were obliged to ride a mile or two out of the town. Nevertheless, Ned slept well in the knowledge that his search for the king was over. He rose early and they returned to Stony Stratford. It did not take long to track down the king and Ned grinned with relief when he found Will Hastings. Since Hastings, as Lord Chamberlain, controlled access to the king the last part of his journey should at least be swift.

"Ned? God preserve us, Ned but you've an unfashionable look!" Hastings appeared genuinely shocked at the sight of him.

"Your pardon, Will. I'd no thought of making the place look untidy," replied Ned with a sheepish grin, "but we've ridden hard and long to find you."

"Ridden? Looks to me like you've been dragged behind the horse not ridden upon it!" Hastings laughed but yet it seemed to Ned that it was a slightly nervous laugh.

"Will, I must see the king, urgently!" The words somehow blurted out.

"What is it Ned? Do you come from Montagu? Is there bad news from the north? We'd heard of a victory."

"No, no," Ned reassured him, "the news from the north is good."

Hastings was visibly relieved, but still seemed wary.

"Why have you come then, Ned? What's this urgent business with Edward?"

"Will, it's Warwick again. He's issued a warrant for my arrest."

"No! On what charge?"

"Several, but chiefly he claims I killed some of his men at arms and raised my sword against him."

Hastings was aghast. "And did you?"

"No! No, of course I didn't! Well, I did raise my sword against him and my man did strike him with an axe head but-"

"Are you mad Ned? We're fighting a war up there! It's not the time to pursue your petty quarrel with Warwick!"

Ned bristled at that. "I think I know more about that war than you do, Will! But Warwick's charges are absurd."

"What then? Answer them in the court? A dispute between two northern lords? The king would have to hear the case - it's unthinkable."

"Why?" Ned demanded.

"Why? You fool, Ned, you could only lose - the king would not, could not, condemn Warwick."

"But Warwick is in the wrong. Let me speak to the king."

Hastings hesitated. Ned could not recall seeing him so flustered.

"Can I not see him, Will?" he persisted.

Hastings said nothing and doubts crowded in on Ned. This was an unexpected hurdle.

"The king is here only for a day or two, Ned," said Hastings. "There are important affairs to deal with today but perhaps you can see him tomorrow. I owe you that at the very least. Then it's up to him."

"But surely you could get me in today, Will. I've been too

long away as it is. I must get back."

"Today's out of the question, Ned. I'll make sure that he sees you tomorrow no matter how busy he is. He'll want to see you, I'm sure - though the matter you bring is unwelcome."

"It must be today, Will," Ned said though he could see that Hastings was losing his patience. "Will, the longer I am away from Lady Amelie..."

"Well, on that score I can reassure you, Ned. I went to Yoredale only a couple of weeks ago and your sweet lady was doing fine in the very capable hands of your two sisters - as it should be. She won't want you loitering about anyway. What possible use would you be? Birth is a woman's world, Ned. All you need to know is whether you've a son or not. Now, kick your heels here for the day - and clean yourself up. I'll find somewhere for you to stay. I suppose you've no money?"

Ned shook his head. Hastings pressed a small purse into his hand. "Here, this should do for a day or two."

Ned looked at the leather bag. "I'm grateful, Will." Hastings had always been generous to him. If Will Hastings said the king was too busy then he must trust that his friend was better placed to know than any other man in the kingdom.

Hastings returned shortly and told him where he could find a room. The mention of Hastings' name opened all doors to him and even Hal and Wulf were accommodated with other servants at the inn. Within an hour he had washed some of the dirt off his face at least and had calmed himself enough to start planning what he would say to the king the following day. In this regard Hastings' reaction, though it had been a shock, was helpful for it made him see that King Edward would find it more difficult to support him than he had first thought. He should have realised that the king relied heavily on Warwick yet he had to hope that Edward could see a way to resolve the problem. He was musing on how this might be done when he heard the sound of many horses riding past the inn on the road north. He went downstairs, half dressed and saw Hal by the door.

"Who was that?" he asked.

"I'd guess that it was the king, his courtiers and plenty of others, lord," replied Hal.

What then, Ned wondered, was the king's pressing business today?

"I'm glad I'm not going," said Hal, "my seat is sore enough already."

"No reason why you would be going," said Ned.

"I've been hunting before."

"He's not going hunting," said Ned.

"Well, why's he taking a great pack of hounds with him then?" asked Hal.

Ned stood still for a moment. "You saw hounds with the king?" asked Ned.

Something in Ned's tone alerted Hal to the importance his lord attached to the question and he paused before replying. "Yes, lord."

"Hunting," Ned murmured, "he can't just be hunting. Unless..." The thought suddenly struck him: Will Hastings was protecting his master from becoming involved in Ned's dispute with Warwick. Hastings was Ned's friend, but he was Edward's friend first. The very first words Hastings said to him when they first met three years before were that he would kill his own brother to protect Edward. So that was it: Hastings was keeping him from the king. More than likely there would be no meeting on the morrow either. Damn Hastings for playing him false; he had expected better - for if he could not trust Will Hastings then who could he trust?

"Hal," he ordered, "get Wulf and saddle the horses!"

"Lord?" Hal looked appalled.

"When did you last question my orders, Hal?"

"Never, lord - and that includes now!" Hal flew out of the door.

Ned ran back up the stairs and retrieved his padded jack which was all the protection he had brought with him. He had been keen to travel light so his battle sword, plate armour and mail had been left in Northumberland with Bear. He strapped on his small arming sword and returned downstairs where Hal and Wulf were already waiting with the horses.

"I want to follow the hunting party," said Ned. His voice trembled as he said the words for he knew if he did catch the king, Hastings would be far from pleased.

"Well, that shouldn't be difficult," said Hal as they set off.

§§§§

The landlord at the inn had told Hal that the king often hunted in Whittlewood forest and they tracked the hunters easily through several copses to the north of Stony Stratford until the royal party splintered into several different groups and suddenly the task became more difficult. The last thing Ned wanted was to draw attention to himself but if he could just have a few minutes with the king he might win his support. First though, he had to find him.

They spent almost an hour in Whittlewood forest and managed to find at least three distinct hunts. Ned even chatted amiably to some of the huntsmen - all local Northamptonshire men - but he was no wiser about the whereabouts of the king for each hunt believed his grace to be with one of the others. They had ridden almost across the breadth of the forest when Ned pulled up in a small clearing.

"It doesn't make any sense," he told Hal, "the king can't just disappear!"

"He could be with another group of huntsmen, lord," suggested Hal. "This is a big forest. We could ride around all day and still not find him."

"He's hunting, Hal! How did we find the others? By their noise. Yes, a hunter might be stealthy or silent at times but there'll be shouts, or a horn or the barking of the hounds. It's not exactly a quiet activity! And the king will always have his household guards nearby."

"Well perhaps he doesn't want to be found," said Hal,

"for kings must have important or secret matters to -"

"Of course!" said Ned. "That would make more sense. That's why Lord Hastings told me the king could not spare the time today: he has privy matters to deal with. The hunt was just a ruse."

"So, do we go back?" enquired Hal.

"Yes, yes, of course. I was a fool to doubt Hastings. There's no point in tiring the horses any more. We'll just ride gently back to Stony."

The more he thought about it, the more convinced Ned was that King Edward must be engaged on some state business. Well, it had been worth a try; he would just have to curb his impatience and meet with the king tomorrow. They skirted the eastern edge of the forest where it broke up into a series of large copses. There was pasture land further to the east as the forest continued its southward sweep. Soon they came upon a meandering stream and Ned dismounted.

"We'll water the horses here before we ride on back," he said.

Whilst the horses paddled idly in the stream, Ned sat down on the grassy bank to rest. The weariness of the past five days had caught up with him and when he looked at his two companions he could see that they too were dog tired. He saw it in their eyes: he should not have dragged the pair of them around half the shire. He reckoned it was not yet noon so they could take their time and still return to Stony Stratford for a well-deserved meal courtesy of Hastings' generosity.

After a while he stood up and stretched. It felt good, he decided, as he glanced across the stream to the treeline beyond it. Then he focussed a little more closely on one stand of trees. Had he seen a flash of movement there?

"Hal? Take a look over there - do you see anything?"

Hal stared at the trees beyond the stream. "No, lord," he said, "what am I looking for, deer?"

"No. I don't know. I thought I saw a glint of something…"

"A glint? It could have been one of the huntsmen," suggested Hal.

Ned remounted. "Come on," he said, "we can take a loop around that way. We need to go back through the forest anyway."

He could tell that the others thought he was imagining things but they followed him across the stream towards the trees. As soon as they passed into the woods they saw the buildings. There were several, some of timber construction and a few of stone.

"Looks like a priory, lord," said Hal.

"Perhaps. Small though, more of a hermitage," said Ned. He had already lost interest. Whatever he had seen, if indeed he had seen anything at all, it was most probably one of the inmates of this small religious house. Emma no doubt would have loved the place but it held little interest for him.

"It's very quiet," said Wulf.

"It's supposed to be," said Ned," that's the point of such a place: quiet for prayer and reflection. They'll be wandering around a small cloister somewhere, reflecting."

They continued on and a few yards from the track past the buildings was a dovecote. The cooing and fluttering from within put Ned at his ease once more. The whole priory or hermitage was small - a simple rural retreat which they should leave well alone. He chided himself for chasing shadows for he'd find plenty of them in any forest.

They had almost left the priory behind them when Ned noticed the horses. He heard them first and then saw them through the trees, tethered fifty paces or so from the nearest building. It awakened his curiosity once more for it seemed odd that the mounts should be there. Surely there was at least a rudimentary stable for travellers to leave their horses.

"Wait here," he told the others and rode over to inspect the mounts. They were still saddled - and what saddles: fine leather work on some of them which could only mean wealthy visitors. Well, good luck to the inmates, he thought, perhaps they would receive a generous donation from their guests. He was about to turn away when he noticed an item tied to one of the saddles, a rather faded red ribbon.

Ned stared at it in disbelief for he had seen it before many times - though not for several years. A young girl had pressed it into Will Hastings' hand as they rode out from Wigmore Castle three years before. He had tied it there before the battle at Mortimer's Cross and after their victory he had been loath to remove it. Ned was surprised it was still there but even more surprised at what it signified: Hastings was at this isolated hermitage. If the Lord Chamberlain was here, then Ned had no doubt that King Edward would be as well.

He should have turned around then but he did not; instead he rode back to Hal and Wulf.

"Take your horses back down to the stream," he said," and wait for me there."

The pair gave him puzzled looks but obeyed. He watched them until they were out of sight then he dismounted and wrapped his reins around a branch. He had no idea what he was going to do. If the king had decided to make a private visit to the priory, he would certainly not be pleased to see Ned. Yet, it was a golden opportunity to catch King Edward on his own for he clearly had few courtiers with him - perhaps Will Hastings and one or two others. He decided he could not pass up the chance. After all, the worst that could happen was that Hastings would send him packing with a kick up the arse for his impudence. It was a small risk.

He entered the building by a small portico; there was a gate but it was, surprisingly, left ajar. The whole place was so quiet that he encountered no-one as he explored the small cloister. It was as if all the inmates had deserted and he recalled that he had seen none either in the fields or outhouses they had passed. It was utterly still, save the sound of his own footsteps on the stone flags of the cloister. A stray thought crossed his mind: what if there had been a plague outbreak in the community? But then the king would have stayed far away, so it could not be that.

On the far side of the cloister there was an archway and a

DEREK BIRKS

door. He laid his hand on the door and raised the latch. Suddenly his mind flashed back to a moment years before when he had opened the door to Mucklestone church. He had found more than he bargained for that day. Nevertheless, he opened the door and stepped lightly inside, leaving it slightly open behind him. He was in a long narrow chapel with the altar at the end furthest from him. His view was obscured by a line of slender columns but he could hear the low murmur of voices.

He took a step forward and saw a small group gathered before the altar. There was a priest facing him but of the others present he could only see their backs. It was enough because he recognised King Edward's tall frame easily, though not the woman beside him. He also realised at once what he was witnessing and started to back towards the door. He passed through it and gently pulled it closed behind him with a sigh of relief.

A hard sharp object dug into the small of his back.

"What in the name of Christ do you think you're doing, Ned?" hissed Will Hastings.

Ned could not bear to face him and could think of nothing to say.

"You fool!" said Hastings and struck him on the back of the head with the hilt of his sword.

§§§§

Ned came to in darkness. His head hurt. He tried to move but his hands were bound tightly behind him, making it difficult to explore his surroundings. He could feel the rough wooden planks on the floor because a splinter dug into one of his fingers.

"Shit," he muttered, "where am I?"

He pushed himself backwards with his feet, which were not tied at least. He found his back against a wall. It felt like it too was made of great rough-hewn timbers. He pushed down with his feet and lifted his bottom off the floor leaning his

156

weight against the wall. He edged upwards and then pushed harder until his head struck some object that jutted out from the wall and he dropped back down again, jarring the base of his spine.

While his legs struggled to get him upright again his mind was feverishly exploring questions of infinitely more importance: what had happened to him after Hastings had hit him? Where were Hal and Wulf? Where was he? His second attempt to stand proved no more successful than the first. As he lost his balance and fell to the floor again he decided to remain there. He dozed fitfully until he became aware of some light, almost imperceptible at first but growing steadily as only dawn could. And with the sun came the birds; so, he was still in the woods… somewhere. He could see his prison now, it might have been an outhouse for a hunting lodge or perhaps he was still near the hermitage. He scoured the room with his eyes but could see nothing that would help him to free himself.

His mind was so befuddled that only belatedly did he remember what he had seen at the chapel.

"A king's wedding," he mused aloud, "but secret, hidden from public view. Why would that be?"

He tried to recall what the bride was like but he had seen little of her. Her back view had been most attractive and he assumed that Edward would not have accepted any but the most beautiful woman for a wife. There had been few witnesses: the priest obviously, several other women - one was older, perhaps the bride's mother? Was she a foreign princess? If so, then surely the wedding would have been a very public occasion, a triumph of sorts, for every man and his dog had been calling for the king to marry.

Try as he might he could not remember any other details for he had only glimpsed the scene before swiftly retiring. Hastings must have been near the door. Ned could imagine him pacing nervously bearing the weight of the world upon his shoulders. Then Ned had chanced along when his friend was watching somewhere else. A moment later and Ned would have got out. He was unlucky. No, Hastings had been right: he'd been a fool. Interrupting the king at prayer would have been unfortunate; watching him marry secretly was on a very different level altogether. He hung his head. It was slowly dawning on him what a grave error he had committed. If the king had married in secret he would want it to stay that way. No-one could be allowed to know…

§§§§

It was late afternoon he reckoned, though it was hard to tell down on the floor. He ached all over: his head was still sore, his wrists were harshly cut into by the rope and his legs were cramped from sitting on the floor for so long. His throat was parched for he had drunk nothing all day. He watched the light begin to fade and steeled himself to survive another night. Then for the first time that day he heard a sound not uttered by a bird: a horse was approaching the lodge.

A few moments later he heard footsteps on the boards outside and the bar was withdrawn from the other side of the door. He held his breath: was this his friend or his executioner?

He breathed a sigh of relief. Hastings had brought a flask of water so he assumed his death was not too imminent.

Hastings looked down at him and shook his head.

"What a wretched, blood-soaked mess, Ned!"

"I'm sorry, Will."

"Sorry? You've no idea, my friend." He put the flask of water to Ned's mouth and he drank eagerly.

"You're still my friend then?" said Ned.

"Don't be too sure yet," said Hastings. "First we need a few words. What did you see?"

"In truth, Will, I saw enough. But surely the king trusts me - I fought by his side for God's sake!"

Hastings forced a smile. "Many men fought beside him, Ned but I wouldn't trust some of them to shit beside him now. Things change. Men change. Your close ally last year might be your worst enemy this year."

"But not me, Will. This is Ned Elder who saved your life too - more than once! Have I changed?"

"Do you think such men would sit where you are now and proclaim their treason - here I sit Will Hastings, take my head if you please!"

"But Will-"

"I know, Ned, I know. Anything you care to say, I've already thought on."

Ned shook his head. "So what's to be done? What does the king say? Does he want my head?"

"The king doesn't even know you were there," said Hastings.

"What? You didn't tell him? Then where's the problem? If it's just between you and me, Will..."

Hastings paced around the room while he spoke quietly. "You've caught his grace out, Ned. This is not some trifling fault. This is not the king found wenching or pissing in a bishop's garden. This is the king marrying someone he's not supposed to be marrying."

Hastings paused for a moment, perhaps realising that his voice had risen above a whisper. Ned thought how shaken he seemed; he couldn't ever remember Hastings looking so worried.

Hastings continued at a whisper. "It was enough of a mess before you walked into it. He sprung it on me last night and I couldn't dissuade him - and believe me I tried! I could see he was set on it and the only thing to do was make sure that it took place privily with as few witnesses as possible. With luck he'll change his mind now he's bedded her a few times. He can still deny it took place - as long as no-one else knows."

"But Will, you know that I'd never speak of it!"

"It's not quite as simple as that Ned, is it? As we speak, you're being pursued as a traitor by the Earl of Warwick - his messenger reached the king this morning. So, what if I let you go? Let's say you go back north. There's a warrant for your arrest. Can you still serve with Warwick's brother, Montagu? I think not. Can you return home - a few miles from Warwick's own fortress at Middleham? I think not! You'd fall into Warwick's hands soon enough there."

"But that was why I came to the king in the first place. I don't see what that has to do with what I saw yesterday," said Ned.

"Don't you? Warwick is the one man above all others who must not discover the king's marriage - for God's sake he's already more or less arranged a French marriage!"

"You know I would never tell him - of all men!"

"Wouldn't you Ned? I've no doubt you wouldn't to save your own life but what if someone dear to you - your sisters, your wife - was threatened? You know you've some priceless piece of intelligence - would you keep silent then? Would you not offer up that tasty morsel to save someone you love?"

Ned did not reply. Instead his eyes studied the floor. Hastings knew him too well: he knew that Ned would value the life of one he loved more than the king's embarrassment.

"Now you see where the problem lies," said Hastings gently.

Neither spoke for a while until Ned gave a weary sigh. "So what are you going to do with me then?"

Hastings first response was to untie Ned's hands and help him to his feet. "I'm going to be a friend to you, Ned - as always. You need somewhere to run to... somewhere safe. Warwick has men everywhere and you can be sure that very soon Warwick will know that you came to Stony Stratford. You can also be sure that every place you own is being watched so you must go elsewhere if you're to avoid a traitor's fate. Don't tell me where now but you'd best get right away - take a ship across the channel, somewhere Warwick wouldn't expect you to go."

"I can't even begin to think..." said Ned. He had not considered himself to be a traitor.

"Your men are outside with the horses - now get yourself as far from here as you can."

Ned embraced Hastings and the Lord Chamberlain turned to go. Then he stopped and turned to Ned again. "Don't let me down, Ned."

DEREK BIRKS

11

1st May before dawn, at Yoredale Castle

It was May Day and the sun was high in the sky, scattering its light at random through the branches. Eleanor was walking with Will through Yoredale Forest, wearing on her head a garland of woodland flowers that he had made for her. She clutched his arm tightly and laughed because in his other arm he held young Will and the boy was laughing too. He giggled every time his father raised him up and pretended to let him fall before catching him at the last moment.

Eleanor smiled at her two Wills: it was so good to see them together. She laid her hand affectionately on Will's chest but when she took it away she found a smear of blood on her fingers. She looked and sure enough there was a small cut in his shirt. Strange she had not noticed it earlier. As she stared at it, blood began to seep from the wound and then, with a suddenness that made her gasp, a crimson flood poured from the raw gash. Will stared at her; he looked shocked to see her.

Young Will was in mid-air when his father crumpled to the ground; the fierce rays of the sun flared briefly and then dimmed until Eleanor could hardly see. She screamed and lunged forward to catch the boy in her arms before landing with a fearsome crack on the forest floor. She groaned and lay still.

She came to on the floor of her chamber and frantically looked about for young Will. Then she realised she had fallen out of bed. She could hardly remember the dream at all. She knew it was about Will, the love so cruelly torn from her, because he was all she ever dreamed about. She had thought of him a great deal in recent weeks, as if he had only died a short time ago; not three years.

She rose and went to the window. It was still dark but the eastern sky carried a pale hint of dawn. Folk in the villages of Yoredale would celebrate May Day this morning but there would be no celebration for those in the castle, no garlands of flowers. Bagot had decreed it too dangerous for the family to venture into the forest.

She wore no night clothing so the cold air brought up bumps all over her bare skin. She sat on the bed but decided it was too late to go back to sleep. Instead she lay down on the huge wolf skin on the floor and caressed the fur gently. Will had presented it to her when she was fifteen; he claimed to have killed the animal with his bare hands. Even at the time she had known it was a lie but she didn't mind. Later, when he confessed he had stolen it from a merchant, she didn't mind that either - a stolen gift was a suitable token of their illicit love.

Now the poor wolf was worn and shabby. She'd no idea how it had found its way to Yoredale Castle but she could not now bear to part with it. She lay upon it, burying her breasts in the pelt, and then she took a deep breath and lifted herself up on her arms. She bore her weight on them until she felt the sinews begin to weaken. Then she lowered herself slowly down again as she released a lungful of air. She repeated the movements rhythmically over and over again until tiny beads of sweat formed on her forehead and trickled down to sting her eyes. She smiled; it seemed the work with Gruffydd was having some effect.

§§§§

In her chamber in the cold northwest tower, Emma contemplated May Day too. She had few memories of it. She had certainly never been chosen as May Queen though it would not have been fitting in any case. One of the village girls ought to be chosen - not that custom had dissuaded her sister Eleanor, who had allowed herself to be chosen several times. She encouraged the worship like some pagan goddess. Still, that was in the past and now the May Queen had her beautiful child of love, Will.

Emma thought of her own son, Richard, the product not of love but malice; a boy formed and shaped inside her by brute force. Then she sighed and shut away the memories that haunted her. There was no order for a woman's suffering, no prized garter awarded by the king for stoic service to men, just the scars. She went down into the Great Hall, where she found Bagot in good spirits.

"My lady, a God-given morn," he greeted her cheerfully.

"Good morning, Master Bagot," she replied dutifully. She had rarely felt less enthusiastic about a sunny morning.

"I have good news, my lady," continued Bagot.

"You've caught Durston?" suggested Emma.

"Well, no, my lady, not that, but Garth is on the mend!"

Her puzzled look must have been clear to him. "Garth, my lady…your escort."

"I know who he is!" she snapped. "But he was killed; I saw the bolt strike him, the blood pour from his breast."

"No, the other two died but not Garth."

"He lives? But you didn't tell me …" Her voice faltered, it felt like the words were being wrung out of her. "Why… why didn't you tell me sooner?" her voice was a hoarse whisper.

Bagot simply looked at her as if she were a fool.

"I thought I had, my lady…I must have forgotten," he stammered. "I didn't want to burden you, to remind you of it."

"You should have told me about Garth. All this time I've been thinking he was dead! I've said prayers for his mortal soul, you fool! Get out!"

After he had gone, her anger quickly subsided for the news about Garth made her spirits soar. She could not keep a grin from her face. Bagot had probably never seen her angry before, distraught yes but not lip quiveringly mad. It had been such a shock though. After Durston's appearance in the forest she had mourned for the loss of her three brave, young guards. But, of them all, she would have wished it to be Garth who survived - how terrible a thought, for the others were sweet boys too. But Garth... was different.

She tried to remember how he looked but the only image she could recall was blood spreading from the wound in his chest. She must send something to him - but what? Some food? Or perhaps some herbal remedies; she had many of those...but no, it would be better to take it to him - see him for herself and tell him that he was not forgotten.

How though? She would look ridiculous if half the castle garrison escorted her to his mother's cottage? It would seem as if he was more to her than just a loyal servant. She did not want that; she must think of another way.

§§§§

For the rest of the day she tried to put the matter from her mind, yet by the evening it was still there, like an apple ripe for the picking. She had her meal served in her chamber that evening, though she merely toyed with her food. Finally she made a decision: she would include Garth in her prayers and leave it at that. No doubt when he was fully recovered he would attend her again and she could give him her thanks.

She felt better for thinking it through and was certain she had made the right decision. She went down to seek out Bagot. It took longer to find him than she expected but she tracked him down in the wine cellar. She thanked him for the news about Garth, seeking to play down her earlier reaction to it. Bagot seemed suitably nonplussed by her visit and she left him shaking his head. She climbed the steps up to the Hall and crossed to the spiral stair by the postern gate. But when she spied Sarah Standlake furtively drawing back the bolts on the gate, her resolve weakened.

"Where are you going, girl?" she hissed. "Don't you know

that Master Bagot has forbidden members of the household to leave the castle?"

"I'm running an errand for Lady Eleanor," Sarah replied.

Emma hesitated. With her sister almost anything was possible but the girl would surely have been more confident if she had Eleanor's permission.

"No, my dear," she said softly. "This is your own private errand, isn't it? Where are you going?"

Sarah dropped to her knees. "Please, my lady. I'm sorry, forgive me. I forgot. I'll go back…"

"No, you won't. Where were you going?" Emma had to know now.

Sarah looked desperate. "I was only going to see … a friend in the village." She began to weep.

"You can stop that," snapped Emma.

The girl sniffled and looked down at the floor.

"How did you expect to avoid being seen?" Emma's voice was suddenly less harsh, for in a tiny fragment of time, an idea had taken root.

Sarah looked wary now, perhaps noticing the change in her tone. "I know where all the castle folk go in the evening - especially Master Bagot. He'll be drinking with old Gruffydd till he's asleep and when he wakes up he'll check the postern. But by then it'll be a few hours till dawn and I'll be back here."

"You've done this before then?"

Sarah knew she had already said too much and said no more.

"You've no need to worry, child; your secret is safe with me."

"But…why?" asked Sarah.

"I was your age once," she said. True enough but age is all they would have had in common; when she was Sarah's age she was running her father's household and had no inclination to have assignations in the small hours.

Sarah stood by the gate looking perplexed. "Are you telling me I can go then, my lady?"

"Yes, you may go."

"And you'll not tell Lady Eleanor or Master Bagot?"

Emma could well understand Sarah's disbelief for it was madness on her part. She could stop the madness now - it would be easy. Just tell the wretched girl to go back to whatever dark place it was she slept and stay there. But the postern gate was half open and the temptation was there; Emma knew she would not be able to resist it.

"No," she said, "I won't tell them…but in return I want a service from you."

The girl's relief was almost tangible. "Of course, my lady, anything."

Emma paused. Even now, she could pull back from the leap she was about to take and nothing would be lost.

"What is it you want me to do, my lady?" asked Sarah.

Emma didn't know. She had a willing accomplice but had not even considered how to commit the crime - and God knew, it was a crime.

"Do you want me to take a message?" asked Sarah.

Yes, a message, thought Emma - thank God the girl had a gift for subterfuge.

"Who's it for?"

Emma flinched at the question. How far could she trust this serving girl, she wondered?

"It's a privy matter," she said.

"Well I can't take a message if I don't know who it's for, can I, my lady?"

Emma hesitated once more. She had not mentioned a name yet; she was not committed to the course.

"It's a young man at arms, Garth. I wish to send him my thanks for his service to me."

Only when she saw the beginnings of a smirk on Sarah's lips did Emma realise how it sounded. "His service saved my life…" she explained.

Sarah nodded earnestly. "I know Garth - most girls in the villages around know Garth." Sarah must have noticed the grimace on Emma's face for she quickly added: "Not in that way, my lady."

"Just give him my thanks, if you will, and tell him… tell him I hope he will soon be fit enough to return to my service."

"Oh he's already up and walking about, my lady. One of the castle garrison told me yesterday - Bagot sends a group of the lads to see him every day or two."

Every day or two - and Bagot had only just seen fit to tell her he was alive! Emma could have throttled Bagot.

"We've been standing here too long, my lady," Sarah told her, "can I go now?"

Practical girl, thought Emma. "Yes. You'd better go."

Sarah pulled the gate wide open.

"Wait!" said Emma. "Tell him also that I'd like to see him."

"My lady?" Sarah probably thought she had misheard.

"Go!" she urged and Sarah flitted outside. Emma pushed the gate closed but did not bar or lock it.

She leant her head against the rough wood, dislodging her coif. Would Sarah think her message was innocent enough? No, of course she wouldn't! She hoped the girl was not a gossip or Emma's reputation would lie in tatters around the may pole tonight. No, as long as she kept Sarah's secret she was certain that Sarah would keep hers: a bitter widow's folly.

12

4th May morning, in Cheapside in the City of London

Ned disliked London. It was three years since he had last been in the city and he had never missed it. He hated its noisy, jostling crowds, its filthy streets and wandering animals and its overwhelming stench of … people. Hal had led them through the streets of Cheap where an assortment of heavily laden stalls spilled over into the street and hampered their progress at every turn. Nevertheless, Hal's confidence that he could find the alderman's house had been well founded. He wondered how the goldsmith would receive him - if he received him at all.

Ned had now been waiting for some time in Alderman Goldwell's privy chamber and he was already regretting taking up Hal's suggestion. He would never normally have stooped so low as to beg a favour from a man he barely knew but an outlaw could not afford such scruples. He was worse off than a beggar. Certainly the merchant had wealth enough: it was a wealthy man who could not only pay for solid oak panelling but also afford to hide some of it behind richly coloured hanging tapestries. He suspected the alderman could get them onto a ship, but would he be willing to do so?

The door to the chamber opened and Ned stood up. A small rust-coloured head peered around the base of the door and stared up at him. Ned stared back open-mouthed. It was uncanny, chilling almost: the boy was the image of young Will, Eleanor's son. His hair was cut longer than Will's, dropping untidily over the boy's eyes, but aside from that Ned reckoned he would have a hard job to tell them apart. His appraisal of the boy was cut short by the entrance of a young woman who scooped the lad up and with only the briefest nod in Ned's direction retreated hastily out of the room. He thought Sarah looked different but it had been three years. Perhaps he was mistaken; he had only met her once and that had been brief enough. There could be little doubt that the boy was Will's though; still, it came as a shock all the same.

The alderman would surely be no friend to him. He was surprised he had been admitted at all but he could see clearly enough now that it would not work. He went to the door to leave but Alderman John Goldwell met him as he passed into the ante room.

"God give you good day, Lord Elder. Do you grow impatient with me?" the alderman asked.

"And you, sir - and no, not impatient at all," stuttered Ned, realising he had just made their meeting even more uncomfortable. John Goldwell ushered him back into the privy chamber and indicated a chair. Ned sat back down again where he had been waiting a few moments earlier.

"I shan't pretend, my lord, that your visit isn't a surprise to me, especially after so long and given what has happened since the last occasion we met."

"Alderman, I'm truly at a loss to know where to start. I shouldn't have come and, having seen the young boy just now, I'm more convinced of that than ever."

"Ah, yes…young Jack," said the alderman, "poor Sarah."

"I didn't know," protested Ned, "Felix should have told me." He silently cursed the wine merchant in Ludlow who had first brought his friend Will Coster into the Goldwell household.

"Now, I beg you not to blame our mutual friend," chided the alderman. "He would have sent to you but I told him not to."

"But Will should have provided for the girl and her child

and, since he could not, I should have done."

The alderman nodded and smiled ruefully. "Yes, my lord, and I'm sure you would have but my daughter's disgrace was not a matter I wanted observed, or discussed, the length and breadth of the land. Felix took her to Ludlow for a year during which time the child was safely born. Now Sarah keeps house for me as she did before your man Will came into our lives. I can well afford to keep her and the boy - two of her sisters were married last year and there's certainly room in the house."

"But do you acknowledge the lad?" asked Ned.

"Acknowledge, you ask? I love the boy as my grandson but to the world he is a foundling, abandoned near this house by some desperate young girl who couldn't afford to raise him - or so the story goes. I begin to forget how we explained it now."

Ned decided that he would still be having a few words with Felix when he saw him next. It occurred to him that he had not seen him since Towton and, given his present circumstances, he might never see Felix again.

"But I doubt my grandson is the reason for your visit," said his host. "Why have you come, my lord?"

"You found me just now on the point of leaving, sir," admitted Ned. "I shouldn't have come."

"Yet ... you have come, my lord. At least satisfy my curiosity as to why."

"Very well. I intended to ask a great favour from you but I see now that I already owe you a debt."

The alderman smiled. "I doubt that, my lord. What's done is done. The Lord has spoken and he has brought you to me and you may be sure that I bear you no ill will at all. It wasn't you who threw your man and my daughter together - if anyone's to blame, it's me. So, please ask your 'great favour.'"

"Well then," began Ned, "I'm in need of a ship to take me out of London."

He expected the alderman to be surprised but then realised that a man who traded in gold would have learned long ago to give away nothing in conversation.

"The city does not lack for shipping," said the alderman, "where do you want to go?"

"North," said Ned, "somewhere north of Newcastle."

The alderman gave a wry grin. "Iceland, perhaps?" he suggested.

Ned shrugged. "I don't know it, Alderman. Is it far from Newcastle?"

John Goldwell smiled. "It's rather too far north of there," he said, "but I fear you won't easily find a ship. There'll be some heading for Newcastle but those going beyond will likely be heading out to the Baltic. There's been no trade going to Berwick for a while but I doubt you'd want to go there in any case. Ships don't just stop anywhere along that coast, my lord. Newcastle's your best chance."

Ned considered how much he dared tell the alderman. He must not forget the man held official rank. He might feel duty bound to arrest Ned if he knew a warrant had been issued.

"Newcastle is a little... difficult for me."

"How is it difficult?" John asked.

"Mortally so," replied Ned, "I'm not wanted in the town."

"I take it you mean that you are most urgently wanted in the town," said Alderman Goldwell drily. He seemed to consider for a moment.

"There are other places you might be landed but I'll need to ask a ship's master I know."

"My name must not be mentioned," said Ned.

The alderman gave him a curious look. "My lord, I'm a goldsmith, discretion keeps me and my precious goods safe."

"Then for your continued safety I urge you not to seek to know more of my troubles. It's best for us all that you don't."

"Very well, my lord. I take you at your word. I shall enquire if passage can be obtained. Do you have coin?"

"Aye, some."

"You'll need a lot I should think," said the alderman, "if you want a ship's master who'll ask no questions - and yet can be relied upon. Where are you lodging?"

"I've yet to arrange that. I wanted to find out first if you would be willing to help."

"Then you must stay here. I've a bed chamber made up for Felix when he stays in London. He's not expected for perhaps a week so you can have that, if it would suit you?"

Ned accepted the offer with alacrity for he had not forgotten what had happened years before when he had stayed nearby at a local inn - he had barely escaped with his life. They agreed that Hal and Wulf would sleep in the apprentice quarters and the alderman promised to begin enquiries for their passage north.

Hal led Ned to the chamber on the second floor. The youth had no need of direction for he had lodged in the house when he had served the alderman with Will. He led the way up the stairway and indicated a work room off the first landing.

"In there I slept with Will and the others," he said, pointing to the apprentice dormitory opposite. His hand rested on the wooden stair rail and he looked down at it for a moment.

"See that cut in the wood there, lord," he said, in a husky voice, "that's where Will struck it in his struggle with the thieves the first night."

"You never told me about that," said Ned, pausing on the stair to glance at the deep mark gouged in the timber.

Hal smiled grimly. "Within a few hours, all of Cheap knew about Will Coster. The 'wild man of the north' they called him. He did for a few men that night!" Hal moved on past the landing and took Ned up to a well-furnished chamber on the floor above. "This is where Felix stayed, my lord. If you need us, we'll be below."

It was not long before Sarah Goldwell brought Ned up a candle. He noted the quality and gave a wry smile. The alderman clearly wanted for nothing if he could afford to provide his guests with a candle fit for a bishop. Sarah set down the candle on a large oak chest.

"My lord, Felix is accustomed to leave items in the chest. I can have them removed if you wish to use it."

"No, mistress," he said, "I shan't need it - thank you, though."

"Is there anything else you need, my lord?" asked Sarah.

"No. Thank you, no."

She turned to go.

"Wait, mistress," he said, "will you sit with me for a while?"

"If you please, my lord," she replied, yet her answer was nervous, her voice strained.

There was a small chair beside the door and she lowered herself into it - awkwardly, he thought. She was younger than he - about Eleanor's age - and like his sister she had reddish brown hair, not as bright, but similar he decided. No wonder the children looked alike. But, young though she was, her face was lined and her skin pale. She was not a warrior like Ellie but she must have some fight in her nonetheless.

"My lord?" He realised he had been staring at her without a word - no wonder she was pale, poor girl.

"Your pardon, mistress," he said, noticing the flush of anger in her cheeks.

"Must I sit here to be looked at, my lord?" she asked. "What do you want from me?"

He wished he knew. Should he tell her that her son had a half-brother? If he did, what would be served by it? Would it help her? No, not at all.

"I'm sorry," he said stiffly, "you're your father's housekeeper - you must be busy and I keep you from your duties."

"Thank you, my lord," she said and swiftly left the chamber.

He heard the relief in her voice. God knows what she thought he was going to do to her. After she left he forced himself to turn his mind once more to his predicament. Newcastle or Iceland? Where in all Christendom was Iceland? It sounded terrible.

§§§§

For several days the alderman was at home very little, though whether that was a consequence of his arrival or merely the nature of the goldsmith's busy life, Ned had no idea. At any rate he remained in the house, fearful of being seen but, as Hal pointed out, since he was not known by anyone in London, discovery was unlikely. Nevertheless, as the days passed he grew restless, fretting over the delay. Occasionally the alderman reported to him that there was no news of a passage but most of the time Ned spent alone or with his two young companions. They of course knew nothing of what had occurred at the Hermitage; they simply knew that the Earl of Warwick was pursuing their master across England - that was bad enough for them.

When he encountered Sarah she was polite but cool towards him. He could hardly blame her. It was thus a great relief when, after a week or so, the alderman brought more welcome news. It was late in the evening, long past curfew, when he sought Ned out.

"Tomorrow morn, my lord! It's all settled," he announced.

"You've found me a ship?" asked Ned.

"Indeed," said John, clearly pleased with his achievement. "You sail on the early morning tide. The master's James Finch - and he won't wait for you so we must be ready at the dock. He's only put in for a few repairs so he's not landing any goods. He's bound for Newcastle with a cargo of wine from Bordeaux. He's agreed to take the three of you. He knows you're in some trouble but he doesn't know your name."

"But...Newcastle? I told you I can't land there in safety," said Ned.

"No indeed," agreed John Goldwell, "it's all arranged. He'll drop you off before the port."

"Are you sure? I thought you said you couldn't just stop anywhere along the coast?"

"You can't," said the alderman, "but Finch has a notion where he might land you for he comes from those parts. You can trust him - he's never let me down," the alderman reassured him.

Ned had been promised trust many times but he had learned only to trust those he knew well.

'Trust no-one' had been Bagot's first words of advice to him. The thought of putting himself in the hands of a stranger aboard a ship at sea did not bear close scrutiny.

"I hope you're right," was all he said.

"I am. Now, we must be off to Old Wool Quay straight after curfew in the morning. I suggest you travel well-cloaked: it can be cool at sea and even at this time of year storms are not unknown. And don't be showing off your weapons too much - the sailors might get nervous and throw you overboard. Now, the last thing: you've a visitor - and he's very glad you're leaving because you're in his lodgings!"

Ned hurried downstairs and met Felix in the hall. Felix wrapped him in a bear's embrace and then clapped him on the back enthusiastically. "Ned Elder! God bless you, Ned, but it's good to see you."

"I should have been to see you sooner," said Ned.

"Hah! This is hardly a visit to see me, Ned, is it? You must tell me all your news and I'll tell you mine."

"Come then," said Ned, "we'd best retire to my, or rather your chamber. It's late. We don't want to keep the whole household awake."

When they sat down upstairs Ned knew that Felix would want to know why he was in London so he tried to steer their conversation on to his friend. "Whatever happened to that comely widow you unearthed in Ludlow?" he asked.

Felix grinned. "Well, I haven't married her - yet."

"And why not?"

"She's a good woman, Ned, but she won't have me! I've asked her countless times but she just won't have me."

"She's got sense then, this widow," said Ned with a smile.

"Aye, perhaps so," replied Felix quietly, "but I understand

why. Since her husband's death she's run the wine business herself - and made a damned fine job of it. As a widow, she's a member of the Ludlow Vintners' Guild - in her own right. If she marries me, she'll lose that and I can't blame her for it."

"Yet... do you live in her household?"

Felix gave a sheepish nod.

"And what do the good folk of Ludlow make of that?"

"The good folk of Ludlow gossip about it, when they have nothing else to gossip about. A black Moor they might stomach but a black French Moor is sometimes a little too much for them!"

When Felix stopped talking Ned filled the silence, he enquired after Holton, his loyal steward at Corve Manor near Ludlow; then he asked of Holton's wife and their young child. Then he told Felix of Amelie, that she was with child and about Ellie and her son, and Emma and her son.

"Enough, Ned," said Felix finally. "I rejoice in your family's good health. Now, why don't you tell me what you're trying so hard not to tell me?"

"It's best you don't know, Felix."

"That'll suit for the alderman well enough, Ned; but not for me, not Felix. I'm your friend. You saved my life and I more than once risked my black hide to get you out of some trouble or other."

"Aye, you've been as steadfast to me as that great ash staff of yours and any debt to me is already well paid," said Ned.

Felix shrugged. "A debt to an enemy might be paid once but a debt to a friend can never be repaid enough times."

Ned met his eyes and nodded but still he hesitated.

"Still you don't trust me? Have you forgotten Towton?"

Ned could see the hurt in Felix eyes. "Of course I trust you...I just don't want to get you involved."

"I'm involved already; perhaps I'll go north with you on James Finch's ship!"

"You know of that..."

"Know of it? You may be sure I know of it: James Finch

is a ship's master I've employed for more than ten years! Now, tell me what trouble you're in."

"You can do no more to aid me," said Ned.

"Let me judge that for myself," said Felix.

Ned gave in. It was a relief to tell Felix. Even so, he did not make any reference to his encounter with Hastings at the hermitage in the forest for that was not his secret to tell.

"So, it's about Warwick again," concluded Felix.

"Aye. I know, I know - the world and his dog warned me about arguing with Warwick. I was so buried in the feud with the Radcliffes that I didn't see that I'd started one with Warwick. I thought after Towton, when peace came, that all the feuds were finished. It turns out that they both continue, with the Radcliffes and with Warwick."

"This Henry fellow sounds dangerous, especially with Mordeur by his side, but Ned he's nothing compared to Warwick. The Earl will simply crush you."

"I know - which is why I didn't want to tell you. There's nothing to be done."

"But surely you have the king's support? Certain, he owes you much."

"Aye, but he owes his cousin Warwick far more…"

"Have you been to see him?"

"There's nothing to be gained by seeing him, Felix. Nothing."

Felix looked truly miserable and Ned regretted telling him the sorry tale - as he knew he would.

"I'd better get some sleep", he said, "we've talked half the night and I've an early start."

"Indeed," agreed Felix, "and in the northern sea it might be the last sleep you have for a day or two."

Ned wondered then what he had let himself in for.

§§§§

At first light, Felix and the alderman led them through a warren of narrow streets towards the quays that lined the waterfront to the east of London Bridge. Fingers of mist crept along the river bank, exploring the warehouses and docks. There were so many ships that Ned wondered idly why it had taken the alderman so long to find him one. Unlike the city streets through which they passed, the quays were buzzing with activity. It seemed utter chaos to Ned as they weaved their way between stacked piles of wool, hogsheads of wine, barrels of salt fish and a thousand other items he struggled to identify. They passed ship after ship shrouded by the morning mist and he expected each one to be his but eventually the alderman stopped beside a vessel which was alive with moving men and snapping lines.

"Here we are," said Felix cheerfully, "the Catherine!"

Somehow Ned was disappointed, for the ship seemed very small.

"Can this go to sea?" he asked.

Felix laughed. "It has done so many times, Ned. Rest assured it will do."

It seemed as if every man was on the cramped deck and at least half were shouting orders whilst the rest hurled back abuse but no-one stopped working for even a moment.

Only one man was still: the ship's master, Ned presumed, who was perched on top of several casks on the deck amidships. Even from a distance James Finch looked a formidable man.

His voice rasped across to them: "Ah Felix! At last! Well, in Christ's name, are you coming aboard or not?"

"Ah, a life of harmony at sea awaits you, Ned," promised Felix. "Now hurry aboard before Master Finch decides to go without you."

He indicated the single gang plank on to the vessel. Ned considered it doubtfully for a moment. He could feel the master's eyes upon him, assessing him, judging his mettle."

"Cast away aft!" the master shouted.

Ned turned to the alderman. "If I can ever repay your favour, sir, you have my word that I'll do so."

He clasped John Goldwell's hand and as he did so he felt

the alderman press a small pouch of coins into it. "This will pay for the horses you've left behind," he said, "and it should buy you some more where you're going." He quickly turned away and left them. Felix gave him a final slap on the shoulder.

"Well, sir?" growled the master.

"Aye," said Ned and stepped up the timber plank and onto the ship. Hal and Wulf followed. Ned tried to appear confident, an impression ruined almost instantly when he gave Felix a wave and tripped over a coil of rope to fall flat on the deck. Felix shook his head and the crew paused long enough to chuckle at his clumsiness and then continued about their business. Any amusement on the part of Hal and Wulf disappeared the moment the ship got under way. None of the three had ever been aboard a ship before in their lives and even in the relatively gentle water of the river they turned slowly green.

"Best keep out of the way," said the master quietly. "There's a cabin below towards the bow. You'd best go there till we clear the port - your lads can stay below aft."

"Bow?" asked Ned.

The master sighed and pointed forward. Ned clambered down a short stair and lurched forward into the cabin whilst Wulf and Hal staggered down a few steps and then sat down on the damp timber.

The master bellowed after them: "If you feel the call to empty your guts then come back topside. That's my cabin you're using!"

Ned sat on the cabin floor and closed his eyes. He was feeling queasy and he didn't like it. He resolved that he would never take a ship anywhere ever again.

§§§§

On the quay side Alderman Goldwell and Felix watched the Catherine slide along the river until it passed out of sight.

"I wonder if we'll ever see him again," said the alderman.

"Don't underestimate him; that young man is strong," replied Felix.

"Strong yes, but his enemies, I fear, are stronger. An outlaw? A traitor? There is only one fate awaits him, Felix. We've done all we can."

"Perhaps not yet all," said the Frenchman.

The alderman drew his cloak about him against the morning chill and studied his friend.

"Tell me you're not going to do something I'll regret, Felix. I wouldn't wish to lose such a valued client."

Felix smiled. "I believe the king is in my debt. Several years may have passed but my service made a difference, I believe. I will petition him - perhaps some mercy may be shown. After all, Ned is still his loyal servant."

The alderman shook his head sadly. "Kings don't pay their debts, Felix. You should know that."

DEREK BIRKS

13

15th May midday, at Yoredale Castle

Emma paused at the top of the spiral stair which led down to the postern gate. If she took another pace and set her foot upon the next step she would put in train a sequence of events over which she would have little control. Along the passage was the nursery where her son was playing happily; yet she was about to abandon him for an afternoon. What if he stumbled and fell? What if he choked and died while she was away? No-one would know where she was; she would not be there to comfort him. But then little Richard knew his nurse and his aunt better than his mother; she would not be missed.

Still she hesitated. When she first sent to Garth, the idea of meeting him secretly had been a far off, half-imagined notion. She had not taken it seriously but if she walked down the steps before her, it would become real. She had been so wrapped up in the difficult part - getting out of the castle - that she had not dwelt on the purpose of the meeting, nor the outcome. Now she was face to face with it and it scared her. After all the horrors she had lived through, how was it that this little assignation could frighten her so? Somewhere along the passage a door slammed and made her jump. Footsteps headed towards her. If she didn't do it now, she would never do it. She hurried down the steps.

She had enlisted the help of the girl, Sarah, to leave the castle unobserved. Even so, she felt like a fugitive when she slipped out of the postern gate. She stayed close to the foot of the castle wall. Sarah had told her that around midday the young lads on the ramparts were hardly ever paying any attention on watch. This had a lot to do with the fact that she and Jane were in the habit of taking them a little food and ale at that time. Still, it was a risk: others might see her.

She stopped at the corner of the northwest tower and put on the cloak she carried over her arm. The moment she was wearing it, she felt safer. Ridiculous though it seemed, the cloak seemed to grant her licence. It also made her uncomfortably hot for it was too warm a day to be wearing a cloak. She set off from the wall taking a direct line across the pasture to the forest. She expected a shout or a challenge of some kind but there was nothing and by the time she was halfway to the tree line, she was grinning like a small child. She reached the forest and then looked around anxiously for Garth but he was not there.

She closed her eyes and leant her back against a tree to wait; in truth she was a little disappointed: he should have been there waiting for her. Worse still, it allowed all kinds of doubts to take root in her head. What if he had decided not to come? A new humiliation; she wasn't sure she could cope with that. What if Durston found her while she was waiting? Her eyes flew open at the thought and she scanned the trees about her but Durston was not there. By the time Garth arrived - if he was coming at all - she would be a gibbering fool. She was alert to every movement. Not ten paces away to her left a low branch twitched, its young leaves quivered briefly and then were still. She held her breath and then, ahead of her, she heard an approach: a slow, measured tramp up the slope towards her. She swallowed hard and held her breath as she waited for someone to emerge.

Relief flooded over her: it was Garth and she drank in the sight of him. He looked tired and sounded out of breath but he smiled when he saw her and his smile seemed to hamper her breathing too.

"My lady," he greeted her rather formally.

"Good day to you, Garth," she replied, her voice suddenly thin and strained.

For a moment they stood together, alone on the edge of the forest.

"Will you walk with me, lady?" he asked and offered her his arm.

"Aye," she said, putting her arm in his.

She noticed him wince. His arm felt stiff and she gripped it less tightly.

"I'm sorry!" she breathed "The shoulder still pains you - of course it does. How stupid of me."

"It mends by the day, lady," said Garth, "but perhaps you would allow me…" He took her hand in his. She nodded and smiled; his hand was warm where hers was cold. They walked slowly for she could see that he was still weak from the wound.

"I'm ashamed to say that I don't know the forest around here very well," she said.

"I know it well enough, lady."

"Garth," she said, "I don't think you should call me 'lady' when we're alone; you should use my name."

"It'll seem strange," he said.

"It's all strange," she replied.

He stopped. "Would you like to go back?"

"No, of course not! Why would you think that?"

He shrugged and winced again. "I'm just not sure how far you want to go today."

"Neither am I, Garth," she said, "neither am I. Show me the part of the forest you like best."

"Very well, Lady Emma."

"Just … Emma," she said and squeezed his hand gently.

They began to talk more freely, as they had before when he escorted her to the Abbey.

He led her through a band of thick woodland and she was glad of the cloak to stop her being scratched by the trees.

"This is your favoured part of the forest?" she said, laughing.

"Not quite. Wait a little - it's worth struggling through this."

187

After a while they emerged into a small clearing where a hillside beck trickled over a short fall and sprinkled water onto the stones below. The falling droplets of water sparkled in the sunlight before dashing themselves into a fine, white spray.

"It's a beautiful place," she grinned.

"It's hard to get to so it's rarely visited - except by me. This is the best time when the sun's on it."

"And do you bring all your girls here?"

"There are no girls. I have no girls - at least, not since I began at the castle..."

He helped her take off her cloak and laid it on the ground for her. When she sat down on it he stood hesitating.

"Are you going to stand there all afternoon?" she teased him.

He sat down awkwardly.

"Show me your scar!" she said.

He looked nonplussed. "It's barely a scar yet; it's still a wound," he said "and it looks ugly."

"I can see it still hurts."

"Aye, a bit."

"Does it hurt if I do this?" she asked, laying laid her head upon his chest.

"No."

"Good."

§§§§

Emma lay on her back and gazed up at the cloudless sky while the warm breeze gently caressed her bare shoulders. Beside her Garth was asleep. She had assumed that they would just talk. God knew that alone would have been enough but then he had put his arm around her and stroked her cheek and somehow - she couldn't quite piece together how - they had become lovers. She did get to see his scar and he was right - it was ugly - but it was the only thing about him that was.

For the first time she could ever remember she had lain

with a man in whom she had every faith, with whom she felt utterly safe. Garth was loyal and brave; true, he was young - too young for her, most would say - and he was of low birth but Eleanor's Will had been low-born and no-one seemed to mind that. No, that was not quite true: everyone had minded but because it was Eleanor they rather expected it. Well, if it was good enough for Eleanor then it was certainly good enough for her.

Yet it was madness and in her heart she knew it. She should not be lying wantonly in some forest glade with her breasts exposed. But for once in this bitter world there was something for her - something other than brutal oppression. Madness it was, yes, but what sweet madness.

A further glance at the sky reminded her that the afternoon was coming to an end: soon she would be missed - if she had not been already. Did she care? No, not really. She was the senior lady of the household and neither Eleanor nor Amelie could gainsay her. Even if her dalliance with Garth was discovered, how could it be worse than the humiliation she had suffered in the years before? If she wanted to she could brave the scandal, take him back to Yoredale Castle - and take him to her bed three times daily if she wished. No-one could stop her. Yet it would not feel right to her and she knew it would not feel right to him either.

Well, that was a notion to consider later; for now, she ought to concentrate on getting back into the castle. Sarah had promised to leave the postern unbarred and unlocked just as the sun set. There was still enough time but only if she moved now; then she realised that Garth had woken up and was exploring her right nipple with his fingers.

"I need to go back," she murmured, kissing his neck, "and you must be exhausted already..."

"I can rest later tonight," he said, "don't worry. I'll get you back by sunset."

She smiled and she was glad she couldn't see it for she knew it was a wicked smile - wicked, though not guilty.

Afterwards they did have to make haste for the light was

fading as they struggled back through the dense thicket. She could see that Garth was tiring fast and stopped him.

"You are gallant, Garth but you are also troubled by your wound. I know the way from here - tis barely a hundred paces to the forest's edge. Save your strength because you're going to need it when we next meet!"

"But -"

"I'll not argue about it: go home to your mother and get another poultice on that wound."

"Alright, lady...Emma. And we'll meet again..."

"I don't know - whenever I can get away. I'll send word by Sarah."

He left her after a long, gentle embrace. She stood for a moment and was tempted to run after him; but she didn't. Instead she carried on her way through the forest which was getting gloomier by the moment as cloud began to roll in from the west. Still, her timing should be perfect: the sun was still glowing red under the dark layer of cloud. Somewhere off to her right there was a crackle as dry stems of bracken snapped. She glanced across and then walked a little faster. When she felt the first spots of rain she thought about running but felt too tired. There were worse things, she knew, than getting a little wet.

Trees rustled to her right; the wind is rising, she thought, and stopped to wrap the cloak around her. She set off again, looking back warily at the sky: the rain would soon be heavy. Close by, she could hear something moving through the undergrowth - too close to the castle for deer and, despite what Garth imagined, there were no boar left in Yoredale. It had been Edmund's pastime to hunt them all down. It was probably a woodland bird or one of the foresters perhaps. If he saw her though, he would surely make himself known.

The cloud swiftly overcame the sun's dying rays and the forest suddenly seemed a lot bleaker. A large raindrop landed squarely on her cheek and others followed as the rain came on heavier. She quickened her step - because of the rain, she told herself - but she kept glancing to the right all the same.

As the rain pattered against the trees, she could no longer hear the rustle of branches or the trampling of bracken but then she saw a dark figure flitting between the trees ahead of her. Durston. His words came back to her: "I'll be watching…always."

All the delight of her afternoon fled in that moment and she broke into a run. She veered away from him and ran on but he was faster and stronger than she was. He seized her from behind and pulled her to the ground. Her cloak fell open and beneath it her linen smock was still untied. The rain washed over her, drenching her. Her clothes clung to her as she struggled to get up but he straddled her easily.

"Well, my lady, what have you been up to, I wonder? You clearly haven't heeded my advice and, unless I'm wide of the mark, you've been a very wicked lady indeed. Now that is a surprise to me - I had you marked as the tight one."

He began to lift up her smock and laughed when he saw how hurriedly she had dressed. "Don't worry, my lady, your little secret will be safe with me - for a favour or two, or three."

She closed her eyes in disbelief; she should have known better after all that had happened to her. Suffering was ever her close companion: she was not born to enjoy happiness without enduring some pain.

"No!" she screamed. "No! Do your worst: hit me, rape me - I've known it all - but I'm not going to make it easy for you."

"What are you going do? Slap me, as you used to try to slap away Edmund Radcliffe? It didn't work well with him, did it? And it won't work with me." He splayed her legs roughly apart. As he began to explore between her thighs, her hand scrabbled around beneath her, searching for anything that might serve as a weapon. She was hoping to find a stone but all she came across was a thin broken twig and her heart sank. She reached up her other hand to scratch at his face but he swatted it away and forced his fingers into her. She was raging then with the cruel injustice of it all.

"I was happy for once!" she cried and brought the broken twig up into his face. It caught him in his right eye and he yelped with pain and pulled away from her.

At once she scrambled to her feet and fled. The castle was not far but she heard him shouting after her. She rushed out of the trees and on towards the castle walls. The main gate was nearer than the postern; she would go and hammer on it if she had to. Anything was preferable to being caught again by Durston. Instead of crossing the open pasture to the wall she joined the track that led to the gatehouse. Only when she reached it did she dare to look back. The trees were covered by a curtain of rain and there was no sign of Durston. He did not dare come along the main approach to the castle.

She was breathing heavily when she banged on the gate. It seemed to take forever for the guards to notice her but eventually they let her inside and she leant against the wall of the gatehouse, grateful to get out of the rain. They stared at her in dismay and one sped off before she could stop him. She knew what was coming next as she made her way to the Hall. They all met her there before she could escape to her chamber: Eleanor, Bagot and Amelie. Sarah ran up from the postern gate her face white with fear. Then came the gasps of sympathy, followed by the questions, the outrage, the disapproval, followed by yet more questions. She sank down under the weight of their anguish.

It was her sister who stopped it all, with one curt word.

"Enough!" said Eleanor and took her up to her chamber, leaving everyone else still wondering. Emma loved her sister for that moment and because she knew she had to explain herself to someone, she chose Eleanor - and she told her everything. Her sister listened without saying a word, and helped her out of the damp, torn clothing and into her night clothes. When Emma had finished she remained quiet for a time - which was rare in itself. Then she hugged Emma to her.

"I'll tell them it was just a walk in the woods then, a pleasant walk that ended badly," she whispered

Emma clung to her, shivering and shaking, until the warmth of the embrace soothed her. It was not the first time her sister had rescued her from despair. She knew the harmony between them would not last and that soon enough they would argue and spit contempt at each other. But she promised herself that, when Eleanor was at her most outrageous and infuriating, she would try to remember this moment.

14

15th May early morning, at the mouth of the River Tyne in Northumberland

Ned eyed the coastline suspiciously. In the early morning light it looked grim and stark. Even the master seemed preoccupied by it, watching the water intently as the ship negotiated its way along the channel.

James Finch spat into the water. "Black Midden rocks," he announced, without any further elaboration.

Ned peered into the dark water but could see no rocks. "Dangerous?" he asked.

"All rocks are dangerous," replied Finch, his eyes still fixed upon the channel, "but it's the ones below the surface you've to fret about."

In the past few days Ned had learned when to leave the irascible seaman alone so he waited in silence whilst Finch satisfied himself that he had found a safe channel.

"Be ready," the master said abruptly. "We've cleared the Narrows. I'm going to heave into the fishermen's quay at South Shields. You three can jump off there but look sharp. I'm not stopping."

"Why can't you stop?" asked Ned.

"My cargo's for the Newcastle merchants and they'd not be pleased to hear that I'd stopped at Shields. They've been trying to kill off trade here as long as there's been a 'here'."

"The alderman told me you're a local man," said Ned.

"The alderman should know better than to gossip about me," retorted the mariner.

"Are you from here - or Newcastle?"

Finch did not reply and the ship passed North Shields as the River Tyne turned south. In a short while, Ned saw the settlement ahead on the south bank and saw too that fishermen were already at work.

"So, this is South Shields?"

"Aye," confirmed Finch. "Now stand by the ship's rail and get ready to jump."

"I should've thought you'd been paid enough to land us safely at least," said Ned.

Finch looked at him. "I'm not fussed about you but I don't want their nets on my keel so get to the ship's rail - unless you want to wait till Newcastle - it's all one to me."

"No, this will do well enough. I'm indebted to you, James Finch."

The master shrugged. "As you said, you've already paid me in full."

"Do me one last service then. Tell me: what day is it?"

Finch was clearly amused by the question. "'Tis the fifteenth day of May, sir."

It was a shock to Ned that he had been away for over two weeks. Only God knew what had happened since he'd left - he'd told Stephen to wait only two weeks. He glanced ahead and saw the quay was close by the bow.

"Good luck to you, Finch," he called as he swiftly crossed to the rail to join Wulf and Hal who were already standing there petrified. The ship was moving only slowly when the master gave them the signal and they leapt from the deck towards a low wooden jetty. Ned had never known such fear as taking the leap. He struck the wooden boards with a painful thump, landing awkwardly on his knees and tumbling over. Hal thudded into him, the end of his bow catching him on the ear. Wulf was not so fortunate, falling on to the edge of the quay and slipping back into the water. He yelped and went under as the keel of the ship passed by. The fishermen nearby jeered and made no move to help but Hal plunged in his arm and pulled him up. Ned helped him drag the sodden youth up on to the quay.

"Thank God for the strong arm of an archer, eh Wulf?" Ned said with a grin.

The ship was already well past them and picking up speed. Finch gave them a curt wave and Ned returned it. They sat and watched the ship until it disappeared from sight where the great river bent westwards once more. Hal stood up and lurched sideways as he tried to walk, causing a renewed outbreak of mirth from the local men.

Ned remained squatting on the platform. "Give it a while, Hal," he advised, "Finch warned me last night that we'd just got our sea legs and would be glad to be rid of them by morning. As usual, he was right."

Ned had developed a healthy respect for James Finch during their short journey along the coast. He was not a man for idle chatter but when he spoke, men listened.

Ned turned to the fishermen who were now preparing to board their boats. "God give you good morning," he called to one. "Can you tell me where we might find some horses?"

The fisherman stared at him thoughtfully. "Good morning to you, sir. Horses you're after? Well, I can tell you where you can find some fish but I doubt you'll find a horse, not here."

"We can buy them," persisted Ned.

"Not if there aren't any," chuckled the fisherman.

He stepped aboard his boat and a younger man cast off and pushed the small vessel out into the river. Ned watched the other boats leave one by one, heading seaward into the rising sun. It would be a fine May morning for there was not a cloud in the sky - just a yellow haze where the sun lay. Yet he had no illusions now about the difficulties he would face in trying to find his way back to his men.

"Wulf, we need to get you dry. Hal?"

"Yes, Lord?"

"We need food and mounts, Hal - in that order. We can't

linger here; we'll have to walk if we can't ride."

§§§§

By mid-morning his spirits had lifted considerably and for once it seemed that the Lord had looked favourably upon him. The fisherman had been right about the scarcity of horses - but only in his own collection of ramshackle shielings by the quay. Further along the river they found several larger settlements and used the alderman's purse to buy all they needed and, though their new mounts would not carry them into battle, the rouncies would suffice for the slow journey along the bank of the Tyne.

It was not too long before they could see the great town of Newcastle ahead of them with its tall church tower soaring skywards. In another age Ned might have paused to admire its beauty against the deep blue of the sky but for now he was content simply to ride on. As they knew, the bulk of the town lay on the north bank and thus they only needed to skirt around the stone barbican that defended the southern end of the bridge across the Tyne.

Beyond the bridge Ned recognised the north road they had used in their flight from the town but this time they crossed it far to the south. The undulating terrain seemed at least a little familiar as they now began to follow the same route as they had taken to Morpeth. On that occasion they had crossed the river at a ford near Bywell but this time they ignored the ford and continued along the south bank of the Tyne. They made good time during the afternoon and Ned hoped they would reach the ford at Corbridge before nightfall. Yet they were hindered by a slow, gruelling crossing of a reed marsh that bordered the river.

"The horses are tiring fast now," he observed.

"It's the only thing they've done that is fast then," muttered Wulf.

It was not just the mounts that were weary, Ned thought. In an hour it would be sunset and they would be spending the night on the river bank.

"Come on," he said, "let's see how much further we can get before dark."

They picked up their pace for a mile or two but by dusk it was clear that the horses were spent.

"A light ahead?" called Hal. "Could it be Corbridge, lord?"

"By God, you're right Hal! What would we do without your eyes?"

They plodded on, dismounting when darkness fell to walk their mounts until they came upon the ford. It was Corbridge, Ned decided. He had been told that further upstream there was a stone bridge but a poor one, likely to be more hazardous to cross than the ford. It had been too long a day. Still, he reflected, at least they had reached their destination.

They camped for the night on the south bank opposite the village but there was no sign of Stephen or his men. Surely they had not already gone home? He counted the days: it was almost three weeks since he had left and he had told Stephen to wait but two.

They remained near the riverbank through the next day but there was no sign of his men and in the late afternoon with the falling sun at their backs they rode across the river into Corbridge.

"You know the tavern, don't you?" said Ned.

"Aye," the pair said at once, "but the Golden Cock's an alehouse not a tavern."

Ned shook his head. "You two could pass for brothers - if you looked anything like each other."

The alehouse identified by Hal and Wulf seemed deadly quiet, almost deserted. Outside was a poorly daubed image.

"If that's a cock then I'm a blackbird," said Ned, "and since when did 'golden' look like dirty brown?"

"Well, this is it," said Hal.

"It looks like the Golden Cock but it doesn't sound much like it," said Wulf. "It used to be a lively place - full of all sorts."

"It seems to be lacking any sorts now," observed Ned.

As they went in he said: "Now, don't call me your lord - just in case."

"What shall we call you then, lord?" asked Hal.

"What do the lads call me when I'm not there?" asked Ned.

"Best not to know, lord," said Hal with a grin.

Ned grimaced. "My fault, I shouldn't have asked. You'd better just call me Ned then - at least I'll know you're talking to me."

They went inside and he appraised the landlord, a tall, thin-faced man. "Do you know our host?" he asked Wulf.

"That's Walter," said Wulf, "he's alright - his wife's a bit more welcoming though." He grinned wickedly.

Walter noted their weapons and treated them with undisguised suspicion.

"I don't think he remembers you," muttered Ned.

"It was his wife served me mostly," whispered Wulf. "She served up a few extra treats, didn't she Hal?"

"Let's hope your friend Walter's hard of hearing or else has a forgiving nature."

Nevertheless, it seemed Walter was willing enough to sell them some hot potage, a chunk of hard bread and a piece of even harder cheese. Once all had been washed down with a jug of ale even Ned began to relax a little.

He had hoped that they might be lost amongst a crowd of soldiers and locals but the room was almost deserted. He was worried too that they might be identified by their badges but it would have invited suspicion to remain heavily cloaked on such a mild May evening.

The few other patrons in the alehouse seemed content to keep themselves to themselves which was as well for it was just a single room with several long benches in it. There was a smaller room attached where the landlord prepared the food and presumably slept with the rest of his family. During the evening a boy wandered around the room hanging a few more rush lights and as some more ale was consumed the gloom was lifted in more ways than one. They negotiated a price for sleeping in the room overnight and, though the landlord did not drive a hard bargain, the remainder of the alderman's coin was used up all the same.

Of Stephen, or anyone else they knew, there was no sign and within a few hours of their arrival, Wulf and Hal were falling asleep. Ned sent them off to sleep on the floor. The landlord's wife made a late appearance and threw them a woollen blanket each - which was more than Ned expected. The pair dropped off to sleep at once and since the local guests had already left, Ned sat alone with the landlord. Walter had already shown himself to be a generous man and Ned hoped he would be equally forthcoming with some information.

"My lads tell me that last time they were in here the place was heaving," he said, "so where is everyone?"

The landlord shot him a strange look. "Where've you been these past few weeks?"

"We've just come back from across the sea," replied Ned vaguely. "What's the news then?"

"The news is that all the pox-ridden soldiers went south towards Hexham - men, horse, banners and all."

"You sound as if you wanted them to go. I'd have thought they gave you a living."

"They gave my business life enough, but I dare say most of them left a dose of something behind - the pox or another bastard mouth for us to feed."

"So, do you think there'll be a battle then?" Ned asked. At least he now knew why Stephen was not at Corbridge to greet him. He prayed the men of his company were safe.

"Might've happened already," said Walter, "a rider came through yesterday. He said the two armies were squaring up for a fight. Still, I dare say we'll know soon enough if anything happens."

The landlady moved around the room extinguishing the reed lights and candles. Ned took the hint and made a show of downing the last dregs of his ale before thanking his host and preparing to join his comrades on the floor. The landlord nodded to him and trudged into the back room.

"Be sure you lock up, wife!" he called out.

Ned stripped off a few layers of clothing leaving himself in his breeches. The landlady crossed the room to the door with the only remaining candle.

She smiled at Ned. "Sir, perhaps you could lend me your hand?" she asked. She held out the candle and he took it whilst she reached up to drag a heavy bolt across the door. When Ned went to return the candle to her, she leant forward and blew it out. In the sudden darkness he felt a hand against his bare chest.

"Good wife," he hissed, "your husband's in the next room!" His words did little to discourage her as the hand stroking his chest wandered down inside the front of his breeches. Now he had a clearer idea what Wulf meant by 'extra treats'.

"Mistress, please… stop!" He tried to keep his voice low but her fingers were beginning to agitate his dormant loins into life.

"God's blood, woman!" he gasped and dropped the candle. At once both bent forward, her with one hand still lodged in his breeches. They clashed heads, temple to temple and fell to their knees.

The landlady cried out.

"What's amiss?" called Walter from within.

"All's well, my dear," she wailed. The warm hand fled from his breeches as she tried to find the candle. He rubbed his forehead. "Are you alright?" he whispered.

"Course I'm not alright! I'll have a bruise the size of an apple," she replied crossly. "What's the matter with you?" The soft winsome voice appeared to have gone.

"You took me unawares," he protested.

"Well, what if I did? You were the one with your shirt off! I'll have to charge for the damage!"

"Damage? What damage?"

"And if you've ruined my good looks, I'll cut your ear

off!" she said.

Given what she had been trying to do, he thought she might have threatened to cut off something else. "I ask your pardon, mistress. But I have no more to give you - I've given every last penny I have to your husband."

There was a grunt of dissatisfaction and a scrabbling noise as she got up off the floor.

His eyes had adjusted by now and he gave her his arm for support. She took it and sighed.

"You're a very sweet young man," she said and kissed him on the cheek. "I might not charge you - perhaps you'll be back in tomorrow night," she said as she passed by into the back room.

Ned sat down on the floor and pulled his cloak up over him. God's death - what next? His head still throbbed a little and it was not the only part of his body still tingling. It was some time before he drifted off to sleep.

§§§§

The following morning they left the Golden Cock and returned across the river to the south bank. Ned was keen not to attract too much attention and in any case he wanted to watch for Sir Stephen. As the sun went down in the evening, they returned once again to the Golden Cock. Ned was not surprised to find that there was no sign of Stephen but they were rewarded with some news. The landlord, Walter, was in loud conversation with one of his patrons - a gentleman, by his dress - who, it appeared, had just returned from Hexham.

Walter was chuckling in tune with his guest. "So, in truth sir, not much happened in the way of fighting!"

"Indeed not, good landlord. There was some drawing up of men on both sides: the Duke of Somerset drew up his men and Lord John drew up his. But then it seemed the Duke did not like the look of his opponents!"

"The Duke's men did not stand then?" said Walter.

"Lord Montagu isn't one to take it slow - he sent his men straight in." The stranger smiled at the thought of it.

"And?" prompted the landlord.

"Oh, the Duke's men pissed themselves and ran! An archer who was there told me a loud fart would have spooked them into flight!" He laughed once more.

"So, what then?" asked Walter.

"All I heard is that the Duke and others were taken - likely Lord Montagu's already had their heads. He's not one to-"

"- to take it slowly," said Walter with a chuckle.

Ned drank in every word of the man's account. The stranger could have been anyone: he did not look like a merchant or a lawyer - he wore a sword so he might have been a knight. He looked older than Ned, his black hair mottled with grey, yet he was not an old man. Ned wanted to ask questions but he knew he must be careful for he could ill afford to raise any suspicion in either man's mind. Just by being there he was doing the exact opposite of what Hastings had told him to do. If he was caught... but that did not bear thinking about.

"The war is over, then," he called out, hoping to encourage the stranger to tell him more.

"Aye, so it seems," replied Walter, noticing Ned and his comrades for the first time. "But I've been remiss young sirs - same as last evening?"

"God give you thanks, good landlord, but we're not drinking tonight. We've friends to meet shortly." Even Ned thought it sounded lame - after all they had come to an alehouse - but his coin was exhausted now.

"But you've scarce arrived," said Walter, looking aggrieved. "A jug of ale each at least?" he pleaded.

"I thank you landlord, but no." He glanced at Wulf and Hal who regarded him with bleak faces.

"Why not join me in a jug of ale, gentlemen?" the stranger suggested. "I'm travelling alone and I'd welcome your company - at least until you go to meet your friends."

Ned paused. It was a risk but without risk he would get

nowhere.

"We'll join you gladly, sir, in the fellowship of travellers, and thank you for your offer."

The stranger sat down beside Ned and Walter soon brought over several jugs of ale.

"Spearbold!" announced the stranger.

"Sir?"

"George Spearbold."

"Ah, well met, George Spearbold," replied Ned, but he offered no introductions in return.

"Does my ear detect a Yorkshire voice?" enquired Spearbold.

"Aye," said Ned, "we're men of Yoredale. And you sir, by the sound of you, hail from somewhere thereabouts."

"Indeed yes, though I come from a mile or two to the northeast of our beloved dales."

"And what brings you so far from home, sir?" asked Ned.

"I'm the seventh son of the Sir William Spearbold of Richmond. There's nothing for me there, sir. I must take whatever living I can find. I'm currently engaged as a messenger, a merchant's factor, if you like."

"So you witnessed the battle at Hexham, then?"

"Not exactly witnessed, but I spoke to some who were there and as I said, the word battle might be a little fulsome, sir."

"What of the army of Lancaster, where did the defeated go?"

"Back into Percy lands, you'd think. They haven't come here, Walter, have they?"

"Not likely to either," the landlord called across to them. "They'll be heading north to Alnwick - and just as well."

"And is Lord Montagu still at Hexham?" Ned asked Spearbold.

"I know little more," Spearbold said, "but when I left Hexham he was still there."

"So when did the battle take place?" asked Ned, relieved that Spearbold did not seem at all put out by his questions.

"Well, just yesterday - where are we? Yes, the fifteenth of the month."

Ned supped up the remainder of his ale and his comrades followed his lead. Then he got to his feet and gathered up his sword and cloak.

"Well, Master Spearbold, we are much obliged to you for your company, your news and your generosity but we must go. God speed you wherever you're bound next."

Spearbold acknowledged his thanks with a nod and a smile.

Ned bade Walter good night and with only a brief smile to the landlord's wife he followed Wulf and Hal to the door. As he was about to cross the threshold, Spearbold remarked:

"Strange time to meet friends - and out there in the dark…"

Ned looked back at him uncertainly but merely gave him a wave before stepping outside. He walked past several merchant's houses contemplating Spearbold's parting observation.

"What now, lord?" asked Hal.

"Aye, Hal. Well said: what now?"

§§§§

George Spearbold remained in his seat in the Golden Cock alehouse. Spearbold prided himself on his integrity - he had never cheated or lied - except where his master specifically ordered it. He had never killed a man though he had fought a few in the course of his work. His skills lay elsewhere. As he was fond of saying: 'sharp wits will ever blunt sharp blades'. Spearbold possessed exceptionally sharp wits and lived by them alone. He was especially talented at rooting out the secrets of others though he would have maintained that it really was not very difficult: one just had to observe carefully and make a few simple deductions.

That was why he was in the Golden Cock and had been in the alehouse every evening until the past few days. The week before he had observed that Ned Elder's second in command had been in the Cock at that hour day after day - and Spearbold thought he knew why. Then Sir Stephen had been obliged to serve Lord Montagu at Hexham and Spearbold had followed him there.

Now by God's most generous hand, the errant Lord Elder had been delivered up to him - well, almost. The only difficulty was that once Sir Stephen returned with his men, Ned Elder would be a great deal more difficult to capture. So, he must hurry to make the arrangements.

His man, Shard, came in. "Ah, Shard, a timely arrival."

"Will you want me again this evening, Master Spearbold?"

"Yes, Shard, I most certainly will." He lowered his voice. "Get me pen and paper and then saddle your horse. I'll want you to take several messages."

The hunt was on now. He had served his master well but this task was more important than any other he had been entrusted with. He had better make a success of it. What he had told Ned Elder was broadly true: he was the seventh son of the prolific Spearbold family and there were no lands or titles for him by that route. Yet, he had been fortunate; he had been favoured. His father had secured him a position in the service of the Earl of Salisbury at Middleham and in the past few years he had proven his abilities to the extent that he was now an agent of Salisbury's powerful son, Warwick. The Earl valued his talents: he was diligent, he was observant and he had a sharp mind. Thus Spearbold had no titles, but he did have power for he knew all the Earl's secrets and when he acted it was with the full authority of the most powerful man in England.

15

17th May morning, at Crag Tower in the North Tyne Valley

Henry sat with Joan in his privy chamber. They sat in silence and the mood was well past sombre. Henry felt sick. Joan glared at him but said nothing - a blessed relief after all the bitter recriminations she had sent his way in the last few days. What irked him most was that this trifle of a girl had been right all along: Warwick was playing him, keeping Mordeur waiting for days before he saw him, then hinting at support only to change his mind a few days later.

The Duke of Somerset had called him to arms - a summons he had ignored. Now Somerset was taken, and probably executed yet still Henry did not have Warwick's support. His very survival was set on a knife's edge. Yet what was he to Warwick? He was nothing and thus Mordeur was still awaiting the Earl's pleasure at York. Without Warwick's help it would be more difficult to get his inheritance.

"Why would Warwick refuse to help me?" he asked. "It costs him only a few men at arms. I can get Ned Elder for him."

"Isn't it obvious?" said Joan. "He must already have Ned Elder."

"No, he doesn't! I swear he doesn't! If he had Ned he would say it loud and clear - the feud between them runs so deep."

"First, he told Mordeur he would welcome your support," said Joan, "then something happened to make him change his mind."

"Yes, yes all that's plain to see - but what?"

"If he doesn't have Ned Elder why else would he reject your offer?"

"Warwick doesn't yet have him but he must know where he is. If that's the case then he doesn't need me."

"Yet he keeps Mordeur waiting around in York. Why?"

Henry sighed. "I don't know - perhaps, just in case. If he fails on his own, he can call upon us."

"So, we wait then."

"Yes, but for how long? I can't even afford to pay the men I have got. They were promised wages and plunder. God knows what they'll do if they're denied both much longer."

"Do we have enough men to take Yoredale Castle?"

"No. I can barely hold this petty tower. The men already know of Somerset's defeat and I've heard their mutterings. They're starting to wonder what will happen now. Soon I'll have to tell them something other than "Wait.""

"Yet for now, that's all we can do," said Joan.

Henry nodded. "But what about the men?"

"Give them a distraction," said Joan. "I think I may have just the thing: Rob Hall."

"What about Rob Hall? He may be outside but he's not hurting us there."

"Give them Rob Hall for sport."

Henry considered the suggestion seriously for a moment and decided it had some merit.

"Your servant, Alice; will she help?"

"Aliena," corrected Joan.

"Never mind what she's called. Is she still willing to give us Maighread's brother?"

"Yes. Aliena says she can smuggle him in the postern gate."

"Is it that easy to get into this place?"

"With help, yes - after all, postern gates are for sneaking out aren't they? It's simple enough to sneak someone in too.

She'll lead him to the cell where his sister is. You can take him from there."

"He's not much of a catch but I dare say he'd amuse them for a few hours. What a worthless wretch - if he really wanted to free his sister he should have tried long before now."

§§§§

Rob leant against the castle wall. He found himself fiddling with his sword hilt. Aliena was a long time coming and if he was nervous for himself then he was doubly worried for her. She was risking a lot to help him - he wondered if she knew how much. It had been weeks since he had left Ned Elder and he had kept a watch at Crag Tower ever since. Once he had almost managed to slip through the gate when a small fire broke out in the castle yard but the gates had been shut before he could make it in. Only the smoke enabled him to get clear again. He hardly dared think how his sister was faring.

Aliena was allowed out occasionally with one or two other servants to get provisions from the village. They were always accompanied by men at arms but once or twice Aliena had escaped their attentions and managed to see him. On the last occasion they had arranged for her to get him into the castle. He had no idea how he was going to get out again with Maighread - but he knew he must try or it would be too late. In his heart he wondered if it might already be too late but Aliena had assured him that Maighread was still alive.

Many times in the past few weeks he had thought of going to their father but he knew what the answer would be. Maighread had been the price of peace with Sir Thomas Elder and you didn't take back the goods once they had been sold. Maighread was dead to their father from the moment he handed her over but Rob's decision to accompany his sister to Crag Tower had taken his father by surprise. He had not intended to lose a son to Sir Thomas as well as a daughter. Since then his father had refused even to speak to him. No, there would be no help from that quarter.

Suddenly Aliena was beside him, wrapping her arms around him and kissing him hard. He had missed her a great deal in the past months. Their few stolen moments together had been all too fleeting and he held her close.

"We mustn't be long," she whispered, "I've left the gate open."

He cupped her pretty oval face in his hands. "This is madness. You know that, don't you?"

"Well, either we do this madness now or we run off into the night - which is what we ought to do!" She gave his hand a gentle squeeze and he held her again in the darkness.

"I've got to do it…" he said.

"Come," she said and led him by the hand through the postern gate and through the small tower that adjoined it. They emerged on the edge of the castle yard and, keeping to the shadows, made their way across to the door which led to the Hall. Rob's eyes darted hither and thither but he saw nothing to worry him. They paused outside the great door.

"You ready?" he whispered. She nodded and gave him another quick kiss on the cheek. She passed through the door first. The Hall was where several of Henry's men at arms slept so Rob waited until she waved him in. He could hear the snoring as they mounted the steps towards the first floor chambers.

"We've not got long," she breathed, "they'll be waiting for us down at the cells and they'll soon get impatient."

She stopped outside Joan's chamber. "This is it."

He hesitated. "If we're caught," he said, "remember: it was my idea. I forced you to come up here." She nodded.

He eased out his sword and motioned her to open the door. Inside there was no light and he had to feel his way to the bed. He stood still for a moment, listening. He could hear Joan's breathing. He laid the point of his sword on her coverlet and slid it across until it reached her. His eyes were still adjusting to the gloom when he prodded her chest gently.

It was strange: she seemed to wake up at once and

showed no sign of alarm. Then he saw she was fully dressed but of course she had known they were coming. All the same she could not have expected him to come to her own bedchamber, yet she took it with ease.

"I thought it was your sister you wanted," she told him, her voice calm and assured. She was a cool bitch, he thought.

"He made me bring him up here, my lady," Aliena blurted out. He grinned: she was certainly playing her part well.

"Get up," he told Joan. "And then we'll go to see my sister." He pointed to the door and Aliena led the way out of the bedchamber. He was careful not to allow Joan to get too close to Aliena nor too far from his sword point. They descended the stairs and went through the Hall. Several of the men stirred and one saw them. "My lady?" he enquired.

"Stay where you are or I'll cut her," hissed Rob.

"He won't," retorted Joan.

The man remained where he was on the floor but Rob saw his eyes casting around for a weapon.

"Shit," he muttered. "It's always easier in thought than deed."

Before anyone else could react he clubbed Joan on the temple with his sword hilt and caught her over his shoulder as she fell. He turned to the man on the floor. "You really need to go to sleep again," he breathed and delivered a sharp kick at his head.

"That should do for a while, at least," he said to Aliena. "Come on."

She led him down a narrow stair to the cells. Joan was no weight at all but if they were stopped he would have to drop her. The passage to the cells went down a short slope illuminated by a flickering torch that seemed about to gutter. It was many years since he'd been down there and the smell was overpowering: a damp, rotten stench. He was expecting to find Henry but the passage was empty except for the rats that scuttled away at their approach.

There were several cells at the end of the passage: tiny, filthy holes in the rock with decaying doors across them. The left hand door lay open and Rob gasped when he saw the occupant.

"Sweet Jesus!"

"It's Lady Margaret..." Aliena's words caught in her throat.

Even in the gloomy light Rob could see that the lady was long dead. When he looked more closely upon her death mask it unnerved him and he could not imagine what it was doing to Aliena.

A muffled croak came from the cell on the right and he knew it was Maighread - she was still alive but he could not make out what she was saying. He laid Joan's body down on the stone flags and examined the door of the cell. He was relieved to find it was secured only by a simple bolt. "Maighread! I'm here! I'll soon have you out."

The low voice inside was sobbing: "It's a trap, Rob."

He heard the words but was slow to take them in. The door to the middle cell swung open and Henry stepped out. Before Rob could take a step, Henry had seized Aliena and put a knife to her throat. She screamed.

"Good even, Rob," said Henry easily. "I think the plan was that you were going to threaten Lady Joan - lying over there on the floor - and force me to release your sister. Well, it's not going to be quite like that."

Rob cursed his stupidity; the shock of seeing Lady Margaret had put all thought of Henry from his mind. He closed his eyes and looked at Aliena's frightened face. He let his sword fall with a clang onto the stone floor and Henry released Aliena.

"Help Lady Joan up!" he barked at her.

He seized Rob's arm, threw him against the wall and then into the cell where he had been waiting. The door creaked shut and the bolt was slid across. Rob's head hurt where it had struck the stonework. He held his hand against his throbbing temple; it felt sticky. He stared at the blood on his fingers and felt sick. A few moments later the only torch gave out and, in the blackness, his sister was still weeping. The cell was cold and wet, very wet. Water must drain through here, he thought, running down the walls and out of the crevices in the rock. He bent down and wet his hand from a puddle that seemed to have formed by his feet. He wiped away the blood but the water smelt foul. It must drain from the kitchen or more likely through one of the privies. Water, sweet water - God how he needed a flagon of ale!

16

17th May late afternoon, south of the
River Tyne at Corbridge

"Another tossing day gone," grumbled Ned. "Two days and still no sign of them."

He hated waiting. It ground him down. He knew he was better on the move, making sharp calls, instinctive not measured. Left to himself he brooded and just now he had plenty to brood about. Even when he found his men, what then? He had promised Hastings he would not go home, he would not get caught and he would not reveal the king's secret. But Amelie would need him, his sisters would need him and his unborn child would need him.

They were still camped near the river but they had moved to the cover of a small wood on higher ground to the east of Corbridge. From the trees they could see the ford and anyone who approached it. They could even see the ramshackle stone bridge further west. If Stephen was coming from Hexham he would have to cross the river somewhere and if he crossed at Corbridge, they would know instantly. All the same, every evening Ned despatched Hal into the town to keep a watch on the Golden Cock just in case Stephen crossed the Tyne further west and entered Corbridge from the north.

They were in a bad way now that the alderman's purse had run out. They had tried in vain to fish the river and in the end had resorted to stealing some eels from one of the wicker traps set along the bank by a mill. At least a few roasted eels kept their stomachs half full.

"We drift and drift," muttered Ned, "and while we drift, the season moves on. In God's name it'll be midsummer before we get home!" Then he remembered that he could not go home.

"The war must surely be over soon, lord," said Hal.

"Aye, lad, and we neglect our lands and loved ones every day we sit here on our arses."

"How long will we wait here, lord?"

Ned only grunted in response.

The war in the north was more or less finished. With Ralph Percy dead and the Duke of Somerset taken, he did not expect the Percy castles to hold out much longer. If they did, Warwick could always bring up the heavy bombards from Newcastle or York; then it would all be over - or so he had been told. He had only seen the effect of smaller cannon at Towton but it had taught him enough. If Henry of Lancaster fought on, his Percy strongholds would be reduced to piles of smoking rubble but Ned doubted he would play any further part in it.

"Lord?" enquired Hal.

"What?" snapped Ned. He had not been listening to Hal - the youth had an irritating habit of filling a silence with every thought that entered his head.

"Sorry, lord. I was just asking how long you thought we would stay here."

Ned shook his head. "I don't know, Hal. I don't know. I expect Sir Stephen soon, which reminds me - time you were off to the Cock."

Hal nodded and went to saddle his horse.

§§§§

Spearbold drummed his fingers noisily on the table. He knew it was annoying the other men who sat at the same long table but he did not care. The delay was getting to him. All was in place: a copy of the arrest warrant had arrived in

Corbridge and the men at arms from the Earl of Warwick were ready to deploy. The only difficulty was that now he could not find Ned Elder. He had expected him to return to the Golden Cock each day - but he did not. Why not he could only guess, but his guesses were usually correct and he was guessing Ned Elder had run out of coin.

Shard had men out searching the town and the lands around it but they had yet to find him. This was not just about Ned Elder; his own credibility with the Earl rested on his success in this task. So he had every incentive to redouble his efforts - and he had, literally, for twice as many men were now out searching. The previous evening he had caught a glimpse of one of Ned Elder's companions loitering outside the alehouse so tonight he had two men observing the building and the alleys nearby and another two watching the west road from Hexham. If Sir Stephen reached Corbridge he wanted to know about it first. Ned Elder was an outlaw and Spearbold was determined not to let him slip through his fingers as others had done.

§§§§

When Hal returned from the town Ned could tell at once that there was something amiss. He had known Hal long enough to notice the signs.

"What?" he asked the young archer.

Hal hesitated. "I'm not sure, lord," he said. "Just a feeling."

"Did you see any of our men?"

"No, but…"

Ned knew not to bully the lad. "But?" he prompted.

"Just… well… there were more men about the town tonight," he said, "in the market place and near the stone tower."

"But you've seen none of ours?" said Ned, "and you took care on your return, I suppose?"

"Of course, lord."

Ned tried to drag his mind from the torpor into which it had fallen, tried to think. Bagot always said: 'keep the bastards guessing'. If there were more men watching then it was possible Hal had missed one of them.

"We'd best be sure," he said. "Wulf, saddle your horse. Hal, get mine saddled too."

"What is it, lord?" asked Wulf.

"Just saddle it!" hissed Ned, hurrying to pull on his boots. He picked up his sword, wishing he had taken a better blade with him - but it would have to do. He was still strapping it on when the others brought up the mounts.

"Quietly, lads. Very quietly." His voice was a mere whisper in the trees.

He led them up the slope away from the town and the river - and away, he hoped, from the merest hint of danger. He picked his way through the forest, stopping occasionally to listen. The forest was his domain - he had been born in the depths of Yoredale Forest so the shadowy trees held no fear for him. The tree cover was thinner than he would have liked but the night was kind, hiding the moon.

On the edge of a small glade he came to a stop; they had looped around in a half circle to the southwest and had thus almost returned to the river. They sat astride their horses, all three straining their ears to pick up the slightest sound. Soon enough they heard it - the sound of treachery. And that night treachery sounded like the rattle of horse harness. Wulf's mare fidgeted noisily. Ned glared at the animal.

"Voices," breathed Hal. Ned shook his head but then he heard them too. Several riders emerged from the other side of the clearing and came towards them. He offered a silent prayer but at that moment the mischievous clouds overhead parted and a shaft of moonlight pointed them out against the trees.

"There!" came a shout.

For a brief moment it crossed his mind that the men riding out of the shadows might be his own come to find him. The hope was short-lived.

"Ned Elder!" another rider called out, "We've a sealed warrant for your arrest."

"You're not the first," muttered Ned. Then, as if by divine hand, the stark column of moonlight was gone. At once Ned turned his mount and spurred it hard. Wulf and Hal chased close behind.

"You can't escape," the cry pursued him, "there are too many of us!"

Under the dark canopy of trees, Ned smiled.

§§§§

Spearbold was raising another pot of ale to his lips when Shard came into the Golden Cock.

"Well?" asked Spearbold.

"We have them trapped up in the forest," reported Shard.

Spearbold frowned. "Did I not tell you simply to follow the youth and mark where they're spending the night?"

"Aye, sir, but... they moved."

"They moved... so you followed?"

"Aye, sir."

"And when they stopped you noted their camp and left a man to observe?"

"No, sir... I told them we had a warrant."

"How very...considerate of you, Shard. We wouldn't want Lord Elder to be worrying about that now, would we? So, let me see: instead of us guessing that he's somewhere in the forest, we now know that he's somewhere in the forest but, unless I've misunderstood you, we still don't have the vaguest idea where!"

"Ah, no, sir," mumbled Shard.

"I'm disappointed, Shard." He gave a curt nod of dismissal but Shard remained. Spearbold sighed and for the first time he felt apprehensive.

"Go on, what else?" he growled.

"Sir Stephen's just ridden into the market place, sir."

"What?" He threw aside the stool upon which he had

221

spent the evening. "You stand there like a fool telling me that as if you describe your sister's wedding! Get my horse round! Now!"

§§§§

Ned, Wulf and Hal waited, tense and alert. Eyes and ears were attuned to the woodland around them.

"Do we just wait it out, lord?" whispered Hal.

Ned shook his head and put a finger to his lips. They could not stay in the forest till morning for then Spearbold or Warwick or someone would flood the woods with men at arms as soon as it was light. With Somerset finished there would be no shortage of Neville men to hunt them down. The night, despite the fickle moon, was their only ally.

"What then, lord? Where can we run to now?"

Hal had a point. They needed a place to hide out but they did not have one. The Percies would not help him and now the Nevilles were hunting him down. There was nowhere in all Northumberland that Ned Elder could look for succour. Or was there? An idea occurred to him - a bold idea - no, more desperate than bold. Slowly, in the absence of any other ideas, the ridiculous notion took hold.

"Lord?" breathed Hal, "they're near…I can hear them."

"So be it," said Ned and nudged his horse gently. "We make for the ford."

Hal exchanged a worried glance with Wulf. "But they're all around us…"

In the darkness Ned grinned. "You should know by now, lad: if you ride with me, it's never an easy road."

He eased his sword in its scabbard and looked at the young pair.

"We ride fast lads, we strike down any man in our path and we don't stop."

They said nothing so he urged his mount forward, driving down towards the river, all pretence of stealth abandoned. Soon they broke cover, leaving the trees behind them and almost at once several riders were in pursuit. Once more the moon dazzled them, illuminating the river as a bright cord winding its silver threads across their path as they galloped down to the ford. There, a knot of men at arms awaited them on foot. As they thundered towards them the group hastily fanned out along the riverbank, bills and helmets glinting in the light of the moon. Ned drew his sword and pointed the blade towards the river.

"An Elder! An Elder!" he bellowed and at once the cry was taken up by Wulf and Hal. They charged the line of men at arms and their momentum carried them through into the ford though their gentle rouncies shrieked in terror. In his haste to escape, Ned had forgotten that these poor nags were not bred to endure such action. The ford became a churning mass of men and horses. A poleaxe aimed at his leg missed and punched into his horse's exposed flank. The beast screamed and reared up driving its forelegs into the perpetrator's chest. There was a crunch as the man's ribs were crushed and he was lost in the dark waters of the crossing. Ned held on grimly as the horse shuddered under him.

Men on foot were usually no match for horsemen but numbers told and they were heavily outnumbered. Worse still, the chasing knights were only twenty paces away. He felt the wound on his mount and his hand came away with hardly any blood - that was something at least. He warded off a sword stroke and carved his blade down onto the assailant's shoulder.

"Into the town!" he shouted and coaxed his horse further across the river. Hal pushed on just ahead of him and Wulf was hacking and thrusting his way through behind. Then at the very moment their mounted pursuers reached them, the clouds drew a shroud across the moon and darkness enveloped the melee once more.

"On! On!" urged Ned. They surged out of the chaos of stumbling men to reach the far bank. But there they were met by more men, some mounted, some on foot.

A deep voice boomed out at them. "Lord Edward Elder! I hold in my hand a warrant for your arrest! Yield and those that wear your livery will be spared!"

Ned recognised Spearbold's voice at once - no longer the voice of a casual alehouse traveller but the voice of authority. He had wondered about such a well-informed traveller appearing at the Cock just when they needed him. He was disappointed though, for he liked Spearbold - or rather the man he had supposed Spearbold to be. Ah, well, had Bagot not warned him? Trust no-one.

Ned knew he could not, must not, be taken. He drove into the waiting ring of horsemen, slashing at the nearest figure and cutting him badly but he could not force a way through. All too quickly they were surrounded though none in the encircling band seemed inclined to strike. Instead they remained at a safe distance.

Spearbold was nearby now. "Give up your sword, my Lord, if you please," he said. "You must see that we have you. I've no desire to harm any of you, nor do I want to lose any more of the Earl's men. So please, give it up."

For the first time that night, Ned hesitated. If it were just him, him alone, he would have ridden at them and tried to cut his way out. He would have fallen, but better that than the grisly fate that awaited him at York or Hexham. But Hal and Wulf had no reason to give their young lives here - and for nothing more than his stubborn pride. He should have made his peace with Warwick long ago and they would all be heading home. He closed his eyes; the very outcome he had laboured so hard to avoid had come to pass.

He held his sword out hilt first and Spearbold was leaning forward to receive it when the cries went up.

"An Elder! An Elder!" the shouts seemed to be all around them. At once Ned snatched away his sword and wheeled around towards the town bank. Stephen and his men were hurtling into the ford. Spearbold was clearly no soldier for his first instinct was to draw back leaving his men at arms in confusion. In the meantime a great swathe of riders wearing the Elder badge rode around Ned, Wulf and Hal and swept them along with them up onto the riverbank and into the town.

"On me!" bellowed Ned, as they thundered past a few startled citizens drawn to the commotion.

Stephen pointed ahead. "The road north, my lord!"

Ned waved him ahead but after a mile or two Sir Stephen slowed up.

"You seem to know where you're going," said Ned.

Stephen laughed. "I've no idea," he said, "but I know where I've come from and at the moment that's where we're heading."

"Hexham?" guessed Ned. Stephen nodded.

He took Stephen's hand and clasped it firmly. "I've never been so pleased to see you."

Stephen grimaced. "Not since the last time I got you out of a hole - at another ford if I recall. You seem to make a habit of getting yourself trapped in them."

"I am grateful nevertheless," replied Ned, "but…I'm afraid my journey to see the king was to no avail."

"So, where does that leave us?"

"It leaves me a wanted man, Stephen. It's no light matter and the more aid you and the others give me, the more you risk."

"We've sworn oaths, Ned. They're no light matter either."

Ned smiled. "Then…we move on."

"But where? There's nowhere that'll take us in!"

"God knows I've had plenty of time to think about it these past weeks. I can't go home to Yoredale whilst I'm outlawed but I can settle my affairs with Henry and Mordeur."

"So, in the end, you're going to Crag Tower."

"One way or another, Henry got me into this mess. If I can bring him, or Mordeur, to account for the Alnham killings then I may be able to settle matters with Warwick. I can't see any other way out."

DEREK BIRKS

17

18th May morning, at Crag Tower in
the North Tyne Valley

Rob came to in darkness but then it was dark all the time down in the cells. It surely must be morning by now. His head still throbbed and his throat was dry. What a fool he had been.

"Maighread?" he called lightly.

"You're awake at last then?" Her throat sounded a lot worse than his. "Little brother, why did you come?"

"To get you out, of course."

She groaned. "You can't get me out! Why do you think I sent you away in the first place?"

He was struggling to understand. "You sent me to get help!"

"From Ned Elder? I knew he wouldn't come - even if you found him."

"I did find him…"

"But he didn't come, did he? I knew he wouldn't. I just wanted to get you out because I knew it was coming. I could see it in Henry's eyes, the anticipation, the longing - the way he lusted after Joan. I knew you'd do some foolishness if you stayed."

"I couldn't leave you in here…"

"But you will, little brother, you will."

We can still get out, he told himself, but he didn't tell her.

"Have you been fed?" he asked, thinking of Lady Margaret's gaunt corpse next door to him.

227

Maighread moaned a reply. "I couldn't tell you ...what they've made me eat... and do. But you should have left me here..."

There was a sudden bang as the door at the far end of the corridor was flung open and torchlight returned. He heard the bolt snap across and his cell door opened. Henry stood there with two of his men at arms and looked at him with disdain.

"There, lads - a new plaything for you. Take your pleasure with him as you will; then throw him off the crag." Maighread gasped. "Still alive in there, then?" Henry grinned, slamming his fist against her door. "Good! I haven't finished with you yet."

"Lord!" pleaded Maighread, "do what you will with me but let my brother go."

"I already do with you what I will with you. Now, say farewell to your brother."

Rob could think of nothing to say, no protest to make or plea to offer. He knew that Henry had no intention of sparing either of them.

They took Rob out and he blinked when he emerged into the daylight once more. He looked around the yard he knew so well. It was a small place: there was nowhere to run and nowhere to hide. The gate was only yards away but it might have been miles for the two men who held him were strong and the gate was well guarded. His appearance brought a half-hearted jeer from the few men on the rampart. He was counting heads when they threw him to the ground and starting kicking him. The first boot struck him in the chest, jarring his ribs; then the blows kept coming, to his side, legs, chest again - good Christ that hurt - his stomach and then mercifully his head and he blacked out.

He screamed himself awake - and shuddered - cold water! They had brought him around by lowering him into the well. Then they raised him up, shivering at the end of the rope that bound his hands. He was tossed down once more onto the yard, then they propped him up against the wooden wall of an outhouse. They untied his hands and pulled him to his feet but his legs felt numb and would not bear his weight. He slumped sideways.

"Stand up!" roared one of them and clipped him around the head. He tried to look at them but his vision was blurred: they were just shapes. One shape came towards him, closer, face to face. He could smell him better than he could see him and he smelt of horse shit and leather.

"Keep on your feet, lad or you'll wish you had," the voice ground each word into him.

Then the shape receded and Rob tried to take a deep breath but a sharp pain in his ribs told him all was not well there. He looked around him without seeing. He was drifting away. Then there was a thud in the board next to his head and he jerked upright. A chorus of raucous laughter erupted in the yard. As it died down there was another sound, nagging, slightly familiar. When it stopped, voices were raised again, raging encouragement but surely not to him. Thud! Something impaled itself into the wood by his hip. It occasioned another outburst of shouting. He looked down. It was a small, black object. He could not focus on it so he reached down his hand and touched it: cold metal.

The other sound began again, an annoying, clicking noise which he still could not place. His hand was still on the piece of metal when another quarrel struck by his right ear. His head was just beginning to clear and he could see them now: a ring of four with two crossbows between them. As the next one was ratcheted back, it dawned on him that they were moving further back with each shot. The next bolt just caught his side and he cried out with pain for it had pinned a fold of his skin to the wall. His legs were shaking and he could not stop himself falling. The flesh tore away from the bolt and opened an ugly wound. He passed out briefly but came to when they lifted him up again.

He was facing the main gate as it opened and Mordeur rode into the yard. He dismounted swiftly and strode across to the Hall door. Then he turned and shouted: "Get rid of him! You'll have other things to do now!"

Rob's wits were shredded. He was manhandled up to the rampart and dragged along leaving a smear of blood on the stonework. "Wait," he muttered but they hoisted him up on top of the wall and he glimpsed the valley floor far below. There was a shriek from down in the castle yard and he glanced back to see Aliena being slapped in the face by Joan.

"Aliena," he said almost to himself. "God protect her."

"Enjoy the fall while it lasts," growled someone and then there was a cheer and he was rolled off the wall over the edge of the crag. He screamed as he fell but when he struck the rock ledge at the foot of the wall, the air was driven from his lungs. He rebounded then onto a grassy bank and for a moment hope returned as he clutched at the foliage but could not hold on.

"Mary, mother of God!" he pleaded. He was turned over and over, jolted to left and right. He thumped into spurs of rock, patches of earth and roots of trees until a flailing arm struck a root and he clung onto it. His shoulder was almost wrenched from its socket but he held on and found himself dangling against the sheer rock face. He gripped the tree root with both hands.

"Oh, holy Mary, thank you. Thank you." He was breathing heavily and every breath hurt but he was alive.

Then the root snapped.

§§§§

Above the din in the courtyard, Henry did not hear the gates open and was taken by surprise when Mordeur burst into his privy chamber.

"Mordeur! At last! You have news?"

"The very best of news, my lord: the Earl has agreed to give you his support if you can give him Ned Elder. He would prefer him alive, but dead will do."

Henry was stunned. The sudden turnaround by Warwick was unexpected. He sat down, slowly absorbing its significance.

"But, I thought... you said you were just kicking your heels waiting."

"The Earl had his own man at work - one Master Spearbold, it seems. But he failed to deliver Lord Elder. I fear Master Spearbold will shortly be in the land of beggars - if the Earl doesn't hang him."

"So, where do we stand? How many men at arms does the Earl send me?"

"Not the fifty you asked for - but he's given you twenty."

"A mere score?"

"Mounted men though and well harnessed," said Mordeur.

"Well, it may be enough," said Henry, breathless with euphoria. "Will they come here?"

"No, they'll meet us at Hexham where Ned Elder was last seen. We are to go south which may draw him to us. The Earl's new agent, Shard, will stay in the borders in case he remains at large here. The Earl will shortly be in York but from there he'll to Middleham for a brief time. If we take Ned Elder, we are to deliver him to Middleham, not York."

"Excellent! That gives us two chances: either we catch him on the road south or he comes to us at Yoredale. Let's hope Durston is well prepared - it's time he delivered on all his fine promises."

"Yes, my lord, but we will need to move quickly now. The Earl is not a patient man."

"Indeed. Rouse the men. Pack whatever stores we need."

"What about the prisoners and ... the servants?"

Henry thought only for an instant. "Too many witnesses here might tarnish the new Lord Elder's reputation. Put everyone into the cell passage under the Hall and bolt the door shut. Anyone who's not coming with us goes in there."

"All? Are you sure, my lord?"

"Yes all of them," shouted Joan. She stood on the threshold, feet planted in a determined stance. "They want us dead! So good riddance to them all - and throw my maid Aliena in there too. The little bitch was lying to me all along!"

Henry was taken aback by her outburst. "I wouldn't want to get on the wrong side of you, my lady."

"No, you wouldn't - but you know that already... my love." Joan grinned at him and his own smile died upon his lips.

"Get on with it then, Mordeur!" he urged. "Oh, and set some fires around the house and stables. Let's burn the place down. We're moving to rather better quarters now!"

18

18th May midday, in the North Tyne Valley, Northumberland

During the early hours of the morning Ned's company made a makeshift camp away from the river and rested until noon, when they set off again following the valley of the northern arm of the River Tyne.

"You know Crag Tower will be held against you," said Stephen.

"Rob told me he had someone on the inside - someone who could get him in… or us."

"And you trust the word of this reiver?"

"He has a sister imprisoned there."

"So he said!" Stephen shook his head. "The truth is, Ned, you don't know that a single word he told you is true."

"I don't know it, Stephen, but I believe it, or I wouldn't be going there."

He glanced ahead at the steep slope of the valley, where the river swung to the west. Wulf and Hal were returning already from their scouting.

"Any sign of Lancastrian stragglers?" he asked.

"No…just a lot of cattle and sheep," replied Hal. "Oh, and some smoke."

"Why so much livestock?" asked Stephen.

"We talked to some drovers," said Wulf, "they've been at Stagshaw Bank cattle fair. There's horses for sale there on Whitsun eve."

"Where's Stagshaw Bank?" asked Stephen.

233

"It's east of -"

"Never mind where it is - what was the smoke?" demanded Ned.

"We didn't get that far," said Hal.

"I sent you out to scout not gossip!" said Ned. "How much smoke are we talking about?"

"Well, there was too much for cooking, or even smelting."

"You said there's a cattle fair - that would cause a host of cook fires," observed Stephen.

Hal scanned the heights above the river ahead. "Lord, you can make out a smudge or two from here."

Ned couldn't, but he took Hal's word for it. "Go and see - and this time look more carefully!"

Hal and Wulf turned and set off again at the gallop.

Ned exchanged a glance with Stephen. "Better warn the men," he said, "and we'll pick up our pace."

Ned followed not far behind his scouts and soon several spirals of smoke became clear to them all. Ahead, on a promontory overlooking the bend in the river, was a small stone castle, half obscured from view by a ring of small trees and scrubland. A pall of smoke hung over it, drifting towards them. Ned watched Hal and Wulf climbing a winding track up the side of the valley and followed their route towards the castle.

"Stay alert!" he shouted as they began the steep ascent.

He found his scouts dismounted outside the castle, which he took to be Crag Tower. The gates hung wide open and the ramparts looked deserted.

"Any sign of anyone?" he asked.

They shook their heads. "Thought we'd better wait for you, lord," said Hal. "It's got an odd smell to it."

That was true enough, thought Ned, for there was a hint of more than just wood smoke in his nostrils. As he dismounted, Bear abruptly slid from his horse and began walking with purpose towards the gates. He sniffed the smoky air several times as if to confirm his suspicions then he turned and walked back to Ned.

"Men burn," he said in his coarse guttural tone.

"Aye, Bear - but what do they burn?" He met Bear's troubled eyes. "Aye, never mind. Men burn."

He walked his horse into the castle courtyard and the rest followed. A tendril of acrid smoke drifted out from inside the tower and the blackened remains of what he assumed had once been storehouses lay at the foot of the curtain wall. There was not a soul to be seen - dead or living - either on the walls or in the yard. Their horses whickered nervously as the smoke stung their eyes and nostrils.

If Ned had any doubts about where he was, they were swiftly dispelled by the Elder coat of arms decorating the stone lintel above the large doors into the Hall.

"This is Crag Tower," he said. "Search everywhere - carefully, for we don't know yet whether we'll come across friend or foe. Hal, Wulf, get up on the wall and keep a good watch. And let's get the fires out!" he shouted. "Come on, Stephen, let's see what Henry's left us to find in the Hall."

He felt strange somehow as he passed under the coat of arms to enter the stone keep. The interior was less scorched than he had expected.

"The fires were hastily set," observed Stephen, "they weren't trying very hard to burn it down."

"Or they were just in a hurry," said Ned, kicking aside the charred debris to get up the steps to the floors above. He sent men on to explore to the top of the tower and John Black was the first to return.

"Less damage up there, lord," Black informed him. "Just a couple of small fires."

Nevertheless, Ned looked over the whole tower until he satisfied himself that it was truly abandoned. "You see, Stephen, we didn't even need to creep in the postern gate. Perhaps the Lord's smiling upon me at last. Let's see if we can clear the Hall a bit and make it fit to live in."

"We're staying here then?" asked Stephen.

"Aye, we'll hold out here for a day or two and while we're doing that we can think about what we do next."

"We can't have missed them by much. How can you remain so calm?" asked Stephen.

"True, I'd hoped to find Henry but the mystery intrigues me … at least a little," said Ned.

"I can't see any mystery here. Henry was a beaten man and now the craven's on the run."

"But why would he go? He doesn't know of me - nor that I was coming. I'm damned sure he didn't run from Rob. Why leave the safety of the stone keep?"

"Fear!" said Stephen.

"And when did you ever see a castle abandoned so?" Ned continued. "There are always folk about: servants, labourers and so on. At the very least we would have seen a few - or their … their bodies. Where are the servants?"

"Henry must have taken them with him or perhaps the servants fled - hardly unknown."

"Possible," agreed Ned, "but answer me this: where are Maighread Elder and the other ladies who would have been living here when Henry took charge?"

"It's good that we've not found the ladies, isn't it? It means there's hope we will."

Ned shook his head. "I'm not so sure..."

"What do you mean?"

Ned's mind jerked back four years to the smoky ruin of a deserted Yorkshire village where he had discovered death in all its cruellest forms.

"I don't know yet, but the smell of death lingers here," he said.

"Lord!" called John Black.

Ned looked up. "What is it?"

Black was standing at the top of the steps that Ned supposed led from the Hall down into the cellars. His voice trembled "I think you'd best come here, lord, if you please."

Ned went down the steps and at once the smell grew stronger and caught in his throat. At the foot of the steps stood Bear, grim-faced.

"We can't open the door to the cellars," said Black. He

coughed. "And there's an evil stench, lord."

Ned stared at the charred door; it looked as if it should just fall apart.

"I smell it well enough," he said. It was an ugly smell, not sweet like a roasting of pork, but sickly and rotten.

"Bear's had a go," said Black, "the bolts are drawn back but the door won't budge. It's still warm to the touch too."

Ned closed his eyes and said a silent prayer. Perhaps they should just leave it shut.

"Lord?" asked Black. His voice was muffled for he held his cap over his mouth and nose.

"Go back up, Black. Send down Sir Stephen - no-one else."

He looked at Bear and met his dark stare. "Use your axe," he said quietly.

"Blood of God!" gasped Stephen as he reached the foot of the steps and heard Bear's axe splinter the door. "Cover your face!" said Ned. If only we could cover our eyes too, he thought.

Bear's second blow shattered the central panels of the door. It was heavy oak but the inside had been incinerated to a thin crust. The appalling stench smothered them like a cloud of death and the three men took a pace back. A yard away were the blackened objects which had stopped the door from opening. Fire-twisted limbs still clung to the door frame, white bones showing through the charred flesh.

"They must have been caught down here," murmured Stephen, "overtaken by the fire."

The cellar entrance was a blackened hole and they could not see beyond the doorway.

"Get someone to light me a torch and bring it down here," ordered Ned. He waited by the door with Bear crouched beside him.

"Men burn," pronounced Bear softly. Ned sighed and nodded his head. As always, Bear's instinct was right; he must learn to trust to it more often.

Stephen hurried back with a torch. Ned snatched it from

him and held it by the door. In the wavering light they discovered the missing servants.

"God's heart!" said Stephen.

"God?" said Ned and took a step into the cellar.

"You're not going in there? Surely, no-one could have lived through it!"

"We must be sure."

"This is beyond evil, Ned."

"Aye, but I must look upon it!" said Ned, his voice harsh. His throat was raw with the smoke and his stomach churned at what lay before them but he would at least look. He would pay these poor souls that respect.

"Stay here," he said, "the last thing we want is a horde of us trampling over these folk's remains."

He eased his way past the bodies at the door, holding the torch high in one hand with the other hand firmly clamped over his face. It was hard to find places to step, to avoid a claw-like hand or blackened skull. His knees felt weak and he paused to lean against the wall, his eyes streaming with tears and not just from the smoky residues.

"Come on you weak bastard," he told himself. "You've seen worse than this." But the truth was he had not and he never wanted to.

He continued to the end of the passage where he could make out the stonework of some small cells. Here there was a mass of tortured bodies where many had tried to escape the flames but now lay in a grotesque tangle of limbs and faces - or what had once had been faces. Those furthest away were less touched by fire but must have succumbed to the smoke. Nothing moved and the only sound was the water dripping down the walls.

There was nothing more to see and clambering over these condemned souls would do no-one any good. He choked suddenly in the thick atmosphere and coughed, racking his chest with a spasm of pain. He was turning to go when he heard a scratching, rustling sound. Rats! They would have found crevices to hide in when the fire came and now it was spent they had come to take its grisly offering.

He took a step further and drew out his long dagger. He would find the little bastards! He stepped carefully over the heap of bodies and waved the torch around nearer the floor. When he stopped moving he could no longer hear anything, except the steady drip of water.

"Bloody rats!"

"My lord?" Stephen called. "Do you need help?"

"No!" said Ned, but he would need help to forget this. What could one do with this?

Suddenly there was more rustling, this time close to his feet. Then something seized his leg and he forgot about the rats. He fell back against the wall in shock, dropped his knife and almost let the torch fall - almost. He stared down at his boots and there, clutching his shin, was a living hand. It was red and raw, but it moved. It lived. Then the hand released him and disappeared. He waved the torch around frantically but could not see it.

He didn't know then what words he screamed but Stephen swiftly joined him.

"Hold the torch!" said Ned and crouched down. There were two bodies in one of the cells, entwined together with a shred of woollen blanket stretched over them. The first one he looked at was dead, her back and head badly burned. He lifted her gently off the second body, another woman. Her hair was burnt in places and the clothes on her back were burned away save some fragments stuck to her skin. She had serious burns but the body was soft to the touch, though cold for it was lying in the water from the drain.

As soon as he touched her, she howled and her hands began scrabbling at the water in which she lay. She lifted her head and he winced to see the burn all down one side of her face. Her eyebrows had been singed off but the water must have kept her alive. It would have been impossible to breathe but somehow she had.

He picked her up and she screamed. He could not see all her burns and his touch hurt her badly. She began to struggle in his arms and every movement was sure to hurt her more.

"Be calm! I'm sorry," he breathed, "I'm sorry." But it didn't stop her screaming. He held her tightly to him and her raw fists pummelled his back. Be calm - you fool, how in God's name could she be calm?

Stephen went ahead with the torch as Ned carried her to the doorway. Her arms had stopped flailing now and the screams became sobs until mercifully she passed out. He mounted the steps to the Hall.

"Find me a bedchamber!" he yelled "and get me some water... and does anyone know what to do with burns?"

Black sped up the stairs ahead of him. "This way, lord, I saw a chamber up here!"

Ned followed him up to the first floor and laid the woman down on the first bed he came to. "Good Christ!" said Black when he saw her.

"Thank you, Black. Now go."

He stared at the woman. He had stupidly set her down on her back and she stirred, taking short tiny breaths and moaning all the while. He stood helplessly over her. I'm watching her die, he thought. Then Bear shouldered his way past and returned him to his wits.

"What is it, Bear?" he demanded.

"Burned," said Bear, "I can do."

He bent down, examined the seared face and then turned the woman over on to her front. Her body went limp and still.

"You've killed her, you fool!" accused Ned.

Bear shook his head. "She still breathes."

Without another word he went out, but returned shortly afterwards with a large flagon of dark liquid and a length of linen cloth he had clearly torn from one of the other bedchambers. There were few men Ned would have allowed to push him aside and fewer still he would have trusted to treat the burns but in his time as a mercenary Bear must have seen more wounds and injuries than anyone else in the company. He watched the big man pour some of the liquid over the linen and press it onto the worst burns. Ned wrinkled his nose at the pungent smell of vinegar.

Bear paused then screwed his face into a deep frown and looked at Ned.

"Need..." he said but he could not find the word to describe what he needed. He puffed out his cheeks in frustration and handed Ned the vinegar. "Wash burns," he instructed and hurried out again.

Ned hardly dared touch the red raw skin on the woman's back. There were strands of wool fused to the flesh. He poured on a little more vinegar and tried to ease off the fragments of cloth but she whimpered at his touch. He was relieved when Bear returned and took over.

He watched Bear work. For a man with such large hands he had a deft, gentle touch. Ned could tell from the speed at which he worked that he had treated such burns before. Having washed the wounds with vinegar, he applied a handful of honey from a pot Ned presumed he had retrieved from the castle kitchen. By the time he had finished the woman was shivering, so he covered her with a sheet of linen. He seemed well pleased with his work, gave Ned a curt nod and left the chamber.

Ned shook his head in disbelief: was there nothing Bear could not do? He called for Wulf and told him to keep a close watch over the woman.

"I'll relieve you later," he told him, "but tell me at once if she wakes."

When he went downstairs, he found Stephen had been busying the men in restoring some degree of order at Crag Tower.

"The gates are shut and the rampart is manned, lord," reported Stephen, "and most of the fires are cleared away except for well... the cellars. What in God's name do we do with those who perished there?"

"I think we need a priest..." said Ned, "and we need them buried. The longer we leave it, the worse it'll be."

"You're right about the priest - but you're going to ask the men to do the burial?"

"No, I'll not ask them, but they'll do it. Take a few men and find me a priest."

He ordered the gates opened and walked around the outside of the castle, calling for Hal to follow him. Towards the river in the west there was a steep fall away from the curtain wall, so he continued around to the eastern side where the slope down towards the fields was gentler. He stood still, looking east: it was a pleasing aspect.

"Here, where the morning sun will warm them. We'll bury them here. Find some shovels or picks," he said.

While Hal hurried back to the castle to find some tools, Ned slowly stripped off his padded jack and discarded his sword and scabbard onto the grass. By the time Hal returned with some digging implements and several men at arms, Ned had already paced out the graveyard he would dig. Within a few moments he had started digging the trench.

He said nothing to the men and at first they watched him work. Then, one by one, they joined him. Others looked on from the walls and a few more came around and helped to dig. Several offered to take over from him and at first he waved them away but as the task neared completion he jumped up out of the pit and left Hal to supervise whilst he addressed a rather more difficult mission: the removal of the grisly remains from the cellars. They stripped out every length of cloth they could find in the household and wrapped it around the charred bodies with reverent care before moving them to the burial site a few at a time on a hand-pulled cart.

It was late in the afternoon before they had taken out all the bodies and by then Stephen had returned with a parish priest in tow. He was a young man and looked ill at ease, Ned thought, but who would not be unnerved by the sight of so many poor tormented souls?

"Father Baston, my lord," said Stephen.

The priest may have been young but he understood quickly enough what was required of him. He had brought up some holy water from his church and he sprinkled it over the remains.

Father Baston was still engaged in this work when a distressed Wulf found Ned.

"She's awake, lord," he said, "but she's weeping with the pain of it."

The priest was in full flow but Ned followed Wulf from the graveside. He had done his bit for the dead; it was time to tend to the living.

§§§§

Her eyes were open, but she was no longer weeping. He imagined that every tear had been wrung from her.

"I'm Ned Elder," he told her softly.

She opened her mouth to speak and winced as the scarred skin of her right cheek was stretched.

"Too late…" Her voice was deep and husky, almost like a man's.

She turned away and said no more to him, resting the undamaged left side of her face on a pillow. He stared for a moment at the angry scar, traces of honey still clinging to it. Then he sat down by the bed to wait.

DEREK BIRKS

19

18th May before midday, at Hexham Castle in Northumberland

Spearbold hurried to the stables and snatched his reins from a startled stable boy. His survival depended upon reaching the gatehouse before someone decided to carry out the Earl's latest orders. He calmed himself and led his horse towards the gatehouse. As he approached there were shouts from the rampart, the gates were opened and a dozen or more men at arms rode in.

Curious, Spearbold edged away from the riders and waited beside one of the storehouses built against the wall. He studied the group carefully - even in flight he could not stop himself from observing, noting and storing memories. He was surprised to see a young lady amongst them whom he did not recognise. Once he laid eyes upon a face, the memory of it never left him and when he scanned the faces of the men he soon found one he did know: the Frenchman with much hair, Mordeur. Spearbold began to piece together what he knew: Mordeur served Henry of Shrewsbury, the new master of Crag Tower. So, here we have Henry, his lady and a clutch of men at arms. What did that mean, he wondered?

Before he could answer his unspoken question, a troop of Warwick's own mounted men entered the courtyard and dismounted. Soon after, he watched, astonished, as Henry remounted and left again accompanied by Warwick's men. He was so engrossed in his observations that he had forgotten that he was supposed to be escaping. He glanced back to the Hall and noticed his own man, Shard, descending the steps and heading for the stables. He had no doubt that his own fall would benefit Shard more than anyone. Shard knew a great deal - in fact he knew far too much about many things, including Spearbold himself.

He must get out of Hexham but he was interested in where Henry was going, so he tagged on behind the men at arms and followed them out of the gate. He followed the party long enough to establish that they were heading south and then he dropped back and turned around to ride north towards Corbridge. He needed to think, yet he also needed to put some distance between himself and Shard.

Warwick had been scathing, almost brutal in his condemnation. The Earl could be generous in victory - he had reaped the rewards himself - but he could be vindictive if thwarted. Spearbold had seen it happen to others, yet his own demise had been so swift, so absolute. He urged his mount to a gallop - the horse was built for comfort not speed and Spearbold had never liked riding at the best of times, but he had to make haste. He travelled light at all times but there were one or two items he needed to collect from an inn in Corbridge - not the Golden Cock where he had waited for Ned Elder, for that was far too indiscreet a place.

In Warwick's service he had gathered a wealth of information and now that knowledge was going to get him killed if he wasn't careful and, above all else, Spearbold had always striven to be careful. He shuddered as he recalled the Earl's final threat: that Spearbold would be 'as a leper' and that no-one would ever pay for his services again. No doubt the Earl would ruin him; and his fine house in Middleham, rented from Warwick, would soon be welcoming a new tenant.

If he was finished with the Earl then he must seek employment amongst the Earl's enemies. Yet the House of Lancaster was all but destroyed: the old King Henry in flight, Percy killed, Somerset and other lords executed - there was only oblivion there. Queen Margaret, he'd heard, was in

France. Who else then? William Herbert, Earl of Pembroke? He was a rising star with the new king and was certainly Warwick's enemy but would he take on Spearbold? Doubtful. Then there was the obvious choice - Ned Elder. But would Ned Elder have him? After all, he had almost brought about his capture at Corbridge. He had to confess that, in their brief acquaintance, he had quite liked the young knight. Perhaps that was the root cause of his failure.

He considered resting overnight at the inn, for he was dog tired after chasing about in pursuit of Ned Elder, but he knew that Shard would expect him to go there. He had never disguised his contempt for the man but he feared him; every man should fear Shard. The Earl himself would not be a problem for several days since his presence was required in York with his brother, Lord Montagu. If he could move swiftly and give Shard the slip then all would be well.

He ate well before leaving the inn after midday for he had no idea where his next meal would come from. As he left Corbridge he was careful to keep a close watch. He saw no sign of Shard but then he had trained the man well. Shard would not be seen until he wanted to be. He was still puzzling over Warwick's apparent support for Henry of Shrewsbury - and where Henry was going. He had only a small garrison at Crag Tower so he must have emptied it. What was he going to do further south with the help of Warwick's men?

Spearbold knew that the Earl of Warwick had more than a few matters on his mind: negotiations for the Scottish peace, he was also in touch with the King of France and he was promoting his brothers' interests with the King. But his private obsession was with Ned Elder, whom he had declared an outlaw for his refusal to face the charges brought against him. It was too much of a coincidence that he was sending out men at arms with the youth who had, it was rumoured, killed Sir Thomas Elder, Ned's grandfather. But if Henry was helping Warwick to find Ned Elder why was he heading south? It made little sense to him. In truth he was more worried about Shard than Henry. Shard could be dangerous and Spearbold found himself repeatedly looking behind him in case he was being followed.

If he was going to offer his services to Ned Elder then he had better find him before Warwick did. At least he had the advantage of having a suspicion where Ned Elder was likely to go and the arrival of Henry of Shrewsbury at Hexham only made his theory all the more likely. But Spearbold dealt only with snippets of information; what did he possess which might persuade Ned Elder to trust him?

The road north through the wall left by the ancients was busier than he expected, with many cattle and horses being driven along a broad trail. Then he recalled that there was a horse market at Stagshaw Bank at the end of the month and many folk would be gathering for that. Because of the congestion what should have been a fast journey became very slow and it was late afternoon when he reached Crag Tower. He approached it with some apprehension; after all, Ned Elder could only receive him with the utmost suspicion.

Crag Tower was already in sight high above the river when something made Spearbold look around behind him: there, a hundred paces or so behind, were three riders. He quickened his pace but his pursuers kept coming. They were not the only riders he had seen along the north Tyne and, with the Fair not too far off, there would be many others. There was no reason to suppose they were after him. He took a well-used track to the east that would take him up the valley side to Crag Tower. He nodded with satisfaction, for he could then watch to see whether they followed him. His satisfaction did not last long as he saw the group of riders take the same track as he had. He turned and hurried on his way but a quick glance back told him that the riders were coming up fast behind him. When he stopped at the top of the rise, an arrow thudded into the long grass beside him. He urged his mount on, for Crag Tower lay only a few more yards further on.

As he rode up he hailed the ramparts. "Ho within! I crave

your pardon!"

"Who are you?" a voice replied.

"I'm George Spearbold! I'm being hunted down! I seek sanctuary!"

He stopped at the gate but silence greeted his request and the gate remained firmly shut.

His pursuers came over the rise and at once he recognised the bulky profile of Shard. The riders pulled up and the archer let fly at him again. The arrow narrowly missed and embedded itself in the gate. He could wait no longer and set off around the castle wall but on the western side found a sheer drop with only a narrow rocky ledge to pass along. He stared down the steep rock strewn slope; he certainly did not want to end up down there. His horse gave a nervous shudder as he guided it close to the wall. He negotiated the worst stretch and continued on a broader, grassier path, daring to look back for the first time. No sign of Shard and his fellows yet.

He pulled up and gave his mount a reassuring pat. Then he looked over the edge of the cliff and wished he hadn't. He could not see the bottom because the spur of rock he was on jutted out a little. Over time he could see that chunks of stone had broken off and no doubt rolled and fallen to the river bed below. There were also roots protruding here and there, the last remnant of a stand of trees that had presumably once crowned the hill.

He was about to continue following the path around the curtain wall when he heard a faint cry. He looked up at the top of the rampart, assuming the voice had come from there, but could see no-one. Then he looked down the slope but there was no-one there either. He listened carefully and heard the cry again. It was coming from further back along the track - the narrower part. He hesitated. He was not keen to go back towards Shard nor did he want to risk falling. He continued once more on his way but then a third cry came, hoarse and desperate. He stopped again.

"I'm going to regret this," he said as he turned back.

§§§§

"Well, where did he go?" demanded Ned, peering over the top of the rampart.

"He disappeared around the sheer drop of the crag," said Stephen.

"And it was Spearbold, Warwick's man?"

"That's what he said. Hal said he spoke to you at the Golden Cock."

"He did more than speak to us yesterday; he damned near caught us! Shit! If he's outside then Warwick must know we're here. What about the others?"

"That was strange: they seemed to be chasing Spearbold and let fly at him a couple of times, so I told Hal to let them have one and they fell back."

"Who would be pursuing Spearbold, for God's sake?"

"Well, whoever they are, we probably need them."

"Find Spearbold - if he hasn't already thrown himself off the crag - and send out a few scouts; there's too many folk turning up here for my liking."

§§§§

Spearbold dismounted and crouched down on the rocky ledge to peer over the edge. At once his head was swimming, for he hated heights. He shut his eyes tight and the vertigo eased; he had come so far he decided he must at least take a look. He opened his eyes and twenty feet below him he saw the crumpled figure of a young man. He was moving his arm but otherwise lay still.

"Can you get me up?" the man called out.

"No, I can't," replied Spearbold, his head spinning again.

"Can you climb down to me then?" pleaded the youth.

"No, I can't!" retorted Spearbold, "Are you hurt?"

"Of course I'm fucking hurt! Do you think I want to be lying here - I think me leg's broken."

"I'll get help from the castle," said Spearbold.

"No for God's sake don't do that! It was them threw me down here!"

Spearbold remained on his knees and hung his head. He was not cut out for this kind of thing. He forced himself to examine the slope below him. Immediately below him it was sheer but across to the right the incline was less severe and descended in irregular steps of rock, their crumbling edges eroded away. He studied the injured man. He had clearly fallen straight over the drop but somehow had rolled to the right onto the shallower slope. Spearbold shook his head, for this dilemma was the last thing he needed. There was already an amber glow to the sky as the sun lowered in the west.

He sighed and lay flat on his belly, spreading his weight across the ground as he stretched his legs out onto the fragile slope. He felt for footholds and was relieved to find several. Carefully he clambered down backwards step by step, resting his hands on rocks or clutching at roots.

Relief flooded through him, for this was much easier than he had imagined, until he slid the last few yards to where the young man lay. He managed to slow his fall by sacrificing the skin on his hands and arms. He came to a stop inches from the drop and scrambled away from the edge.

"Thank you, sir," said the youth.

He looked pale even in the glow of dusk. Spearbold examined his leg. He knew a little about curing ills but not much about broken limbs.

"Which leg is it?" he asked, lifting one. The youth fainted.

"Ah," muttered Spearbold, "that one then."

He looked at the sky. "Not much to be done now till morning," he said to himself with resignation and settled down on the bank beside his young charge.

§§§§

"So, let me be clear about this, Hal," said Ned wearily, "you've found his horse wandering around the perimeter but you haven't seen him?"

Hal nodded. "Aye, lord, but the light's going. He might have fallen off the edge."

"Well, if he did his horse seems to be more intelligent than he is. Leave it now, we'll search for him in the morning - but keep a good watch tonight. If anyone wants me I'll be with the Lady Maighread."

20

18th May the early hours, at Crag Tower in the North Tyne Valley

A flame flickered nearby. It hurt her eyes. There was a pungent smell in the air, a strange blend of vinegar and honey. Maighread watched the flame, mesmerised by its wavering beauty. She had watched the flames before, through the iron grill of her cell door. A firebrand was thrown from the door of the cellar onto the wood and kindling piled across the narrow passage. The wood was dry and the fire was swift. It wrought panic amongst the servants: some hammered in vain on the door whilst others drew nearer the cells, nearer to her.

The fire engulfed them for fire was ever stronger than flesh. One anguished cry became two, three, many, as the fire sizzled and cackled. It had seemed so loud, but not as loud as the screams. She had moved away from the door grill then, unwilling to bear witness any longer. She had fallen upon her knees with a trembling prayer, not for life but for a swift death for all.

She put her hands over her ears to shut out the sound but it made little difference. She got to her feet again but the heat through the grill drove her back against the wall. In the passage outside her cell, Hell was brought to earth: shapes that once were people twisted in agony, flared for a moment like torches and then fell to be charred and consumed in the flames.

With a crash a figure fell against the cell door, a girl with her shawl on fire and her hair smouldering, a girl who had combed Maighread's hair and brought her wine, a girl who had loved her brother.

"Slide the bolt across!" she had cried.

She looked into Aliena's eyes as the fair curls about her neck glowed red and the girl's hair caught fire.

"Aliena, open the door!!" she had pleaded. The young girl's hands scrabbled at the bolt. A gust of fire sucked the door open and hungry flames explored the cell. Maighread already had her shawl off and threw it over Aliena. She pulled her screaming into the cell and slammed the door shut. It wouldn't stay shut. She took the shawl again and soaked it in the water that ran down the wall. Aliena's scalp was burned black and her face glowed red raw.

"Don't touch me! Don't touch me! Don't touch me!" the girl screeched.

The smoke was thicker now, billowing under the door, and through the grill. Maighread's eyes stung and her hand holding the door shut began to burn. She tried to hold Aliena but the young girl battered away her hand. She let the door go and dragged Aliena down to the floor with her. They lay in the drain with the cold water trickling beneath them.

The fire ate through the wooden door and frame but the wet walls offered it no sustenance and the disappointed flames seemed to retreat a little. She soaked the shawl again and again, wringing out the water over the pair of them as they huddled low to the floor. The shawl was too small to cover them both. She turned them around so that the clothes and skin sodden from lying in the drain faced the fire. Steam rose from their bodies and mingled with the smoke and the stench of roasted flesh. In the end Aliena stopped screaming.

§§§§

Ned was awoken by gentle weeping. Maighread was lying on the coverlet, swathed in strips of linen. She lay on her left side, with the burned skin uppermost. There was only one candle in the chamber and the light played upon her face, her tears glistening as they ran down her nose and cheeks onto the bed. He knew he should hold her but he dare not. If he touched her burned skin she would surely scream and… he had never found comfort easy to give.

He realised that her eyes were open and staring at him. She said nothing. Her face held no expression; she might have been dead - but she was not. She continued to stare at him without speaking. Unnerved, he broke the long silence.

"I'm Ned-"

"- Elder," she said softly, "you told me."

"You are Maighread Elder?"

She nodded. "You look just like your grandfather."

"I'm sorry I didn't get here in time…" His words sounded lame, inadequate even to his ears. How must they seem to her?

"I didn't expect you to come at all," she replied.

"Then why send the message?"

"Did you ever wonder why I got him to learn the message? I knew Henry wouldn't delay much longer. I thought if Rob spent weeks looking for you he'd be safe from Henry. Henry really hated my brother…"

"Well," Ned ventured a smile, "it worked at least: it kept Rob away."

More tears dropped onto the bed cover. "No, I failed there too: Rob came back for me … and his little Aliena." She wept again and said nothing more.

He wanted to ask her about Rob. He wanted to reach out and take her hand but the linen bandages rebuffed him and he drew back. He could not leave her alone though - God knows she must have felt alone enough in the past weeks - so he sat down once more by her bedside.

He awoke in the faint light of early dawn and when he looked across to Maighread he saw her eyes were open again.

"Did you sleep at all?" he asked. She shook her head

"Henry had Rob thrown off the Crag; it's where the castle always used to send its prisoners."

He thought he had misheard her.

"Rob's dead?" The news affected him more than he would have expected.

"Aye, he's dead," she continued, "and there's nothing can be done about him. But if I was you and I knew that Henry had left here yesterday, I'd not be sitting here beside some burnt out widow. I'd be in the saddle after him before it's too late."

"It's not too late. I'll hunt him down for what he's done but a day or two will make no difference."

Maighread gave him a strange look - a look of pity.

"You don't know, do you?" she breathed. "You don't know who he is?"

"Does it matter?" he asked. "He killed my grandparents. Now, I've tired you greatly, my lady. You should rest."

She laid her bandaged hand firmly upon his, though he could see the pain in her face.

"My Lady? What is it?"

"Henry. Henry claims he is your half-brother."

There was a split second when he doubted it but she had loosed a demon which had been lurking in his mind for over three years. He recalled every one of Lord Radcliffe's words from a cold scaffold in Hereford: 'You've a bastard brother - of Radcliffe blood. He'll come for you and you won't even know him!' The memory struck him like a poleaxe.

Maighread's hand clutched his more tightly. "I'm sorry," she whispered.

"He'll go to Yoredale," breathed Ned. He clasped her hand in his until she cried out and he released it with mumbled apologies.

21

19th May before dawn, at Crag Tower in the North Tyne Valley

It was still dark and Spearbold had slept very little, finding it hard to forget where he was. The youth too slept fitfully and, when he was awake, he groaned with the pain. Spearbold was worried about the leg, though he could not entirely explain his concern for the leg of a complete stranger. Still, he could do nothing for the lad until he could get off the ledge and he was certainly not going to try that in the dark. They had barely conversed except to introduce themselves but Spearbold had told Rob that Henry had left. He was hard to convince.

"And you think that Ned Elder has the Tower now?" Rob asked.

"I can't be sure, but whoever does have it, it's not Henry of Shrewsbury," replied Spearbold, "for I saw him yesterday with his entire garrison at Hexham."

"If it's Ned Elder, then we're in luck."

"You know him?" asked Spearbold.

"Well enough."

"That'll help at least," said Spearbold. It would certainly help him if Ned knew and trusted the youth.

When the cool dawn came both men were still awake and Spearbold was dreading what he must do next.

"Do you think you can get up the slope?" he asked Rob.

Rob tried to lift himself up and his face contorted with pain. "Blood of Christ!" He sat down again, ashen faced.

257

"As I feared," said Spearbold. "We need to bind that leg - you'll get nowhere if we don't."

"But bind it with what?" Rob looked around their small patch of earth and rock. "There's nothing here."

Spearbold took off his baldric and the sword it held. "This is all I have."

Rob regarded the length of leather doubtfully. "I can't see how that'll do it," he said.

"No," admitted Spearbold, "neither can I."

"You'll have to go up. If it's Ned, he'll help me."

"Ah, now there's the problem," said Spearbold, "Lord Elder may know you but I doubt he'll trust anything I tell him. We had a bit of a run in a day or two ago."

"Why, what did you do?"

"I tried to arrest him."

"And failed, I gather," said Rob. "Well, you'll just have to make him believe you."

"It's not going to do either of us much good if one of his archers plucks me down, is it?"

"Well, unless you can carry me, that's what you'll have to risk."

Spearbold considered carefully for a moment: his situation was not much different from where he started. He had set out to speak to Ned Elder and this way at least he would have a legitimate way in. It might even help his cause by proving Ned could trust him. In any case, he couldn't stay on the ledge forever.

He nodded. "Very well. I'll leave my sword and belt down here."

He started to clamber up the slope but all too soon he came slithering back down to where Rob lay. He frowned and puffed out his cheeks. "Not so easy getting up," he observed.

"Don't tell me we're both stuck down here now!" said Rob.

"No, no. Don't make a hasty judgement, Master Rob," Spearbold sought to reassure his young companion. "I'm just getting the feel of the task, that's all."

He addressed the rock strewn slope once more, looking in vain for handholds. He remembered now that he had slipped the last few feet on the way down and there was nothing within reach to get any purchase on. He jumped up a little but he could see that the nearest tree root was a foot higher than he could reach. He could feel Rob's eyes upon him.

"Thanks for the rescue," said Rob, shaking his head in disbelief.

"Well, perhaps you should have waited for a taller fellow to come along," said Spearbold, aggrieved, "I should have carried on and left you!"

Rob grinned at him. "No, I'm glad you came by," he said, "at least I can starve in good company."

"I suggest we abandon our pride and shout as loudly as we can," said Spearbold, though in the back of his mind the memory of Shard and his archer stirred.

"Alright," agreed Rob, "we'll both shout together."

§§§§

Ned sat in the Hall with Sir Stephen and Hal.

"So we reckon that Spearbold came here yesterday evening, hailed the gate and then rode off again and all we've found of him is his horse? Do I have the right of it, Hal?"

"Aye, lord. Strange isn't it?"

"No, Hal, it's not strange it's beyond belief!" said Ned.

"And there were a few arrows flying about as well, don't forget," said Stephen.

"Hal, there are important decisions to make and I need to know if Warwick's men are out there. Now take your bow - and Wulf - and a couple of others who won't get themselves lost and find out what's going on!"

"Yes, lord!" Hal bolted from the Hall.

Ned gave Stephen a wry smile. "He reminds me of how he was the first time I laid eyes on him: a cheeky young colt, eager to learn and eager to please."

"You're too hard on him sometimes; he takes your reprimands to heart."

"Believe me, Stephen, he only takes them to heart for the beat of a sparrow's wing then he forgets." He wrinkled his nose. "We'll need to air this place out… get rid of that vile smell."

"Are we staying then?" asked Stephen.

Ned had been wrestling with that question since the early hours of the morning.

"I've an idea of what to do, Stephen, but I need your counsel on it."

Stephen bent forward to listen.

"Our situation is this," Ned continued, "I am declared an outlaw and any who travel under my banner are also outlaws. We're far from home, in a hostile land. We have few provisions and barely enough horses to carry us all. The Lady Maighread is too ill to ride and must stay here."

"'Tis a nasty situation," agreed Stephen in a sombre voice.

"There's more," said Ned, lowering his voice. "The man we have heard of as Henry of Shrewsbury claims to be my bastard half-brother -"

"What?"

"- and if Lady Maighread is right, he's going to Yoredale."

Stephen said nothing at this last revelation, but Ned knew that he would realise its significance. They sat for several moments then Stephen said: "So, we ride south?"

"But that's the issue, Stephen: do we?"

"But we must! The estates? The people? Your wife, your sisters and their children? How can you even stop to think? Your path is clear."

"No, not so clear, I'm afraid. There is also the Lady here to consider. Even if we had enough mounts, she can't ride and she needs more care if her burns are to heal. She must stay and if she must stay then so must some of us."

"I see. Of course, you're right." He looked at Ned and smiled grimly. "But you've made your mind up?"

"Aye, but it asks much of you… and others."

Stephen nodded. "You want me to stay and hold Crag Tower?"

Ned took his hand. "I ask it as a friend, not a lord," he said.

"Then I answer as a friend, Ned. Of course I'll stay. I have no kin at Yoredale. You take with you the men with wives and children on the estates. The younger ones can stay with me."

Ned grinned. "So, my friend, we're of one mind. Bear too, will stay with you."

"But surely you'll have need of him more than any man?"

"Aye, but he knows how to treat the Lady's burns and I'd rather he carried on doing that. I'll not say I won't miss him. He's been a rock for us all." Ned looked his friend in the eye. "This is no easy task I set for you, Stephen. You'll endure much risk and you'll be in the dark. I may not be able to get word to you how we've fared."

"Bad tidings come fast enough, Ned."

"I suppose…"

"So, it's agreed then," said Stephen. "You should go with all speed."

"Aye, Henry already has at least a day's start on me but first we must know if Warwick's men lie in wait for us outside. I'm hoping Hal can solve that riddle quickly."

§§§§

Hal and his four companions left Crag Tower on foot to do a thorough search of the castle perimeter. They first investigated the sloping path which traversed the valley down to the river. From the top of the rise they could see the whole area around to the south and west. They saw one craft on the river and watched a small herd of cattle being driven north along the valley but otherwise they could see no signs of movement. All the same, if Hal had learned anything from his lord, it was to be cautious.

"Wulf," he said, "you keep a watch here while we take a

look to the east."

Wulf sat down on the grass and prepared for a lengthy stay. Hal trotted off with the others around the crown of the promontory until they reached the crag's sheer drop to the north. Here the castle walls were close to the edge and the upper stone had weathered from exposure to the northerly winds. The foot of the wall was overgrown with tough, wiry ivy but a trail of broken stems showed Hal where Spearbold's horse had passed along the narrow ledge. Soon after, he began to hear the sound of voices.

§§§§

Inside Crag Tower, Ned took the time to speak to each of his men, to tell the married ones of the threat to their loved ones and to share their concern. He also explained to his young lions why they must remain at Crag Tower. He could see the disappointment in their eyes and the hurt as it dawned upon them that they might not see their homes or their lord again. He could not promise them either a short or easy sojourn at Crag Tower; he needed it to be defended and he might never return to thank them for their service.

Whilst Ned talked, others prepared; some for the journey south, others for a long defence of Ned's northern stronghold. The prospects did not seem promising for either. Ned employed Stephen in taking an inventory of the castle's provisions: it was meagre fare, for Henry had left little behind. They soon realised that the castle garrison would be hard pressed after only a few weeks.

"We'll just have to hope that all is resolved by then," Ned told him. "If I'm taken, Stephen, your only duty is to Lady Maighread and the men. Crag Tower might make a handy bolthole if we're still on the run but it's not worth their lives if I've already lost."

"You can rely on us to do our duty, my lord," said Stephen, "whatever fate befalls you or Yoredale."

"I just hope I've left you enough men," said Ned.

"You've left me Bear - he counts as several, I think."

Their preparations were disturbed by Hal's return at the gate. When Ned saw Rob hobble into the castle supported by Hal's men, he was astonished. And the appearance of Spearbold with his hands bound behind his back was doubly surprising.

"Rob! Rob!" Ned greeted him like a long lost brother. "Maighread will be relieved to see you alive. We all thought you were dead."

Rob managed to combine a rueful grin with a wince of pain. "I thought I was done and that's true but by God's grace this fellow Spearbold came along."

"And what exactly did he do to help?" demanded Ned.

"On the face of it, not much," conceded Rob, "but when I thought it was all over, he was there to keep my spirits up and make sure I didn't go over the edge during the night."

Ned gave Spearbold a cool stare. "That may not be enough to persuade me to spare him, Rob. This man's made a deal of trouble for us all."

"He seems honest enough to me," said Rob.

"And what do you base that judgment on - your wide experience of consorting with honest men?"

Rob looked aggrieved but did not protest.

"Go to your sister," said Ned, "she's alive, but… she's badly burned, Rob. I'm sure your deliverance will give her some encouragement. Then we must see to your leg."

He turned to Spearbold. "Well, master Spearbold; I need not guess why you're here. You've found me once more but again you'll get no cheer from it. How in God's name did you know I'd come here?"

Spearbold gave him a look of disdain. "Lord Elder, I worked it out: that's what I do. If I might speak a word, my lord," asked Spearbold.

"You've spoken a word and that was enough!" snapped Ned. "I've better things to do than listen to you. Wulf, take our guest to the stable. He can keep his horse company for a while. Then he'll ride out with me."

"Lord Elder!" Spearbold threw himself to his knees before Ned. "The Earl of Warwick has dismissed me! I came here to yield to you and seek to serve you in any way I can."

Ned shook his head. "That won't work, Spearbold - it makes no sense for him to dismiss you but it does make sense for you to try to gain my trust... Take him, Wulf," he ordered.

Whilst Spearbold was led away protesting his innocence, Ned asked Hal to report what he had seen.

"We saw none but those two, lord; but I've sent a rider north and south along the valley to keep watch. They'll ride in if there's any sign of trouble coming."

"No sign then of the men who loosed an arrow or two at Spearbold?"

"No, lord."

Ned considered for a moment. It looked as if the plan was to place Spearbold within the castle, presumably so that he could betray the garrison at a vital moment and allow Warwick's men to get inside.

"Very well, Hal. Get yourself ready to ride; you're coming with me to Yoredale."

Hal's face brightened. "Oh, I thought…I'd heard… only those with wives were going back with you."

"Aye mostly, Hal, but I want you with me."

"Thank you, lord!"

"Thank me if we're both still breathing when all this is over," said Ned. "Now go. I want to leave by noon."

Poor Hal, he thought, he doesn't know yet how much he's going to miss his shadow, Wulf, but they can't all go.

He mounted the steps to Maighread's chamber and smiled as he heard her loudly berating her brother, who was in the chamber opposite having his broken leg set by Bear.

"Give the lad a rest, my lady," he said as he strode into her room, "and save your voice. He tried to save you and you're both still alive. So give thanks to God for that much and strive to stay alive."

Her face softened, though the scarred right side still

looked raw and swollen. At his glance he noticed she turned her chin away from him a little.

"Lord Elder, I must thank you now for my brother's life too," she said. Her voice was hoarse and she looked drained. Too much of her brother's company would likely finish her off.

He sat on the bed beside her and explained swiftly why he was leaving and the plans that had been made to protect her whilst he was away. She asked no questions but merely nodded: she understood better than anyone what he was about to undertake.

"So," she said after a while, "it may be that we shan't meet again... nephew."

"I will return ... as soon as I can to bring a relief for my men here... if for no other reason."

"When you've secured your castle, Ned, and protected your lady and your new child, you should stay there with them. Let others deal with your affairs up here."

"Perhaps," he said, forcing a smile.

Her expression clouded suddenly and she took his hand. "You'll need to be careful, Ned: Henry's not as strong as you but he can make more mischief - and Joan..." It seemed to pain her to mention her niece's name. "She has ... disappointed me."

He looked down at her hands, freshly wrapped up and reeking of vinegar and honey.

"Take care, lady," he said and kissed her gently on her left cheek where a tear had formed. She released his hand and he left her.

DEREK BIRKS

22

19th May afternoon, on the road south from Crag Tower

They left Crag Tower in bright May sunshine. It could have been summer, Ned thought, were it not for a cool, persistent breeze which pursued them south along the valley of the North Tyne. They were not alone, for many folk were on the move coming from all around for the Stagshaw Bank Fair. Some brought strings of horses to be sold; others were keen to sell their wares to the crowds who would be attending the fair.

"It's one of the biggest livestock fairs in the north - the land even," said Spearbold.

Ned found Spearbold was beginning to annoy him, feeding him useless information all afternoon.

"Why don't you tell me something I'm not privy to!" he said.

"I've been trying to, my lord, but you won't listen," replied Spearbold. Ned could tell from his tone that Spearbold was genuinely exasperated, so he rode alongside him for a while longer.

"Well then, I'm listening now," he said. After all, there wasn't much else to do.

"My lord, there's a man called Shard," began Spearbold, "and I can tell you exactly where he is now and what he's doing."

"Go on," said Ned, though he was sceptical.

"He'll wait for you at a key place - perhaps a river

crossing. He'll be waiting to catch you off your guard and then he'll hit you with every man he's got."

"And how do you know that if you're no longer giving him his orders - unless perhaps you are?"

"It's what I've trained him to do," said Spearbold.

Ned smirked. "Well I escaped you, so that doesn't say much for his chances does it?"

"You had a great deal of help, as I recall," replied Spearbold, "but it was Shard who tracked you then, not me."

"You said Shard will be watching us but my men searched the area around Crag Tower - there was no-one within miles."

It was Spearbold's turn to look smug. "I suppose they watched to the south and west? And perhaps the north?" he said.

"Indeed they did," Ned assured him, "and saw no-one."

"Shard's man would have been to the east of Crag Tower because you would not have expected an approach from the east. All he needed to see was where you were going. Shard is not a thinker. He's a hound, a tracker and when he gets your scent, he'll never let you go. Don't regard him lightly, my lord."

"You make him sound like a spirit, Spearbold. Is he flesh? Does he live and breathe? Or perhaps he doesn't exist at all...eh?"

"But...why would I invent such a man?" protested Spearbold.

"To get me chasing shadows - is that your plan?"

"By God, you're an untrusting sort of fellow, my lord." said Spearbold. "I told you: the Earl has rid himself of me! I put myself at risk simply by joining you! Shard is a concern to me too - perhaps it'll be to your satisfaction that one of the first to be cut down will be me!"

Ned began to wonder about Spearbold after his outburst but dared not trust the man: he was more than capable of deliberately causing confusion. By late afternoon they were approaching the bridge across the river and Ned had a decision to make. He decided not to cross at the bridge and they continued along the North Tyne valley.

"Hal," he called, "take Tom and two others. Scout up the valley and see if you can find a place for us to camp tonight."

"Very well, lord," said Hal.

"And Hal -"

"I know, lord," laughed the youth, "I'll take all care!"

Ned grinned. "I know. I always tell you that, but I still mean it."

He despatched two men to drop back a mile or so to watch for a pursuing force. Spearbold followed his commands with interest.

"It occurs to me, my lord, that if Shard wanted you to divide your company up, you've already begun to do so."

"Too much occurs to you, Spearbold - for your own good!"

"I'm only urging caution, my lord, but I'm sure your precautions make much sense."

Ned gave him a non-committal grunt.

"My fear is that Shard is already close, my lord, very close. Will you at least untie my hands?" he asked.

"No!" said Ned, "now be quiet for a while!"

Spearbold looked scared, thought Ned. Perhaps this man Shard was to be feared. But then perhaps Spearbold could dissemble like a travelling player and play the worried man.

They met Hal and his scouts halfway up the slope away from the river. Hal pointed further up the rise where Ned could only see a broad band of woodland.

"Camp in the trees?"

"There's an outcrop of stones and a ditch amidst the trees," said Hal.

"What do you mean: an outcrop of stones? An old house? Sheep fold?" asked Ned.

Hal shrugged. "It's just a great lump of wall in the middle of nowhere - it's taller than a man and broad too."

Spearbold coughed.

Ned sighed audibly. "What?"

"I've ridden through here before," said Spearbold, "it's part of the ancients' wall than runs across the north - part of an old wall tower, I think."

"And has your hero Shard been through here before too?" asked Ned.

Spearbold nodded. "Indeed. He'll know about this place."

"Do you think Shard is behind us or could he have got ahead of us?" asked Ned.

Spearbold hesitated. "Do you ask me as a captive or an adviser, lord?"

"It matters not; if you're going to give me any advice, you'd better make sure it's sound," growled Ned.

"In truth then, my lord," said Spearbold, "I don't know - but I do know that he'll be close."

Ned shook his head. "So you've said - not that it's much help! Come on then, Hal."

Ned examined the short stretch of stonework and scratched his head. The land beside the wall was overgrown with low scrub and littered with pieces of loose stone. On its north side behind the ruined turret a deep ditch ran through the trees and on up the slope.

"What in God's name did they build a bit of wall here for? Still, it'll do for us. We'll camp here. We can hide the horses away in the trees."

He looked at the darkening sky: the day had cooled rapidly and now clouds were rolling in. It would be a murky night, he thought. He turned to the men.

"Hal, get a fire lit. Black! Stringer! Tom! Go down to the river and get some water."

Will Stringer and Tom were quick to answer his call but Black took his time, his reluctance pitched just short of insubordination. He merely suffers me, thought Ned, and he doesn't quite see himself as a water carrier. The thought annoyed him but in some way it also amused him. There was something almost admirable about the taciturn Black - almost.

Ned posted more sentries than usual, admitting to himself

at least that he was nervous about how close Shard might be. Several of Hal's archer comrades foraged for firewood along the forested ditch. He watched Hal building the fire and noticed that Spearbold was shaking his head.

"You think a fire unwise, Master Spearbold?" he said.

"Aye, my lord, I do."

"If Shard's nearby, he'll already know we're here and if he's not we may as well have a fire."

"He'll see us all the better though," remarked Spearbold.

Ned shrugged and looked at the night sky again.

"I'm not so sure about that," he replied. "Build up the fire, Hal. I suppose you'd better untie our friend Spearbold too."

He walked amongst the men as was his habit, offering a word here and there but also taking stock of how they were holding up.

"Take your rest, lads," he said in a low voice, "but keep alert when you're on watch. We've no friends here." They were words he had said a hundred times since they had come to the northern borderlands and he suspected that his weary men had stopped listening long ago. All the same, if Shard came he wanted them to be prepared.

He wandered into the trees to inspect the ditch when it began to rain. At first it was a gentle pattering through the canopy of young leaves but it was not long before the branches were rattling with sound of torrential rain. Men scattered seeking shelter from the downpour. Rainwater cascaded off the wall and splashed onto those trying to take cover beside it. Where Ned was the ditch, already boggy in places, began to fill with rainwater draining down the hill. The trickle soon became a flood and Ned retreated up to a large oak nearer the wall. From there, his cloak wrapped around him, he waited for Black and the others trudging back up from the river.

"Water!" barked Black. "It's been stick dry for weeks and it has to piss down on us now - now!"

Ned gave a grim smile; for once he was in complete

accord with his man. He stared down towards the North Tyne but now he could barely see it. Indeed he could see little in any direction. He certainly didn't see Shard coming and the first he knew of it was a strangled shout from the far end of the wall up the slope to the east. Spearbold was right.

"To arms!" he shouted but others were already on the move.

Hal struggled to string his bow as the unrelenting rain lashed into them.

"Forget that and use your sword!" snapped Ned. Through the curtain of rain he could now pick out a few shapes hurrying towards them.

"Shit! They're amongst us!" roared Black, drawing his sword.

He was grateful he could not see Black's face for he had a fair idea it would be wearing a thunderous expression. Whoever got in Black's way in the next few minutes was in for a hard time.

"Come with me, Black," he shouted. He too drew his sword and ran around to the ditch side of the wall. He was worried about the ditch. True, it would be muddy now, but it provided a direct path to where his mounts were tethered and he couldn't afford to lose them.

He went to the edge of the ditch and immediately lost his footing and slid down into it on his backside. Black stood above him laughing - until he too found himself slipping and joined him at the bottom.

"Come on," said Ned and headed up the ditch.

Black did not move. "Where are we going? We should be out there! They're attacking at the wall!" he grumbled.

Ned ignored him and continued along the ditch. It was treacherously slippery and he had to concentrate to avoid falling. He glanced back. Black had started to follow him. It was hard to ignore the fearful clamour from his camp but he trusted that his men would hold their own. He emerged into some low scrub higher up at the head of the ditch. At once the rain slammed into him and so did the enemy.

There were three men at arms descending into the ditch and they had seen him first. They struck him all together and he fell back head over heels into the ditch, just managing to hang onto his sword. He was winded and slow to rise but the first man to him was moving too fast and slid past him into the undergrowth. Ned clubbed his sword down on to the man's neck and then swivelled to face the others. More now, for others were jumping into the ditch.

"Lord!"

He glanced behind him and saw Black and beyond him Stringer was hurrying to join them. Black stabbed the wounded man as he tried to get up then he joined in the melee that had formed around Ned. There was little room to swing a blade but the fight was brutal and bloody. Ned abandoned his sword and used his long knife, pulling a man down onto him and plunging the knife into his unprotected belly. He was locked together with his victim until a torrent of rainwater washed them off their feet and further down the gully. Above him, Black was wrestling with his opponent. Black was a strong man and his arm forced back the man's head until it snapped back and fell forward.

Ned ripped his knife from his own adversary and stood up. The noise was confusing: everywhere men shouted or screamed and above it all was the rain, never easing, never relenting. The men that faced them were shocked by their quick losses and tried to scramble back up the ditch.

"Keep pushing them back!" ordered Ned. "I'm going back to the camp!"

He left Black and Stringer to hold the ditch and slithered back down until he was amongst the trees. Then he climbed back up past the nervous horses to the wall. Still the cursed rain fell; he might as well be blind but he could hear the bitter struggle taking place on the other side of the wall.

Suddenly a man at arms dropped down off the wall and landed beside him. He drew his sword but was relieved to see that it was Tom!

"There are too many of them," cried Tom, "and much use

the wall is!"

"Aye and more coming," replied Ned. "Go and help Stringer and Black in the ditch."

Tom nodded and disappeared into the trees.

Ned felt his way up the wall and climbed up on one of the lower parts to lie on top of it. He expected to see what was happening but all he saw was smoke and rain. They had sited their fire in the ruined turret but it had hardly caught before the rain came. Now its half-charred carcass hissed and sputtered as heavy droplets drowned the dying flames. The result was a haze of steamy smoke.

"God's Blood," he breathed in despair. The clash of arms below him sounded murderous. The rain poured down on to him but soon the smoke cleared and he could see the men below, swaying and staggering as they fought. His men were fighting with their backs to the wall, the archers crammed into the small turret and the rest spread out all along the wall. Although the wall was too high to scale in the central part by the turret, elsewhere they were being outflanked by men at arms clambering over the lower parts. He could delay no longer.

"Ned Elder! An Elder!" he cried as he leapt down into the fray, wading into the attackers. Here at least there was room to use his sword. He rallied and cajoled his men.

"Press them back! Send them back to Warwick without their heads!" he bellowed, pushing forward to drive the enemy back. His arrival gave his men renewed belief and soon the assault began to falter.

He heard a call of "Fall back!" and scanned the hillside for the man who had given the order. The attacking men at arms tried to pull back but in the poor light they tripped over stones and slid in the mud churned ground, cursing as they stumbled into each other. Ned harried them as they retreated raggedly up the hill to the east, leaving behind them a dozen or so dead.

It took Ned a long time to account for all of his men: six were dead, another was hanging on to life by a thread, his stomach ripped open by a sword, and seven others had serious cuts or wounds. One of the dead was the man Ned looked to, in the absence of Bear, for the care of the wounded. Others tried but lacked both his knowledge and expertise.

Of Spearbold there was no sign and Ned cursed himself.

"Where's that shit Spearbold?" he demanded of Hal. "I should've left him bound."

"I didn't see him go...sorry lord," answered Hal, "should I go after him?"

"No, it's my fault," said Ned bitterly, "I should have known he'd betray us. He'll be long gone by now."

"Not so very far," croaked a voice. Everyone turned to look as a sodden, mud-smeared Spearbold climbed shakily back over the wall.

"I hid," he admitted, "I'm not a warrior by nature, my lord. Yet... nor am I a 'shit' either."

Ned gave him a nod of approval and clapped him on the back. "Very well, Spearbold, consider yourself Ned Elder's chief counsellor - no skill with a sword required."

Spearbold gave a low bow by way of thanks and began to offer advice at once.

"I warned you not to underestimate Shard, my lord," he said.

Ned was bending down to examine one of the enemy corpses. He patted the badge the dead man wore; no surprise to find a bear and ragged staff.

"Shard, or someone else - what does it matter? They're all Warwick's men and he'll keep sending them after me. I'm an outlaw, charged with treason. My fate is sealed, whether I get back to Yoredale or not."

"He'll pursue you there easily enough - he expects you to go there," said Spearbold. "If it's escape you want, you need to head north - or for the coast, take a ship."

"Of course, I know that! But how can I flee north when my family's at Yoredale."

"Warwick isn't a monster; he won't harm your wife and

family."

Ned gave him an icy stare. "Well, Spearbold, that rather depends on your point of view. He'll marry off my sisters, make the children his wards and wait for my wife to deliver her child. When she's a widow he'll find a husband for her, and so on. My wife and sisters have suffered enough. Anyway, it's not Warwick that worries me; it's Henry of Shrewsbury. He, I assure you will have fewer scruples than the Earl."

Spearbold nodded in silence.

Ned was finding that, without either Stephen or Bagot, sound advice was something in short supply. He removed his sword and scabbard, then wandered over to a chunk of wall and sat down with his back against it. Spearbold rubbed his sore wrists and came to squat down beside him.

"Tell me about Shard," said Ned.

"Shard is a tracker, a born tracker - that's why I used him. I never found anyone better. But he's not much else: he's certainly not much of a soldier. That's why he botched the attack on your camp."

Ned grunted. "You think he failed? He's taken half a dozen of my men!"

"My lord, I know you must make haste to return to Yoredale but Shard will press you at every turn and he'll be reporting to the Earl, who'll supply more men if they're needed. You will lose more men. All I am urging you to do is to be cautious."

Ned shook his head and Spearbold said no more. Both sat against the wall in silent contemplation until exhaustion took them off to sleep. Around them the camp slowly settled down to survive the remainder of the night but no-one slept soundly.

§§§§

Dawn brought Ned little solace. As well as the six men who had been killed, the badly wounded man had died during the night; it was probably a blessing. The other wounded could all ride but if such losses continued, Ned's company would not get anywhere near Yoredale.

"How well do you know the area to the south of the wall?" Ned asked Spearbold.

"Well enough to guide you home, my lord. I've served the Earl all over the north, remember."

Ned frowned in irritation. "We'll get on a great deal better if you mention the Earl a great deal less," he said.

Spearbold nodded. "Your pardon, my lord…thoughtless of me."

"So, can you suggest a route?"

"Aye, my lord. I suspect you would go by the North Road?"

"That would make sense to me," agreed Ned, "it's the quickest way."

"Indeed it is but it is also the main way south to York where the Earl will shortly be heading. Nothing would please Shard more than to hand you over to the Earl on the road to York."

Ned shook his head. "Haste, Spearbold. Haste is what we need if we're to catch Henry!" Perhaps Spearbold's advice would not be as helpful as he had imagined.

"Aye, my lord… but if you are taken you'll catch no-one," said Spearbold.

"At the very least I must get to Yoredale before Henry. Nothing must stop me and I expect you to use your wits to help me, not put more obstacles in my way!"

"I have been considering it, my lord. We should follow the river - almost to Hexham - we'd better give that a mile or two's distance. Follow the river to Corbridge and cross there."

"I've bad memories of Corbridge - as you know very well," said Ned.

"We must cross somewhere," argued Spearbold, "Corbridge will be quieter, believe me. Then, if we must, we'll take the ancient road south."

They set off with a little more optimism as all the men were glad to be on their way home but their enthusiasm slowly waned as they made their way along the sodden riverbank where their horses slid in the treacherous mud. Like the men, the poor beasts were tired. Ned had hoped to make a good pace but the wounded could only ride slowly and the rest trotted alongside.

Despite Ned's fears they forded the Tyne at Corbridge without incident and rode through the hay meadows that lay beside it for several miles. When they left the Tyne there were fields of summer wheat with a sea of green stalks eager for a month or two of sun to ripen them. By the afternoon they reached the foothills that led them onto the uplands where cattle grazed on the low rolling hills. On the face of it, Ned thought, they might just have been taking a gentle ride, but for the whole day they knew that they were never alone.

From the outset Ned had sent scouts both ahead and to their rear, as was his custom, and every few hours they returned to report. When they camped in the evening Ned told Spearbold what he had learned.

"We have men ahead of us and men behind," he said. "Behind is probably Shard but ahead, who knows? I'd have expected Henry and Mordeur to be further on by now."

"Could it be Henry?" asked Spearbold. "It doesn't make sense though. Surely, if what you say is true, then Henry should be making all possible speed to Yoredale? But in any case, do you want to catch him?"

"Spearbold, all those I love are in Yoredale. All these men have families at risk at Yoredale. If we can't get there ahead of Henry then we must at least try to catch him."

Spearbold stared at Ned grimly. "Well I'll speak plainly, my lord, and risk your wrath. There is only one way to do what you want: you must leave your wounded and ride. Ride so hard that your mounts fall, spent beneath you the very moment you reach Yoredale Castle. That's the only way you have a prayer of catching Henry of Shrewsbury!"

Ned stared at Spearbold in surprise, seeing him in a new

light. His words, however, struck home.

"You may be right," he conceded, "unless he stops…"

Spearbold threw up his hands. "Why in God's name would he stop?"

"He might stop if we got close to him and he thought he could finish us…"

"But we won't..."

"Yes, we could - as you said. A few of us - the archers - ride ahead and catch him, slow him down, trim his numbers a little. Give the rest of us a chance to get to him."

Spearbold regarded him thoughtfully, his face a mask of doubt.

"It might work, my lord, but every part of your design would have to work, every last detail. And the risks…"

"I know the risks but just blindly following Henry isn't enough - he'll get to Yoredale before us."

"What do you wish me to do, then?" asked Spearbold.

"At first light, ride ahead and find Henry for me! Take Hal and the other archers with you. I'll shepherd the rest along as quickly as I can."

"Are you certain, my lord? Stripping away your archers…it's a -"

"Aye, I know, a risk - but it's our only hope."

DEREK BIRKS

23

20th May evening, at Bishop Auckland, near Durham

Spearbold had never ridden so fast for so long and he had never felt so weary. It was not what he was born to do; he was not a rider of horses. True, he rode a horse quite frequently but usually without either haste or desperation and today had seen a deal too much of both.

So, here he was in the evening at Bishop Auckland, saddle-sore from hunting a man he didn't know and accompanied by only a handful of archers. What Ned Elder expected him to achieve with such limited resources he did not know. They had stopped outside a small tavern, the kind where good local ale would be served and a night's accommodation might be obtained on a stretch of rush strewn floor. It was a far cry from the standard of inn he had come to expect in the Earl's service, when at worst he might have been sharing a room but at least he would have had a bed.

Not only was he forced to accept such limited hospitality but he also had to pay for it himself with what little coin he still possessed, for his young lord was penniless. He wondered how it was that a lord with such extensive estates could be so badly provided for and resolved to offer counsel upon the shortcoming as soon as he could. For now, the tavern would have to suffice. It was crowded too; they were fortunate - or so the landlord put it - that he had room for them at all.

He squeezed himself down next to Hal at one of two long tables. As they ate a thick unappealing potage he absorbed the idle banter around him. He had impressed upon Hal and the others that they must give nothing away in the tavern about their own business, but listen carefully to that of other patrons. Yet he heard nothing, no snippet of news that encouraged him to believe that Henry had even passed through the town. He did hear plenty about the Earl of Warwick, who was expected at any time. It was thought possible that Warwick might even break his journey at the nearby residence of the Bishop of Durham, Laurence Booth - the local man of power. Spearbold was almost as anxious to avoid the Earl as he was to find Henry of Shrewsbury. He was also concerned lest somehow Shard had already informed the Earl that his former servant - one George Spearbold - was now in league with the outlaw, Ned Elder. He shivered at the thought of it and sought a distraction.

"Hal," he said, "I'm going to take a walk around for a while to clear my head."

Hal got up at once. "I'll come with you," he said, a deal too quickly Spearbold thought.

"Are you under orders to watch me, Hal?" he asked.

"Watch out for you, rather," replied Hal with a grin. "Lord Elder said you might need some protection."

"Did he now?" Spearbold wasn't sure he believed Hal but the lad would be good company, nevertheless.

The early evening light was only just beginning to fade but Bishop Auckland was a very small place and before the sun truly began to set they had walked all around it twice.

Spearbold rubbed his sore buttocks and wondered how he would face mounting his horse once again on the morrow. Hal leant against the high stone wall as if he had not a care in the world. Spearbold assumed that he didn't and yet when he studied Hal's face he saw a look of concern in those kind, blue eyes. No, he realised suddenly, that was not concern; that was alarm. Hal's jaw dropped and he raised his arm, pointing behind Spearbold.

Spearbold's head spun around to look. Riding through the town towards them was the Frenchman, Mordeur - a man who had attended upon the Earl and had to his knowledge met Shard in Hexham. If Mordeur was here, then so was Henry. They were in the shadow of the church porch and Mordeur continued past without noticing them. He rode north out of the market place towards the Bishop's palace, stark against the sky's sunset glow. Spearbold followed, pulling Hal with him. There were few abroad now and, but for Mordeur's sudden appearance, they too would be back at the tavern.

Ahead of them Mordeur was admitted through the palace gates and they stopped to conceal themselves in some trees opposite.

"What's here?" asked Hal in a whisper.

"Why are you whispering Hal? The nearest pair of ears is at the gate," replied Spearbold.

Hal shrugged.

"The Prince Bishop of Durham is here," continued Spearbold, "at least he is sometimes."

Hal looked unimpressed. "So?"

"The prince bishop is the most powerful man hereabouts - aside from the Earl of Warwick."

"So what's the bastard Frenchie doing here?"

"Splendid question," admitted Spearbold. His eager mind was already shuffling through a whirlwind of possibilities.

"Does Mordeur know the bishop?" asked Hal.

"Bishop Lawrence Booth? I doubt it," said Spearbold. But it was all a muddle in his head: surely neither Henry nor Mordeur could have had dealings with Bishop Booth... but the Earl of Warwick certainly had. "The bishop is a closely watched man," he told Hal.

Spearbold knew from Warwick's correspondence that Booth had only just received back his lands and rights from King Edward - for Booth had been a staunch man of Lancaster until Towton. If Booth wanted to keep his head he would need to be well disposed towards both the king and his leading nobleman, Warwick, yet there was no love lost between Booth and Warwick. King Edward had pardoned Booth, and Warwick had to put up with it but Spearbold knew the Earl would grind every last concession he could out of the bishop… even perhaps helping to capture Ned Elder.

"Hmm. Bit of a mystery," observed Hal.

Indeed, thought Spearbold, and for the first time that day he was actually glad that he had ridden to Bishop Auckland. For here was mystery, here was intrigue and such areas were the domain of George Spearbold. The saddle sores were justified after all.

"Mordeur came in from the north, did he not?" said Spearbold.

"Aye. Must have come down the North Road as we did…" Hal gave him a quizzical look.

"Hal, Henry's company must have passed through Bishop Auckland long before us. They should be well south of here. So how is it that Mordeur is back here this evening and approaching from the north?"

Hal shrugged. "So, what do we do?"

"You go back to the tavern and I'll keep a watch tonight," said Spearbold. "Come back at first light."

"You're staying here all night?"

"We need to know who's in there, Hal. We dare not miss them leaving."

Hal nodded and left. Spearbold watched him go with regret and settled down to wait. He sensed that something was going on and wrestled with it well into the night. He knew Warwick had provided men at arms for Henry, for he had seen them at Hexham. He knew from his own experience that Warwick did not give such favours to men like Henry unless he could see a clear advantage. Spearbold was in no doubt that the prize for Warwick was still Ned Elder - but that had been obvious all along. There must be something else he wanted - but what? That was one mystery.

Always his thoughts led him to more questions. Why Mordeur? Was Henry there too?

He sighed. More puzzles but, for all his wits, he could do nothing without information. He needed facts.

§§§§

Spearbold woke suddenly.

There was a clatter of hooves on the cobbled gateway opposite as a rider cantered out. For a moment Spearbold doubted his own eyes. Shard? But Shard was tracking Ned Elder and couldn't reach Bishop Auckland until noon at the earliest. Yet he was already leaving! Spearbold was still pondering the implications of this when Hal arrived.

Spearbold frowned; it was well past dawn. "You're late," he muttered.

"Overslept," said Hal, "sorry…oh, a horseman passed me in the market place -"

"- that was Shard," said Spearbold bitterly.

"But… it can't be Shard. Can it?"

Spearbold did not care to answer. In fact he did not care to even think about it. He moved to get up and felt a pain shoot through his back and neck as if someone had rammed a spike through them. He must have slept awkwardly and his body had seized up. He slumped on the ground like a sack of corn, a large dog turd at his feet. He kicked it aside irritably, sending a further jolt of pain up his spine. This was not how Spearbold lived, propped against a tree with turds round his ankles. "Help me up, Hal," he said.

The youth reached down a strong hand and pulled him up. He brushed himself down and glanced across to the palace. What he would not give for a look inside.

"What's Shard doing here?" asked Hal again. "Wasn't he supposed to be behind us?"

"Something's amiss, Hal. It's very much amiss."

The palace gates groaned open once more and a column of horsemen swept out of the gateway - there must have been at least a score of men at arms and archers, perhaps as many as thirty. At their head rode Henry of Shrewsbury and beside him was Mordeur.

"Thank God!" breathed Hal. "They're still here! So they're hardly any distance ahead at all. If Lord Elder makes good speed we might even catch them on the road later today!"

Spearbold was unmoved by Hal's enthusiasm and dropped his head in his hands.

"What's wrong?" asked Hal.

For a moment Spearbold could not speak as the enormity of his error struck him.

"What is it?" demanded Hal, worried now. "What's wrong?"

"Everything's wrong, Hal, everything," Spearbold mumbled. He felt empty inside but he must pull himself together. Perhaps the situation could yet be retrieved.

"Get the others and the horses," he ordered, "and hurry! I'll follow as speedily as I can."

But his limbs were reluctant to move freely and Hal soon disappeared ahead of him into the town. Sweet Jesus! How wrong he had been! How foolish and puffed up with his own pride. His first advice to his new lord would likely be his last. He'd been so obsessed with mysteries but there was no mystery to solve here: indeed it was now all too clear to him. He cursed his stupidity: he had seen them himself at Hexham - Shard and Mordeur - deep in conversation. They must have arranged it all then.

All this time he had been obsessed with Shard the tracker but he had forgotten Shard the horseman. The man was not tracking them, he was just finding them! Then he had ridden south through the night here to Bishop Auckland to report where Ned Elder was and what he was doing. And now Henry and Mordeur were heading back towards Ned's company with only one aim in mind: to kill or capture the outlaw, Ned Elder. To do so they had not only their own men but Warwick's and now others wearing the livery of the Prince Bishop of Durham.

He broke into an ungainly run as he neared the tavern where Hal and the others waited with his mount. He was so out of breath that Hal had to help him up onto his horse.

"Ride!" he croaked at them. "Ride hard or your lord will be destroyed!"

§§§§

Ned was hot and tired. Some of his men had taken off their surcoats or breastplates while others had loosened their gambesons. It had been an uncomfortable night, knowing Shard must be close behind them, and the morning sun brought them little comfort. He wished the Lord would make up his mind about the weather. It was too warm for May now and he could see that his men had had enough.

They were a battle hardened crowd but they were older than those he left behind at Crag Tower. They had borne the brunt of the fight at Hedgeley Moor and they were tired. Tired of running and tired of fighting for their wounds healed only slowly these days. They wanted nothing but to get home to wives they had not seen for months but now their horses were tired or lame and they were weighed down with carrying all they needed. As a fighting unit they were in poor shape.

He glanced back the way they had come - still no sign of Shard's pursuit and yet they were travelling painfully slowly. It didn't make much sense, unless Shard had given up - but from Spearbold's description that did not sound very likely.

On the road ahead he saw John Black riding towards him. He had again sent scouts ahead and Black no doubt was returning to make his report. With Black the news was never good; he managed to make every success sound like a disappointment.

"There's a ford ahead," announced Black miserably.

"That's good," said Ned.

"I've been through it. There's a wayside cross on the other side of the stream, but I wouldn't stop there for long."

"A wayside cross should be a sign of hope at least," observed Ned.

"Well, the trees close in on either side of the road so I've sent Tom to scout the woods."

"We need to stop somewhere for a rest," said Ned. "Will it do?"

Black gave an indeterminate shrug. "As I said, I wouldn't stop there for long…lord."

Ned dismissed him with a curt nod and rode on until he reached the ford. The recent rains had strengthened the current though it did not seem to trouble his horse unduly. He followed the road - little more than a track as it wound up the side of the hill. The cross was sited half way up the slope and he pulled up beside it. Beyond it lay a wall of trees and here the forest was thick and dark.

"We'll rest here a while," he told them all, "but don't get too comfortable and keep a sharp look out."

The men paid little attention; they were too weary to care.

He dismounted to examine the cross: it was small and quite recently erected, he decided. You didn't see so many new ones now - most were old and weathered. It lifted his spirits a little to see the white stone cross and he wondered if it had given similar encouragement to other travellers. That was what it was for, after all. He bent down on one knee to offer a silent prayer -perhaps at last God had forgiven him and would hear his prayers.

As he rose up again a small dark missile ricocheted off one of the arms of the cross and chipped a piece from the stone. He turned on his men.

"Who threw -"

"Crossbow!" shouted someone. God had clearly ignored his plea.

More bolts and arrows fell upon them, punching into men and beasts alike. He threw himself to the ground as all around him men fell, plucked from their mounts or struck down where they stood. Several of the horses were hit: one thrashed its head upon the ground in a vain attempt to shake free an arrow lodged in its neck and another fled back into the ford. Ned stayed put on the ground.

"Here, lord!" shouted Stringer as he darted his horse through the carnage and seized the reins of Ned's mount to drag it along with him. Ned got up and ran to meet him. Will was almost there when an arrow struck him in the chest, knocking him back; then another shaft sliced through his shoulder and pulled him spinning to the ground. He landed awkwardly but got onto his knees and began to crawl towards Ned. He was barely a yard away when a quarrel struck him on the side of the head.

Ned looked away. His company was being cut to pieces and he had yet to glimpse a single enemy. A score or more were dead and he could see only four, perhaps five, still moving. The sudden barrage had stopped but, unless his assailants had run out of missiles, he couldn't see how any of his men could escape. He knew why the archers had stopped: they would have nocked their next arrow or rewound their crossbows and now they were waiting for someone to move.

He stared at the treeline: many eyes would be watching - and not just the attackers. He could feel the eyes of his surviving men on him, seeking a sign, a way out. To remain where they were in the open was to invite certain death but there were several horses still within a few yards. He weighed up his chances, scanning the road to locate the men he thought might still be able to make an escape. How long should he wait? All thoughts of getting back to Yoredale were gone; he would settle for just getting off the road.

He closed his eyes and sucked in a lungful of air. God help us all, he said to himself. Then he looked towards the heavens - if not me Lord, you might at least help them. He braced himself and leapt to his feet, darting sideways to reach for the reins of Will Stringer's mare.

"To horse!" he yelled, mounting the animal and hunching down low over its neck. Arrows filled the air. Most flew past him but one buried itself in the mare's flank. The animal shrieked and bolted straight ahead into the trees. Ned clung on as his mount bundled aside a startled archer hidden in the undergrowth. He tried to pull the horse up but, maddened and hurting, it was beyond any man's control. It wasn't the first time Ned heard a horse scream but no matter how many times he heard it, it sent a shiver through him. It was a sound beyond man, perhaps even beyond God.

Mounted men crashed through the forest after him but whether they were his or not he could not tell; it was all he could do to stay in the saddle. Green-tipped, wiry branches of beech whipped against his face; his right knee cracked hard against a sapling and went numb. Finally the wounded mare slowed up and walked unsteadily to a standstill. Then it stood: spent, quivering and quiet.

To Ned's right hand a horseman broke through the trees and veered towards him. Another appeared behind him to his left. No friends, these men. He drew out his sword and his horse collapsed under him. Rolling clumsily to one side he banged his helm against a thick tree root. The chasing riders moved to trap him between them but he let them come. He leant his back against one of the thicker trunks and held his sword out in front of him.

"Come on, lads," he said softly, "let my blade take away all your cares..."

They came at him from both sides but were forced to duck under branches and check their speed. He had a tall beech at his back but that was no good. He glanced around and saw an oak with two low branches a few yards away. Better, he thought, and scrambled across to it. One of the riders was close now, sword ready in his hand. Ned took a step back, putting a thick branch between him and his opponent. As he anticipated, the knight had to bend to avoid the branch and as he did so he lost sight of Ned's sword. In that split second Ned thrust the blade up through his adversary's groin. It did not penetrate far but it did not need to. Bright, arterial blood splashed down Ned's arm as he drew out the sword. The rider stared at him in shock and could only watch his lifeblood flow away. He let fall his weapon and slid from the horse, leaving a slick of blood on the saddle.

His companion dismounted at once and came at Ned on foot. Ned nodded with approval. His opponent carried a short handled poleaxe and moved surprisingly fast for a big man, putting every ounce of his strength into his first strike. Ned was slow to parry and the force of the blow crushed him back against the tree trunk. His sword just held the shaft of the axe but the steel point carried on and punched into his helm. His adversary wrenched the weapon clear to deliver a killing blow, whilst Ned reeled back against the tree.

He could feel warm blood trickling down inside his helm. His vision blurred and he shook his head, hoping to clear it. It just made it hurt more. He move back around the tree, knowing he was in trouble. The other knight would have to step over his fallen comrade to get to Ned. It was his only hope.

Ned tried to dart forward and chop down the arm that held the poleaxe, but he managed only to stumble forward and fall to his left, in doing so he completely wrong-footed his opponent. Ned was lucky: the cut he had intended for a wrist became an off balance uppercut to an armpit. It sliced through muscle and tendon and rendered the arm useless.

Ned staggered to his feet and wrestled the other man to the forest floor. Both men were hampered by their wounds and, though Ned had the use of both arms, his head felt as if it had been cloven in two. He found it hard to focus and it took all his strength to club his opponent with his sword hilt until he lay still.

He didn't know if the man was dead but he didn't care - he had never felt such pain. He tore off his helm and cried out aloud but that only made it worse, so he kept quiet.

"God's death," he whimpered.

He crawled to the oak and lay against it. Tears streamed down his face and mingled with the blood. He tried to take short, shallow breaths, tried to shut out the raw agony. He looked up at the canopy of branches and was dimly aware of distant shouting. This must be death, he thought.

He passed out but when he woke up he found he was still alive and the sharp pain was still there. Gingerly he got up onto his haunches - so far, so good. He put his hand to his forehead. The blood there felt dry. He stood up and at once lost his balance, flailing an arm at the tree for support.

"Steady," he said. "Not too fast...steady."

His head cleared and he felt a little better until he reached down to pick up his sword and the stabbing pain and dizziness returned. He leant on the sword, waiting for a wave of nausea to pass. He was breathing hard; for such a brief fight this encounter had taken much out of him. He glanced down at the perpetrator, his face crumpled beneath the sallet where Ned had stove it in. Brutal, merciless - that's what he had become again, just as he had before. He had to be without mercy, he knew it and just as surely he knew that not every part of him hated the bloodshed.

He listened for the first time. How long had he been out?

"Oh, good Christ...," he murmured. What had happened to his men? When he had stopped at that bloody cross he'd had twenty-six men: loyal soldiers, weary men with lives still to lead and children to feed and watch over. He had to get back to them - surely some must have survived. But the ambush was hardly an accident and other men would be coming for him. He was the prize Warwick wanted. Was he really worth any of this blood?

He looked around for a horse but they had gone - probably as well for he doubted he could ride. Carefully he sheathed his sword. He found a sturdy fallen branch to support him and began to walk slowly. Getting his bearings was not easy but he started off towards what he thought was the east. Then he stopped. Twenty yards ahead, half-hidden behind a beech was a man he would know in a crowd let alone a forest. Tom! Of course, he'd been scouting in the forest before the ambush.

"Tom!" he hissed, mindful there could be others nearby. He dared not call out yet nor did he want to creep up on him. He skirted around in a circle to approach Tom in his line of sight. Five yards away he stopped. Tom could not see him, for Tom was pinned to the tree by a brace of arrows and was long dead.

"This is madness," he muttered to himself, "they're all dead and I can't even find my way out of the damned forest."

He felt a fresh dribble of blood on his scalp; he wiped his forehead and set off again. The forest was spinning around him once more - it would not keep still. He stopped to lean against a tree, staring at the bark as he struggled to remember what sort of tree it was. That shocked him for he thought he knew every tree you could find in a forest - perhaps he didn't. His legs wouldn't move a step further and he dropped to his knees.

Hot tears ran down his cheeks once more. He had led his men into that ambush; Black had warned him but he had ignored him because it was Black. Time to admit it to himself: his men were gone and if he wasn't dead, he damned well ought to be.

He thought he could hear voices nearby and soon the dry forest undergrowth crackled as men tramped through it. No horses then, they were seeking him on foot. He could not stay in the open where he was for he was far too visible. He clambered to his feet and nearly lost his balance. He stumbled a few more yards. He could not get far like this. He cast about for somewhere to hide and noticed a fallen tree, cracked in two by old age and rot. He lay down beside it and slid half under its decaying trunk, covering himself with old bracken stems. It smelt foul but he was past caring: whatever happened to him now, he deserved it.

Men seemed to be trampling on top of him they were so close by. Yet they passed him by and the sounds of searching drifted away. After a while they seemed to have gone completely. He was about to move when he heard the bracken rustle only a few yards away. He lay still, head throbbing and eyes glazed. He gripped his sword hilt tightly and the dizziness returned. Then a hand pulled away the dissolving bracken fronds he had drawn over him.

It was all over.

DEREK BIRKS

PART THREE: YOREDALE

DEREK BIRKS

24

21st May dawn, in Eleanor's Chamber at Yoredale Castle

Eleanor was not asleep. She had awoken from another dream: they all ended the same, with her lover, Will, dying. The look on his face was always the same too: he stared at her as he fell, his face frozen in a mask of shock. It was her fault. Now she lay in her bed and awaited the dawn. Soon its first hesitant glimmer would creep by her east window and another day without him would begin.

When dawn came, it came swiftly and the sun's awakening was greeted with a wretched ungodly screech from the other side of the Hall. She leapt up, ran to her chest and seized a sword; then she glanced down at her bare breasts and stopped. She reached for her linen shift on the bed, threw it on and raced out of the door where Becky met her, carrying young Will who was crying.

"It was -" Becky began.

"I know who it was!" shouted Eleanor, "I'd know my sister's scream anywhere! Stay here with little Will!" she ordered and ran along the passage that led to Emma's chamber. When she got there she found it empty but she had only to follow the screams. The wailing voice led her to the nursery where Emma's son Richard usually slept. She burst in to find Emma sobbing over the boy's cot. His nurse cowered against the wall muttering a prayer.

The boy must be dead, was her first thought, but then she knew at once, without even looking into the cot, that Richard was still very much alive for he was howling in sympathy with his mother.

Eleanor seized her sister by the shoulders. "What is it? What ails him?" she demanded.

Emma just pointed at her son and plunged her head into her hands. Eleanor pushed Emma aside and lifted Richard out of the cot. Only then did she see it: on his forehead, a little cross had been painted. She knew blood when she saw it. She held the boy to her, trying to calm him but his bawling subsided only briefly.

"He needs his mother, Emma!" she said sharply but Emma just stared at her.

"It's a punishment," she muttered, "a punishment...for my sins, my wickedness."

"Emma!" Eleanor could have slapped her sister then. She turned to the nurse but she was still sitting on the floor intoning with her eyes tight shut. Bagot rushed in followed by Amelie and half-dressed men at arms appeared in the doorway. Suddenly the tiny room was choked with people.

Eleanor felt like screaming too. "Get out!" she roared above the confusion before recovering her composure a little and lowering her voice.

"All is well," she said calmly, except it wasn't. "Master Bagot, Lady Emma is unwell. Please send everyone about their duties and then wait here. Lady Amelie, a word if you please."

Still carrying the crying boy, she swept out of the nursery and took Amelie with her into Emma's chamber. There she pointed to the daubed cross on the boy's forehead and Amelie sat down on the bed, her face grey and drawn. For the first time Eleanor saw how her sister-in-law had been weakened by her pregnancy. How did she not see it before?

"Leave this to me, sister," she said. "It'll be nothing of consequence: a poor jape of some sort by one of the servants. Bagot! Help the Lady Amelie back to her chamber! I'll find you later."

He looked up at her stern tone and then nodded before

leading Amelie away.

Eleanor pushed the door closed, sat Richard on Emma's bed and looked down at him. He was the same age as young Will and had been talking for over a year but what could he tell her of this? She tried to ask him, stroked his forehead and asked the questions but the boy said nothing: he just sat miserably on the coverlet and sobbed his little heart out.

She flung open the door. "Nurse! Get in here!" she bellowed. Richard began howling again.

The nurse came reluctantly to the door. "It's the devil's work," she breathed.

"Since when did the Devil hand out crosses?" Eleanor retorted savagely, handing the boy to her. "It's not the Devil's handiwork; it's the work of a man – a hateful, bitter man, that's all! Now wash it off and do your job!"

The nurse beat a hasty retreat and Emma came back into her chamber. She stood stiffly and stared at Eleanor without speaking. Eleanor wanted to hug her, to comfort and reassure her, but she didn't. Something about her sister's cool aloofness stopped her.

"It had to be my son, not yours," muttered Emma.

"It was your son because Durston doesn't know me. He knows you – and it's you he wants to hurt. It means nothing. Richard is not harmed. We must ignore it."

"Ignore it?" cried Emma. "You wouldn't be saying that if it had been little Will!"

Eleanor paused. Emma was right about that at least.

"I'm sorry, Em. Of course, I'd be as angry as you. Yet… all the same, we must at least pretend to ignore it. In the meantime, I'll speak to Bagot. We have to be certain that no-one gets in again, or something worse may happen."

The two sisters stood for a moment on the threshold but no touch or gesture passed between them. Eleanor quickly went to her own chamber and the first thing she did was to go to her son and wrap her arms tightly around him.

"Careful," said Becky, "let the poor little bugger breathe!"

Eleanor explained what had happened and Becky brushed

her hand lightly against Eleanor's cheek. "I'm sorry, Ellie."

"We must keep the children close day and night," said Eleanor. "Will can sleep in here with me. Make up a small bed for him."

She did not locate Bagot again until the middle of the day but it seemed he had been busy. He was in the castle kitchen with Gruffydd and on the large table before them was the body of another lamb – its throat cut like the first.

"At least we know where the blood came from," said Bagot.

"Where did you find it?" asked Eleanor.

"In the courtyard," he replied gravely.

"It's distressing, lady" said Gruffydd soothingly.

"Never mind 'distressing'! How in God's name did it get there? It didn't just wander through a locked gate and slit its own throat!" snapped Eleanor.

"We don't know," conceded Bagot.

"Well whoever it was – and I assume it's Durston – has wandered through this castle at will!" she said. "Were there no guards?"

"They were posted, but they're boys mostly," replied Gruffydd, "and if a man knows his way around in the dark…he could go anywhere."

"But how would he get in at all?" she demanded.

"We don't know," repeated Bagot, "but it wasn't the main gate – we can be certain of that!"

"Where then? The postern?" she asked.

"No, it was locked and barred. I check it myself several times every night," said Bagot.

"Does he fly in then? Is he a spirit?" Eleanor railed at them.

"It couldn't have been him - not unless he has someone on the inside helping him," Gruffydd said.

Eleanor shuddered. "That would be worse still," she said, "to know that we're being betrayed by someone we trust…" Her voice faltered. "Then we wouldn't know who to trust…"

"We must be on our guard," said Bagot, "Durston

claimed he wasn't acting alone. With the Cliffords back at Skipton, there could be a few more men of Lancaster around here too."

"What you mean is: if a man could get inside to do this, he could easily open the gates," she said.

"Aye, I do."

"Double the guards then; put someone on every floor," she urged.

"We don't have the men, my lady," Bagot said. "We don't even have enough boys. All we can do, we will."

"I'm sorry Bagot, but ... it's the children, you see, that's the worry – and Lady Amelie too. She's not well. I should have seen it earlier. I don't want you worrying her, or Lady Emma, with any of this. Speak only to me."

"Aye, my lady, we will."

"I know we can depend on you two to do all you can to protect us." She gave them what she hoped was an encouraging smile and left them still pondering over the dead lamb.

Pray God, she said to herself, we do not end up like the lamb.

25

21st May morning, on the road north from Bishop Auckland

Hal suddenly reined in his horse and stared at the road ahead. Spearbold and the others pulled up alongside.

"Riders!" announced Hal. "Coming this way fast."

Spearbold strained to see but could make out nothing clearly. They had encountered few travellers so far on the road from Bishop Auckland but he had expected to meet Ned Elder by now.

"Who is it?" he asked. "Can you tell?"

Hal studied the distant group, squinting at the pennants they bore.

"We'd best get off the road, Master Spearbold," he said quietly, "just in case."

"It could be Lord Elder," ventured Spearbold.

"Red banner…" said Hal.

Spearbold felt sick. "You might be mistaken," he suggested.

Hal gave him an incredulous look. "No," he said firmly.

"What if we just ride on past them, heads down?" asked Spearbold.

Hal shook his head. "If Mordeur's amongst them, he'll know me - and you too. Come on! Best be quick!"

"Of course," conceded Spearbold, "it's not worth the risk."

Hal turned and led them back the way they had come until he reached a thicket of low trees and bushes fifty yards or so away from the road. The others followed him into the thicket and dismounted.

"Keep still and out of sight!" ordered Hal.

They held their horses on a tight rein and waited. It seemed an age to Spearbold but finally the column of horsemen passed them and he studied them closely. He recognised Mordeur at once with his distinctive melee of black hair - not quite so black these days - and Henry of Shrewsbury alongside him. But there were fewer men there than he anticipated. Had they fought Lord Elder and been rebuffed? They did not have the look of men who had just been beaten in combat. There appeared to be no prisoners but they led some riderless horses. The group sped on beyond his view towards Bishop Auckland, leaving him none the wiser. He glanced at Hal. The lad was sharp and would have noticed as much as he.

Hal stared back at him. "Which way now, Master Spearbold?"

Spearbold might as well have pointed blindfold … but he had only one thought.

"There's no choice, Hal," he said, "we must continue north. We must find our lord and pray that all is well."

Hal nodded but there was a grim expression on his face suggesting that he did not expect all to be well. Nonetheless, Spearbold knew that, whatever he said, Hal would have ridden to look for Ned Elder. So they rejoined the road and carried on but it was already mid-afternoon and if they weren't careful they would find themselves still on the road into the night. Spearbold was not keen on that so he hurried them on past undulating fields for pasture and on into a swathe of woodland and down into a steep river valley.

Even before they reached the wayside cross Spearbold knew something was wrong. He wrinkled his nose: there was a certain smell in the air.

Hal, alongside him, slowed his mount and then came to a halt.

"What is it?" asked Spearbold.

"Do you smell anything?" asked Hal. His face was as white as a swan's wing.

"I think I do," said Spearbold.

Hal nodded slowly and restrung his bow. "Nock an arrow, lads," he said.

"Be careful," said Spearbold as Hal nudged his horse forward.

At the white cross they found the killing ground. Hal dismounted and Spearbold followed suit. Ashen faced, he forced himself to examine the bodies with Hal and the others. Someone might just be hanging on to life, he told himself, just waiting for a friend to come. But no-one was waiting. Spearbold did not have to be military man to see that almost all the wounds were from bows or crossbows - an ambush then.

Hard though he found it, Spearbold realised it was harder still for Hal and the rest. The dead men were friends - some they would have known all their lives.

"No sign of Lord Elder," mumbled Hal, "or one or two of the others." He walked away but his words hung in the air. No-one dared name the missing in case they found them, as if to speak of them might somehow cause them harm. Yet, Spearbold reflected, it could hardly get much worse. Men that were comrades, men he had sat next to only the day before, lay cold and grey. He would never forget the smell either: the smell of blood, festering in the warmth of the afternoon sunshine.

They lingered by the cross until Spearbold felt the eyes of the others upon him; they were expecting him to show the lead. He knew they must look for the missing men and bury the dead, but which first? The poor men's bodies would still be there later; Ned and the others might not. Yet, there were only a few hours left before sunset.

"Shard will be searching these woods now as we stand here," he said.

"How do you know it's Shard?" asked Hal.

"Shard's lord and master is the Earl and he does what the

Earl wants - and the Earl wants Ned Elder."

"We should bury our comrades," said one of the archers.

"Aye, we should," replied Spearbold, "but we're not going to - not yet. If we don't pick up the trails now, it'll be too late - if it isn't already. Hal?"

"Master Spearbold's right enough," agreed Hal. "Come on."

The youth led his horse on foot into the forest to try to find some clear tracks to follow. There were so many sets of them just beyond the tree line that at first he found it impossible to follow any. Spearbold realised that Hal was no mean tracker himself as he began to describe what he thought had happened.

"You can see where men have been waiting," Hal explained. "They were there long enough to flatten the grass and bracken where they stood. Look. Some were more nervous and wandered around but others must have just lain down to wait." He moved further into the trees. "Look. Here's where their horses were tied."

Spearbold, stepping over the dung, reckoned that even he might have noticed that.

"Now," continued Hal, "see where several tracks lead off here to the north and there's more over there, to the west. Difficult to tell who's who though."

"So, are we any wiser?" asked Spearbold.

"Patience, Master Spearbold," said Hal, "there are fresher tracks too - could be Shard, or at least someone following after the first riders."

"So which ones should we follow?"

"Both. They twist along together. If Shard's hunting down some of our friends then we might as well follow his lead: he's probably a better tracker than I am."

"Very well," said Spearbold, "lead on then."

As they walked their horses through the trees, Spearbold could not recall ever being so ill at ease. He disliked forests at the best of times with their dark shadowy places and cunning branches and roots that sought to ensnare the unwary.

"Be on your guard," whispered Hal. "We should be as quiet as we can." He looked at the others as if to reinforce his point. "And keep the man nearest you in sight all the time."

"How many with Shard - assuming it is Shard?" asked Spearbold.

"I should say somewhere between ten and a dozen."

"And we are but five…"

"Stop!" hissed Hal. It was so sudden they all obeyed instantly and began to scan the trees close by. Spearbold could hear nothing and was about to say so when a voice sounded behind them.

"Thank Christ for that! I thought you were never going to stop."

Out of the trees to their rear stepped John Black, leading his mount.

As one, they all sighed with relief. Black had taken an arrow in his shoulder but was otherwise unscathed. He told them quickly what had happened, though they had already worked most of it out for themselves.

"Did Lord Elder get away?" asked Hal urgently.

"If he did then he's a lucky bastard, because no-one else did!" Black spat out the words.

"You don't know then," said Hal.

"I don't - and I don't fucking care, either!"

"He's your lord," said Hal, "you should remember that occasionally."

"Aye, tell that to Will Stringer - and all the rest! I told him not to stop at that cross…"

Spearbold was anxious to get moving again. "Is there anyone else you've seen alive?" he asked Black.

"No." It was a sullen response. "A few of us tried it when Lord Elder made a move but God knows if anyone else got away. The only one who might have made it is Tom - he wasn't there when we were hit. He was scouting ahead."

"Best we move on then," said Spearbold.

"Who put you in charge?" demanded Black.

"I did!" retorted Spearbold. "Feel free to leave us - you

don't owe me any loyalty."

Black said nothing but when Hal led them off, he followed.

They had just started off when Hal stopped again and turned towards Spearbold with a grin. He pointed out two bodies.

"Lord Elder's been this way," said Hal, "this looks like his handiwork."

Black glanced at the corpses, which had been stripped of armour, boots and weapons. "Whoever's tracking him didn't leave much behind."

They moved on but though they noticed some traces of blood they found no more men at arms, dead or alive. Spearbold glanced up increasingly often, keeping an eye on the light: it would soon start to fade, he decided. He took Hal gently by the arm.

"We should stop for the night," he said.

"We'll not reach the forest's edge before sunset in any case," said Hal. "We may as well follow as long as we can then make camp for the night."

"Very well, Hal," said Spearbold, "but it'll soon be dusk."

Black nodded without enthusiasm. "And pray that Shard doesn't find us first! Can you still see a clear trail?"

Hal shook his head. "It's confusing," he said, "Shard's men have taken different paths from here so he must have lost Ned's tracks."

"Well, can you find them or not?" asked Spearbold.

"Perhaps," said Hal, "if you leave me to it and stop asking me!"

Spearbold watched as Hal circled the area and then moved further away. "Wait here," he said.

"Excellent," muttered Spearbold. He thought it seemed a lot darker already. Did darkness come earlier in the forest? He squatted down on the ground, his legs aching from the slow walk through the undergrowth. Hal had drifted from view though if he listened carefully he could hear muted sounds of movement.

"Where's he gone now?" asked Black.

"Just wait quietly," said Spearbold.

"Piss off!" said Black.

It seemed as if they had waited for hours but eventually Hal returned and he seemed a good deal more optimistic.

"I've found a clear track to follow," replied Hal, "two men, or a man and a boy perhaps. Let's see where it takes us."

"A man and a boy?" said Black. "Well it can't be Ned Elder then, can it?"

"I think it is," declared Hal.

"What do you know anyway? You're no better tracker than I am," said Black.

"I know Lord Elder…"

"But do you know shit stinks, boy? I'm not following you anymore."

Hal shrugged.

"Good!" said Spearbold, "it'll be a lot quieter without you. Come on, Hal. We'll follow your trail until the light goes."

He shepherded the others after Hal and then tagged on behind them. After a moment or two he looked back to find that Black had decided to follow. But all too soon the light faded and Hal had to admit he had lost the trail. Spearbold called a halt. As the night descended, he regretted they had no fire or torches to lift the gloom a little, though at least it was warm. It could have been much more uncomfortable than it was. All the same, with darkness the forest began to come alive with noises he did not like much. Hesitant footfalls came towards them but then seemed to veer away at the last minute. Animals? Did they have wolves in Northumberland? Surely they would have howled. If they didn't, then it would hardly be fair.

They settled down for the night but Spearbold could not sleep and he could see that Hal too was restless. Spearbold could not think of anything to say so they lay in silence on a pile of bracken they had gathered. Was Shard sleeping? Spearbold hoped so.

§§§§

There was no sound but Ned could sense someone there. Then something brushed his arm - a light touch. His eyes flicked open: a hand lay on his shoulder - a small narrow hand. He looked up.

The girl said nothing. She did not cry out nor run away; she just stared back at him. Her silence unnerved him and he found himself wondering if she was real. Was this what death brought: an angel to take him to purgatory? He looked at her more closely and noticed she was dressed in a dirty smock - no angel, then. Yet she had a kind oval face and her hair was plaited neatly to the side. He listened to the forest: not a sound out of place. But Shard's men could still be out there.

"Who are you?" he whispered, trying not to sound too frightening. She gave a half smile and pulled at his arm. She was gentle and stronger than he expected.

He shook off her arm. "You'd better go, lass," he said. He had enough dead souls on his conscience and he didn't want another. But the girl did not leave.

"It's not safe, lass! Go!" he said and pushed her away.

She shook her head and held out her hand. She couldn't have been much more than twelve, perhaps not even that. He shook his head and at once regretted it. His hand flew to his head where the throbbing pain suddenly turned steely sharp. It felt as if the poleaxe was still embedded there.

She bent down to kneel beside him and he saw to his surprise that she carried his discarded helm in her other hand. The girl must be simple - for what in the name of Christ could she want with him? She got up and took his arm, trying to pull him up again. Reluctantly he let her help him to his feet and once there she put her arm through his and coaxed him away from his hiding place.

"Alright then, I'm coming," he conceded with poor grace. He stumbled along beside her for several paces and then she stopped to examine the wound on his head. She reached up and touched his forehead where blood had begun to trickle as soon as he had got up. She looked at him and he could see the concern in her eyes.

"Why do you care about me, little one?" he asked. Again she made no answer and took his arm once more. He felt decidedly groggy and blood now dripped steadily onto his chest. He was past caring where she took him or why she cared enough to bother. By God, there was nothing to her but she was a strong girl all the same. He felt weaker with every step and yet she bore much of his weight. Most girls would have run away screaming seeing him lying there broken and bleeding. It beggared belief. Then he staggered and fell; the girl could not hold him and fell with him.

"Leave me, lass," he mumbled and passed out.

§§§§

Ned awoke lying on a stack of logs - or so it seemed to him. He was in some sort of timber outhouse, he thought. He tried to remember how he had got there. He'd been wounded. He felt his temple. Someone had put a poultice on it. He pressed on it and winced. It was still sore enough then, but not the persistent, lancing pain of before. He tried to sit up but all that happened was that several logs slid from under him to roll onto the floor and he nearly passed out again. He steadied himself and looked about him. Where in God's name was he? Wait. The young lass - where was she? Perhaps he had conjured her up?

He abandoned his attempt to sit up and lay back again. Someone had gone to some trouble to treat his head wound and it did feel a little better. There was nothing to be gained by destroying their good work. It followed that he was in no immediate danger and he saw that the door was ajar so he was no-one's prisoner either. His weapons were gone but he could not remember whether he had cast them aside himself or not.

He was in a woodshed, by the look of it. He could hear

voices outside. He listened more carefully: not voices, just one voice - a man's voice. He could not make out what was being said but the tone was gentle. A spider dropped on to his leg towing a silvery thread. He brushed it carefully aside and it swung out hanging impossibly by the single thread. He knew how the spider felt.

The light was fading - it had to be around dusk. He must have dozed off for a while and when he opened his eyes the girl was there, sitting calmly on a chunk of tree trunk, watching over him. Seeing him awake she smiled, a broad warming smile; he smiled back.

"God give you good even, lass," he said. She laughed - at least it looked as if she was laughing but it was a strange, soundless laugh. Then she hurried out of the shed.

"Wait!" he called out but she was gone. He thought about running after her but he wasn't sure he could run and in any case he did not want to frighten her. He tried sitting up again and to his great relief he found he could do so without the room swaying. Small steps; he would just sit still for a while and see how he felt. Then to his surprise the girl returned but this time she was not alone. With her she brought a tall, well-built man - a forester by the look of him. He stooped as he passed through the doorway, the girl pulling him in. Did she never stop smiling? The man with her was not smiling: he looked rather worried. He took the girl gently by the shoulders and turned her to face him.

"Leave us, Agnes," he said. She threw her arms around his neck and hugged him. Then she flashed another beaming smile at Ned before flitting out through the door.

The two men stared at each other for a few moments without speaking.

"Agnes didn't bring me here on her own, did she?" said Ned.

"No," said the man and sat down on the log. "She came and got me. She's a strong lass but you were a bit too heavy."

Ned could see ten kinds of distress etched on his face. "And you're her father?" he asked.

The other nodded. "Aye, I'm Walter."

"Why didn't you just leave me, Walter? Take your girl home and leave me in the forest."

Walter shook his head. "I didn't leave you in the same way I didn't leave the bird she found with its wing broken, I didn't leave the hare, or the deer with an arrow in its haunch that a huntsman had lost the track of. Agnes collects wounded animals and tries to nurse them back to health - to her you were just another one to be mended. It's not easy to argue with Agnes."

"Is the girl simple?" Ned asked. Her father's face flushed with anger for a moment but then he calmed himself. Ned cursed his bluntness.

"She can't speak," said Walter, "but tell me, stranger, do you think she's simple?"

"No, I don't, Walter. I think she's as bright and as strong as steel - a little angel."

"Aye, she is."

"But this time she's given you a problem, hasn't she, Walter?"

"Aye."

"It's a bigger problem than you know. I'll leave at once but you must remove all trace that I've been here - there'll likely be someone tracking me. And they won't care about you... or Agnes."

Walter nodded miserably. "But if they're any good at tracking they'll know you were here, whatever I do to hide it."

"There'll be too many to fight off," said Ned.

"Aye." There was an air of resignation about him now.

"Get Agnes away," said Ned, "Have you kin she could go to?"

Her father laughed. "Kin? The only kin Agnes has is me. Her mother died when she was five and she's not spoken a word since."

"And you've raised her alone? How old is she?"

"Must be thirteen soon. I don't rightly recall..."

313

It was nearly dark when Walter stood up to go. "Who are you running from?" he asked.

"You don't want to know," said Ned, "but they could find me any time. Take Agnes into the forest for a day or two. Don't wait till morning - go now, before it's too late. Did you find my sword?"

He nodded. "I'll bring it. I took your dagger as well - just in case."

"Then fetch them please and then go. Make Agnes understand and take her as far from here as you can - and be careful."

"Aye."

Ned felt a chill though the evening was warm. A crushing memory stole unbidden in to his mind. An unwelcome, loathsome memory he would carry with him all his days. A memory of children's broken and bloodied bodies, of folk who had put their trust in him only to be cut to pieces in Edmund Radcliffe's rage. He could not bear to think that Agnes might join that company of lost souls.

Suddenly, as if she had known his thoughts, Agnes flew through the door and hugged him. Then she pulled away and he could feel her tears on his cheek. Walter came in with Ned's weapons and pushed her outside.

"Thank you and God be with you both," said Ned.

"Aye," said Walter. He stopped in the doorway. "There's some food in the house…and the road north lies to your east - if that helps you."

"I thank you. Now, go - while you still can."

When they had gone, Ned sat up in the dark and listened, attuning himself to the forest sounds. He tried moving his head; it still hurt. He tried standing and found he could walk slowly without too much discomfort. He sheathed his sword and dagger then stepped outside.

The forester and his daughter had a tiny cottage, hardly worthy of the name. The land around it was uncleared with trees cloaking it on all sides. He went into the cottage and found a simple interior, sparsely furnished. It was dark inside, the only window roughly shuttered. Part of the floor was strewn with dry rushes but the rest was beaten earth. There was a straw bed and above it under the eaves was a narrow loft where he assumed that Agnes slept. By the window there was a small table - fashioned by Walter he imagined - where Agnes, or her father, had laid out some bread and cheese for him. Once his eyes had adjusted to the gloom he sat down and ate.

He tried to put himself in the boots of his opponent. He had no doubt that Shard would be searching for him; Warwick would never accept he was dead without a body. According to Spearbold, Shard was an excellent tracker and if that was the case he would find his way to the cottage, sooner or later.

Ned knew he should move on but he needed rest. He sat on the bed then he practised feeling his way from the bed to the door in the dark. He drew out his sword and laid it down upon the straw. His head ached a little but young Agnes had done a good job. With luck she and her father would be far enough away by now. He was tempted to remove his mail but he would never get back into it in a hurry and he was afraid he would scrape his head wound. The mail was outdated and very worn in places; he ought to get rid of it when he returned to Yoredale - if he returned. Yoredale seemed a very long way away just now. He lay down on the straw and it felt warm. He would just lie there for a while and then go south.

26

22nd May in the early hours, outside Yoredale Castle

Sarah Standlake was shivering in the chill night air. There was no friendly moon to light their way as they stumbled along the uneven path. She clung to him lest she tumbled down the steep bank but soon they reached the castle wall where they could feel their way. Sarah stopped by the corner base of the northwest tower and leant against the wall, pulling him to her. She kissed him with wet, eager lips and ground her pelvis against him, feeling him respond.

But he pulled away from her. "Not here," he whispered, "you said we'd go somewhere warmer."

"Aye, come on then," she said and took his hand to lead him around the tower onto the path that led to postern gate. He seemed tense and unsure but why he was making such a fuss she didn't know because he had been all over her a few minutes before. After all, they could do it all again when they got inside. She giggled to herself: how good it would feel to be with him on a straw bed. She wanted this one to be more than a quick wrestle in some damp hollow in the bracken. She knew this youth was the one: she did not know him well yet but she had fallen for him from the moment he had walked into the village.

They arrived at the postern gate and she found with some relief that her sister had left the door unbarred. That had been her greatest worry - not to be able to gain entry after all the trouble she had gone to. She pushed open the heavy door and smiled to herself: as they had agreed, Jane had left a torch burning in the alcove just inside the door. God love her sweet cousin!

"Hurry up!" she hissed, drawing her young companion swiftly through the gate after her. "I must be mad," she continued, "bringing you in here again – Becky'll kill me if she finds us!"

Sarah glimpsed his face in the wavering light as they hurried quietly in: he still looked nervous and she smiled back at him encouragingly.

"There's nothing to worry about. It's all arranged with Jane. Becky will never know."

"Good. You've done well," he replied and kissed her on the lips, cradling her face gently in his hands. As she smiled up at him he gave her head a sharp twist snapping her neck as easily as a shaft of summer wheat. "Sorry, Sarah," he said softly.

He scooped her up as she fell and laid her down on the stone flags.

Then he crouched beside her to wait, leaving the gate ajar. Her shocked, lifeless face stared up at him under the flickering torch, silently accusing him. After a while he stood up, puffing out his cheeks. Abruptly he picked up her body and tossed it out of the gate. Then he waited just inside again, listening carefully.

§§§§

It was late in the evening when Gruffydd and Bagot sat down at one of the long trestle tables in the castle kitchen, to finish off the last of the best ale. Bagot put two flagons on the table and they swiftly drank them down.

"We must've talked to every man on the estate," concluded Bagot, "and we're no wiser. Why can't the women of this household stay within its damned walls for a few weeks?"

"Aye," grunted Gruffydd, reaching for another flagon.

"Well, do you believe the Lady Emma just went for a

walk?" asked Bagot. "There was more to it than that - she's not dared go out since her last visit to the Abbey. Mind you, I'm glad they've stopped."

"Don't see it matters much why she went out," snorted Gruffydd, emptying the flagon.

"It matters," said Bagot, "because every time I lock this place up tight as a virgin, I turn round to find some idle pisspot has left a gate open!"

"Hmm." Gruffydd nodded sympathetically.

They continued drinking steadily, effortlessly draining flagon upon flagon and when any of the servants or cooks ventured into the room they flung an empty pot at them.

"Lady Eleanor won't be satisfied with nowt, though," said Bagot ruefully, "she'll want neat answers, not more mysteries. Dog's shit! That's all the best ale gone."

He started on the second best ale, pouring some for Gruffydd who took a large swig and at once spewed it out onto the table.

"God's breath man, that ale's been drunk once and pissed back into the barrel!" declared Gruffydd. He spat out the last dregs.

Bagot sniffed at the pot of ale. "Surprised you noticed but let's have some wine then - no-one'll know."

He tapped a barrel and poured out a generous amount for each of them.

Gruffydd was staring at him. "What do you mean: 'surprised I noticed'?"

"Well, what did you drink in your ... cave, was it? Goat's milk?" he suggested with a laugh.

"I drank ale if I wanted to - or wine ... but the water of a Welsh mountain stream is sweet and clear."

"Water!" guffawed Bagot. "Only beggars drink water!"

"Enough of your insults! We've still a mystery to solve…"

"Not really, that lamb must've been put there at first light when you took over the watch and opened the gate; I thought you looked half asleep."

"What! You could hardly stand when I arrived," retorted

Gruffydd. "You were nodding and the only thing keeping you awake was your soft head banging against the portcullis!"

"Well it must have been shut then, you stupid Welshman!"

"Aye, but did you really check the postern in the night? Most likely you didn't bother – or forgot."

Bagot stood up and fetched more wine, ignoring Gruffydd.

"Where's mine then?" the latter enquired.

"No more wine for careless Welsh tosspots," muttered Bagot.

"Stop calling me Welsh!"

"You are Welsh!"

"Not the way you say it!" Gruffydd snatched Bagot's flagon of wine and stole a deep draught before Bagot could wrest it back and the pair grappled for it. Gruffydd kept hold of it and drank again.

"Keep it then!" shouted Bagot and he fetched another, brim-full with Ned's best Rhenish wine and proceeded to drain it. They both got up to refill their flagons but Bagot got to the barrel first.

"I'm Ned's trusted man – you're just an unwelcome guest, Welshman!" Bagot crowed loudly and as he raised his flagon it smashed against Gruffydd's chin and he bellowed with laughter. "Clumsy…sodding…Welshman," he pronounced the words slowly.

Gruffydd, stunned by the blow, grabbed one of the iron kitchen pots and tossed it at Bagot, who ducked so that it caught him only a glancing blow on the shoulder.

"Trusted man?" Gruffydd roared. "You one-legged English fart! You aren't a trusted man anymore – you can't be trusted to fucking stand up!"

Bagot glared at him and threw aside the trestle table, almost losing his balance in doing so. Then he lunged at Gruffydd. The latter intended to sidestep his opponent, but somehow his body did not respond and Bagot landed on top of him. Both fell to the stone floor, cursing and shouting.

Then both attempted to stand but only succeeded in dragging the other down again. They rolled about the floor, trading insults and lashing out at each other with any object that came to hand.

"Get off me, you lame Yorkshire turd!" shouted Gruffydd.

"Hie back to your shithole of a cave with the other hairy animals!"

"You'd know more about shit than me - you talk little else!"

Bagot swung a fist as he tried to pin the Welshman down but Gruffydd brought his knee up into Bagot's midriff, winding him briefly. The two were breathing heavily, the ale and wine beginning to take its toll, but both men got to their knees and prepared to launch into a fresh fusillade of insults.

§§§§

Bathed in the candlelight, Eleanor stood naked by her bed, her hand resting lightly on Will's small wooden cot.

"He looks so peaceful," she said.

"Now he's finally asleep!" groaned Becky.

"I think you're right: he will be as handsome as his father," said Eleanor, sitting down on the edge of the bed.

"Well, his mother's looking very sleek and strong these days," teased Becky, putting her arms around Eleanor's waist. "Your work with Gruffydd must be doing some good."

"Your hands are like ice," Eleanor said, turning and drawing her legs into the bed, "but you don't look so bad either," she said with a grin. "We're survivors, you and me."

"It's like it used to be," said Becky, with a guilty laugh, "in a bed together."

"Ssh. Young Will might hear you! You're an evil influence, Rebecca Standlake. Anyway, it's not like that anymore. We were wicked girls then and our lives were ... I don't know... breathless."

They both lay back on the straw mattress and Becky

wriggled to get comfortable.

"Mmm, I wish you'd kept the down bed," she said.

"Too soft! Anyway, I didn't let you into my bed to pass comment on it."

"Why did you then? We haven't shared a bed in years."

"Just company…at a difficult time."

Becky raised an eyebrow. "If it's company you want, one of the dogs would have lain on your bed."

Eleanor stroked Becky's bare arm. "A young widow has certain needs…"

"Well, I would have thought the young widow knows more than enough to manage her own needs," murmured Becky.

Eleanor leant across Becky and blew out the candle. In the darkness she whispered: "I thought we might both have the same needs… and I thought we might manage them together."

"Stop talking then… my lady," said Becky softly.

Eleanor was glad no-one could see her broad grin. Somewhere below a boor banged. She kissed Becky's cheek. Then she heard a man's voice, calling. Could she never have some peace! She prayed someone would shut the fool up. Silence returned and it seemed her prayer had been answered. Then came a single cry of alarm, cut short.

"Shit!" said Eleanor and leapt from the bed at once. "Get your girls!" she ordered, "then bring them here and stay with Will."

She tugged on her breeches and jerkin then went to the oak chest against the wall and threw it open. She reached inside and pulled out the bundle of cloths in which Will's swords were bound. In her blind panic she could not unwrap them, angrily threw them aside and rushed from her chamber.

Everywhere there was noise, echoing in the confined spaces within the walls. She had no doubt that the castle had been breached - but by whom? She could do nothing alone: she had to get to Bagot and Gruffydd; they would know what to do. She ran, almost falling, down the spiral stair from the gallery outside her chamber, trying to think. Where would they be? She ignored the Hall where many of the servants usually slept and turned into the butteries.

There she found a clutch of young girls, who were cowering on the floor.

"Have you seen Bagot?" she demanded but they only shook their heads.

She went on through the butteries and burst into the kitchen to find Bagot raising a greasy spit iron above his head.

"It's your fault!" he raged at Gruffydd, "you idle Welsh churl!"

"Bagot!" Eleanor's voice seared across the room.

Both men snapped their heads towards the threshold where she stood.

She sobbed, fell onto her knees. "Look at the pair of you!" she screamed, tears streaming down her cheeks. "The two upon whom all our hopes rested… God help us for now we are truly lost!"

Bagot and Gruffydd cast their eyes down and Bagot let the iron spit clatter to the floor. They sat on the floor paralysed with shame as they became aware of the clamour nearby. Then, from somewhere deep in the castle, there came a single scream.

Eleanor brushed aside her tears, took a breath and slowly drew herself up, recovering her composure.

"You've failed us," she breathed and ran out. She had to get back to her beloved Will. She must get her swords and fight for him - he was all that mattered now.

DEREK BIRKS

27

22nd May at first light, in the Derwent Valley north of Bishop Auckland

Agnes blinked and came wide awake. She looked around the clearing where they had stopped to rest in the early hours. Dawn's light filtered through the trees, softened by early morning mist. Her father was gone but there were angry shouts from nearby. She knew one voice was his - then she heard the clash of weapons and ran in the direction of the noise. Her father came stumbling through the bracken towards her. He dropped beside her onto his knees and she reached out her arms to throw them around his neck. Blood flowed from a wound in his chest - too much blood, she knew. Her mouth opened wide but no scream sounded.

"Run, lass!" said Walter in a hoarse whisper. "Run!"

Agnes stared back at him, willing him to get up. She understood: the wound was too great, but she could not leave him. He staggered to his feet. "Agnes, be gone!" he urged.

She could hear others crashing through the trees. He thrust her roughly away and stood in front of her, waving his hunting knife as his assailants appeared. They began to circle around him and he turned to push her again. "Go, Agnes. Please, for your mother's love, go!"

She fled, evading their outstretched arms, and she kept on running. She ran, though the low branches whipped her face, though her lungs were bursting and her heart was breaking. She heard others coming through the forest after her, but she was quick and nimble. Her father had given her a chance, given his life to let her escape.

She carved a path where there was none, flitting between the trees in the thickest part of the forest. Where could she go? She knew only the woods. But Agnes was not one of life's runners. She had never run so far or so fast before and her legs already ached. The sound of her pursuers drove her on. They were getting closer. She must get her bearings. She must find somewhere to hide. The forest was hers not theirs, but her mind was in such turmoil she could not think.

She darted a glance behind and glimpsed at least one man at arms. They were close. Then from nowhere a youth appeared in front of her and she hurtled straight into him. He looked as shocked as she was and clutched her to him as they fell to the ground together. The breath was punched out of her as he landed on top of her in the bracken. He rolled off her and she willed her limbs to move. She could not get to her feet. They had her: she was lost. How had this man got ahead of her? She scrambled onto her knees and faced him. If she could have screamed at him she would.

Behind him she saw the chasing man come into view and her head dropped. Then, to her surprise, the youth lifted her up, tossed her over his shoulder and carried her off. As he ran she was buffeted from side to side. He carried a bow and her face kept slapping hard against it. The youth was quick and strong. She could feel the power of the arms that held her. Perhaps he was not one of her pursuers. She clung on to him and to hope.

Without warning he flipped her off his shoulder and threw her down into the bracken. She tried to roll away as despair gripped her once more.

"Stay down!" he cried as he snatched an arrow from his bag and raised his bow. The man at arms appeared between two thin trunks barely twenty feet away. He was breathing hard and he must have seen the archer only at the last moment. Agnes watched in fascination as the arrow disappeared through his neck leaving only a spurt of blood in its wake. By the time the man was falling, her rescuer had reached down and hoisted her up onto his shoulder again.

He ran on but after a short while he stopped and listened. She beat lightly on his back and he set her down gently on her feet.

He stared at her for a moment. "I'm Hal," he whispered, "who are you?"

She opened her mouth, knowing that no words would come but hoping it would show him that she could not speak.

"You're frightened," he said. "Where are you hurt?"

At first she did not understand but then he pointed at her smock and her hands. She looked down at her hands. She had forgotten. Her father's blood was on her hands and the smock was stained with it. She shook her head.

"Were you with someone else?" he asked.

She nodded, staring blankly at the dried blood. Yes, someone else…someone who used to be her father. He took her hand then and wiped her tears away.

"Don't worry," he said, "I've comrades in the forest."

He smiled. It was a warm smile. She knew he was trying to reassure her but then he had not seen the men who had killed her father. She forced a smile back at him.

He set off again, taking her hand to pull her with him. She stopped. He might not realise it but he was heading for the cottage. Would the cottage be safe? She thought not and tugged at his arm, shaking her head vigorously.

"My friends are this way," he insisted and dragged her with him. She dug in her heels but all she could do was shake her head. She felt foolish. She needed words and she did not have them. It was the first time she had ever had such a thought. Her father had always known what she wanted to say but now he was gone.

The young man stopped tugging at her. "You know this forest well?" he asked.

She nodded.

"And you don't want to go this way? Do you know of a safe place?"

She had no answer but she never had time in any case. An arrow thudded into the branch next to him and he picked her up once more. He continued on in the same direction and she was powerless to stop him. They burst into a small clearing where several other men were waiting. Hal set her down.

"Where in black hell have you been?" one of them demanded. He looked and sounded angry. These men seemed little different from the ones who had killed her father.

"We're being followed," Hal told them.

"How many?" asked an older man. He had a kind face, she decided, and though he carried a sword, he did not have the look of a soldier.

"Don't know!" replied Hal.

"Who's she?"

"Don't know that either, but we should move or we'll be making a stand here!"

"Against who, for God's sake?" demanded the angry one.

Agnes' keen ears could hear the men approaching now. Hal and his comrades seemed to take no notice of her as they argued. What were they thinking? Did they not see they must go? She seized Hal's arm and tried to pull him away.

"Wait," he said, brushing her aside.

She let go of him and ran away from them, away from the others, from all these men of war who had killed her father and destroyed her world.

"Wait!" She heard Hal's call but she didn't stop. She had her legs back now and she knew where she was going: home, back to the cottage. If she took a long route around, she might still lose them all. No-one had come to the cottage before, except for one or two her father knew; she was certain now that she would be safer there.

She slowed up, moving more stealthily and taking care to leave few marks of her progress. A sudden thought struck her: she could go down by the river. She could lose a tracker there more easily. She changed direction, taking a line which led her down a steep incline into the river valley. Here the trees thinned out but there was still some cover. When she reached the river bank she stopped and scanned the forest behind her. Nothing moved; the deer would be watching nervously, for deer knew all about men. She could hear voices far off.

She stooped down at the water's edge and rinsed her hands in the cool stream, washing away the blood and with it the last trace of her father. The river here was narrow and it got deeper as it passed down through a short gorge. She waded into the cold water up to her knees and then, as she found the middle of the stream, up to her waist. She gasped with the sudden chill of it. Her thin linen smock clung to her as she walked carefully along the river bed, feeling the stones beneath her feet.

Before she reached the point where the stream descended steeply through the ravine she climbed out of the water on the opposite bank and made her way up the side of the valley through a wall of oak and beech. Her smock dribbled water down her legs as she walked. She felt colder out of the water and the sun had no warmth to it.

At the crest of the rise she looked briefly into the ravine where the river plunged down then she descended the long, gentle slope. It would take her down to the ford where the water was always shallow but before she reached it there was a shout from the other side of the valley. She looked back up the slope; Hal and his comrades were closer than she expected. He shouted to her but she ignored him and hurried on to the ford.

When she reached it she came to an abrupt halt. Everywhere she looked there were dead men: on both banks of the river, in the ford, by the cross. She did not know these men but she recoiled at the sight of them. Some must have bled to death in the water; one had slumped over the cross, his congealed blood a dark scar on its white face. Others lay on the muddy banks where flies buzzed and clustered busily around their corpses. She waved away the flies but she could not mend these punctured bodies. She trudged from the ford back into the forest, her legs suddenly more weary than ever. She saw the web of tracks in the undergrowth and made use of them to obscure her own as she made her way back home.

She stopped in the trees by the cottage. It was the only home she had ever known, where her mother had died and where she had grown with her father. It was her home yet she approached it with hesitant steps. Her eyes flitted from place to place: the wood store, the small pen which the goats shared, the coppiced area to the west of the cottage and finally, almost reluctantly, the doorway. There was no sign of anyone but she noticed that the door was not latched; the knight must have left it open.

She paused on the threshold. She hoped she had lost them all but any one of them might stumble upon the cottage. If they did, they would look inside but perhaps they would not trouble to look in her special place, where she always bolted to when she was troubled. She was more than troubled now.

§§§§

Ned woke up with a throbbing head. It was already light - he had slept through the damned night. He should have been halfway to Bishop Auckland by now! He knew he was tired but even so. Now he was stiff and cold; he got up, massaging his legs to get himself moving. His head still ached. He had hoped it would feel easier by now but it didn't.

He stuffed the last crumbs of cheese into his mouth and swallowed; then he picked up his sword and paused mid-stride. Had he heard the scuff of a boot outside the door? He moved to it and stood, listening. The door was flung open and instinct made him bring up his sword. It only just parried the sword of the first man through the door. They froze and stared at each other for a long moment, swords locked together.

"Black!" said Ned. "I thought you were dead."

"My lord…" Black did not take a backward step. "I was…

I was one of the lucky ones…"

"Put up your weapon, man," said Ned.

Black held his sword pressed against Ned's for a moment longer than was acceptable.

"Black?"

"Aye," conceded John Black, and sheathed his sword.

Hal and Spearbold pushed past him into the room.

"My lord!" Hal greeted him warmly. "You're a sight for us to see. We were starting to think you'd been killed."

Ned was relieved to find that at least some of his men were still alive. "Not so easy to kill…How many others are there?" he asked.

"Hah!" retorted Black and shouldered past the others to go outside.

"This is all…" said Hal quietly.

"Black has every right to be angry. I made a mistake," said Ned. "Hardly my first and most likely not my last."

"They would have ambushed you somewhere, lord," said Hal, "if not there, then somewhere along that road. We're your men, lord, wherever that may take us. Black forgets that too often."

One by one, all of the rest came into the cottage and Ned clapped each of the archers on the back in turn. "Geoffrey, Dickon, Will Cross, glad to see you all!"

The archers acknowledged their lord and soon the small room was heaving with armed men.

Ned nodded to Spearbold.

"My lord, I am relieved to find you alive," said Spearbold, "after what we found at the river…"

"It can't just have been Shard's men," said Ned.

"It wasn't," replied Spearbold, "Henry was the one who led the ambush. Mordeur was there and Shard too."

Ned shrugged. "They're all Warwick's creatures in any case," he said, "but at least it tells us that Henry's not too far ahead."

"He wasn't," agreed Spearbold, "but he will be now. He's already got a day's start on you and you'll need to ride hard just to keep it at that."

"And Shard's men are not far away," said Hal.

"So we need to escape Shard first," said Ned.

Spearbold frowned. "Don't think it will be easy," he warned.

"I know. You've told me enough times!"

"Shard will pursue you for as long as it takes. You're his path to advancement. He'll have assured Warwick that he could find you and bring you back. He knows he can't return to Warwick without you or your head. He knows he must not fail."

"Very well then, let's get moving. We'll head east to the road. Hal, send a couple of the lads ahead; Shard's out there somewhere and I don't want to run into him without warning.

"Aye, lord. Come on!" He cajoled the archers outside. Looking at him Ned realised with a start that Hal was no longer the orphan boy Amelie had found at Corve Manor. At Towton and now in this campaign the boy had become a man, a valued man, a trusted young warrior upon whom he had come to rely a great deal. Amelie would be proud of him; she had fussed around him like a mother hen these last few years. 'Keep Hal safe for me, won't you Ned?' she had told him when he left for the northern marches. Well, Hal was kept safe so far but it was little thanks to him, he thought bitterly.

There was a shout outside and the door was flung open. Black stood on the threshold.

"They're coming!" he growled.

"You can't let him trap you in here, lord!" warned Spearbold.

"How many?" asked Ned.

"Dickon says about a dozen."

"Any archers?"

"Aye - a couple," said Black. He waited by the door, his expression bleak while Ned pondered: run or fight? There was no point in fleeing for Shard could run as fast as they could.

"We must take them on," he said. "There's no time to dwell here."

There was a cry of alarm from the back of the cottage. Black did not move.

"Get round there!" Ned's order was like a slap in the face to Black and he stormed out. Ned drew his sword and followed him outside. As Black disappeared around the back, three men at arms approached the cottage from the front with only Hal in their path. The young archer had an arrow nocked and loosed it at once, bringing down the first man. Ned leapt over the fallen one and threw himself at the other two, slashing at one and shouldering aside the other. The first parried his sword stroke and the second clutched at his thigh where an arrow from Hal had cut an artery. The sudden spurt of blood distracted his comrade and Ned slammed his sword hilt into his face, knocking him off balance. He chopped the blade down across his opponent's shoulder and he collapsed to the ground. Ned turned to see Will Cross stumbling back towards the cottage, blood dripping from his arm.

"Help Will in!" shouted Ned to Hal.

The wounded man at his feet started to get up. Ned thrust his dagger into the man's throat: this was no time for half measures.

Black appeared around the cottage wall, backing away from two opponents. Ned cursed silently. Where were the rest of his men? Dickon was at the other end of the cottage by the wood store but where was Geoffrey? He couldn't see him; perhaps Hal had sent him forward to scout. Black was giving ground, strong though he was.

"Lord!" he bellowed. It was unlike Black to ask for aid even when hard pressed.

"Dickon!" cried Ned. "Keep your eyes open!" Then with a quick glance towards the forest he hurried to help Black, launching himself at the nearest man at arms with a thunderous blow. Black grunted a reluctant acknowledgement and plunged his sword under the other man's breastplate.

Ned's onslaught had broken his man's sword but he shuddered as he felt the impact in his head and jerked back in agony. He felt faint but Black, with his own adversary down, battered the man into submission.

There was a shout from Dickon. Too late, Ned saw him fall under a series of poleaxe blows. He tried to clear his head and stumbled towards Dickon. An arrow from the trees flashed across him as he ran and half rolled, half fell to avoid it. As he lay on the ground his head slowly cleared again.

"Hal!" he shouted. "Root out that archer!"

Hal appeared in the cottage doorway but ducked inside as another arrow thudded into the door frame beside his head. Ned got up and staggered to the wood store. Dickon sat against the wall, his bloodied body still, eyes fixed. The owner of the poleaxe was gone. Ned edged his way past Dickon and surveyed the small animal pen and coppiced area away from the house wall. He peered into the low trees; if there was anyone there they were well hidden.

Then he heard a noise behind him. He twisted round facing the door of the wood store. There was a sudden cry from inside and he wrenched open the door. He was greeted by a cascade of logs and two figures tumbling out of the store in a frantic struggle. He stared in amazement as they landed at his feet: the man with poleaxe screaming and Agnes; thin, mute Agnes. He lay on top of her, his breeches around his thighs and soaked in blood. Her smock was torn to shreds and there was blood all over her. She had plunged a knife into his groin and she was forcing it up into his belly. She didn't look much like an angel just now.

Ned kicked the wounded man off Agnes and seized her around the waist to lift her up. She was mad with anger, her hands still wrapped tightly around the knife handle. She brandished it wildly and it took all Ned's strength to wrest it from her. Then he carried her into the cottage and laid her down on the straw in the loft.

"What's she doing here?" asked Hal.

Ned stared at him. "Agnes? She lives here. What do you

care?"

"Well…I ran into her in the forest; she was all bloodied - not as much as now - but…"

"Good Christ, her father…"

Hal said nothing.

"Come on Hal, we've still more of the devil's work to do! Spearbold - keep an eye on Agnes."

He moved towards the door, her knife still in his hand. He paused and turned to look at her. Then he reached up to the loft and she watched him as he buried the blade up to its hilt in the straw.

"She doesn't speak, Spearbold," he said and then went out.

Spearbold nodded.

Outside an arrow buried itself into one of the frame timbers and Hal dropped to a crouch.

"What are you doing down there, Hal?" said Ned.

"There's an archer about," said Hal.

"Well, you're an archer; go and find the bastard! We need to find Shard too - and where's Geoffrey gone?"

"I sent him on ahead," said Hal, getting warily to his feet.

"How's Will?"

"Not good."

"Black! God's Blood! Where are you?"

Black ghosted up to them. "I'm not hanging about in the open," he replied gruffly.

"Seen anyone else around the back?" he asked.

"No, just the first two."

Another arrow struck the door. Hal flinched but Ned did not move. "Hal?"

"I know! I know, go and find the bastard!" said Hal and he dashed off, running a ragged course into the trees.

"Come on, Black," urged Ned, "I want Shard."

Yet another arrow thudded into the door - he began to think the archer was aiming for it. He would surely run out of arrows soon.

They followed Hal into the trees. It was eerily quiet there.

He trod carefully and Black, two yards to his right, shadowed his every move. He studied every tree in his path; the sun was behind him, still quite low and offering dappled light at best. Easy to miss a man in dappled light. Where was Shard? He doubted he would even know him if he did see him. Black was too close; he waved him further over to his right.

A sudden cry of pain sounded ahead of them and they hurried forward, all pretence of caution abandoned. Thirty yards further on they found the last archer, pinned to an oak by an arrow loosed at short range by Hal. It had been a swift death.

"No sign of Shard, Hal?" asked Ned

"He didn't come past me."

"Shit! Where is the bastard? How many do you think are left?"

"There could be five or six…" said Hal.

"There could be a thousand - but there aren't," said Black.

There was a shout from behind them.

"That was Spearbold!" said Ned.

Hal was already moving. "They're at the cottage!" he yelled.

§§§§

Agnes buried her head under the sheepskin that she kept up in the loft. When it was bitter at night she would wrap it around her. Now it was worn and did not cover much of her. She peered down between the rough boards of the loft floor, watching the man they called Spearbold. His name did not suit him, she thought: he didn't look much of a spear carrier. Spearbold had opened one of the shutters a little and was keeping watch.

Suddenly he jerked his head back and called up to her. "Keep still and lie low!" He moved towards the door and then glanced up at the loft once more. Then he sat down on the bed and for a while nothing happened. Despite herself, Agnes jumped when the door was kicked in and two men strode in.

"So, you show your face at last, Shard," said Spearbold.

"Surprised to see you've thrown in your lot with a doomed man," replied Shard smoothly.

"Ned Elder's already gone," Spearbold said.

"Aye, but he's going to come back for you."

He prodded Spearbold hard with the point of his sword and Spearbold cried out in outrage and pain. Agnes gasped and Shard looked up to the loft, noticing her for the first time.

"God's Grace! Not you again - about time we were rid of you," he growled. "Come down here!"

She shook her head and shrank back into the eaves, dislodging a large spider from one of the roof beams. She liked spiders and watched it scuttle to safety. Take me with you, spider.

Shard turned to his companion. "Get her down here," he ordered wearily.

Spearbold moved towards her but was struck down.

"Sit down. You're too old for this," said Shard.

Perhaps Spearbold deserved his name after all, she thought: he had only stayed there because of her. Outside, she could hear sounds of a struggle; so could Shard and his companion.

"He's here! Well, our three should hold him for a while. Get that little bitch down and bring her to the door," Shard ordered as he moved to the window.

The man at arms climbed up to the loft and took her by the arm; she knew him instantly, knew every line and hair on his face: she was hardly likely to forget the man who took away her father. Struggling was pointless but she struggled anyway, clamping an arm around the nearest beam. He prised her off it and dragged her down with him. She banged her chin on the loft floor and blinked. Protruding from the straw was the hilt of the dagger she had used earlier.

The man tugged at her hard just as she grasped the knife and then everything seemed to happen at once. Her momentum caused her to fly out of the loft onto her captor; the outstretched knife struck him in the eye and lodged there. He screamed and let her fall. Spearbold leapt up to try to catch her and helped to break her fall as she landed on top of him.

Shard whirled around and cursed. "Not again! You little witch! But it'll be the last time, I promise you." He raised his sword.

"No!" shouted Spearbold.

The door imploded with a deafening crash and Ned stood in the doorway, drinking in the scene. He ignored Shard, who stood transfixed with his sword still in mid-air, and looked at her. "Are you alright, Agnes?" he asked.

Agnes, sitting on top of Spearbold, found a grim smile. Her knight was bleeding again, she noticed with sadness. Then her mouth opened wide as Shard's sword arced down at Ned. Most men would probably have stepped back, she decided, but Ned didn't. He took a swift pace forward, seized Shard's blade with his gloved hand and plunged his own sword up through Shard's side.

Agnes knew nothing of fighting but she knew Shard would die because the tip of Ned's sword poked out of his back. Ned ripped out the sword and pushed Shard to the floor.

"Well met, Shard," he said, "well met." Shard coughed up blood and Ned sheathed his sword. He looked weary.

Spearbold leant down to examine the body. "He's dead."

"Aye, and a quicker death than he deserved," replied Ned.

"Shard was not an evil man, Ned," said Spearbold.

"Aye, but you don't have to be an evil man to do evil."

Agnes rushed across to him and hugged him tightly. She felt her eyes well suddenly with tears and her grief came then in a flood, no longer held in check by blood and fear. She sobbed her heart out on Ned's breast. He held her tightly and spoke gently.

"He's gone, hasn't he, little angel, Walter's gone. You can take us to him and we'll give him a good burial, here where you loved him. You can say a fine daughter's farewell, but you mustn't be afraid. I'll take you with me and I'll look after you, as you looked after me."

DEREK BIRKS

28

25th May morning, in the Great Hall at Yoredale Castle

The bloody remains of their household men at arms, bearing the pale blue badges of Elder livery, lay discarded in a stinking heap in the centre of the floor. Eleanor was drawn to their young faces – they were just boys really. Some of the older men had succumbed at once but the younger ones believed they could win if they only tried hard enough. They had fought on to the bitter end and they deserved better than to be thrown onto a pile like scraps of offal. Their faces were grey now; their bodies had been left in the Hall for two days whilst the surviving members of the household had been locked in their chambers. They could have been moved but clearly their captor had decided to make a point.

She sat with Emma and Amelie at one of the long tables; on the floor nearby were Becky and Jane Standlake with the two small boys: Will and Richard. Sarah had not been seen since the start of it all - she hoped the girl had escaped. The rest of the household were there: the cooks, the servants from the kitchens and buttery, the nurse, the alewife and the stable lads. But not one fighting man was left.

In the end Eleanor had done nothing to prevent it. How they came in, she did not know but as soon as the children were taken she had capitulated. If her son was to die, then the least she could do was to be with him.

By the door that led up to Ned's bedchamber stood the one they called Durston – she couldn't remember him from years before but the mere sight of him had cast Emma into a pit of silence. Becky too looked terrified every time he spoke. A dozen or so of his men at arms were spread around the Hall, mostly leaning with a casual air against the walls. They were all waiting, though she was not too sure for whom since Durston was already there. On the raised platform at the end of the Hall two chairs had been placed and, despite their dire situation, she was intrigued: two chairs, not one.

A moment later the wait was over and their conqueror swept into the Hall. Amelie gasped, Emma cried out and fainted onto the floor as Henry of Shrewsbury ascended the dais and sat down on one of the chairs. Eleanor barely noticed the diminutive girl who followed him in and sat down beside him for her own eyes were fixed firmly on Henry. She had seen him only twice before but on each occasion he had brought her misery. Becky and Jane helped Emma back up on to the bench. For once she shared her sister's pain: Henry had hurt them both.

"This is how it will be," he said. His voice was deep and cold but he spoke with assurance, with the confidence of knowing he was master of the castle and everyone inside it.

Amelie stood up and looked Henry in the eye.

"Oh, shit, don't," Eleanor muttered to herself and reached out a hand to pull her sister-in-law back down but it was too late.

"You have no right to enter this household," Amelie declared, her soft French voice calm and even. Henry said nothing but turned his head to glance across at another who had followed him into the Hall. Eleanor knew him well enough: Mordeur, the Frenchman who had inflicted so much pain on her family. He stepped forward and struck Amelie hard in the chest with his fist, knocking her to the rush floor. There were cries of fear from some of the servants. As a demonstration of Henry's intent it could not have been more powerful: to publicly mistreat a lady with child was unthinkable.

Eleanor stood up at once.

"Stay where you are!" Henry told her. She shot him a fierce look and went to Amelie's aid anyway.

"Leave her!" ordered Henry and Mordeur seized her wrist to pull her away.

"She's with child!" Eleanor shouted angrily, slapping away Mordeur's hand.

Henry seemed unperturbed. "Yes, I'm glad you mentioned that," he said, "though I had noticed."

Eleanor ignored him and helped Amelie to sit up. She wheezed and wept with the pain, feeling her chest gingerly and gasping for air.

"Breathe slow and shallow," soothed Eleanor, "and don't try to speak."

"You can get her up," said Henry, "but keep her quiet. If she interrupts me again she'll not live long enough to give birth!"

Becky darted forward and helped Eleanor raise Amelie onto a bench. Eleanor sat beside her with an arm around her shoulder.

"As I was saying," Henry continued, "this is how it will be. I now hold this castle which I claim along with all the lands around it and the titles that presently are held by my half-brother, the traitor Ned Elder, as mine of right, due to me by right of my lineage from the Houses of both Radcliffe and Elder."

"No!" The scream from Emma rattled them all. She looked as if a bolt of lightning was coursing through her. She screeched at Henry, wild-eyed and incoherent; then she fled towards the Hall door where Mordeur stuck out a boot and tripped her. She fell forward, cracked her head on the door post and dropped like a stone. Even then she was neither still nor silent, trying to raise herself by clinging to the door frame, all the while muttering what sounded like a prayer.

"Take her up to the solar," said Henry. His face showed almost no emotion which surprised Eleanor for even Mordeur seemed taken aback by Emma's reaction. Perhaps Henry knew the reason for it.

Of all of them in the Hall, Eleanor was the only one who was not stunned by his announcement. She had been expecting it. After Towton she had assumed he had perished there but now, seeing him again, she remembered Edwina's words. Of course she had not believed it at the time, but now she could see the resemblance to Ned clearly enough.

"Your lives are in my hands," he continued, "I would kill any of you without a second thought. So, see you do as you're told. The women are to go to the solar." He pointed to Becky. "You, take the children to the nursery."

Becky stood up. Will and Richard had been cowering on the floor and she offered a hand to each of them. Will looked to his mother and Eleanor nodded and brushed her hand against his cheek. "Go with Becky," she told him.

Richard looked around the Hall in vain for his mother, his shoulders sagged and he began to sob. Jane took his hand and moved to follow Becky.

"Not you," said Henry, "Mordeur, take that one up to the garrison dormitory."

Mordeur smiled and nodded, seizing her by the arm.

"No!" pleaded Becky, "please lord, send me. Let Jane take the children!"

"Your turn will come soon enough, woman. Now, take the children out!"

"But…" Becky watched Jane being led away by Mordeur. At the foot of the spiral stair Jane turned to Becky with a look of desolation. Becky took a step towards her but Eleanor pulled her back and breathed in her ear.

"You can't help her, not yet, my dear… but soon."

Becky met her eyes then she took the boys out.

Eleanor helped Amelie up from the bench and took her arm to lead her out. Henry got up and stepped off the dais to leave but he waited for them to walk slowly towards him. As they passed in front of him, Eleanor turned to stare at him. He gave her a look as cold as stone.

"Don't think I've forgotten you, Eleanor Elder," he said. "You should be more terrified than your sister - I've not forgotten what you did to my mother. She will be avenged, I promise you."

Eleanor had expected nothing better from him so she turned instead to the young girl by his side, appraising her for the first time. She had remained silent whilst Henry talked and seemed almost insignificant, yet something about the way she held herself shouted a warning in Eleanor's head. The girl met her gaze and returned it with wordless venom. Yes, Eleanor decided, here was a force to be wary of.

Henry took the girl's hand and they walked out together. Eleanor guided Amelie along the passageway through the west range to the solar and pondered on who the girl was. She had a smug, proud look to her; could she be Henry's wife? She would have to wait to find out but she knew it would not be the last time she encountered the girl.

One of Henry's men at arms loitered outside the door to the solar. He gave her a lascivious leer when they approached and as Eleanor passed through the doorway she felt his hand squeeze her rear. She stopped and turned to smile broadly at him. She laid her hand on his face and caressed the dirty stubble on his cheek. She knew that he was drinking in the look of promise she was giving him. She slowly turned away as if with a hint of reluctance and reached down to explore his groin. "Not yet," she told him softly, "perhaps later though."

He grinned and closed the door behind her.

Amelie looked at her in alarm. "Ellie, what are you doing? Don't make yourself a whore to them!"

"Believe me sister, I would if I thought it would help but I've no intention of doing that yet. But nor am I just going to sit and wait for Henry to dispose of us."

She guided Amelie to a seat. Her sister in law was already out of breath though it had been but a short walk from the Hall.

"You can't know what Henry's planning," said Amelie, still wheezing.

"Yes, I can."

"Do you…know him then, this Henry?" asked Amelie, "I don't remember him from… before."

Before answering, Eleanor glanced across to Emma who had been dumped on the bare floor by the men at arms. She was either asleep or unconscious.

Eleanor took Amelie's hand in hers. "We thought the feud with the Radcliffes was over," she replied, "But it's not. What Henry said in the Hall is true: his mother, Edwina, was Lord Radcliffe's sister. Henry is my half-brother: my father's son with Edwina."

Amelie took a moment to absorb her words. "You know this to be true?"

"I've seen no document to prove it but Edwina told me so herself – I didn't believe her then but now…"

"We must get word to Ned at once…" Amelie looked pale, drained.

"You need to rest. I shouldn't have told you," said Eleanor. "All I've done is worry you more."

"How can I not worry about all of this?"

"But you have enough… with the baby. You are not strong, my dear."

"We've borne more trial than this before, you and I – and survived."

"Yes, we have but there are so many this time and so few of us," said Eleanor. "Lord knows what's become of Bagot and Gruffydd. With their help, escape might be possible. Perhaps they are in hiding."

Amelie shook her head, tears on her cheeks. "No, they're not. I saw them taken and they must have been hurt for they could hardly walk."

Eleanor felt like screaming. They were hurt - but by ale, not steel! But the knowledge would do little to calm Amelie so she held her tongue.

"If they still live, they'll be in the oubliette," said Amelie.

"Oubliette?"

"It is just a hole in the rock on which the castle rests," explained Amelie. "Ned and I explored every inch of this place when we first moved into it. But if they are there, it is a wretched place…"

Emma suddenly came to. She sat up and looked around her in confusion and then she climbed to her feet, barely glancing at them and retreated to the far end of the room.

Eleanor was losing patience with her sister: after all, had not she and Amelie suffered as much in the feud with the Radcliffes? In the last few hours the shock to all of them had been great but Emma seemed strangely devastated by Henry's reappearance. Although Eleanor was inclined to leave her to stew for a while, Amelie was not. Before Eleanor could stop her she got up and went over to Emma.

"Emma?" she ventured. Her soft enquiry broke the dam and Emma fell upon her knees, tears coursing down her cheeks and dropping onto the floor. In a small, terrified voice over and over again she begged God's forgiveness. Eleanor joined Amelie, sat down on the tiles beside Emma and gently took one of her hands.

"Sister?"

Emma stopped her muttered incantation and turned to Eleanor for the briefest of instants; then she snatched her hand away and turned back to continue her prayers.

"You told us at the time that Henry betrayed you," said Eleanor, "but he's not worth this torment. He's just … a man!"

Emma showed no sign of having heard.

"We all suffered, Emma, but we've put it behind us," said Eleanor getting up and returning Amelie to the bench. She meant it. It had been hard but she had put aside all the anger and hatred she had felt in the wake of Will's death. For a long while she had assumed that Emma had done the same but recent events had proven her wrong.

"Why should it make any difference that this Henry now claims to be your half-brother?" asked Amelie.

Eleanor was about to agree until a sudden, awful thought struck her. Emma had trusted Henry and been betrayed but just how close had she let Henry get? One glance at Amelie told her that her sister-in-law had just made the same deduction.

"Sweet Jesus, surely not," breathed Eleanor.

"I am afraid to even think so," whispered Amelie.

Eleanor stalked back across to her sister and dragged her whimpering to her feet.

"Did you lie with this Henry?" she demanded. The blunt question struck Emma like a cudgel. She pulled herself away and cowered again into the corner of the room. She could not say the words but she nodded, still sobbing.

"You stupid, stupid bitch! You were already carrying a child, you were married to Edmund and yet you lay then with Henry? What were you thinking?"

Emma stopped weeping, pulled away from Eleanor and sat sullenly below the sill of the large window. Eleanor sat down beside her and wrapped her arms around her.

"I know. I know I am none to chide you," she said, "and this is the sort of punishment that should have been mine, not yours."

"How could I know?" cried Emma.

"You couldn't have," replied Eleanor.

"Yet it is a mortal sin," whispered Emma. "I am truly damned."

"The Church declares many things to be mortal sins," said Eleanor, "but men still commit them every day. Besides, you didn't know, so how can it be a sin?"

After that no-one could think of anything useful or comforting to say and they lapsed into a long silence, each dwelling on their own terrible thoughts.

As the afternoon light began to fade Henry walked into the solar flanked by two of his men at arms. Emma fixed him with a look of pure loathing.

"You knew, didn't you!" she spat the words out. "You knew who I was and you lay with me anyway."

"I don't recall you complaining about it at the time," said Henry, "but I think you'd lain with a number of men that year – I can see how you might have been confused."

Emma got up from the window and went to stand in front of him.

"I may have sinned," said Emma, "but the Lord will see the wickedness of your part and will burn you for it!"

"Don't tell me what the Lord will do! I had fifteen years of hearing what the blessed Lord was going to do – from my own mother! And He didn't do any of it!"

"Lady Amelie's in pain," interrupted Eleanor, "This is no place for her. She needs to be in her bed. It's not right for her to be here. If you don't let her go to her chamber the child may die!"

"Mmm. Children die," replied Henry, "but you're all free to return to your own chambers now – in fact, I insist upon it. I don't need to keep you locked in. You're not going to take any risks because I have the two boys in my … care. They are your surety: as long as you do as you're told no harm will come to them."

"Aye, but for how long?" asked Eleanor.

He stood there smug and smiling; if she'd had a knife she could have cheerfully stabbed him in that grinning mouth.

"If you're thinking of getting out or if you're thinking that our dear brother, 'Lord' Ned, will soon be back, forget such fanciful thoughts. He's dead, lying in some forest in the north – so it's just you three and the children."

"Ned is not dead," said Amelie softly, "for I would know it, I would feel it. Ned is not dead."

"Whatever evil you do, Ned will surely kill you," said Eleanor, though she did not believe her own words.

Henry looked confident. "He's dead - but, even if he isn't, while I hold you in my grasp he won't try anything. If Ned Elder lives, he'll get no joy from these estates ever again – that I swear to you."

The door suddenly opened and Mordeur strode in.

"My lord, a messenger … from… " he hesitated.

Henry nodded. "Alright, wait. Ladies, you may go where you like within these walls but remember what I said about the children - so be careful."

349

He walked swiftly out taking Mordeur and the other men at arms with him.

29

26th May in the early hours, in the oubliette at Yoredale Castle

Bagot opened one eye but could see nothing. He opened the other eye but it didn't help. There was not a glint of light in the tiny place where they were confined. He ached all over. He had stupidly put up a token resistance and they had given him a good beating. Still, all his limbs seemed in working order – or at least working as much as they ever did these days.

He felt his way around: he was squatting in a rectangular hole, not quite square and not very big. It was hewn out of the very rock on which Yoredale castle stood so it was damp. It was probably the cold water dripping onto his head that had eventually brought him awake. It surprised him that after nearly three years at the castle he had never bothered to inspect the cell. Not that it would have made much difference for it held few mysteries.

A rasping cough sounded close by. "Gruffydd?" he whispered.

"I've a terrible head," growled Gruffydd.

Bagot laughed humourlessly. "That'll be that last flagon of wine you drank."

"No, it was the last flagon of wine you hit me with," moaned Gruffydd.

"Well, for my part, I'm sorry," said Bagot. He was sorry about a lot more besides.

"Ah, the fault lies with us both," conceded the Welshman

ruefully, "and between us we've doomed this household because we're not going to get out of here."

"Aye, shame's got a bitter taste to it," agreed Bagot.

"How long do you think we've been here?"

"Hours? Days? Weeks? Only the Lord knows how long but you're right: we're not going to be getting out."

"If I had a blade, I'd cut my throat," muttered Gruffydd.

"If I had one I'd cut it for you! Isn't it bad enough being here without you groaning on about it?"

Gruffydd did not bother to answer and they remained sitting in the filth. In the silence they heard a scratching noise.

"Is there any other soul in here?" asked Bagot aloud.

"There's no room in here for anyone else!"

The scratching became rustling.

"Rat," observed Gruffydd.

"No shortage of meat then..."

"Can't be bothered to try and catch him – he can see a lot better than we can!"

"Shit. We've been bloody fools..." observed Bagot.

"Aye, do you think they're treating the ladies well?" asked Gruffydd.

Bagot didn't really want to think about it. "Depends who they are and what they came for... and we know shit about either..."

"Well I'm not going to just sit here and die," said Gruffydd.

"You are if we don't find a way out," said Bagot, with a weighty sigh, "come on, let's cast about and see what we've got."

It would be a token search but they might as well do something. They both leant forward on their hands and immediately clashed heads.

"Watch out!" Bagot barked, rubbing his forehead.

"If I could see, I would watch out," retorted his companion.

Bruised but undeterred, they shuffled around to explore the tiny cell.

There was a sharp crack. "By St Stephen!" said Bagot after a moment.

"What?"

"I've found a friend." He rattled the bones he had knelt on. "Dear Lord - this fellow was in irons – pinned to the rock floor, poor devil."

"Oh, shit…"

"What?"

"Just shit… a mess of fresh rat turds," reported Gruffydd.

"By St. Michael, they'll come in handy," said Bagot drily. "This place could be worse, you know."

"I can't think how."

"In France, I found a terrible one, just a long tube in the rock. Once in, you never got out. You couldn't even sit, only stand."

"You're not making me feel any better," grumbled Gruffydd.

"Why do you think our friend was chained down to the floor?" mused Bagot. "Don't you think it's odd? Throwing him down here would surely be enough."

"He's your friend not mine and any friend of yours must have been an annoying sod. Perhaps he annoyed the Radcliffes too."

"The Radcliffes were a bad lot at the best of times," replied Bagot. He shuddered as he was reminded of the events of three years before. He didn't want to go through that again! Except… it seemed that perhaps he was. "I'm going to stand up," he announced.

"Oh, please don't."

"You can stand up too."

"Thanks very much," said Gruffydd.

They helped each other to their feet but their legs were so cramped they struggled to stand.

"Well, we're standing up. Now what?" enquired Gruffydd.

"You're taller than most wouldn't you say?" said Bagot.

"Taller than you, that's certain. What of it?"

"I think our friend was tall too; that's why he was chained

down," observed Bagot.

"But I can't even see the ceiling, let alone reach it?"

"Not quite, no, but I should think you'd be close enough if you reached up."

Gruffydd raised an arm in the darkness. "No, can't feel anything."

"You could lift me up then," suggested Bagot.

"Hah! You weigh too much! I'd need a God-damned trebuchet to lift you!"

"All we need is for them to open that trap door once," said Bagot, "but the pity of it is, they don't need to open it ever again. This is an oubliette: a place where you're forgotten and left to die. There'll be no food, no drink, no light; just damp air. Then we'll end up like our friend – a pile of bones, picked clean by the rats."

"Well it's just as well I've got a cheerful bastard like you for company!"

"We could make a noise," suggested Bagot, "force them to come down to quiet us?"

"What's to stop them ignoring us?" Gruffydd pointed out.

"They're not used to this place; they may want to check on us – just in case."

"They'll not even hear us," protested Gruffydd.

"Now who's being miserable?"

30

26th May, at Warwick's town house in

York

Henry shivered. There was a chill in the morning air and summer still seemed a long way away. He felt like a small boy again, back in France where his mother had sent him at the age of seven. His uncle, Lord Radcliffe, had arranged for him to be a page in the household of a Norman baron. Looking back he supposed he had been quite fortunate; a bastard could have no genuine expectations after all. At least he had been schooled in the essentials of knighthood - even if it was an honour he had never achieved. Yet, his strongest memory was of his tutor, a sharp witted and equally sharp mouthed cleric. Henry had been made the butt of every jibe imaginable by that man; even the thought of it made him shudder though he knew the cleric was long dead.

Now he sat waiting in a cold ante-room to see the Earl of Warwick and it daunted him more than he had expected. Warwick was an earl of great power but he was surely just a man all the same. The door to Warwick's privy chamber opened and when he was admitted by a servant he resolved to be confident from the outset, after all he was in a position of strength. He could give the Earl what he wanted: Ned Elder's head.

"God give you good day, my lord," he said, announcing his entry to the room.

The Earl of Warwick said nothing. He sat behind a large table, littered with scrolls and documents of all sizes. He held one of them in his hand and continued to peruse it in silence.

"My lord," Henry continued, "I am pleased to tell you that I have captured Yoredale Castle."

Warwick looked up from the piece of vellum in his hand and leaned back in his chair. He stared impassively at Henry as if he had not heard. His cool demeanour sent a shiver through Henry.

"My lord? It is good news is it not?"

Warwick returned once more to his document and said nothing for another few minutes. By the time he put it down, Henry's confidence seemed to have drained out of him, but he persisted nonetheless.

"I came at once to bring you this news myself ..." he said but he was sweating now, wilting under the weight of Warwick's stare. His throat felt dry.

"You came because I sent for you," said Warwick simply. "I ... sent ... for you." The Earl emphasised the words as if speaking to a child. "A man with any sense would realise that I had news to impart, not to receive."

"My lord..." Henry fumbled the words out.

"Do you know what this is?" asked Warwick, picking up the document once again.

Henry shook his head, not daring to speak any more.

"It's a death warrant," he said. "I shall shortly be overseeing the execution of a dozen or so of the King's enemies: men who lately fought against my brother John. If you don't stop talking and start listening, I'll be adding your name to the list - after all, you also fought against us, did you not?"

Warwick measured his words to the letter and though the words themselves should have been harmless, Warwick's tone cut Henry to pieces. He trembled in silence and a trace of a smile crossed Warwick's lips.

"So, to the reason I summoned you. His Grace, King Edward, showing extraordinary mercy, has decided not to execute Ned Elder and has instead sentenced him to five years in exile. This, in case you have forgotten, is the same Ned Elder whose head - or person - you promised to deliver to me. Had you done so then he would already be dead and the King's admirable inclination towards clemency would have been of no consequence. As it stands, however, Ned Elder is no longer an outlaw with a price on his head and he has until the first day of June to get himself away from these shores. If he does not, he'll be killed."

Henry assumed he should say something in response. "But what of Shard?" he scratched out the question. "I thought he would have finished off Ned Elder by now."

"Shard? Shard is most likely dead. I've heard nothing from him but a man of mine in Bishop Auckland claims he saw Ned Elder on the road south two days ago. That may or may not be true but Ned Elder is likely to be heading your way from Durham. He probably does not even know he's been reprieved. I have put some expensive men at arms at your disposal - it's time you earned them."

"I still have his sisters at Yoredale -"

Warwick nodded almost imperceptibly. "You have them at Yoredale - well and good. But if you want to keep that castle and his lands and titles then you'd better make sure he doesn't leave Yoredale before the 1st June comes and goes. The safest course for you would be to kill him."

Henry trembled as he replied. "But is he not protected by the King's order until then?"

"Yes, but he doesn't know that yet and neither will many others. Perhaps word of his reprieve did not reach you in time - unless of course, you fear him too much?"

"My lord; I shall take his life with pleasure. I have dreamed of it most of my life."

Warwick's expression did not change. "Your dreams are of no interest to me. Unless you kill Ned Elder, you're just another worthless bastard pissing out my coin. If you fail me, I'll hang you - and I'll hang that pretty little Elder wife you've got too."

"I promise you, my lord…"

Warwick interrupted him: "Promise me nothing; a promise disappears quicker than a fool's fart. All I want to hear from you is that Ned Elder is dead - only that. If you aren't able to tell me that, then you'd best throw yourself off one of Yoredale's highest towers."

Henry nodded.

"Oh, and one other thing: I'll be sending my own men to search for Ned Elder too. Don't expect anything from me if they find him first. Now, go. Your time is already running out."

Henry nodded. Now came the part he had dreaded most but Warwick had already turned his attention to the documents which covered the table in front of him.

"My lord?" Henry found his voice, if not his confidence. His stomach churned and his bowels felt loose.

"Have you forgotten something?" Warwick asked without looking up. Was there a trace of a smile there?

"We haven't discussed, my lord, how I should dispose of …"

"The spoils?" said Warwick. "We're not going to discuss it either."

He scanned the contents of his desk and picked out a small scroll. "These are my terms - not for discussion. They assume Ned Elder is dead and this document is therefore worthless if he escapes."

He handed Henry the scroll. "I suggest you look at it carefully - on your way out."

"My lord," conceded Henry and almost ran from the chamber. He hurried from the house stumbling as he passed the impassive guards at the gate. Then he walked briskly away and unsealed the document. It took him a moment or two to grasp the essentials for Warwick's terms had been set out by a legal hand. He leant back against a wall and almost cried with relief.

Warwick had secured a grant from the King of Ned Elder's lands in Yoredale to Henry. The power of the man!

He had feared that either King Edward would not have agreed, or worse that Warwick had not asked at all; but the Earl had kept his word. Henry was elated as he read through the rest of the provisions for the surviving members of the Elder family. Lady Emma was to have Corve Manor, wherever that was. He laughed out loud at the next part - Lady Eleanor and her bastard were to have Crag Tower - much good the smoking ruin would do the bitch! Let her rot up there in the far north where she could not interfere.

When he read the next two lines of the terms, the smile froze on his face for therein lurked a dark cloud. It was a small cloud, to be sure, but a worry nonetheless. Henry recognised that this was the shrewd Warwick making sure that his investment did not lose its value - planning for the future as a great lord should.

The grant of the lands to him was clear enough and if he died childless then his cousin Joan would inherit the Yoredale estates. Yet there was no mention of Ned Elder's titles, only the lands. That was odd; but what choice did he have? He was not going to return to Warwick and argue the terms - and Warwick knew it. The outcome might have been far worse: after all he had got what he wanted and he was relieved not to have joined the condemned men awaiting imminent execution. He was still in the hunt but he must despatch Ned Elder or he would have nothing. The design he had drawn in his dreams was still being built, stone by stone. He had always intended to draw Ned Elder to Yoredale to kill him. Still, if Ned Elder had been on the road for two or three days, he could not be far from Yoredale. Warwick was right: his time was running out.

31

26th May in the early hours, in

Eleanor's chamber at Yoredale

Eleanor searched Becky's face in the dim light of the single candle. "Am I being foolish?" she whispered.

Becky smiled and shook her head gently. "No, you give us hope, as always… but if you fail, I don't like to think…"

"Well don't. Just carry on with what you're doing!"

Becky frowned but finished binding the layers of linen around Eleanor's upper body, pulling the cloth tight across her scarred breasts.

"This won't be enough," she observed quietly.

"With the leather, it'll serve," said Eleanor, "and it's all I have."

Held in place across her stomach was a small but sturdy piece of hide Becky had filched from one of the workshops.

"Men fight with a padded jack at least," said Becky, "… or full plate."

"Men would," replied Eleanor with a grin. She pulled on her leather jerkin and Becky handed her a pair of dirty grey breeches.

"Where did you find these?" asked Eleanor.

"On one of the stable lads," replied Becky

Eleanor wrinkled her nose.

"Sorry about the smell."

"And he just gave them to you, because he has a dozen other pairs? I don't think so."

"It was more of a trade," said Becky awkwardly, "he's only a boy; it doesn't matter."

"Oh Becky…" Eleanor met her eyes for a moment and then looked away.

"Come on," said Becky quickly, "just that troublesome hair of yours to deal with now."

She had already plaited Eleanor's long hair and now she wound it carefully into a tight ball and pinned it at the back of her head. Then she picked up the simple white coif, placed it over her head and tied it under the chin.

Eleanor drew herself upright. "Now, how do I look?" she asked.

Becky laughed. "You look like … no maid – or man – I've ever seen!" She stopped laughing then. "You're as you used to be, in our sweet youth: part maid … part man…"

Eleanor sighed. "I wasn't even part maid for very long, was I? I shouldn't have asked."

She picked up Will's swords which she had wrapped in linen cloth and thrown under her bed before she was taken. She drew out each blade: they were dull and the one she had used for practice with Gruffydd had a rough edge. Will used to keep them so bright and sharp; she should have taken more care of them. Still, it was not going to matter much now.

Becky helped her strap the two leather scabbards to her back and then guided her hand as she carefully sheathed each sword. "You'll never sheathe them on your own," said Becky.

"Oh, Becky!" Eleanor stifled a laugh. "I've a feeling that'll be my smallest worry!"

Becky laid a gentle hand on her shoulder. "Could we not wait for your brother?"

Eleanor shook her head. "Who knows when, or if, Ned will get back? He could be up in the marches for weeks, even months. My sister will do nothing. There's no one else."

"But the Lady Amelie seems worse – and the birth can't

be far away now," said Becky.

"All the more reason to get her away from Henry; if he wants Yoredale, he won't let Ned's heir live!"

Becky nodded, her face taut with worry.

"Now, are you ready to play your part?" asked Eleanor.

"Yes, I know. I'll get Jane from the guardhouse and meet you at the nursery."

"Yes, but you stay hidden and do nothing until I get there."

"I know," repeated Becky. She suddenly seized Eleanor by the shoulders and hugged her close. "Take care, Ellie."

Eleanor flashed her a smile, kissed her on both cheeks and then took a deep breath.

"I always take care, my dear. It just doesn't seem like it to anyone else!"

"Wait," said Becky and opened the chamber door. She peered outside into the passage. "Clear," she said.

Eleanor nodded and left the chamber at once, worried that any further talk might lead her to change her mind. She knew if she was wrong she would condemn them all but she put that from her mind and made her way silently down the spiral stair to the first floor. Behind her was the kitchen and, assuming Henry had not confined all the servants, they would soon be up and about, lighting ovens or whatever else they did at this ungodly hour of the day. This was the difficult part: she needed to pass through the butteries and down into the vault below the buttress tower in the centre of the north range. Someone was bound to be sleeping in the adjacent Hall and she could not afford to disturb them.

She had rarely visited the butteries but her recollection was that they were usually well ordered with every item stored in its proper place. She had a feeling the cook was quite particular about such things. Now the butteries looked as if Bear had taken an axe to them: sacks of milled flour knocked over, a barrel lying on its side smashed open and the hooks for hanging the meat scattered across the floor. She stepped carefully around the debris to get to the partition at the rear of the Hall. She stood behind it, listening but all she could hear from the Hall was snoring.

She turned away and descended the next curving flight of steps down into the wine cellar where there was further evidence of ransack and small pools of wine still lay on the stone flags. She stared at the low vaulted ceiling and a thought suddenly struck her. She stopped and reached over her shoulder to draw out a sword. She couldn't. She stooped awkwardly and finally managed to do it. She puffed out a sigh of relief. Will's scabbards might look impressive but they were utterly useless in a cellar.

She moved on, the blade held out before her, expecting with every step to run into one of Henry's men at arms. She crossed the chamber to the well where a single torch shed some flickering light. Almost burnt out, she thought as she entered the next cellar. Ahead of her lay the passage which ran under the Hall. It was so gloomy she could not see the end and her breath hung in the air beside her. She continued along the passage, nerves as taut as bowstrings. She was about halfway along when she sensed a movement behind her. She turned quickly but kept the sword at her back, held firmly in her right hand. A figure stood about five yards from her. She could only see his outline against the glow of the torch behind him but he wore a sword which told her he was one of Henry's men. She could afford no delays. She tightened her grip on the sword and began to walk towards him, stopping barely a yard away. Now she could see his face: young and uncertain. Shit!

"God give you good morning, sir," she whispered in what she hoped was her huskiest, most seductive voice.

"I think He already has," replied the youth. Her manner of dress clearly confused him at first but as she came closer he must have realised that she was no man. When she spoke, his face cracked into a broad grin. Eleanor smiled back and leaned in towards him. It was not the first time a man had underestimated her, and he carried on grinning as she brought her sword around and thrust it straight up through his throat. His mouth froze open in shock but he made no sound. She pulled back the blade and he dropped to his knees. Blood spurted crazily onto his chest and the splashes that landed on her chin and neck seem to sting her.

She leant on the sword, gulping in deep breaths as she watched him die. It did not take long. She was not sure how she felt: she had killed before but this seemed different. He didn't look vicious, or brutal. He hadn't struck her first yet she had done for him. Forget him, you stupid bitch, she told herself, forcing back the tears. There's no turning back now.

The youth stopped twitching and she sighed. Then she wiped her bloody sword on his shoulder and inspected the corpse swiftly, relieving it of the small axe she found in his belt. He was too heavy to drag out of sight, so she moved on swiftly.

She paused for a moment by the door which she hoped led down to the oubliette and then carried on along the passage until she came to a stair which she expected would bring her up by the postern gate. She stole up the first few steps with her sword held upright, close to her breast, ready. She was careful not to scrape the naked blade against the stone; she did not want to disturb any more men at arms.

The postern was important: if a hasty escape was needed, the postern would be it and she wanted to know how many men guarded it. She was lucky: two men were at the gate but both had their backs to the stairs. She retraced her steps back down to the cellars and returned to the door she had passed earlier. For a moment or two she rested her head against the door and listened. Nothing. She tried the door; it was unlocked but it creaked alarmingly as she opened it. To her relief she found no-one on the other side of the door. She found no torch either.

The dim light from the passage showed a flight of rough steps immediately in front of her; they seemed to be hewn from the very rock. She closed the door behind her and was plunged into darkness.

Foolish child, she scolded herself.

She crouched down and began to edge her way down the steps using the tip of her sword as a guide. The musty air was cold but her hands were sweating.

A sudden volley of shouts from below shattered her nerve, She cried out in shock, dropped her sword and slipped down the remaining steps to land with a heavy thump on a platform of wooden boards. Then, in the darkness, there was silence again, just the sound of her own breathing and somewhere the distant drip of water on stone. Her limbs felt intact but there would be some bruises. Best think before you move, she told herself. She thought about the voices - she knew them both and she almost wept with relief.

"Gruffydd? Bagot?" she whispered, her face close to the wooden floor.

There was a pause before she heard Gruffydd's muffled reply. "Lady?"

She wiped away a tear. "Stop weeping like a child!" she berated herself aloud.

"Are you alright, lady?" asked Gruffydd.

"Never mind that," said Bagot's voice, "can you get us out?"

"Well, it's what I came for," she replied, "but I can't see anything down here."

"Yes, we'd noticed," said Bagot.

She explored the floor and quickly found a raised edge of timber: the trapdoor.

"Shit," she muttered, clutching a hand now embedded with splinters. The door didn't seem very large so she tried to lift it but, although she could raise it a fraction, it was held firmly down.

"Haste is needed, lady," urged Bagot from below, "the noise we made will draw the guards."

"Really Bagot?" she replied. As if she didn't know that better than he did. In the blackness she investigated the fixing: it was held in place by a short length of rusty iron. She tried to move it with her fingers but it was too stiff. Then she remembered the axe which she had stuffed into her belt. She drew it out and swung the head of the axe at the iron. Missed! She felt for the iron again. Missed again! She touched the end of the bar once more and swung again moving her hand at the last moment. "Shit! Oh, good Christ!"

"What is it?" asked Gruffydd, his voice full of concern.

Eleanor said nothing. If she made any sound just then it would be a scream of pain. Instead she trembled, her hand clenched between her legs as she waited for the pain to subside. Then she tried to flex her hand. Not shattered then, nor even broken; just yet more bruises.

"I'm alright," she said.

"Well come on then, lady," Bagot hissed impatiently.

"I should leave you here, you impatient bastard," she muttered. She stopped for a moment and listened once more. Had she heard movement on the other side of the door above her?

If so the need for speed was greater still. She swung the axe a dozen times in succession: some missed, some hit and made a dreadfully loud clang; but gloriously, several blows loosened the bar and she was able to force it through. She gripped the edge of the door and began to lift it. It was a struggle but its small size meant she could just do it. Thank God!

Then the cell door above her swung open with a bang and torchlight flooded the small dark place. She shut her eyes – she couldn't see anyway. Where was her sword? She had put it down to use the axe. Oh, shit! Where was the axe? She flicked open her eyes: there were two of them, one by the door holding the torch and the other coming down the steps towards her with his sword drawn. She suddenly remembered that she had another sword and managed to drag it out in time to parry her opponent's first blow. There was no room to move on the narrow landing and he easily grasped her sword arm and punched the hilt of his sword into her forehead. She fell back against the wall, stunned, beaten and already starting to grieve for her son and the others. She looked at her opponent, no callow youth this time.

He shook his head. "You shouldn't play men's games," he said coldly. He called up to his comrade: "Come and take her upstairs; I'll close the trapdoor."

Eleanor sat on the platform waiting for her head to clear. When it did she saw the other man at arms descending the steps. He still had the torch in one hand; his sword was in its scabbard. He reached down to the floor to push herself up. Her hand touched metal and she smiled. With his assistance she came up fast and swung the axe hard onto the first man's sword hand. For once she hit what she was aiming at and he cursed, dropping the sword. At the same time his right leg disappeared through the open hatchway and he screamed as his crotch struck the edge of the wooden frame.

The man who helped her up could not draw a weapon without letting go of either her or the torch. Thus he released her hand and she drove the axe onto his wrist. She knew at once that she could only wound him but it was enough. He fumbled for his sword with the injured hand but she found her own first and drove it hard up between his legs - and he screamed too.

Between them they had made so much noise that many must have heard it so she had to be swift. She sliced her sword across the neck of the other struggling guard. Bagot pushed him aside as she helped him up with Gruffydd pushing from below. It seemed to take forever then to raise Gruffydd's bulky frame from the oubliette even with Bagot's help. She kept glancing up the steps but could not see the doorway. The torch lay guttering on the bottom step. She picked it up and ran up the steps. The door was shut but surely the cries must have been heard. Gruffydd and Bagot staggered up after her. Gruffydd handed her the second sword. "We are in your debt, lady," he said.

She put a hand on his arm and beamed at him.

"You're bleeding," he said, his voice gruff with concern. She put her hand to her forehead and it came away smeared with blood.

"Just a little," she dismissed it.

"Now what?" enquired Bagot, strapping on the scabbard he had acquired.

Quickly she explained to them what she intended to do.

"St Michael's Blood!" breathed Bagot. "Are you sure?"

"You don't think we can do it?" she asked.

"I think if we tried it fifty times, we might do it once and live," replied Bagot.

"What then? Any better ideas?" she asked.

"Not a one!"

§§§§

Bagot led them along the passage to the now unguarded postern gate and they pounded up the steps in the northwest tower. Whilst he darted off to go to Amelie's chamber on the first floor, Eleanor and Gruffydd went up to Emma's chamber. Eleanor woke up her sister whilst Gruffydd ran on to the nursery. Emma looked horrified and for once Eleanor could understand it: bruised and bloodied, she must look a hideous sight.

"Come!" she ordered. "We'll get the boys and then we're going."

"Going? Where is there to go?" breathed Emma. "We can't escape these men!"

"Coverham Abbey. It's the nearest sanctuary. Come, dress yourself! And quickly! Bagot and Gruffydd are with me."

Emma hesitated. "Coverham? Yes, yes, the monks will take us in. But a pair of women and two old men; how can we even get there?"

"Don't you want to save your son?" Eleanor's anger flared.

"You'll kill us all," whispered Emma.

"We're going; stay if you want to," said Eleanor and left.

She ran through the empty guest chamber and reached the nursery where Gruffydd had subdued one of the guards but was still grappling with the other. She did not hesitate but stabbed the soldier in the back. He fell to the floor and she stared at the bloody wound she had made.

369

"I am a bitch; I am born of hell's fire," she muttered, struggling to control herself.

"Don't think about it, lady," advised Gruffydd. "You may yet do worse things to save your son. You've done this once before – you can do it again."

The nurse screamed when they entered the room.

"I've had more than enough of your whining," said Eleanor, knocking her to the floor, "A far braver girl than you has been spreading her legs all night for Henry's men! Think on that!"

She lifted a troubled Will and tried to soothe his fears.

Gruffydd scooped up Richard but paused mid-stride. "Lady Emma?" he said.

"I don't know if she's coming," replied Eleanor, tight-lipped.

"But she must… we've got her son."

Becky ran up with Jane. The girl looked half dead: a large bruise covered one cheek and her eyes were red rimmed. Her grey shift was torn and stained.

"Sorry," said Becky, "Durston wouldn't let her out of the guard room without a few more favours … from us both. But we're here and my girl's still alive." She kept her arm tight around her cousin, who said nothing.

Gruffydd swore colourfully. "Your pardon, lady, but I'll have that bastard Durston!"

Eleanor looked at Becky. "How many others were in the guard room?" she asked, unable to keep the sadness from her voice.

Becky shrugged. "A couple, I think."

"I'm worried we haven't seen Henry or Mordeur," said Eleanor, "they're the ones to worry about!"

"Aye," agreed Gruffydd, "they could just be waiting for us at the main gate or the stables - they'll know we'll make for the horses."

"You go on down with the boys," said Eleanor, "I'll get Emma up. I'll carry the cow if I have to!"

"No!" The Welshman was adamant. "Lady, there are few

enough of us as it is. We'll go together."

So they hurried back to Emma's chamber. To her surprise Eleanor found her sister dressed and waiting for them at the door.

Eleanor interrogated her with a glance. Emma looked pale but determined.

"I'm not quite the weak fool you think," whispered Emma. Eleanor gave her a curt nod and went on to descend the spiral stair. At the first floor she paused.

"Bagot should be here by now with Lady Amelie," said Gruffydd.

"Go on," said Eleanor, "he may need some help with her. Wait for me below."

Gruffydd hesitated.

"Go," she hissed, "time's too short, Gruffydd. Get the boys down to the stables!"

Gruffydd nodded reluctantly and carried on down the steps. Eleanor ran along the passage to Amelie's chamber where she found Bagot bending over his mistress who still lay in her bed.

Eleanor stared at him.

"She can't go anywhere!" said Bagot, "her hour has come... the birth will be soon."

Amelie, pale as ice, lifted her head up and looked her sister-in-law in the eye. "If you can get out, you must! Take the boys and go. You must! Henry will kill us all anyway..."

Eleanor felt crushed, thwarted at every turn.

"I'll stay here, lady," Bagot said to Eleanor. "Gruffydd can see you safely away."

"You can't stay here! She's birthing... you're a ..."

Bagot raised his hand. "A man, yes. But please, don't argue about it, my lady. Lady Amelie and I've chewed it about: there's nothing else to be done. Just go."

Eleanor looked at them both in disbelief. Then she ran to Amelie and flung her arms around her. "I can't leave you," she said, "I just can't!"

Amelie was weak but still strong enough to give voice to

her will.

"Sister, you cannot leave. And yet … you must not stay. I, and my child… we will be safe in God's hands." She smiled. "He has not let me down yet and neither has dear Master Bagot." She moved her hand to rest on Bagot's arm.

At that moment Eleanor knew that, whatever she did next, Ned would never forgive her. She kissed Amelie softly on the forehead.

"You sat beside me and took my hand when Will was born. I will come back for you," she said simply. "I will help you…"

"God speed to you, my lady," said Bagot.

Eleanor nodded and ran out of the chamber. She fled down the stairs, almost tripping as her eyes blurred with tears. Be strong, she told herself. Be strong!

She joined the others in the large paved passage by the postern gate.

"Do we wait?" asked Gruffydd.

"No!" She brushed aside their questioning looks with a fearsome stare. "You should've saddled the horses by now!"

Gruffydd shrugged. "Very well, lady. Keep close and keep quiet," he ordered them as they passed through the small door to the stable feed store. Two stable hands lay on the floor against the far wall. Gruffydd nudged them with his boot.

"Don't pretend you're asleep – we've made enough noise to wake the dead!"

They opened their eyes. One of them stared at Eleanor. "Lady?"

"What?" she snapped.

"Are those… are those my britches?" he asked.

"You've been paid well enough for those!" said Becky.

"I was just asking…"

"Well don't!" said Becky.

"Show some respect, boy!" said Gruffydd.

Eleanor was not surprised how empty the store was: winter fodder was in short supply. It had been another hard winter and none of the latest crop of oats had yet been harvested.

"Lady!" Gruffydd hissed at her. He stood by the door leading into the stables. She slid a sword from its scabbard and took up station beside him. He motioned the others to remain in the shadows and carefully lifted the latch. The door swung open easily for it saw frequent use. They crept into the darkness and felt their way past the stalls which lay on their right hand. The only sound was the occasional snort or cough from one of the horses. To their left were several pairs of tall doors which could be opened onto the castle's central courtyard.

After they had explored to the end of the stalls, Eleanor stopped. "Most of these stalls are empty," she observed.

"Aye, so where are the rest?" asked Gruffydd. "They can't have put them all out to the farms!"

They retraced their steps back to the store.

"Only five left," said Eleanor.

"The new lord went out last night with quite a few," volunteered one of the stable lads.

"Henry went out? He's not here?" said Eleanor, "what about Mordeur?"

"Didn't see the Frenchie with him."

"Shit," said Eleanor. Mordeur was more dangerous than Henry.

"It's still good news, my lady," said Gruffydd. "That explains why there were so few in the guardhouse. We might just do this, my lady. By my count we've already taken out four."

He turned to the grooms. "Now, the pair of you, saddle the horses – five should do for us. Quickly, mind!"

The two lads hurried to saddle the mounts and then opened one of the high doors into the courtyard to lead out the horses.

"Wait!" warned Gruffydd but it was too late. One of the lads cried out and was thrown back through the door to land with a crash against the boards of a stall. Eleanor stared at his still form, thinking he had been kicked. She stepped forward to take the reins of the wandering horse but Gruffydd dragged her back and a bolt punched into the stall. They crouched to the floor and the other stable hand dived into a nearby stall.

"Crossbow," mouthed Gruffydd.

A voice sounded out across the courtyard: "Go back to your chambers! You're not leaving here tonight. You're not leaving here any night." He laughed long and loud.

"Durston!" Becky ground out the word.

"Are you sure?" asked Gruffydd.

"Of course I'm fucking sure!" Becky spat back at him.

"Where is he?" Eleanor asked Gruffydd.

Gruffydd pointed up. "Best place would be the south rampart: near the guard house and with a perfect field of fire over both the stable doors and the main gate. But I doubt if he's on his own: there were two bolts one after the other; one man couldn't reload that fast."

He stood up. "I'll have to go up there."

"No," replied Eleanor, "I'll go. Stealth is hardly your strength; they'll hear you coming! And surprise has worked quite well for me so far."

"Very well," agreed Gruffydd, "but remember Mordeur is around somewhere and…."

"I know: he's more dangerous than all the rest put together," said Eleanor.

"You'd better warn Bagot on the way," said Gruffydd.

"Give me your long knife," she said.

"Are you sure?"

Eleanor nodded grimly. "I'll need to get close…"

"Aye, I suppose so." His hand trembled as he handed over the blade. "Take care, lady."

She grinned then set off through the fodder store pausing only to hug Becky and plant a large kiss on Will's tearstained cheek. He looked utterly forlorn when she left but she put him from her mind as she hurried up the steps.

Bagot was waiting on the first floor landing. "I thought

you'd have gone by now. When I heard the footsteps, I thought ..."

"No matter," interrupted Eleanor and told him quickly about Durston and Mordeur.

"Aye. Mordeur, eh?" he said, "I'd better come up with you."

"What about Lady Amelie?"

"She's holding on well and there's a girl in there with her now. She should be churched with women now."

Probably the saintly nurse, she thought. About time the craven bitch did something useful!

"Anyway, you're not going up against Mordeur without me," said Bagot, "I know that bastard better than anyone!"

Bagot led the way up the steps, though more slowly than Eleanor would have liked. He ignored the narrow stair that led up to the tower battlements and headed for a door which accessed the rampart of the west wall.

"From here I can walk along the curtain wall to the southwest tower and on to the south rampart," he explained. "You take the same door on the east side to work your way along the north curtain. We'll meet either side of the southeast tower. But take care and keep low – we know they're there somewhere. And if you find Mordeur, back away."

She left him and went out onto the rampart above the north curtain wall. It was a simple, low crenellation and she moved along it bent almost double. Fast and silent. She reached the northeast tower which she knew well for it gave access to her own chamber and went through it onto the east curtain wall. She stopped. Someone could be a few yards away with a crossbow pointed at her. She wouldn't see death coming and the bolt would pass right through her. She crouched, shivering a little, and scanned along the rampart ahead. There was a faint glow at the far end by the tower – the door to the tower must be open. Of course! The crossbowman would need some light to reload.

She realised in alarm that she could now see her own

breath in the cool air – and if she could, so could others.

§§§§

Bagot rubbed his leg ruefully as he crouched by the rampart wall. The doubts were closing in on him: he was getting too old for this sort of thing; everyone thought he didn't know it - but he did. He knew better than anyone how he wheezed with the effort of simply climbing the stairs and how his damned leg throbbed with pain day and night unless deadened by the relief of beer or wine.

He might take on Durston, though it would be hard against the younger man; but Mordeur? He would need God to play a part if he was to live until morning but, as a lifelong blasphemer, he had long since abandoned hope of assistance from that quarter.

This would be a severe test of him and his leg, perhaps too severe. Yet, was this not why Ned had left him there - trusting his most loyal captain to keep his wife and sisters safe? He had let his lord down and it had been left to Lady Eleanor to lead the fightback. She had risked all for those she loved; now it was time for him to earn his corn.

He looked along the rampart; there was little light and he could barely see to the other end of it. He suspected that Lady Eleanor would be moving a good deal faster than he was. Come on, you old bastard. He urged himself forward. Let's see if you've still got some steel in that rusty backbone. So what if his leg already hurt, he wouldn't feel it when he was dead. He thought about drawing his sword but up there, in the darkness, a dagger would be more use.

"I suppose a silent prayer couldn't hurt," he breathed as he started slowly along the rampart. He looked up at the night sky. Well, Lord, if you're seeking out some old soldier to aid tonight…perhaps you could overlook a few of my past faults: the mistakes of my youth and… also my middle age… and, even more so, my latter years. I'm not making any promises mind, but I might try to forget the countless times

You've left me in the shit.

He could see a faint glimmer now in the eastern sky. "Well, at least You're not still abed," he muttered. He stopped and listened. Close by, he could hear a crossbow being reloaded. He wondered idly if the crossbowman could see him so he pressed himself back against the wall. He tried to crouch down but his leg would not bend and he found himself neither up nor down. Any doubts about his visibility were soon dispelled as a quarrel seared a cut across the top of his ear as it flew past.

He grunted and struggled upright, hearing the ratchet of the crossbow as it was rewound again. Run, you stupid bastard, he told himself. Run? He hadn't run for three years. He set off towards the far end of the rampart and collided clumsily with his attacker as he was raising his weapon. The bolt flew off into the air and Bagot, man and crossbow smashed with a dull thud into the door of the southwest tower. Bagot lay on top of his opponent who tried to batter him with the bow.

"Nothing wrong with my arms," growled Bagot. He pushed the bow down with his left hand and stabbed swiftly with the knife in his right. He chuckled to himself, partly with relief and partly because it occurred to him that if all his fights could be accomplished lying down, he would still be a formidable warrior... but then that was the easy part of his task.

He staggered to his feet and opened the door which led onto the tower's spiral stair. There were footsteps below - shit! He should have met up with Lady Eleanor at the southeast tower by now but he dared not leave men at arms behind him. Well, she would have to manage on her own a while longer. He slid his falchion from its worn leather scabbard and waited on the top step for the man to come to him. The only dim light was coming from a torch somewhere below and it got dimmer as the bulk of the man filled the lower part of the stairs. His shadow preceded him as he mounted the steps and Bagot braced himself on his good leg.

§§§§

Eleanor started moving along the rampart slowly on all fours with her knife held in her right hand. Down below in the courtyard a single torch burned low and she could make out the open stable door. Suddenly someone, she thought probably Gruffydd, darted across the doorway and a she heard a deep thwack as a crossbow fired nearby. She crouched motionless and in the darkness she heard the snapping noise of a crossbowman reloading.

Gruffydd had not crossed the doorway for exercise; he had given her a chance. She got up and ran along the rampart. By the tower door a shadowy figure was bent over with his back to her. She was a step away when he half-turned towards her and dropped the bow to fumble out a sword. He was too slow and his sword was still half in its scabbard when Eleanor drove the knife down onto his back. It met some resistance from his padded jack so she stabbed again and plunged it up to its hilt down through his neck and into his chest. His anguished cry cut the night and then died with him.

She moved to the door and risked a glance inside. No-one. She swiftly examined the dead man. Was it Durston? She was not sure but she thought not. She waited by the door to catch her breath and settle her jangling nerves. Where was Bagot? He should have joined her by now - yet Bagot moved slowly so perhaps he was still on his way. She could not wait forever. She looked to the east and was horrified to see a thin sliver of light on the horizon. Darkness, their friend, would soon be gone: she could not afford to wait any longer.

She slid through the door into the southeast tower; it was not a part of the castle with which she was familiar. It housed the castle garrison and there could be men in any room on any floor. She took the passage around the tower to get to the south rampart. The door to the rampart was ajar. She stepped out onto it and advanced carefully along the boards. Soon she was at the far end having encountered no-one. Perhaps she had already killed Durston and he was the only one up there? She opened the door to the southwest tower and at once she could hear the faint clatter of combat below her. Durston and Mordeur were not on the battlements; they must be in the west range and Bagot was there on his own.

She sheathed her knife and drew a sword to descend the spiral stair. She slipped, almost fell and gratefully clutched the central pillar of the stair to save herself. She searched through the second floor chambers but they were empty except for the nurse, still lying on the nursery floor. Oh, shit! Perhaps I killed her, she thought. Then she realised that the sounds of fighting had grown fainter. They must be on the floor beneath her. She returned to the stairs and went down to the first floor. The solar door was shut but she could hear the clash of swords beyond it. She hesitated and then opened the door.

§§§§

Durston must have only seen Bagot when the heavy sword battered him on the shoulder. He fell back down the steps with only a grunt of surprise and Bagot went after him. But by the time he had limped down to the first floor landing, Durston was on his feet. Even so, he looked in a bad way and there was enough blood on his jack to tell Bagot that another such blow would finish it. Durston backed away out of the stairwell and through the door into the solar. Bagot followed him, still cautious. He couldn't believe his good fortune but perhaps God had smiled on him after all. All the same, his leg was complaining already and he had hardly got started. Durston might be wounded but he was still dangerous.

"Shoulder a bit sore?" he said to Durston.

"You always were a lucky bastard, Bagot," said Durston, "but I'm not finished yet."

"The blood dribbling down that shattered arm tells me a different story," replied Bagot with a bitter smile. "You'll answer now for those young lads you slew in the forest - and for the cross of blood you daubed on poor Richard. Cowardly acts they were but then you've always been a coward."

"If you think you can kill me, then go ahead and try," said Durston.

Bagot heard unhurried paces rap a harsh rhythm on the stone nearby. Durston heard them too and continued to back away around the solar, knowing that Bagot could not move swiftly enough to cut him off. Bagot followed, keeping one eye on the door to the tower steps. When he saw Mordeur framed in the doorway his heart sank. Mordeur slammed the door shut and grinned.

§§§§

When Eleanor entered the solar she saw at once that Bagot was in trouble, trying to fend off both Mordeur and Durston. Bagot saw her come in but the others had their backs to her. She flung the door open wide so that it crashed back against the wall and just for an instant Bagot's opponents hesitated. He seized the opportunity and sliced his falchion across Durston's neck. Mordeur ignored the falling Durston and hacked at Bagot. Eleanor hovered nearby anxious to intervene.

"Go, my lady!" Bagot told her. "I've got him! Go whilst you can!"

It seemed to her that the struggle was a good deal more evenly balanced than Bagot claimed but she took him at his word and went out and on down the steps back to the stables.

The others greeted her with relief but she pushed straight on to the horses.

"Mount!" she ordered. "Gruffydd, we'll go out the postern; we've no time to fuss with the main gate and portcullis!"

"Aye, dawn's coming and there'll still be men about," he agreed. He helped the women up onto their mounts and then lifted up the boys to Becky and Jane. Eleanor leapt up onto the side of a stall and swung herself into the saddle. Gruffydd shook his head and mounted his own horse.

"Take the forest path to the west first," ordered Eleanor.

"Aye, we'd best ride a drunken path first to lose any that follow," replied Gruffydd.

"I'm sure you know more about drunken paths than the rest of us," remarked Eleanor, "so you'd better lead."

He threw her a sheepish look and then took them out into the courtyard, through the covered stone passage that led to the postern gate. Eleanor hesitated and then turned to the stable lad.

"I'll be back!" she called to him, "and I'll bring you your britches!"

He gave her an uncertain grin and she followed the others out through the narrow gate. They had stopped.

"Get on!" he cried. "What are you waiting for?" But then she saw what had halted them. Becky and Jane had dismounted and knelt beside their cousin's body. Eleanor joined them. Sarah lay facing the sky, her neck at an unnatural angle yet there was not a mark on her.

No-one knew what to say; they just wept. Eleanor glanced up at Gruffydd.

"Lady…" he pleaded.

"I know," she muttered. She lifted up Becky and hugged her. "Be strong, my dear," she said softly.

Becky shook her head. "It's too much," she cried, "too much…" Then he picked up the sobbing Jane and saw her remounted. She passed Richard up to her again; the girl stopped crying and took him in silence.

They rode off across the fields towards the forest but the light was improving all too quickly. Eleanor steeled herself against all grief. She had killed several times before dawn and Gruffydd was right: she would need to do it again, whatever the cost. As soon as she had seen the children to sanctuary she must return for Amelie and Bagot. She could get the midwife and hope that she arrived in time - or at least before

Henry returned.

When they reached the edge of the forest several men stepped forward out of the trees with bows levelled at them.

"Halt!" cried one. As all of them pulled up, Eleanor reached for one of her swords and almost lost her balance. She gripped the horse tightly with her knees to stop herself slipping from the saddle. Finally, she dragged out the sword with an angry flourish; she was not going to be taken at this final stage of their escape.

"Lady Emma?" said one of the men, lowering his bow.

Eleanor thought he looked familiar – in fact most of them looked familiar. She looked across at her sister who was staring in disbelief at the youth who had spoken.

"Garth?" breathed Emma.

Eleanor frowned and tried to interpret the look on her sister's face; it was an expression she had never seen there before.

"Lady Emma," said Garth, "what a relief!" Eleanor had no difficulty with the look on Garth's face.

The other men facing them also put aside their bows and Eleanor studied the small group. They were mostly very young but one that stepped forward she did recognise.

"Ragwulf? Isn't it?" she said.

"Aye, Lady Eleanor, it is."

"But you're one of Lord Elder's men at arms. How is it you're still in Yoredale?"

"I fell ill with a fever before he left. My son went north with him in my stead. Since the castle was taken I've been keeping a watch. Last night they tossed the bodies of my friends and brothers outside the walls in a godless heap, so I gathered some help."

Eleanor recalled the pile of corpses displayed on the floor of the Great Hall. "They were very young," she said, "and very brave…"

"Those here are even younger," replied Ragwulf, "but they don't lack for mettle."

She looked doubtfully at the young men: boys, only boys -

some carried bows taller than themselves. She looked hard at Ragwulf - he was a different matter altogether. Thank the Lord for his fever. She thought he had been with Ned since before Towton, so he was a veteran of sorts. He was tall and quite good looking she decided - if a little grey in places. He was probably more than twice her age...

"Lady, dawn is already here," urged Gruffydd.

"Ragwulf," she said, "your comrades will escort the others to Coverham Abbey but I want you to come back to the castle with me to get the Lady Amelie out. She is ... well, we'll need a litter of some kind and we'll have to fetch the midwife to take with us."

"Of course, my lady! Harry, John - cut some staves," he ordered.

As Eleanor expected, Gruffydd was not happy. "I'll come back with you too," he said.

She laid a hand on his arm. "I want you to take my son to a safe place, old friend," she said.

"But my place is with you - stopping you getting yourself killed!" he complained.

"Take Will and keep him safe; Will is all I have," she said.

He nodded with only a glimmer of protest. "But take care, lady," he warned, "our attackers could return at any moment."

"Yes," said Emma, "and Henry left his whore behind, so he'll be back!"

Eleanor paused thoughtfully. "You saw the girl?" she said. "Where was she?"

"I saw her pass my chamber. I thought it was you at first."

Eleanor was still for a moment, piecing together what she had seen in the past hour. What had Bagot said? He had mentioned a girl. She suddenly felt very sick: what had she done?

"Lady?" enquired Gruffydd.

"Ride on!" she snapped at him. "We'll follow as soon as we can. Come Ragwulf, hurry!"

She turned back towards the castle without even stopping

to say farewell to her son.

"What about the midwife?" asked Ragwulf.

"There may not be enough time!" shouted Eleanor. "Now ride on, all of you! "

She hoped she was wrong; she even prayed she was wrong. But if she was right, she hoped they would be in time.

32

26th May at dawn, in Amelie's chamber at Yoredale Castle

Amelie woke with a start. It was dark in the chamber, the window shrouded by tapestries hung to dim the light ready for her confinement. Her back ached; a dull, deep-seated ache. The pain must have woken her. No, she could hear someone in the chambers further along: boots scraping on stone flags, steel ringing on steel and harsh voices too - Bagot's among them.

Her hand lingered over the child. She knew about childbirth: she had witnessed it enough times. She had played her part with Ned's sisters. She had held Eleanor's hand when they had brought young Will screaming into the world and cradled Emma's son, Richard, moments after his birth. She knew all about birthing, but still... she had never given birth before. She knew it was the most natural act for any woman. It was simple. Yes simple, but never safe. She had seen what could go wrong in many a cottage across the estate. The midwife from the village should have been with her. All had been arranged but since Henry's arrival the gates had been shut – no-one came in or went out. She should have women around her, but surely, if needs be, she could do it herself – with God's help.

She found herself staring at the doorway. Joan, small and still, was leaning against the door, her face expressionless.

"Lady Joan?" said Amelie.

"Lady Amelie," responded Joan, "you've woken up. Pity."

She remained by the door, as if considering her next move.

Amelie tried to sit up but a sharp pain lanced up her back...that had not happened before. She fell back, taking shallow breaths, but her eyes never left the figure in the doorway.

"Will you help me birth my child?" she asked.

Joan seemed to make up her mind and took a step forward into the chamber. "The birth is near?" she asked.

"Will you help me?" repeated Amelie.

Joan looked around the chamber. "It seems there is no-one else," she said.

Her voice was light, matter of fact, but Amelie was wary. She slid her right hand under the bedclothes and found the hilt of the small knife that was hidden there. Her mother's blade, though much good it had done her mother. She had put it close by to cut the baby's cord if it fell to her to do so. She watched Joan walk slowly towards her and she gripped the knife more tightly.

"You know this child is the very worst thing for Henry," said Joan.

"An honourable knight does not make war upon women or children," said Amelie.

"I don't think anyone who knew Henry would describe him as 'an honourable knight' – not even his mother - that would be the mother that your 'honourable' family killed," said Joan, smiling. It was a thin smile and her voice was cold as winter. She stood beside the bed and rested one hand on the linen head sheet that covered the pillows.

"A fine bed, lady," she observed softly, inspecting the coverlet and rich hangings.

"Will you help me or not?" demanded Amelie. The words came out harsher than she intended, fuelled by another spasm of pain.

"I certainly won't kill a child," said Joan, "so I fear ... it will have to be the mother."

Amelie grasped what she had said only slowly but then brought the knife out from under the covers. She held the knife point aimed at Joan's throat but once more her body was racked by pain. Joan seized her hand and the knife flew skidding across the floor. Joan ran to recover it but after a cursory search she gave up and returned to Amelie who screamed, convulsed again with pain. She tried to calm herself: her boy was taking his first steps into the light and she must bear the hurt for his sake.

Joan moved to the bed once more and Amelie tried to raise an arm to push her back. Her arms felt like lumps of wood. How weak she had become. Joan easily pinned down her arm and reached for a pillow.

"Bagot!" Amelie screamed as Joan carefully placed the pillow over her face. Amelie wriggled under it but Joan was strong, stronger than Amelie would have imagined. Fear swept over her but the instinct of a mother fought its way out. She forced up the pillow and gulped a breath of air. Then it was pressed back down again; once more she willed it off her mouth to snatch some breath only to find it clamped down upon her.

§§§§

Bagot knew he had dealt Durston a mortal blow but Mordeur's blade was already singing through the air at him and he only just parried it in time. He swatted away the next blow more easily and confidence coursed through him. Mordeur might be fitter than he, but he was not necessarily any stronger.

His illusions did not last very long as Mordeur pressed him back against the door to Ned's Great Chamber. The door was ajar and he stumbled backwards through it into the room beyond. He kept his balance - just, but his leg screamed and the pain seemed to claw at every part of him. Mordeur must have seen his weakness for he struck again and again, forcing him across the chamber.

Bagot felt weary, his falchion seemed heavier with every block he made. The room spun around him and he realised that he was falling - falling onto the dais where his lord had looked down upon his tenants. Behind him the Elder pennant, a blur of pale blue, hung still against the wall. Here Lord Elder gave his judgements. Ned would judge him ill if he did not protect his lady, he thought. Lady Amelie was his prime concern - a solemn trust given him by his lord. Whatever it takes, he thought, I must keep Mordeur from her. Then he hit the floor of the dais.

Mordeur stepped onto the dais sword raised for a killing blow. Bagot swung his falchion low and it cracked into the Frenchman's knee. He cried out and twisted as he fell, his sword thrust taking Bagot high upon the chest. Bagot grunted but he was no stranger to pain and dragged himself back against the wall. Mordeur lay on the dais; he was breathing heavily and glaring across at Bagot.

Mordeur might be down but he was by no means finished. Still, now at least neither of them could stand properly. They lay at opposite ends of the dais and looked at each other. Mordeur examined his left leg ruefully and sighed. Bagot was not surprised: he could tell that the knee was broken at the very least. Bagot was bleeding down his chest but the wound would not kill him - not unless he bled to death.

"Ah, Bagot," said Mordeur, "we were comrades once; how is it we find ourselves here - at each other's throats?"

"It's a long time ago that we were on the same side," growled Bagot. In his youth he and the Frenchman had fought side by side in the French wars. Both had fought under the banner of Sir John Elder, Ned's father - the banner that hung on the wall now between them.

"It was after Castillon - that was the end of it all," said Mordeur.

"Castillon," murmured Bagot. He would never forget the disaster at Castillon when the great old warrior, Lord Talbot, had fallen. He and Mordeur had fled with all the rest - those who survived.

"We took different paths," said the Frenchman.

"Words now will change nothing," said Bagot, "too much has happened; too much blood, too many lives lost."

Mordeur nodded. They both knew it was too late for reconciliation now.

Mordeur moved first: he drew out a dagger and staggered to his feet using his sword as a crutch. Bagot did not bother with his dagger; he was going to have enough trouble holding his sword. He got up by pushing his back against the wall and relying on his one good leg. They faced each other but neither made a move, each knowing that a single mistake now would be the last. Bagot knew the ragged wound in his chest was weeping steadily; perhaps his opponent was waiting for him to lose a bit more blood.

They held each other's eyes for a heartbeat longer and then both took a painful step forward. Bagot's falchion was half-raised but his arms trembled with the effort; Mordeur's dagger was held out in front of him. A short blade against a long - it was surely no contest.

They were barely a sword's length apart now, eyes still locked together. An image flashed into Bagot's head, an image of hand to hand fighting at Castillon, amidst the carnage wrought by the French cannons. He remembered the last time he had seen Mordeur: in the centre of it all, surrounded by blood smeared blades, fighting on. Mordeur had been a hard man to kill - he still was.

The Frenchman's dagger moved swiftly but so did Bagot's falchion, fizzing through the short space between them and carving down through Mordeur's shoulder and neck. The stroke was only halted by the edge of his steel breastplate. Still it was enough; Mordeur's face went white as bright blood flowed and his legs crumpled under him. His hand released its grip on the hilt of his dagger, leaving it where he had plunged it at the moment of impact - in Bagot's side.

Bagot let his weapon clatter to the floor. He leant back against wall again and examined his new wound. He glanced down at Mordeur; his body was already still. The Frenchman was a hard man to kill, but so was John Bagot. He tried to reach down to pick up his sword but he almost blacked out as he bent forward. He really should bind up his wounds.

Lady Amelie cried out in the chamber next door; he could not trouble her at such a time - the birth chamber was a place for women now in any case. The second cry was different for, though he could barely stand, he still knew his own name when he heard someone scream it. He cursed himself roundly and took a step back towards the solar. That one step told him that if he did nothing to attend to his wounds he would not take many more. He summoned his remaining strength and lunged for the chamber door; his Lady was only a short passage away but that passage seemed endless. The door to the chamber lay open and he looked on in horror at the scene being played out within. He was spent but heart alone got him across the room and he seized Joan, hurling her aside and the pillow with her.

§§§§

Amelie gulped in short breaths and stared at Bagot: he looked utterly spent. If he had won his battle he had done so at a high price: his breast was red with blood and a knife was still lodged under his ribs.

"I came when you called, my lady," he wheezed. She knew it was bravado but she loved him for it. She glanced at Joan who lay on the floor by the door.

"Oh Bagot," cried Amelie. "You are the one that needs help now." She clutched his arm. "Where are the others? The boys?"

"They've gone to the abbey, my lady, to Coverham - you remember?"

"The abbey," said Amelie. Yes, of course; how had she forgotten that?

"But Lady Eleanor will come back for you," said Bagot.

"But I need help now Bagot. I am frightened for my child. For God's sake, help me birth my son!" It would be a son - of that she was in no doubt.

"Of course, lady," he said, but she saw the utter confusion on his face and it did little to reassure her.

"What shall I do?" he asked.

Searing pain gripped her again - was it supposed to hurt so much? She said a silent prayer as more waves of pain shuddered along her spine. She spoke between short breaths: "Take my hand, Bagot. Stay with me. The child is coming … Ned's boy is coming…"

Bagot took her hand in his - still grimed with blood. "I'll not leave you, my lady."

Amelie saw the tears filling his eyes but she felt the strength draining from her as her body convulsed and her baby began to move.

"He's coming, Bagot…" She couldn't speak any more. She tried to remember what to do. She wanted to scream but instead she panted through the pain. Bagot still gripped her hand but his terrified face was not helping. She shut her eyes and pushed hard hoping it was the right thing to do. Then Bagot released her hand.

"Bagot!" she groaned and tried to reach for his hand. She opened her eyes and saw Bagot falling in a spray of blood. Joan's blood-spattered face hovered a foot away from hers. Amelie saw the knife in her hand and flapped her arms in vain as Joan stabbed her in the breast. She willed her baby on but her chest seemed to contract. Joan plunged the knife into her again. She screamed to push her child out into the world. She could see the blood seeping from her wounds, running down the linen coverlet.

Downstairs, a door slammed. Joan stared at her, then looked down at her own blood-stained hands. "God forgive me," she murmured and fled from the chamber leaving the knife in Amelie's chest.

Amelie couldn't breathe. She felt no pain in her chest but the core of her body was in agony. She could feel the strength draining from her; she was too weak … her son would not be born. Oh, Ned, our loving labour was in vain. She squeezed her eyes shut and darkness engulfed her.

33

26th May, early morning at Yoredale Castle

When Eleanor reached the postern gate with Ragwulf it lay half open, just as she had left it. They dismounted and left their horses outside. She knew they must be careful for she had no idea how many men were left or whether Mordeur was still there to lead them. Thus they had agreed to stay together and to make straight for Amelie's chamber.

Eleanor drew out a sword and Ragwulf looked at her strangely

"My lady…forgive me, but do you know how to use that?"

"If we had more time I'd show you," she said crossly, "but for now you'll just have to believe me, won't you?"

He shook his head and pulled a face but she did not know him well enough to interpret it.

"Lead on then, my lady," he said.

Eleanor passed through the gate and along the short passage into the courtyard. She scanned the doorways and battlements but saw no-one. Ragwulf stopped close beside her.

"Could Bagot have got them all?" he whispered.

She recalled Bagot when he last saw him, already bloodied and weakened. "No, I don't think so."

Ragwulf nodded. They moved back to the door at the foot of the spiral stair. "Lady Amelie's chamber is up there," she said softly.

She took a deep breath, opened the door and climbed the steps quickly. Though they tried to make as little noise as possible, their boots sounded on the stone treads. At the top of the steps Eleanor touched Ragwulf's shoulder and urged him into the passage beyond Amelie's chamber. He nodded and moved swiftly on. She hurried towards the door of Amelie's room. It was open and she stepped inside but came to a stop after only a few paces.

Bagot lay on the floor in a pool of blood, his face a grim, final mask of despair. She ran to the bed. Amelie's white linen shift was soaked with blood, her face had a deathly pallor and her eyes were shut. The hilt of a small knife protruded obscenely from her breast but the blood no longer flowed. Eleanor touched her cheek. It was cool to the touch.

"Oh, Amelie…not you…"

Ragwulf came in. "Durston's dead and Mordeur too; there no sign of Bagot…"

His voice tailed off as he took in the scene. At once he bent down to Bagot. Eleanor looked at him and shook her head. She slumped onto the bed and sobbed, her arms wrapped around Amelie.

"It shouldn't have been you," she cried, "of all of us, not you."

"Lady, we should go," said Ragwulf, "we can do no more here but die."

She ignored him and he laid a hand upon her shoulder; Eleanor whirled around, her face full of rage. "Don't touch me!" she yelled at him. "Did I give you leave to put your hands on me?"

"I only meant…we should go," he said, taken aback by her reaction.

"Well go then; I don't need you now!"

"Be calm, my lady, or whoever did this -"

"Whoever did this? I know who did this! Do you hear me, Joan?" she screamed the accusation until she felt her lungs would burst. "The bitch that did this will feel my sword run the length of her body. I will spit you for this!"

"Hush, lady!" said Ragwulf.

She turned on him. "I'll spit you too if you dare hush me again!" she cried.

But he did dare. What's more, he seized her and clamped his hand over her mouth. She struggled in his arms but he was stronger. She tried to reach a blade, any blade.

"Stop fighting me," he said softly, his face close to hers. She tried to jerk her head at his but could not move it from his tight grip. She thought of biting his hand but he had clamped her jaw shut.

"Listen!" he hissed at her, "In the name of God, listen!"

Since she could not break free she had to humour him but later she would kill him for it. Perhaps he had heard men stirring nearby - even so, no-one was going to manhandle her and live to tell the tale in some tavern. She could hear nothing.

She waited for him to release his grip; he did not.

"Are you listening?" he demanded. She growled at him but then fell silent.

He turned her towards the bed and she heard it, a faint sound like a lost lamb bleating for its mother. And at once she understood. Ragwulf released her and she swept aside the bloody coverlet and blanket. There was more blood underneath.

"Oh, sweet Jesus…" she murmured.

Amelie's son looked up at them and cried.

Ragwulf swiftly seized the knife from Amelie's breast and cut the birth cord. Eleanor lifted the baby and wrapped it in a piece of linen cloth already laid out for the purpose.

For a moment they could only stand there in silence, Eleanor hugging the mewling child to her breast. Tears streamed down her face and she did not know whether she cried for joy or sorrow.

Eleanor held the baby before Amelie. "You gave your life to your son, sweet girl. And I swear to you I'll keep him safe until Ned comes."

She turned to Ragwulf. "Thank you. You're a strong man

- who has good ears," she said. Then she reached up and lightly kissed his cheek.

"God has given us a miracle," he said. "But what are we to do with it?"

The baby nuzzled unhappily at her breast.

"We must find a wet nurse at once," she said.

"This is no ordinary child," he said, "we must be careful."

She knew he was right but she could feel herself irritated by how often he was being proven right. She nodded. "No-one else must know of this birth - at least not until we can get the boy to Ned."

"It won't be easy," said Ragwulf as he pulled the coverlet up over Amelie's face.

They moved towards the chamber door but somehow she could not bear to leave. Poor Bagot lay where he had fallen and they had unwittingly walked his blood around the floor. Eleanor sighed. "I know. Staying here won't bring her back."

They had all promised Ned that they would keep Amelie safe - and they had all failed.

"I should never have left her," she breathed. "If I'd stayed she wouldn't be dead."

"Her life was always in God's hands, not yours," said Ragwulf. "She died for the boy. He's the important one now."

She did not know whether to hit him or kiss him again. Instead she passed through the door way and into the passage. She wrapped the infant as close to her as she dared to try to keep it well hidden but she didn't want to smother it.

"If we meet anyone, I'll do the fighting," said Ragwulf sternly.

"Well, just now I've my hands rather full in any case," she said. "But if any man - or woman - sees the child, you will have to take them with us or kill them. Do you understand?"

"I understood before you said it." He started down the steps.

"Wait," she said, "what became of Amelie's blade?"

"I have it."

"Then give it to me."

"Why? We just agreed I'd do the fighting -"

"Give it to me," she said, "so that I can defend myself and the child."

He shrugged and handed it to her.

"And should I see Joan, I can bury it deep inside her wretched heart, if she has one!"

They reached the base of the staircase and turned towards the postern gate. There were now two men at the gate and they looked up in surprise. Eleanor stood behind Ragwulf so that they would not see the tiny bundle against her breast.

Ragwulf had drawn his sword at once; she hoped he knew how to use it.

"If you let us pass through that gate then there's no need for any of us to take a hurt," he told the guards. There was enough uncertainty on their faces to suggest they might just step aside; they must have known by now how many casualties they had suffered. Yet they were powerfully built and well-armed men; they might fancy their chances against one man and a woman.

It was a tense moment. The two men exchanged a glance and she could tell that they had decided not to fight. They stepped aside and she moved closer to Ragwulf as they walked towards the gate. At that moment the baby decided to lend a hand and started to bawl.

"Oh, shit!" breathed Eleanor. Then a lot seemed to happen at once.

One of the men at arms said "Wait!" Ragwulf struck hard and fast with his sword, stabbing him between his legs. He crumpled to the floor, clutching his groin but his companion dealt a blow at Ragwulf and cut him on the shoulder. He was better harnessed than Ragwulf and battered him several times. Ragwulf seemed unable to do anything but parry.

The baby cried louder; she was worried others might hear. Clutching the child in one arm, she took out the knife. The man at arms was so preoccupied with finishing off Ragwulf that he paid her no attention. He never saw the blade as she thrust it through the side of his neck twisting it as she pulled it out. He dropped like a stone - aye, a stone that spurted blood. Ragwulf stared at her in disbelief.

"I thought we'd agreed: I'd do the fighting," he said. It was the first time she had seen him angry.

"Well you weren't doing it very well!" she retorted and bent down to the wounded man.

"I'll do it. Get mounted!" ordered Ragwulf.

She obeyed meekly but loitered long enough to hear the man's last rasping breath. It gave her no pleasure but she knew she would have to get used to it.

They rode out as far as the trees and then stopped. She checked on the baby and was relieved to find him unhurt.

"I don't suppose you know of anyone who might be a wet-nurse to the boy?" she asked.

He offered her a withering look by way of reply.

"Well, we must find one within a few hours, or the boy is lost."

"The child has been saved once, God will see him safe," said Ragwulf.

"No. We will see him safe!"

"How in God's name can we find a wet-nurse?"

"I'm not asking you to find a two-headed beast, Ragwulf - just a wet-nurse!"

He said nothing after that so she took his silence as agreement.

"We need to move," she said.

Still, he said nothing and his expression was stern; for an awful moment she thought he was going to ride off and leave her. Her manner had clearly displeased him; well, he would just have to put up with her.

"When you've finished sulking, perhaps you could fulfil your obligation to Lord Elder and help his sister keep his son alive!"

Her words stung him to respond. "I need no reminders of my debt to Lord Elder," he said sharply.

"You're a great brute of man; surely you can put up with a

foul-mouthed woman for a few hours? I need your help…where can I take the child - a safe place where we might at least find a midwife who'll keep her mouth shut?"

"No-one will keep their mouth shut if Henry asks the question," he said.

"Oh, don't trouble yourself any further; I'll find somewhere myself!" said Eleanor and she rode away from him into the forest. She had no idea where she was going but she heard him following her and soon slowed to allow him to catch up.

"I'm sorry, my lady," Ragwulf said. He didn't look very contrite but it was enough.

"We must work together if we're to save Ned's child," she said. "You may disapprove of me but we are not the ones who matter here…now…"

He nodded. "There's an abandoned place by the river which might serve us for a while and it's not far from Carperby - there might be someone there…"

"Carperby's a busy place - too many wagging tongues," she said.

"We'll head south to Thoresby and take a quiet path west. We won't pass through any villages that way."

"Very well. Let's do that. I fear this poor child's hours are running out."

DEREK BIRKS

34

26th May, midday in Yoredale Forest

Emma pulled up her horse and stared across at the remains of the curtain wall. Beyond the wall lay Elder Hall, or what was left of it, which wasn't much. She felt a tear meander down her cheek and brushed it gently away. What had once been the centre of her life was just a pile of rubble and burnt timbers now. Her late husband, Edmund, had decided to level it as a gesture of his power both to her and her brother. Edmund's gestures were always lavish.

Gruffydd had decided they would take a circuitous path to Coverham Abbey, avoiding the shorter, but busier, route to the southeast and instead keeping to the heavily wooded areas of the valley. Although it more than doubled the length of their journey, it would, he argued, make it more difficult for any of Henry's pursuing men to discover where they had gone. Emma was inclined to argue - she wanted to get to Coverham without delay - but when Garth had agreed with Gruffydd she had acquiesced gracefully. She had forgotten though that they would pass so close to her old home and when they did the sight of it took her unawares.

Despite living in the Vale all her days, Emma remained a stranger in its vast expanse of woodland. She had not spent her youth exploring the forest paths, as her brother and sister had done. On the few occasions when she had ventured into the forests she usually managed to lose herself - one leafy glade looked much the same as another to her.

"Lady?" enquired Gruffydd.

"A moment," she said, drinking in the devastation.

As long as she could remember she had run the household at Elder Hall. Her mother had died when she was but a child - six was it, or seven years old? For several years she had learned her role and then, on her tenth birthday, her father had appointed her mistress of his household. She remembered that day well enough: a chasm of fear at dawn and a flood of tears at dusk. Yet she had learned quickly and in the end made herself indispensable to her father. She had been happy then, knowing her own place in the world and knowing that she was valued by her father for what she did. Then one day she had opened the gates to Lord Radcliffe and all that she had was ripped away from her.

The very thought of it sent a chill through her. She glanced at Garth for reassurance; she knew he would have his eyes on her - he always did. He grinned at her in response and her heart gave a flutter of excitement.

"Lady, we should get on," said Gruffydd.

She frowned at his impatient tone but nodded and urged her horse on. The others followed and Garth moved his mount closer to hers; she darted a grateful smile at him. Had the others noticed? Gruffydd stared straight ahead - his face a tapestry of misery; it was not hard to guess who he was worrying about. The two boys looked relieved to be out of the castle; and the servants, Becky and Jane - well, they wrestled silently with their grief. The other youths with Garth looked nervous; she reminded herself that Garth was older; the rest were lads from Redmire and Aysgarth who were too young to serve in the castle garrison - most were no more than fourteen.

She gave silent thanks that Garth was still alive; God had watched over him for her. If he had not been wounded by Durston in the weeks before then he would have been on duty at the castle the night Henry took it. He would have fought bravely and then he would have died and his cold, mutilated corpse would have been among that terrible pile of young bodies in the Hall.

He rode comfortingly close to her now and she could not

resist looking across at him again for it was not just her heart that was aroused by his nearness. Her hand reached across and rested for a moment on his shoulder; it was an instinctive gesture and she drew back hastily. What was she thinking? She did not dare look back to see who had noticed. Yet since that day spent with him in the forest they were bound to each other; she felt it and she knew he did too.

They made good time from Yoredale and crossed the river at a ford not far beyond the ruins of Elder Hall. They followed the south bank of the river eastwards then struck away from it to avoid the village of Aysgarth where tongues might wag of their passing. Then they returned to the river bank again before riding up over the moorland and on down into the Cover valley where the abbey lay.

The sight of the mill on the banks of the Cover warmed her heart for the abbey church would soon come into view through the trees. The abbey was like her, battered and bruised by the wickedness of men, but rebuilt and still standing proud. She grinned like a small child when she saw the familiar round archway of the gatehouse. She had passed through it many times in the past. Now she would ask Reedman - or more particularly his abbot - for sanctuary within the abbey's stout walls until her brother could free her and the children from the threat of Henry. But how long, she wondered, would they be there?

Gruffydd interrupted her thoughts. "Lady, someone must go back to the castle."

"Why? That would be foolish!" Gruffydd could be tiresome at times.

"Someone must go back to the castle," he insisted. "Someone must watch for Henry's return, for the Lady Eleanor, or Bagot or Lord Elder, when he comes back."

He was right, she realised. "Very well, you go then," she said.

"I would gladly go," said Gruffydd, "but I'm not getting any younger and there are others who know the forest better than me - besides I should stay with young Will."

"I'll go," said Garth.

"No - not you," said Emma sharply, "you must stay here. Your place is with me - and my son."

Garth looked at her fondly, but she could see the determination in his eyes.

"Gruffydd is right, my lady. I know the forest well and I'm not sending one of the younger ones. It has to be me."

Emma hesitated. "Very well, if you think so," she said. She saw the sense of it and the way he looked at her perhaps it was best that he was not so close by - not yet.

"But you will take care, Garth," she said quietly.

He turned his horse to pass by alongside her and stopped. He took her hand gently in his and kissed it. There was a wicked twinkle in his eye as he said: "I will ever be your loving servant, my lady."

She wanted to embrace him, to hug him to her breast, to kiss his sweet face; but she did none of those things. She just nodded and he let fall her hand to ride away. She bit her lip as he disappeared into the trees.

"Lady, we should go in," urged Gruffydd.

If she had held a dagger just then she might well have plunged it into him, hard. Instead she showed him a stony face and rode in silence towards the abbey gate.

35

26th May afternoon, at an old mill south of Carperby in Yoredale

Eleanor sat on a pile of straw that Ragwulf had gathered with the baby against her breast. Her tears were running down onto the linen shawl she had wrapped him in. His cries were getting weaker now, but he was still fighting, clinging to life by his tiny little finger tips. If Ragwulf didn't return soon she would just have to run into Carperby and scream for a wet-nurse. There would be little point in keeping the boy's birth a secret if he died because of it.

Ragwulf had taken her to the old mill, long ago burned down with the miller in it. That was a sad tale too. Little remained of the building: the water wheel lay rotting on its supports, barely scorched; but the mill itself was mostly a charred patch of earth - all save the part she was now sitting in, which boasted a roof at least and two lengths of wall. It did not look safe and she had told Ragwulf so but he had insisted that it would serve. Serve for the baby to die in, it seemed.

She heard footfalls nearby and picked up her knife... Amelie's knife. She was relieved when Ragwulf put his head around the edge of the wall. He came in but he had brought no-one with him.

"You were supposed to find a wet-nurse!" she said. The baby stirred, feeling her anger, and she tried to calm herself.

"Where do you expect me to find a wet-nurse, my lady? What girl wanders around the villages crying: "wet-nurse for hire?" He held out a leather flask to her.

"What's in there?" she asked.

"Goat's milk, my lady; it was the best I could do…"

"You can't give a new born goat's milk!"

He looked genuinely distraught. "Why not? It's milk, isn't it?"

"It's not the same as a mother's milk…"

"My lady, I heard of a shepherd's daughter gave birth out in the hills - she gave her baby goat's milk."

"What happened to it?"

"I don't know… I suppose it was alright…"

"You expect me to feed my brother's son goat's milk?"

"Aye…if you want him to have a chance."

Eleanor pulled out the stopper and sniffed the liquid inside; it smelt rank. She rammed the stopper back in. "Where did you get it?" she asked.

"From a horse - where do you think? Are you going to feed him with it or not?"

Ragwulf was angry now - well that made all three of them.

"It smells odd. What was in the flask before you put the milk in it?"

"Mead," he said flatly.

"Mead," echoed Eleanor, "you want me to feed my nephew on mead and goat's milk…"

She had been weeping before when there seemed no way to save him. Now she had one poor hope for the boy and her tears came out in a flood. She was always so certain, direct; now she did not know what to do. She still held the leather bottle in her hand but it shook so much Ragwulf took it from her. She looked at him and shook her head.

"Will you help me?" she asked, choking back her tears.

"I'll do whatever you ask, my lady," said Ragwulf. He looked pale.

"It'll be a new experience for both of us then," she said. "Hold him, if you please." Ragwulf took the child warily. "And don't drop him!" she said but he nearly did when she uncovered her breasts.

"Close your mouth, man. You must have seen a breast before."

"Aye, but not ... a lady's breast," he said.

"Do you mean not a pair of breasts with an ugly great scar across them?"

He turned away. "I don't know what to say, my lady."

"You don't have to say anything - just help me. Give me the child."

She settled the baby against her breast and he nuzzled gratefully against her nipple only to find she offered him nothing and he grumbled weakly again.

"What are you doing?" he asked.

Eleanor looked at him for a moment. "Well, he can't drink it straight from the flask can he? You don't know me very well, so this is going to be difficult. But, just for now, imagine that I'm not Lady Eleanor. Pretend I'm...your wife, or a woman you know well."

He looked utterly confused so she carried on.

"I want you to dribble the milk onto one of my breasts and the baby can take it from there."

He looked at her in disbelief. "Why don't I just dribble it onto your little finger and he can suck it from there?"

Eleanor said nothing for a moment. She felt a complete fool. "Well why didn't you suggest that sooner?" she snapped. She handed him the child and quickly covered herself.

Once a whore, always a whore, Becky would have said. One moment's panic and you bring out your goods. What must this man think of her? Well he couldn't think any less of her than he already did. .

"I suppose now that you'll boast to all you meet that Lady Eleanor needed no invitation to show you her breasts."

He disarmed her with a smile. "I don't recall seeing the Lady Eleanor's breasts... only those of a woman I know well." His eyes met hers; she saw the humour there and could not help grinning at him.

She cradled the boy once more and Ragwulf held the

bottle over her finger letting the thin white liquid drip along it whilst she tried to coax the baby to take it. It was easier than she expected for the child was so hungry he would probably have drunk anything - that did not mean the goat's milk would do him no harm though. Yet, when the milk ran out, the infant was still craving more.

Ragwulf nodded and disappeared with the flask. She wondered whose goats he was milking so freely. When he returned she had fallen asleep and so had the child. When Ragwulf woke her she thought the boy had died but he was still warm against her when they fed him again.

"This might keep him alive for a few hours more but it doesn't solve our problem," she said. "I'll have to take him to a midwife; she would know who might be able to nurse him."

"If anyone in Carperby sees you with that child they'll know at once whose it is; there was only one woman with child at the castle. They'll know it's Lord Elder's son - and that means that, sooner or later, your enemies will know too."

"But we must have a wet-nurse; no matter what it takes! He can't live on goat's milk!"

"I've an idea," he said, "I've thought about it - while I was milking the goat - and I think it'll work. You must leave him with me."

"No!" she said at once.

"Hear what I've to say first, my lady. I'll take him to Goodwife Harding in Carperby. She knows near enough every girl that gives birth around here. She'll find me someone - and there'll be no connection with the Elders."

Eleanor frowned. "So you'll just amble up to Goodwife Harding and say: look, I've come across this baby - she'll want to know where it came from!"

"Be calm, lady. I've thought about that as well."

"For a fighting man you've been doing far too much thinking," said Eleanor. "The boy's staying with me."

"Listen to me," he pleaded, "I'll tell her I got a young squatter girl with child and her family disowned the babe… and she brought it to me… and I fed it goat's milk on my finger to keep it alive so far."

"She won't believe it," retorted Eleanor. "Forget that idea; he's staying with me!"

"It matters little whether she believes it or not, she'll still help me find a wet-nurse for him. And how else can we do that?"

For the first time Eleanor allowed herself to consider his proposal seriously; she owed him that much. The more they talked about it, the more she came to believe he might be right. But could she trust this man at arms with Ned's heir? He had been loyal to Ned for years, fought alongside him; now he had not baulked at helping her to get the child away - even milked goats. She smiled at the thought.

"Can I trust you?" she asked, looking him in the eye. She bit her lip as she studied him and he held her gaze.

"Swear to me," she said in a low voice, "swear that you'll never leave him - not for a second - even when he's at the breast of a wet-nurse."

"I swear to you that I will keep him from all harm and return him to you or to his father."

She did not drop her eyes. "What do you swear by, Ragwulf?"

His voice was solemn. "I swear by my faith in the old Norse gods."

"The old Norse gods - what are they to you?"

"My blood is the blood of Norsemen; my family has lived in these dales for centuries and my father taught me of the old gods. They are not the faith I wear on a Sunday but they are the faith in my heart."

"Well, it's a weak oath if you swear by something I don't believe exists," she said.

He frowned. "So be it. I swear by my faith in the old Norse gods and ... by the breasts of a woman I know well."

She laughed out loud. "That oath will serve very well but if you don't keep it, these breasts will hunt you down and kill you."

"I've no doubt of it," he replied, "but you won't need to

for if I break this oath I'll already be dead."

"I'll go to Coverham and tell my sister about Amelie and Bagot. Where will you be?"

"I'll take the child and wet-nurse to my cottage at the west end of Carperby. Any of the lads who are at the Abbey can tell you where it is."

"Well then…" She handed him the child and shook her head. "I've shed more tears in the past day than all the rest of my days together." She bent over the child and kissed him on the head. Then she reached up to Ragwulf and pressed her lips to his cheek.

"Take care, my lady," he said.

She stood for a while longer; reluctant to leave the boy now that it came to it. Then she steeled her heart, went out, mounted her horse and rode off. She did not call out, she did not look back and she did not shed any more tears.

§§§§

When Eleanor arrived at the abbey she intended to tell her sister all that had happened since they had parted after their escape from the castle. Emma had taken up residence in the Abbey's guest house which though not exactly opulent was very comfortable with an open Hall, strewn with fresh rushes, and sleeping cubicles for several guests. Emma herself slept in a small chamber off the Hall whilst the children, Becky and Jane took the cubicles and the young men slept on the Hall floor, as did Gruffydd. Eleanor saw at once that there was little space for any more fugitives let alone an infant and a wet-nurse.

She sat down with Emma in her chamber and spoke of Amelie but the moment she described the scene, Emma cried out and others rushed into the room. Emma blurted out at once that Amelie and Bagot were dead and a sudden gloom descended upon them all. Eleanor had not had time to mention the child. Several times afterwards she tried to tell her sister but something held her back - did she trust Emma not to tell someone?

Soon enough everyone knew that Lady Amelie and Bagot were dead. Amelie was looked upon fondly by Ned's tenants and the canons of Coverham, who also fulfilled the role of priest or vicar in several of the local communities, were well aware of her reputation for kindness and humility. Her death could not pass unnoticed, nor that of Bagot who had become something of a legend amongst the young men of Yoredale.

Gruffydd took Bagot's death especially hard. "I should've been there," he muttered to himself, when heard how his old warrior comrade had died. He remained unusually quiet for the rest of the day, Eleanor thought. Well, he was not a young man; the oubliette and the escape had taken their toll on him. She was not surprised when he took himself off to a corner of the Hall and tried to sleep. Later in the evening, she covered him with a blanket as he snored fitfully on the floor.

She had some hours to reflect upon what she had done with Amelie's child. She realised that just as news of her death would spread quickly, any mention of the birth of a child would be seized upon with desperation by those who loved Amelie. If the child was in danger now, how much greater would the danger be if every man knew of his existence? So, she decided, she would tell no-one until Ned returned: he would be the first to know.

PART FOUR: BROTHERS

36

26th May evening, on the road to
Yoredale Castle

Henry was weary. He had ridden hard and was simply relieved to see the square towers of Yoredale Castle in the distance. It was late in the afternoon but he reassured himself that they would reach the castle by dusk. Then he could rest, plan and prepare.

As they rode closer to the castle, however, he began to feel uneasy. He could see no-one at the battlements; they had clearly become careless in his absence - he would have to do something about that. By the time the walls rose ahead of him his anxiety had deepened into a feeling close to panic for there was not a man to be seen anywhere on the ramparts. His banner still flew above the northwest tower and the gate was firmly shut but there was no sign of life.

He heard a few murmurs of disquiet around him as several of his men made similar observations. He quickened his pace but with every yard of ground he covered, his fears increased. When he pulled up outside the main gate, no-one challenged him - or even seemed to notice him. Now he was really worried - what if Ned Elder had somehow managed to overtake them and had already retaken the castle? But he realised quickly that if Ned Elder had the castle he would have it well guarded and would certainly have noticed his arrival.

He pounded his fist on the gate and waited impatiently. He looked at the men with him; their horses wandered noisily on the cobbles but it was the riders who were nervous. He drew out his sword and hammered its hilt against the gate until the timbers shuddered. He waited for what seemed an age and then, when he had almost given up hope, he heard the portcullis inside being raised and breathed a sigh of relief. Still there was a further delay and silence - no welcoming shout from within. Why was it taking so damned long, he wondered? Were they all asleep - or still making whores of the servants? He would instil a better discipline once he got inside; some were Warwick's own men - he would have expected better of them. In fact he would have expected better of Mordeur too.

Abruptly the great gates began to move slowly apart and he rode inside. He knew at once that all was not right. The only men he could see were the two who had dragged open the gates; the courtyard was deserted and the stable doors lay open.

"Where is everyone?" he demanded.

One of the men who wore Warwick's livery spoke first.

"We're all that's left of the garrison. They're all dead - save one other - and he'll be stiff by morning."

Henry knew this could not be true. "But where's Durston?" he asked.

"Dead."

"What about Mordeur?"

"Dead."

"Now that I can't believe - Mordeur isn't dead! How do you know?"

The man looked at Henry stonily. "Because I kicked a rat off his butchered body not two hours ago."

Henry put his hand on his sword. The man leaned against the gate and watched him, shaking his head. "What are you going to do, lord? Kill me? You haven't got enough men left to waste one of them! Still, now that you're back, I'm going to get some sleep - if you want to know what happened I suggest you ask your good lady...my lord."

Henry was barely in control of himself in the face of such

insolence but he let the man go.

"If you're lying, I'll have your miserable hide flayed off you!" he roared after him.

If the man heard he showed no sign of it and disappeared up the steps to the garrison dormitory.

"Shut the gates," snapped Henry to his men, "and then see who's left!"

He crossed the courtyard to the southwest tower and swiftly mounted the steps to the guest chamber on the second floor where he had installed Joan before his departure for York.

He flung open the door of their chamber and found her lying on the bed. She looked up when he came in.

"Thank God you're back, Henry; but you come too late," she said wearily, "many hours too late."

Her voice was strained and he could see even in the dying light that her eyes were swollen and red. He seized her by the shoulder and shook her roughly.

"What happened? Tell me! What happened?" he demanded.

"They got out… they all got out," she murmured. "I don't know how they got out, but they did." Her voice sounded flat, unnaturally frail; this was not the same Joan he had left less than two days before - the hard-nosed bitch who would squeeze a man's parts until he screamed for mercy.

"Who got out? The two old men? But they couldn't get out, not without help - it's not possible!"

"She helped them - that she-wolf. I saw her covered in our men's blood."

"Who, damn you?" But he knew she could only mean Eleanor, for Emma didn't possess such skills and Amelie was heavy with child.

She told him what she knew, though by the sound of it he could have pieced it together himself. It was a blow but all was by no means lost.

"It's a setback, my dear, but we are still alive and we still have the castle. Ned Elder must still come to us. There is surely no need for so many tears; we've lost a few of Warwick's men but that's all."

She remained silent and that concerned him. "Is there something else?" he asked, "something you've not told me?"

Joan gave a slow nod. "I can't find the words to tell you...I have done something terrible...I can't say it..." She shrank down onto the bed and began sobbing, her whole body convulsed with weeping.

He gave up then and left her. He walked through the chambers and passages of the west range. All were empty including Emma's chamber. He descended to the floor below and the first room was Lady Amelie's bedchamber. The door was shut but even so he could smell the stench of blood. He opened the door slowly and looked inside. He leant against the doorpost and puffed out his cheeks. He took several paces into the room and, stepping over Bagot's corpse, went to the bed. He drew back the coverlet and stood there for a little while. Then he went out and closed the door behind him.

He leant back against the cold stone of the passage wall.

"Joan. What have you done, Joan?" he murmured. Drops of sweat ran down from his forehead and he saw that his hands were shaking. He tried to shut out the image but couldn't and before he knew it he had emptied the contents of his belly onto the floor. He felt ashamed and angry. It was fully dark before he left the passage and wandered into the Great Chamber next door. There he found Mordeur; it was certainly a day of shocks. Mordeur was a heavy loss for he had relied upon him greatly. He still could not quite believe that the Frenchman was dead, even seeing him there; he expected him to rise up at any moment protesting that he was alive - but he didn't.

He sat down in the darkness next to the body on the raised platform. In one way it changed nothing: he always knew he would have to kill Ned if he was to take his lands and that was still the case. Yet, it changed everything: the guilt for Joan's crime would hang around both their necks for ever and when Ned Elder found out he would shake the very earth apart to find and kill them both.

He must have sat there for an hour or more. There was no light in the house; it seemed that all the servants had fled too so there was no-one to light torches or fires. Well, at least we won't freeze to death in May, he thought. He stumbled out through the solar and up the steps back to Joan's chamber; his chamber too, he supposed. Joan had stopped weeping - that was a blessing - and was sitting up on the bed. He sat down beside her.

"So," he said, "you've killed a mother and her unborn child; you are damned - and so am I. But I was damned when I was born, so what do I care? My mother was killed, my father and uncle executed, so what do I care about someone else's wife? The whole family is damned to hell: you, me - Ned Elder and his sisters too. We've all got blood on our hands - do you think it matters too much whose blood it is?"

Joan remained silent.

"Well I don't think it does," he said. "You did it to kill one of our rivals, our enemies - and you succeeded. Kings do it and call it policy - what's the difference?"

He lifted her chin with his hand. "You're no use to me like this, girl. I thought you were the hard one - God knows you always told me I was weak."

She looked at him but still said not a word.

"If you want to win Joan, you'd better get used to the blood under your fingernails; because there'll be a lot more of it. If you can't live with that, then you may as well crawl back to Crag Tower - it'll be a ruin by now, but you can have it if you like." He got up, laughing to himself: she could fight Eleanor for it - that would be some contest!

She suddenly seized his arm and pulled him back. "No," was all she said.

Then she pulled him towards her and kissed him on the lips with a passion he had not felt from her before. She drew him on to her and held his head in her hands. When he uncovered her small breasts and cupped them in his hands he half expected her to push him away but she did not. Instead she tore at his clothes desperately and allowed him to undress her.

§§§§

It was long after dawn that he awoke beside her. He considered getting up but when he moved he could still feel every bruise, scratch and bite she had left on his body. God knows he had needed less recovery time from some bouts of armed combat. It occurred to him then that she had merely been using him, turning her anger into unbridled passion. She certainly knew what to do with a man - he wondered idly how she had learned such ways under the watchful eyes of Lady Margaret and Maighread Elder. He suspected there must have been some well satisfied stable lads at Crag Tower. Still, it was a lot better than her wallowing in guilt; she seemed to have put that behind her - at least for now.

She stirred and got up. Had she been awake for some time? He admired her nakedness as she looked for some clothes to wear. After a few moments she gave up and dragged the coverlet off the bed to wrap around her.

"You look very smug," she said.

Her voice was cool; that was not a good sign.

"Don't think you're going to get that every night, Henry," she continued, "you just caught me at a weak moment. I don't have too many of those - as you know."

He was not entirely surprised and hid his disappointment. "You didn't seem too weak last night," he said.

"Well, we both have to make sacrifices if I'm to bear you an heir. Now, tell me what happened with Warwick."

Back to business, he thought wistfully.

"Warwick was not very helpful," he began and explained how the meeting had gone and the terms he had been presented with at the end.

§§§§

Joan smiled as she watched Henry rushing about in the courtyard below. It was what he was best at: shouting at and cajoling his men; insulting their manhood until they did as he told them. She had always thought him weak, but they feared his sword; they must have seen something in him that she hadn't. Perhaps he was only weak with women?

She looked again at the document Warwick had given her husband and frowned. Henry had not shown it to her; she had stolen it from his privy chamber. He had not told her the part about the boy, Richard. She sighed. Did he really think she was going to run off and hunt the boy down? She had killed Amelie when her blood was running hot, when all around her were falling. There was no haste to deal with young Richard; Warwick could raise him at Middleham but still it would not do for him to become another Henry, angry and desperate to be restored to his 'birthright.' It wasn't so hard now to contemplate killing a rival. Henry was right: she had already taken the first and biggest step; one more would make no difference now.

DEREK BIRKS

37

27th May early afternoon, on the moor

south of Swaledale

"Blood of Christ, what a mess!" Ned spat disconsolately into the beck. "And you're sure?"

"Aye, lord," replied Hal, "I'm not likely to forget that banner in a hurry."

"No, none of us are." He felt empty; Hal's words had ripped the guts out of him.

"Leave me a while, Hal," he said and the youth retreated up to their camp.

Ned closed his eyes and tried to imagine how it must have been when the castle was taken: Bagot would have fought stoutly but there had not been enough with him. The ladies should have been safe enough for they had some value to Henry but for the rest...he had only to recall Crag Tower to know the limits of Henry's mercy. He hoped Eleanor had done nothing reckless but motherhood seemed to have changed her. Above all, his thoughts were of Amelie; she must be close to giving birth now. He had told her he would return in time - another rash promise broken...

Spearbold was walking purposefully down towards him. He sighed and leant forward to splash some of the beck's cool stream onto his face. Then he stood up and walked up the slope to meet Spearbold.

"I know what you're going to say," he said before Spearbold had opened his mouth. "We can't stay here all day, it's too open. I know."

Spearbold looked a little put out. "If you know what your valued councillor is going to say before he says it then he ceases to be of much value."

"Well, you said it," retorted Ned. Then he relented. "Listen, you do always offer me good advice; it's no fault of yours if I sometimes choose to ignore it. Come on, it's past midday already. We'll ride over the ridge into Yoredale, closer to the castle. We can wait in the forest - we should get there before dark. We'll feel more secure there."

He walked back to their camp with Spearbold muttering behind him. "Another night in a forest... one of us would feel more secure under a roof."

"Stop moaning," said Ned, "you're better off than most."

Spearbold did give him sound advice: it was his suggestion to take the road to Richmond and then skirt the town to ride up the Swale valley. This morning they had ridden across the open moorland to approach Yoredale from the north. The journey had been slow going, especially because poor Agnes was unused to riding and however they sat her upon the horse, she seemed to find a way to fall off.

Ned had sent Hal and Black to ride ahead over the moor into Yoredale to take a look at the castle and their bitter news had shaken him. The brightness of the morning could not lift the darkness in his heart or remove the raw fear of what he would find if he ever got back into Yoredale Castle. What sort of a lord fails to protect his own? A bad one. One glance at Black was enough to tell him that at last they were in agreement about something.

They set off on a path well to the west of the castle before descending craggy slopes etched with fast flowing becks and waterfalls. By late afternoon they found sanctuary in the dense forest of the Yore valley. Amongst the trees it was cooler and Ned was glad to once more breathe the familiar woodland scents; he felt that he had come home. Yet these lands, the forests and the castle were no longer his; all was lost, he was attainted and outlawed. Anything he did now was against the law simply because he did it; yet he had to do something.

"Hal, go to the forest edge and keep a watch: I want to know everyone that enters or leaves that castle. Black, get some rest - you can relieve him later tonight."

Black did not seem overjoyed at the prospect of a nocturnal stint but he contented himself with a glowering nod.

What was he to do now with Agnes? He thought she could have served one of his sisters or Amelie at the castle but he no longer had a castle. She had made the journey with them obediently for mile upon mile, though her own heart must still be full of grief. God only knew what she thought of them all.

They had barely set up camp in a hazel grove when Hal returned. He was not alone.

"Young Garth, isn't it?" said Ned, genuinely pleased to see the youth, embracing him like a long lost friend. "God's blood! It's good to see you, Garth."

"He was doing the same as me," said Hal, "and we sort of … found each other. He knows all about the capture of the castle, lord."

"Aye, lord," confirmed Garth; his voice was muted, solemn.

"Tell him about the Abbey," urged Hal, "and Lady Eleanor, and Lady Amelie, and Bagot…"

"Peace, Hal, or we shall hear nothing!" said Ned.

Garth told them all he knew and Ned was relieved to hear that most of his family had escaped; but on the matter most important to him, Garth had little to say.

"The last I saw was Lady Eleanor and Ragwulf going back into the castle to fetch your Lady and Master Bagot."

"Bagot was with her then?" asked Ned.

"Aye, lord, Bagot was with her for certain; he would have kept her safe."

"How long ago was that?" asked Spearbold.

"Yesterday morn, early."

The best part of two days, thought Ned. A great deal can

happen in two days. He should have made better speed; if he had, he might have got Amelie out himself.

"And you've heard nothing more since?" he asked. Garth shook his head.

"And you've not seen my sister, Lady Eleanor or Ragwulf since?"

"No, lord," said Garth sadly.

"You two had best return to your watch on the castle. I'll join you shortly."

When the two youths had ridden off into the forest, Spearbold took Ned aside.

"What is it you're planning, my lord?" he asked, a worried frown on his face.

"Planning? If only I had a plan, Spearbold. Sadly, I don't. I'm just going to walk up to that castle gate and knock upon it."

"You jest, my lord?"

"Do I have a look of humour about me, Spearbold?"

"But that would be madness, lord; it's exactly what Henry would want. You're giving him your head for nothing."

"No, I'm giving him my head in return for my wife's freedom!"

"No, lord; think again, I beg you! There must be another way - you don't know he will trade her for you; you don't even know she's there!"

"If there is a chance she's there, then I must take it. I am nothing Spearbold, nothing. I'm a condemned man; tell me what I have to lose."

"What if she was rescued by your sister and is safe and well?"

"It's possible. Ragwulf is one of my best men but surely if they had got her out, Garth would have known by now? Still, it changes little. If she lives, she'll be better off without an outlaw as a husband. King Edward will treat her well - I know he will. I can't keep running away - it's not how God made me!"

"But -"

Ned swept aside his protests. "Black! Wake up!" he shouted.

"I've not got a wink's sleep yet!" Black shouted back.

"Well get up and come here!" This was one man he would not miss.

"What is it?" demanded Black.

"You're released from my service; you may go where you will."

Black gave him a puzzled look. All he said was: "Oh."

"Spearbold, I give you two charges to undertake, if you will."

"Anything I can do, my lord!"

"Make sure my sisters and their children are safe and …find a suitable position for Agnes. God knows she has suffered enough."

"Of course, my lord, but -"

"No more to say," said Ned.

Agnes ran to him and buried her head in his chest, giving a long moan which shocked him to the core; it was the first sound he had ever heard her make. Yet he had to go to Amelie.

"I'm sorry, Agnes," he said softly and pushed her gently towards Spearbold. She would not go until Spearbold took her hand and pulled her away. Ned quickly untethered his horse, mounted and rode off without another word.

He knew the forest trails as well as any man and made good time but he soon realised he was being followed. Surely Spearbold would not; and indeed Spearbold had not, but Black had. Ned stopped to intercept him.

"God's blood, what are you doing here, Black? I told you: you're free to go; any oaths you swore to me meant nothing from the moment I was outlawed. I should have released you sooner."

"I was always a free man, lord; the oath may mean nothing to the law but it means something to me."

"Well, even so, I release you from my service."

"I choose not to be released," said Black.

Ned shook his head. Was nothing straightforward with this man?

"What do you want of me, Black? You complain at every turn; you bristle when I tell you to carry out even the smallest task and now, when I release you, you refuse to go!"

"I swore to stand by you and fight for you, lord. That's what I've done so far and I intend to carry on doing it and neither the law nor you will talk me out of it."

Ned could not help smiling. "I swear, Black, that if I told you to live long and happy you'd take your own life just to spite me. If it pleases you to ride with me, I'll be glad of it but when I enter the castle I'll do so alone. Agreed?"

"Of course, lord; I'm not fool enough to go in there - even if you are."

They found Hal and Garth squatting in the trees, their eyes on the castle. Ned joined them.

"Well hidden, lads; I'd never have found you had your horses not been tethered next to you."

Hal smiled. "We wanted them close by, lord."

Ned shook his head.

He looked at Hal for a moment. "I'm going to go to the castle - now I know that you would want to come with me, but you're not going to."

"But they've crossbows, lord," protested Garth, "they'll put a quarrel in you before you get anywhere near."

"I don't think they will," said Ned. In fact he was almost certain that, as long as Henry knew who was coming in, he would let him do so unharmed. If Henry was indeed his half-brother then he would want to talk to Ned - at the very least for a moment or two.

"Hear me well, you three," he said, his voice calm but solemn, "Garth, you are to go to my sister at the abbey and tell her I have returned. They cannot stay there forever; if I do not return then Spearbold will come to help them get away. Go now!"

"Yes, lord," said Garth and, with a final glance at Hal, he rode off.

"You two are to stay here until I come out, or my lady comes out. Watch and wait but don't try to get into the castle. Do you swear to that?"

"Aye, lord," they agreed though he could see that neither gave his assent willingly.

"However it ends, I would ask you to give my lady or my sisters your loyalty… but that will be your choice."

He could see the misery in Hal's eyes for the youth worshipped Amelie; he would have given his life to help free her. If he got Amelie out then at least she would have Hal to protect her.

"I'll leave my horse here; do with it what you will." He turned to go when a sudden thought occurred to him. "Give me your sword Hal," he said and handed Hal his own weapon. "That was my father's - I don't want Henry to have it. You keep it."

Hal was too stunned to protest further.

Ned walked out of the forest and up the track which led to the main castle gate. He stared up at the walls. As Hal had told him, his banners had been removed. Those draping over the walls now were the old ones, the blood red banners of the Radcliffes. So, Henry saw himself as more Radcliffe than Elder.

It was already dusk; he hoped that Henry's men were not too eager. Just in case, long before he reached the gate he called out: "I am Ned Elder. I want to see Henry the Bastard and I want to see him now!"

DEREK BIRKS

38

27th May evening, at Coverham Abbey near Middleham

Eleanor lay awake on her straw mattress. Outside in the Hall she could hear them all snoring their way through the night but for her sleep seemed harder to come by. All she could think of was the child. How had she even considered leaving him with Ragwulf? A hundred things could go awry. She made up her mind that on the morrow she would set off early for Carperby; she could not leave it all to Ragwulf.

Having made her decision she felt more at ease and was just slipping into sleep when the night was shattered by a hammering at the abbey gate. Ragwulf! Something had gone wrong! She was the first one out of the Guest Hall and barely half-dressed but still she hurried to the gate. By the time she reached it, the banging had stopped and the shouting had started. A heated argument was being conducted through the small hatch in the main door, but she was relieved to find that it was Garth, not Ragwulf, outside the gate.

"The abbot's instructions were quite clear," declared the gatekeeper, "no-one's to be admitted after dark or when the canons are at prayer."

"That's nonsense!" replied Garth. "Now, let me in!"

Eleanor shook her head: it seemed to her that it would be hard to find a time when at least some of the canons were not at prayer.

Garth caught a glimpse of her in the torchlight behind the gatekeeper.

"Lady Eleanor!" he shouted.

"Let him in," she told the gatekeeper.

"I dare not, my lady," he replied, "for the abbot was most clear in his orders. He said…" His voice tailed off as he absorbed the look on Eleanor's face.

"I've already heard what he said," said Eleanor. "Just open it."

He shook his head miserably. "I'll be dismissed, thrown out, if I do," he mumbled.

"Then stand aside and I'll lift the bar myself; then you won't have disobeyed your abbot."

In desperation, he threw himself in front of the gate. "The abbot won't see it that way, my lady!"

Eleanor groaned. Why were men always so keen on having rules, she wondered? Well, she would see what fear could do. She must have been a dreadful sight in the flickering torchlight: dressed only in a thin linen shift, with her feet bare and her blood red hair hanging around her face and down her back in long, angry tangles - and that was before she took out the knife.

She took a pace towards him and he flinched.

"If you don't let me open the gate, I'll cut off your fingers, one by one…and after your fingers, I'll have to cast about for something else to cut off…"

The gatekeeper shot aside and disappeared into the cloister, presumably to fetch his master.

Eleanor sighed wearily and went to raise the bar across the gate but it was much heavier than she expected and she would have looked very foolish if Gruffydd had not come along to help her.

"You took your time!" she snapped at him as they let Garth in. She had not meant to be so brusque; her anxiety over the child was driving her mad.

A moment later the abbot arrived with a gaggle of canons in tow before she could take Garth to the Guest Hall.

"Lady Eleanor!" the abbot cried, "Is it not enough that we house you, feed you and give you the protection of these holy walls… that we suffer women and children, not to mention armed youths, and comings and goings at dead of night? Do you now seek to threaten our people, ransack our property and change the order of our worship? Perhaps you'd like us to abandon our abbey until you've finished abusing it?"

"I ask only that you open the gate when required! Is that so much to ask? It need not have disrupted your worship at all!" shouted Eleanor.

"Those who claim sanctuary do not come and go as if they are in some tavern! And I will not be railed at in my own abbey by one such as you…my lady," said the abbot.

In the silence that followed the last echo of his words Eleanor could feel the eyes of everyone upon her, imploring her to bend her knee to the abbot and beg his forgiveness. That would have been the sensible course of action to take but it was not one that she was willing to contemplate.

"One such as me?" she repeated softly. "One such as me? My brother freed this valley from the tyranny of the Radcliffes - he shed his own blood so that your canons would not have to hear the suffering of the Radcliffe tenants whose souls they prayed for! And I too shed my blood to remove the Radcliffe scourge. So don't speak to me as if I'm some idle whore, abbot."

The abbot, however, looked as if he too was just warming to his theme and he opened his mouth to reply.

"My lord abbot!" Everyone looked around at the sound of Emma's voice.

"We are all grateful to you for your hospitality and those of us who claimed sanctuary have remained here in good faith; but our friends and servants, who work only to free us from the dangers outside this house, must be allowed to come and go - else we are likely to rest here forever."

Becky sidled up to Eleanor and gripped her arm tightly. "I swear if you say another word, I'll strike you myself," she whispered. "Now, leave it."

Eleanor glared at her but she had cooled down a little and merely pulled her arm free and gave her a non-committal shrug.

Emma continued before the abbot could think of a response: "I'm sure that when my brother returns, all will be settled, my lord abbot; and the Elders will show their gratitude for your aid."

"But that's what I'm here to tell you, my lady," said Garth, "Lord Elder has returned!"

In the uproar that followed his announcement, Becky guided Eleanor back to the Hall and all the rest of their party followed, anxious to hear Garth's news.

§§§§

Eleanor swept aside the curtain that divided off her sleeping area from the main body of the Hall and Becky followed her in. Eleanor rounded upon her at once. "You shouldn't have done that!" she hissed, "you presume too much!" She slapped Becky's face hard; instantly she regretted it.

Becky recoiled in shock and Eleanor, seeing at once the hurt in her eyes, walked back out into the Hall. Every face was turned towards her in trepidation.

"Get back to sleep!" she yelled at them and they scattered like startled hares. Within a moment only one was left there: Will. She stared at him, standing alone, his lower lip trembling with fear. Oh, good Christ…the anger left her at once and she opened her arms to him. He gave her a reproachful look, as well he might, then he came running up to her and clamped himself to her knees. She bent down and swept him up into her arms, holding him close to her breast. "I'm sorry, Will," she said softly, "I don't always think before I do things. It's not something…to take pride in…" She cradled him for a while and then took him into Jane who settled him down with his cousin in the sleeping space next to hers.

In her own cubicle she found Becky sitting on the floor, head in hands. She stood up at once when Eleanor entered.

"Does my lady want me to sleep with Jane and the

children?" she asked. Her tone was cool, a sure sign of the depth of her hurt. Eleanor stood in front of her, close; they stayed there, face to face, for a few moments then Becky lowered her eyes.

In the candlelight Eleanor could see the angry mark on her face. She bit her lip. "No. Stay, please."

"I've been foolish, my lady," said Becky, "I began to believe I was more than your servant... I was wrong."

"Stop it! You know very well the fault is mine," said Eleanor, sitting down on the mattress. "Come sit here with me while I grovel to you."

"You're not going to be very good at it," remarked Becky, perching at the far end of the bed.

"You can hit me if you like..." said Eleanor.

"I do believe you're serious," murmured Becky, shaking her head. "How would that help? It'd just give them all something more to gossip about. You never, ever hit me before."

"And I will never, ever do it again. Please, forgive me."

"The lady does not need forgiveness from the servant."

"You stopped being my servant years ago; you're my only friend..."

"Sometimes, perhaps - when you want it to be so."

"No, always! Always."

"You have a gift for raising the fires of hell out of nothing; yet...you're like your brother: you try so hard to do what's right but your fire burns those who are closest to you..."

"... like Lady Amelie," said Eleanor. "If I had not begun the escape..."

Becky laid her hand down on the mattress between them. Eleanor closed her own hand gently upon it and looked across at her.

"There's something else troubles you though, isn't there?" said Becky.

Eleanor nodded. "You know me too well..." She pulled Becky to her and sobbed on her shoulder. "It's not only

Amelie… and I must tell someone else in case anything happens to me. She lowered her voice to whisper. "But you must never breathe a word of this to anyone …anyone." So she told Becky about Ned's child.

"I can't sleep for worry; what if the child dies and Ned never even sees him?" she breathed. "Ned won't forgive me for leaving Amelie in the first place. If I let his child die…"

"Hush," soothed Becky, "you have a friend…"

"I told myself there would be no more tears," she said, as her sobs subsided.

Becky gently stroked her hair, "You're a strong woman; no-one is stronger than you."

Eleanor kissed her forehead and forced a smile. "I can't sleep. I must see Ragwulf - I need to know that all is well with that child. Then I can go to Ned. I'd better find Garth; he can tell me how Ned is."

She peered out into the Hall and looked at the slumbering bodies on the floor. Becky stood by her shoulder.

"I don't think he'll be there… do you?" whispered Becky.

Eleanor met her mischievous eyes and grimaced. She stepped across the sleeping youths to get to Emma's chamber. She knocked lightly on the door but heard no reply. She opened the door and passed through, closing it behind her. A single beeswax candle fluttered in the draught - no expense was spared for her sister, she observed. The closure of the door caused Emma to stir. She started when she saw Eleanor. She hastily disentangled her bare legs from Garth's and covered her breasts. She nudged Garth who came slowly awake.

"Don't look so guilty, sister," said Eleanor, "I've seen your nipples before and I'm hardly the one to cast stones, am I?"

"Why do I feel guilty then?" said Emma.

"Because you're you; but you shouldn't. Who wouldn't want to curl up in the arms of young Garth? He's a sweet boy!"

Garth reddened and looked around for a hole to

disappear into.

"Don't start," warned Emma, throwing the coverlet over her lover.

Oh dear, thought Eleanor, I'm making a mess of this already. She bent down to pick up a linen shift that lay on the floor and handed it to her sister. Emma got up and threw it on. Eleanor gave her a warm embrace.

"Believe me, I'm pleased to see you happy; and thank you, for your help with the abbot."

Emma took a step back and looked at her. "You're my sister - and the abbot was in the wrong."

"So," said Eleanor, "what of our brother?"

"He's back in Yoredale," confirmed Garth, lifting the coverlet off his head. He did not sound exactly jubilant.

"There's something else," said Eleanor. "Is he wounded?"

Emma took her hands. "Ellie, he's gone into the castle to get Amelie out…on his own. He doesn't know she's already dead. He's given himself up for nothing."

"Then we must go in after him," said Eleanor at once.

"Go in …how, my lady?" asked Garth. "They might let him in alone but they'll not let us in so willingly and we'll never storm the place. There's only a handful of us left."

"Did Ned not bring back the men he took?" demanded Eleanor. "He must have taken near a hundred men with him - where are they?"

"I don't know, my lady; I saw but one or two only."

"One or two…" Was the manhood of Yoredale to be reduced to one or two; there would be more widows in the valley than wives. "But we must do something…"

"He said he wanted no-one else with him. It was what he wanted, my lady."

"Well, it's not what I want!" replied Eleanor. "There are things he doesn't know -"

"What things?" asked Emma, but her question was overwhelmed by another pounding at the abbey gate.

"Oh, shit!" declared Eleanor.

"What now?" said Emma.

"I'll go," said Eleanor and dashed to the door.

"Don't you dare!" said Emma sharply. "I'll go this time; Garth get dressed and come with me."

Eleanor followed them out into the Hall.

"Stay here," Emma ordered them all. Eleanor struggled to remember the last time she had obeyed her sister but this time she did, despite the dark fears she harboured. She went to Becky and waited. It seemed like hours before Emma returned but when she did Eleanor could never have guessed who she would bring in with her. On the threshold to the Hall stood a tall figure she had not seen for years.

"Felix?" she breathed, "what are you doing here?"

"What else would I be doing miles from home, my lady, but digging my friend Ned out of a very large hole?"

"But how did you find us?"

"I stumbled over Hal in the woods near the castle. Just as well or I might have blundered into the castle without a thought."

"You'll have heard then - as we have - that Ned is in the castle on his own," said Eleanor.

"Yes, lady."

"Well, do you have any ideas, Felix?" asked Emma.

"I thought I might go in and get him out..." said Felix.

"Then you're as mad as my sister," said Emma.

39

27th May evening, at Yoredale Castle

Henry was in his privy chamber when Ned Elder's voice rang out in the still night air. He had only to glance out of one of the two narrow windows to see the ground beyond the gatehouse and there he was. There, alone, outside his door was the man he had wanted to meet for most of his life. He glimpsed him once in the bloody aftermath of Towton, ghosting through the mist amongst the trees of Castle Hill. He seemed then relentless, invincible; yet here he was below, utterly at his mercy. Henry had but to say a word and all his troubles would be over.

Joan came in and joined him at the window and, since only one could see out at a time, he moved back into the room.

"You can kill him where he stands," she said.

"I thought I would feel triumph to have him in my power," said Henry, almost to himself.

"You should do; isn't this what you wanted?" She moved behind him and wrapped her arms around his waist. "Kill him," she whispered, "and Yoredale is finally yours."

He shrugged her off and walked to the door. "Don't you think I know that? I know that far better than you." he said on the threshold.

"Then get it over with!" she said.

"This is not a moment to be rushed," he said softly, "and... I would hear what he has to say." Outside he could still hear Ned shouting as he walked along to the gatehouse.

"Open the gates and hand me a sword," he said to the

men at arms on watch. "I want some crossbows on the ramparts too," he ordered. Then he slowly dismounted the steps down to the courtyard. He was in no hurry since it would take some time to raise the portcullis and get one of the gates open.

At the foot of the steps he strode out into the main courtyard and took a deep draught of the May evening air. He wanted to be able to remember every smell, every sight and sound of this night. He swept his sword in great circles in the air as he walked towards the far end of the yard.

"Get some more torches lit down here!" he shouted.

The portcullis was up and two men were dragging open the gates; it would not be long. There was movement above him and he looked up in satisfaction to see half a dozen men scurrying into position on the rampart. He was surprised to see Joan up there too but he supposed she wanted to witness the moment. It was her victory too, after all.

Ned Elder stepped through the open gate and at once it was shut firmly behind him. Henry and Ned studied each other in the gloom. Henry noticed how similar they were: in stature, colouring and yes, in their faces too. He was sure that Ned would have made the same observations.

"Brother, you're a wanted man," he began, "do you come to surrender to me?"

"I've come for my wife…and, if you are truly my brother, you'll release her in return for me."

Henry had not expected this; he had assumed that Ned would already know of his wife's death. At once he felt an unwelcome pang of guilt for, though the killing was not his doing, it could only be laid at his door. Yet, the woman was dead; what else could he say? Somehow this meeting he had envisaged for a lifetime had not started as he intended.

"I am your brother - don't doubt for an instant that we share the same father."

"Then release her," replied Ned, "you have me; you don't need her."

"You come armed," said Henry.

In response Ned took out and threw down his sword. "Now that obstacle's gone; release her."

"I can't do that, Ned. I truly wish I could."

"Those are the weak words of a craven, Henry, not a lord - and certainly not a brother."

"I can't release her Ned, because ..." Why was he finding it so difficult to say those words?

"He can't release her because she's dead," shouted Joan from the rampart, "stone, cold dead!"

The fool, he thought, why had she blurted it out like that?

Ned stood very still. When he spoke his voice was as cold as death. "Does she speak truly, Henry?"

Henry's mouth was suddenly so dry he could hardly speak.

"It was not meant to happen, not on my part..."

"How then?" demanded Ned, "was it the birth?"

Henry looked at his brother; it would have been so easy to say yes. One small word would have settled it; yet, he could not do it. He felt his brother's pain; how or why, he didn't know, but he felt it.

"How did she die?" Ned's voice was strained; he must be barely under control and who could blame him? Ned took a step towards him and a crossbow bolt took him in the calf, dropping him onto one knee on the cobbles.

"No!" bellowed Henry. "No-one is to act without my order!"

His angry words reverberated around the courtyard. He walked towards Ned, the sword still in his hand. Ned was up on his haunches ready to spring forward.

"I see you come armed, brother," said Ned, grim-faced in the torchlight. Henry took another step closer and then dropped his sword.

"Henry, what are you doing?" Joan cried from above them.

Henry did not answer her but bent down to talk to Ned. "It was not childbed...she never gave birth."

Ned winced. "Then what?"

"She was killed - not by my order Ned, believe me, not by my order."

"One of your men killed my wife, heavy with child?"

"It matters little who killed her; the act was carried out in my name and we both know the blame rests with me. I can't undo it - all I can do is beg you to forgive me."

"You've brought death, dishonour and ruin upon me and my family," said Ned, his voice slow and hoarse, "I could forgive a brother for all of that, but not this!" Ned ripped out his dagger and drove it into Henry's side. Henry staggered back, barely keeping to his feet; he looked down at the tear in his jack and touched the blood that flowed from it. Several crossbow bolts struck the cobbles around them; if the fools weren't careful they would kill him themselves. One quarrel punched into Ned shoulder and knocked him off his feet.

"Hold, damn you!" Henry bellowed up at the rampart. Christ's blood; the wound hurt! He bent down gingerly to retrieve his sword. "I suppose it was bound to end this way," he told Ned as he stood over him.

"I'm tired, Henry, just finish it quickly."

He nodded and raised his sword but it never fell. The quarrel struck him in the chest and he toppled slowly backwards, hitting his head on the cobbles. Stunned, he stared at the offending bolt; he had told them, ordered them, to stop. Joan was up there, she could surely have stopped them. Joan… The same Joan who had killed Lady Amelie and her unborn child because they stood in her way. Joan.

He was dimly aware of more crossbow fire; one of his legs jumped as if kicked. Then suddenly he was being dragged across the yard towards the corner of the courtyard. Ned, his brother Ned, was pulling him under cover.

"Why bother?" he croaked and then he wept as the night was filled with shouts in anger, the whirr of reloading crossbows and the snap of quarrels on stone.

§§§§

Why bother, indeed, thought Ned. Henry was as near dead as made no difference; and for his part, death would be welcome enough. He should have stayed in the courtyard; death would have come more swiftly. He had no weapon but they were in the armoury - it was the first room he had found off the courtyard. He stared about him - it was more of a workshop than a store so there were few serviceable weapons: two blunt sword blades without hilts and what seemed like random pieces of plate armour mostly with torn straps.

Urgent steps sounded on the stone stair a few yards away; he looked into the passage outside the room. A smear of blood gleamed on the floor where he had dragged Henry in; they would be found at once. He rummaged about and discovered a long handled poleaxe - well, the handle had once been long, but was now a splintered stump. He tried its weight and balance; it would serve better than nothing.

Henry stirred and Ned crouched down beside him. He looked dreadful and so he should; yet he felt pity for this man, his half-brother. He was no Edmund Radcliffe - born with much and always wanting more; Henry was born with nothing, his very existence a sword thrust in the heart of his mother. He was trembling, his eyes open, blood welling from his several wounds.

"Say that you forgive me, brother," Henry pleaded softly.

"Where is she?" asked Ned.

"Still in her chamber… I'm sorry for it, Ned."

"Aye, you say that now easily enough," replied Ned.

A man at arms hurried past the armoury and Ned swivelled around to face the door. The footsteps paused and then began to come slowly back towards him. He stood up; the crossbow bolt through his calf had done little damage but the other one was still lodged in his left shoulder and the arm would hardly move. Just as well he used his right. He raised the poleaxe and took a step to the door. The man who had run past appeared in the doorway with a sword in his hand then hesitated. Ned did not; he brought down the axe, embedding it in the man's neck. The doomed man stood for an instant until his legs buckled beneath him and his lifeless body dropped onto the threshold.

Ned returned to Henry. "I'd like to give you the forgiveness you seek but…"

Henry had fallen onto the floor on his side. Ned bent down to him but Henry had no more to say and his eyes delivered a bleak stare.

"So brother," he whispered, "you die unforgiven after all."

He picked up the fallen man's sword and thrust it in his belt. He knew now what he wanted to do: he wanted to join Amelie. With the poleaxe in hand, he started up the spiral stair to the floor above. He could hear someone on their way down; if they met halfway, Ned's right arm would be hampered by the stone pillar that was the central core of the staircase. He retreated back down and waited below; his opponent barely saw him before the axe struck him on the chin, removing most of his lower jaw. He fell forward screaming until Ned buried the axe spike into the back of his skull. The sound would have told them all where he was. He snatched up the dead man's sword and sheathed it. He pushed past the body and mounted the steps; his calf, he found, disliked going upstairs.

He entered the solar but it was in darkness and he stumbled several times as he crossed the room. He passed into the Great Chamber and was surprised to find a torch burning brightly within. He could tell at once that there had been fighting there; the bodies had been removed and the floors washed but there was still blood on a tapestry by the door and on the raised dais.

The door opposite him led to a short passage and then on to the chamber he and Amelie had shared for three years. He took a step towards the door; the passage was unlit. By the time he was questioning why the Great Chamber was lit and the spaces either side of it were not, another quarrel knocked him off his feet. The range was short and the bolt tore into his body, ripping through the soft flesh of his side. Sweet St. Michael, it hurt, but it would not kill him. Joan was clearly no fool; she had set him up. She had expected him to go to Amelie's chamber.

The torch hung from the wall not far away. He tried to roll to the side towards it and nearly passed out as he rolled right over on the wound. He let the wave of agony pass and got to his feet; when he reached the torch, he stared at it in confusion for a moment. Then he put down the axe and wrenched the torch from its iron bracket. Slowly he made his way along the side of the room towards the passage door. They would not be able to see him now; if they wanted to get him, whether with sword or crossbow, they would have to come into the chamber to do it.

How many were there, he wondered? Then he laughed - a short, painful laugh, curtailed by the excruciating pain in his shoulder. Yet it was a grim sort of humour: Joan had men waiting to kill him and it would cost them some blood to do it. She didn't realise that if she just let him get to Amelie, he would accept death willingly.

If they had any sense they would have noticed the change of light in the room when he moved the torch; they would work out that he was by the door. So be it. He reached out his right hand and hurled the torch through the open doorway into the passage; a crossbow bolt flew past him. A waste. He quickly took a look around the edge of the door: there was only one man at the end of the passage, hastily reloading his crossbow; it would not be his weapon of choice in the confined space of the passage. The torch lay on the floor boards in front of Amelie's chamber; it might gutter but then on the other hand it might set fire to the door.

He retrieved his poleaxe and moved back to the door, carefully because sudden movement caused his shoulder to throb more than it already was. He took a few deep breaths and stepped out into the doorway; the crossbowman swung up his bow as Ned threw the poleaxe. The quarrel cracked into the stonework and ricocheted into the chamber. Ned was already moving forward, one slow step at a time. He drew the sword out and so did his opponent. Ned reached the torch and kicked it aside keeping his eyes on the other man. He half expected him to run; but he didn't. In the glimmer of torchlight he saw the badge on the man's breast: the bear and ragged staff; it seemed he was destined never to break free from Warwick.

How good was this man? He was no callow youth; he looked capable. Ned knew he would not last a prolonged fight.

"Just walk away," he said to the knight.

"Lady Joan's orders were quite clear - and they were the same as the Earl's - 'if you see him, kill him'.

"Who would know?" asked Ned.

"God would know," replied the other.

"Yes, I suppose He would," conceded Ned. He was weary now; there was no fight left in him; even his anger was spent; he just wanted to see her again.

"What if I were to go into that chamber and leave my sword outside with you?"

The knight looked puzzled. "But you wouldn't do that, Lord Elder."

"Do you know what's in that room?" he asked.

"Aye."

"Then let me make peace with my wife. I'm a dead man however I look at it; I just want to spend some time with her. You'll be able to boast then that you were the man that killed me."

"I don't boast," replied the knight.

"Good. I like that in a man. Will you let me into the chamber for a while?"

The knight looked at him warily, still clearly expecting a trap of some sort.

Ned sighed finally. He reversed his hold on the sword and held it out by the blade. His adversary leant forward no doubt expecting Ned to spring at him. But when he took Ned's sword there was no sudden lunge, no last ditch attempt at escape.

The knight stepped back from the chamber door. He indicated the flickering torch on the floor. "You'll need that."

Ned picked up the torch. The chamber door was ajar and he could smell the death within.

"My lord," said the knight in a gentle voice, "in there, it's not pretty…"

"I've never seen a death that is," murmured Ned. "How long will you grant me?"

"As long as you need; when you are ready to die you have only to come out. I shall give you a swift death."

Ned gave him a nod and he passed into the chamber and closed the door behind him. The smell of blood was overpowering. He lifted the torch and gasped, leaning back against the door for support. It looked as if no-one had touched the room: Bagot's corpse lay on the floor by the bed and at first he could not look beyond it. He mounted the torch on the wall and crossed to the bed, screwing his eyes up so that what lay there was just a blur. When he opened his eyes fully he saw that someone had pulled the coverlet up over the body.

He lifted its edge and slowly began to pull it back. He could go no further the moment he had uncovered her face. In his heart he had stored a tiny shred of belief that Henry and Joan had lied to him. How he wished that they had.

Her face felt hard to the touch, not like stone but like a piece of pale dried vellum; a face that had been soft and was no longer. Now that he was beside her, he could think of no words that made any sense. He had fallen in love with her in an instant and he had never stopped loving her; yet he had not been there to save her. When the knight had asked him how long he wanted with her he had been tempted to answer: a lifetime; but no lifetime was long enough to tell of this woman's virtues.

He rested his hand on her swollen belly where his child still lay, never to take a breath, never to see him; and his grief was suddenly unleashed. He fell upon the bed weeping and the salt of his tears stung his eyes until they were red raw.

How long he lay there he did not know, but the torch had burnt out and there was a glow of light coming through the narrow window. The knight had been generous and now he must keep his own promise. He sat up and replaced the coverlet. He felt drained, ready for death. God knew it could not come soon enough. For abandoning his wife he deserved a traitor's fate; at the very least he had betrayed her.

He went out of the chamber and glanced at the knight who was sitting on the floor leaning back against the wall.

"You're a patient man," said Ned.

"I'm never in haste to kill someone," said the knight.

"Perhaps not the best quality for a man at arms," replied Ned, sitting down beside him.

"I hope I'm more than just a man with a sword."

"We're all just men with swords; it's just that some of us do more damage than others."

The knight smiled - a thin grey smile.

"I'm surprised your mistress did not send you in to kill me earlier," said Ned.

"She did, but she is not my mistress; I answer to a greater power."

"Which one: God, or the Earl of Warwick?"

The knight fingered the badge upon his chest. "I've had some hours to consider that - both, I hope."

The eastern sky looked lighter now, a long, bright blade of sunlight slicing away the last shadows of night.

"Let's get to it then," said Ned, "if you're ready."

They both stood up and faced each other, a yard apart. Ned's calf felt sore when he moved.

"I'm not comfortable with this, my lord," said the knight. "I would rather we fought."

"What would be the point of that? I'd probably kill you." Ned wished the fellow would just do it; he had prepared himself for death. There was no more to be said.

"Perhaps not, you're carrying several wounds…"

"I'd still kill you - and I don't want to. We agreed! I'm an

448

outlaw - you can kill me without guilt."

The other man looked him in the eye. "You are not an outlaw at the moment."

"I am. I'm an outlaw till I die; now let me die here. If you love God then you'd be doing Him a service - I don't doubt that."

"But I do; I do doubt that. And you ceased to be an outlaw two days ago. The king has sentenced you to exile but only if you leave England by the end of the month."

"But..."

"It does not suit the Earl for you to go into exile. He would rather know that you are dead."

"So, the reprieve changes nothing: your master wants me dead - not that I could get to a port by Sunday in any case; but most of all, I have no reason to live! Now do as you said you would."

The knight sighed and slowly drew out his sword. Even so Ned was not sure the man had the nerve to do it.

He laid his hand on the knight's arm. "Sir, is your blade sharp? You will do me a service if you give me a clean, swift death."

"It will do well, my lord ... have you a last prayer?"

"It's done! Now, in the name of God, do it. Take my head."

Ned loosened his jacket and the knight let his blade rest lightly against his exposed neck. Ned felt it nick him and smiled: the sword was indeed sharp enough. He watched the knight lift the sword high and then he closed his eyes.

PART FIVE: A TRAITOR'S FATE

40

28th May before dawn, near the village of Carperby in Yoredale

Eleanor rode so hard that the youth she had brought to lead her to Ragwulf's cottage was in frequent danger of being left behind. She wanted to get there fast for she had arranged to meet Felix and the others at Yoredale Castle by dawn. Only Gruffydd and Garth would be left at the Abbey to protect Emma and the boys. Gruffydd because Eleanor thought he was not fit enough to ride, let alone fight; and Garth because her sister refused to allow him to go. What Garth made of that Eleanor did not know but she had an idea that the youth did not welcome such special treatment.

As they neared the village of Carperby, she slowed her horse to a walk and her companion caught her up.

"What are you called?" she asked the youth.

"Tom, my lady."

"There are too many called Tom…" she said, "what do your friends call you?"

He hesitated before responding: "Tom… 'Shortpipe', my lady."

She grinned and decided to seek no further explanation.

"Well, Master Shortpipe," she said, "we're nearly at the village - time you played your part."

They dismounted and tethered their horses in the trees; the nearest farm was not far away.

"Which garth is it then?" murmured Eleanor as they stopped at the tree line.

The youth at her side said nothing.

"Which one?" hissed Eleanor.

"I've not been here when it's dark, my lady," said Shortpipe, "it looks different…"

"You'll look different if you don't soon find it! Come on - and mind you keep quiet!"

Eleanor crossed the open stretch of field with Shortpipe trotting behind her. The cottages were scattered over a wide area each in its own garth whereas she knew that at the other end of the village, the east end, they were more ordered. No wonder Ragwulf had told her to bring someone who knew where he lived - if only young Shortpipe did know.

She stopped. "Well?"

She watched him struggle to get his bearings.

"It'll soon be broad daylight and I can't wait that long," she said.

Her sharp tone seemed to concentrate his mind a little and he gave an eager nod. "I see it now, my lady," he said excitedly.

At once Eleanor wrapped her hand around his mouth. "Quiet, you fool!" she whispered. "If you're sure about it you can join the others at the castle."

"Aye, my lady," mumbled Tom.

She grinned; the poor boy looked positively relieved to get away from her.

She hurried to the building he had pointed out and crept alongside the wall towards the door. She knocked as quietly as she could and, when there was no response, she knocked again, a little louder. No-one came. She moved to the window; it was small and a piece of hide was draped across it on the inside. She listened at the opening: nothing. She went back to the door and pushed it; it opened easily. She drew out a knife and crossed the threshold, silent like a cat, ready for anything - except she found nothing - and no-one.

She was sweating with worry; she wanted to scream. Where in the name of God was he? And where was the child? If the boy was harmed she would kill Ragwulf; then she would kill herself. She sat down on the floor and tried to calm herself. Where might Ragwulf be? He had gone to the midwife; with luck she had pointed him to someone who could suckle the babe. Then what? She did not know.

It struck her like the spike of a poleaxe, piercing her heart: she had handed over Ned's child and she had no idea where he was.

"What have I done?" she breathed, "pray God forgive me; but He won't - and neither will Ned."

She did the only thing she could: she sat down to wait. She watched the dawn creep into the valley, knowing the others would worry when she did not arrive but still she waited in the hope that Ragwulf would return.

§§§§

This is a shambles, thought Felix. He might carry with him the hope of salvation for Ned but the days were running out now and he could not even get to Ned - if indeed Ned was still alive. Dawn had come and gone without any appearance by Lady Eleanor. He glanced at those around him and it gave him little encouragement: a mute girl, the supposed 'adviser', Spearbold, and a few young boys, pretending to be men at arms. That's all he had aside from Hal and the taciturn Black. The last two he thought would make an attempt but the rest...

He was beginning to believe that the Lord had abandoned his cause and yet all was in place - all he needed now was to get his hands on Ned before someone executed him. Every moment he waited here reduced his hopes of success. When he had petitioned the king to sentence Ned only to a short exile, he thought the hard part was done. He was beginning to understand that getting Ned out of the country was going to be more difficult still. He was not going to let all his good work be wasted now without a last effort. He would just have to act without Lady Eleanor.

He went to his horse and checked the straps that held his

quarterstaff in place - they must not be too tight. He explained to Hal and Black what he was going to do.

Black simply laughed in his face but Hal smiled and said: "Just like three years ago, Felix - a lost cause and no hope of success."

"Just be ready," said Felix solemnly. He didn't want to remember three years ago; it had nearly killed him. He mounted his horse and cantered down the track to the castle. Up close it was an impressive pile of stones, he had to admit. He could see a few men on the ramparts and red banners billowed down some of the walls. He knew he would be seen at once and lost no time in hailing the gatehouse: "Ho, within! I have a letter from the king! Open your gates!"

He expected his announcement would cause concern in the castle - at least he hoped it would. It was a brave castellan who refused entry to a horseman claiming to bring a message from the king. Yet he did not look much like a messenger; albeit his clothes were not poor he wore no royal livery.

"Approach the gate!" A woman's voice, now that was a surprise; but Felix obeyed and rode to the gate. There he dismounted but wound the reins around his arm. He heard the portcullis inside being raised and waited.

The customary small door was set in one of the gates at head height; when it slid to one side it was not a woman who faced him but a stern looking man at arms.

"Pass your message through here - if you are indeed from his Grace." He sounded sceptical and Felix could not blame him.

"I cannot give this to any but the one who is master here," said Felix.

"Wait." The door slid shut.

Felix waited patiently. He must not show concern; he must be polite, but firm. It was a long wait but the small door eventually opened again.

"I'm still here," he said, with what he hoped was a genial smile.

A woman's face appeared; she was young, very young -

just a girl really.

"God give you good day, sir. My husband is away in the King's service," she said, "thus, you will understand my caution. You may deliver your letter to me and I'll see it reaches my husband when he returns."

"Good day to you, my lady. I shall happily leave the message with you but...I have ridden from York. Surely a King's man might expect some hospitality for his trouble." He looked around him. "I am but one man..."

He could read people as fast as any man and he saw the uncertainty in her eyes now as she contemplated how much of a risk he presented.

"I will gladly surrender my sword if it would reassure you, my lady." That made the difference as he knew it would; giving up his sword was a ploy he had used several times before.

"Very well," she said and stepped aside. Felix drew out his sword and passed it through hilt first to the man at arms he had seen before. Then after a few minutes there was a banging and the gates opened slowly inwards. He took a deep breath; this was the moment and he prayed to the Lord that Hal and the rest were paying close attention.

As he passed through the gate his horse suddenly appeared to be startled and reared up. Indeed she had been startled by Felix pulling back on her mane. She was a long suffering mare but she could give as good as she got and it was all he could do to control her.

"Come on," said the man at arms. "If you've ridden the animal from York, you can manage to get her through an open gate!"

"Give me a hand," beseeched Felix, feigning fear.

"Alright, alright, let me take the beast," ordered the man. Felix backed away to the other side of his unsettled mount.

"Thank you, good sir, thank you," he said, "thank you for your patience." The horse was suddenly still and Felix drew out his staff rapidly. Before the man could say a word Felix had driven the iron cap of the staff into his head. He dropped like a stone and Felix quickly rolled his body between the two gates. Then he stepped forward with the staff in both hands. Unfortunately he was in plain view of the young lady of the house and she screamed orders to her men as she backed away across the yard. Two men ran at him with swords drawn. Too close together lads, he muttered to himself and pushed them both back with the staff. One fell on his back on the cobbles and Felix felled the other with a sharp blow to the shoulder. The first found his feet and charged only for the deadly end of Felix's weapon to meet him at the throat. Felix meant only to stun him but the force of the man's momentum all but impaled him on the staff. Men scattered away seeking the shelter of the several doors in the courtyard.

"Come on, Hal; are you asleep?" he murmured. A missile flew towards him and clattered against the stone wall beside him. Crossbows, oh good!

"Take that man down!" the girl screeched. Good Christ, she sounded wild now. "Lower the portcullis!"

The next quarrel plucked at his sleeve and he heard the rumble of chains above him. But he also heard the shouts from the ramparts: Hal and the others were riding towards the gate. Swiftly he thrust his staff into the stone groove where the portcullis was descending and braced himself against it. The ash staff held and stopped the heavy gate's progress but he knew it would not hold for long.

"Watch out! Crossbows!" he shouted as Black and Hal ducked under the portcullis and thundered past him. The young lads followed and Felix leant against the wall with relief. It was short-lived as his comrades came under attack from the ramparts with bow and crossbow.

They were in but they may just have come in there to die.

41

28th May dawn, at Crag Tower

Maighread shivered; it was a grey dawn and the east wind was cold on the tower battlements. "He's not coming back," she said

"He's only been gone a week," said Sir Stephen. "Give him time, my lady; he'll come back."

Maighread shrugged her shoulders and turned away.

"You know him far better than I," she said.

"By now he'll have reached Yoredale, God willing. He'll have secured the castle and he'll be waiting for Henry."

"And what if Henry has already taken his castle at Yoredale?"

"Impossible. The castle might be lightly manned but Bagot's a canny old soldier. The walls and gates are strong enough to hold out for months. If Henry did get there first, all he'll be doing when Ned arrives is sitting outside it."

"You seem so certain." Maighread was far from certain. True, she knew little of Ned Elder, aside from his reputation, but she did know Henry. Henry was cunning; somehow, he would have found a way in. Sir Stephen was loyal - loyal, but blind.

"You should go after him," she said. "There are a score of you here. What do I need with so many men at arms?"

"I'm not leaving here," said Sir Stephen bluntly.

"But you must see that you're not needed here - and you may be needed at Yoredale. You could make the difference between life and death for your lord."

She meant it as kind advice but she knew it sounded

harsh. It still hurt her to speak and every word she said came out as a growl.

"Just because he told you to stay… what if you're wrong? There are too many against him - he needs you."

"Ned didn't tell me to protect you and hold here at Crag Tower; he asked me to, as a friend. And, as a friend, I'll do what he asked."

Maighread wanted to leave him there on the cold rampart; her burns ached and speaking was making her feel sick. She moved to the wall and leant out.

"And what if I were to throw myself into the ravine?" she asked.

"My lady!" Sir Stephen went to seize her arm and then stopped uncertainly.

Maighread tried a grim smile and it brought tears to her eyes - well, her good eye anyway.

"If you'd touched that arm, I'd certainly have jumped," she said.

"Your pardon, my lady, but you must not think of such a thing!"

"Believe me, Sir Stephen, if half your flesh was seared away, you'd think on it too. But… I've not got so low yet. My point was that, if I were to leave, you would have no cause to remain. You could go to support your lord. My brother and I could slip away into the borderlands."

"But, my lady…"

"Your young men are restless and bored in any case - you know they are. They have the appetites of youth: they get into fights and they stare at the serving girls with their tongues hanging out. It's all you can do to keep them in check."

"And where would I take them, my lady?"

"Take your men home, Stephen," she said. She turned to go. She had said her piece and the chill breeze was beginning to bite.

"Home? Ned might be there, it's true and he might need me; but he could still be fighting up here. If I go south to Yoredale, he may come here expecting to meet his fighting men and find only a stone shell."

"You hold the fate of many in your hands," she said.

"But I answer only to one and he'll be better served if he can be sure that I'll still be here when he needs me! If your brother asked you to wait for him here, my lady, would you leave Crag Tower?"

His words were quiet, spoken from the heart, she could tell. "It's not the same," she replied.

"Why not? Ned is my brother in arms - a brotherhood forged in the blood of battle and I'll hold this place until I die or he returns."

She shook her head and her ravaged skin felt sore. She leant against the stonework waiting for the pain to subside.

Sir Stephen wasn't looking at her; he was staring down below to the main gate. She followed his gaze and saw two men on foot supporting a third between them.

"Did those three not just ride out?" she asked.

Sir Stephen nodded. "I think we've just lost another three mounts," he said.

§§§§

Maighread followed Sir Stephen down to the Hall; she urged him to hurry ahead and took her time descending the spiral stair. She walked gingerly, always careful not to extend her leg too far lest the scars should stretch and weep afresh. Bear would be most displeased with her for going up to the rampart at all. He would say nothing of course but he would grunt at her in a way that clearly conveyed his displeasure. Once she banged her leg against the curved wall and stopped in agony, waiting for the wave of fire to burn itself out.

In the Hall, Sir Stephen was talking to two young men - one she knew was Wulf but the other was not yet known to her. Sir Stephen's face told her that there were no good tidings.

"You'd better get off," he told them.

Maighread waited for him to explain.

"Come," he said gently and sat her down on a chair upon the raised dais.

"What is it?" she asked.

"Warwick's men are nearby," he said. "They're watching the track southwards - the one Ned took - and they have enough men to keep us penned in here as long as they please - so Wulf tells me. They have archers and crossbows; they could have killed Wulf and the others but they just took the horses and gave young John Swift a beating."

"But why has Warwick done this now?" she asked.

"It must mean he's closing his grip on Ned, leaving no possibility of escape. He knows Ned isn't here but he wants to be ready in case he does come."

"It doesn't sound good," she said.

"I don't know. It tells us that Warwick hasn't yet got Ned."

"So there's still hope?"

"Perhaps," acknowledged Sir Stephen, "but it ends all discussion of whether we go or stay."

"Because we can't get out now - even if we wanted to?" she said.

"No, at least not without a high cost - and certainly not with you."

She stared down into the North Tyne valley. "So, when Warwick withdraws his men, we'll know that, one way or another, the matter is settled. But we won't know whether Ned's alive or dead."

"On the contrary, Lady Maighread," replied Sir Stephen gravely, "if Warwick withdraws his men we'll know that Ned is dead because I don't think the Earl will give up until he is."

42

28th May dawn, at Yoredale Castle

"To arms; to arms!"

Ned heard the cry and opened his eyes.

"Wait here!" said the knight and ran along the passage into the northwest tower. Ned did not wait; instead he followed him up the steps to the top of the tower. They both looked down in amazement upon the courtyard below where a furious melee was in progress.

At once Ned picked out the tall black figure who wielded a great staff. "Felix of Bordeaux?" he muttered. Then he saw Hal and Black; the very last of his men - the fools.

"Your men, it seems, have a good deal more fight than you," said the knight. He held out Ned's sword. "Now, perhaps you will fight me."

Ned looked down to the courtyard once more; boys were dying down there - dying in the forlorn hope of getting him out.

"No!" Joan screamed at them from the west rampart only a few yards away. "I told you to kill him! Strike them both down!" she yelled to the men beside her.

Ned took the sword offered. "I'll not fight you," he said.

"You must," said the knight, smiling, "if you want to help your friends."

Reluctantly Ned took up a guard but two quarrels flew at the pair of them. The knight was unlucky for he took both of them. He dropped his sword and cannoned forward into Ned, knocking them both down onto the boards. Ned could see a quarrel in his neck but he could still take a breath and only a little blood welled from the wound.

They sat against the wall out of sight of the rampart just below them.

"Shall I try to take it out?" asked Ned.

"Don't be a fool!" snapped the knight.

"I need to go to my men. Join me; I'll help you down."

"I can only be forsworn once in a day," said the knight. "Sweet Christ, it hurts to talk."

"Don't then; stay here. I'll get you help when it's over."

"Just go."

"I would know your name, sir?" said Ned.

"I am Thomas of Redesdale," said the knight, "you'd best hurry, lord."

"Wait for me here," said Ned.

The knight shook his head. "Go now!" he cried and staggered to his feet. Another bolt struck him in the chest before he had even stood upright.

Ned clambered onto his knees and dived through the doorway, almost throwing himself down the spiral stair. His injured left shoulder thudded into the stone pillar but he clung on and then half ran, half fell down the steps. The best way to aid his comrades was to take out the crossbows. Thomas had taken another bolt for him to give him a chance; he owed it to the knight to make the most of it

The door to the rampart was on his left and he crashed through it, keeping low. The crossbowman was only a few yards away along the rampart, still reloading his bow. He tried to fend Ned off with his crossbow and Ned took the blow on his shoulder - the same shoulder which was now a bloody pulp. It did not stop his weapon as it sang through the air and sliced across his opponent's chest. The girl ran along the battlements with the other man and disappeared into the southwest tower beyond. Good riddance! He could worry about her later. He scanned the other ramparts - there were no other men at arms up there, with or without crossbows. All were down in the courtyard.

He hurried down the stairs but saw no sign of the girl.

When he burst out of a doorway into the courtyard, Felix nearly took his head off with his staff.

"Well-timed, my lord," he said breathlessly, "we've stopped them up in the stables!"

"How many?" he asked.

"Three at most - and the wench has just fled in there too," said Black, leaning on his blood-smeared sword.

"Well, Black, if they decide to leave the stables, try to get in their way - if it's no trouble," Ned added.

John Black gave him a curt nod. "If it was any trouble, lord, I'd not be here at all."

Ned pulled a face and looked about the yard.

"You're hurt, lord," said Hal, running up to him. "I'll see to it."

"No, Hal, not yet; there are others…"

Hal nodded and joined Felix who was kneeling beside one of the young lads.

"They're just boys," said Ned.

"They always are, lord," said Black, with a grim smile, "But we took all the older lads with us, didn't we? They'd have come in handy but we left them up north to defend a worthless castle and a burned woman."

"Enough man!" growled Ned.

"Still, they'll get older… if they live long enough," said Black.

Ned made no answer; he'd been in Black's company for only a few moments, but it was already too long. He had released the man; why wouldn't he just go? Did he enjoy tormenting his lord so much?

Ned turned away and went to the youth Felix was examining. The expression on Felix' face told him all he needed to know; it was a bad belly wound - though all belly wounds were bad. They could not stop the blood flow and the boy was growing paler as they watched.

"Who's this, Hal?" he asked studying the youth's face.

Hal swallowed. "It's … Tom Shortpipe."

Ned knelt down beside him. "Tom," he said, "you've

been a brave lad." How empty his words sounded but the boy opened his eyes and looked up at him.

"Lord? Thank you, my lord; did I fight well? I tried to fight well, to make you proud."

"Rest, lad; and you'll fight for me again." The lie came easily enough and the boy fell silent and then a sudden thought seemed to occur to him. "She never came in the end, lord," he said.

"Who never came?"

"The Lady Eleanor," he breathed.

Ned was going to ask him what he meant but he saw there was no use; the boy was already staring up at the morning sky.

"Was Eleanor supposed to be here?" Ned asked Felix.

"That's what we agreed," replied Felix, "the lad Tom took her somewhere and she sent him back to meet us; but then... she never came."

Ned threw down his sword and anger flooded through him.

"Garth told me she went back to get Amelie, yet my wife lies dead in her chamber. Now she doesn't keep her word to you. It seems my sister is not quite ... with us."

"You cannot doubt the Lady Eleanor," said Felix, "she would never desert you. Never!"

"I know her better than you do, Felix; she's ruled by her passions...only her passions. Aye, when the fire's in her she can carve her way through any hazard you put before her but when she's in a dark mood... she knows not what she does."

There was a crash as the stable doors were suddenly thrown open; a moment later several horsemen burst out into the courtyard, battering Black to one side. Ned stumbled into their path as they headed for the gates his attention drawn to the girl in their midst. He did not see the poleaxe coming and its steel hammer caught him on the side of the head with a fearful crack. The riders drove on past and hurtled out of the gates.

Black picked himself up from the cobbles.

"Shall we go after them?" he asked Ned.

Ned lay on the cobbles, seeing only through glazed eyes. He tried to speak - and couldn't move his lips; he tried to rise - and couldn't get his arms to respond. He looked up at Felix - he knew it was Felix, tall and black against the sun. Then other figures crowded in on him and they were all tall and black against the sun.

43

28th May dawn, at Ragwulf's Cottage in Carperby

Eleanor sat on Ragwulf's bed, not knowing whether to go or stay. Felix would be waiting for her but the child must come first. Where was the child? She was alert to every sound and stood up at every bird call, every shout in the village nearby. She went to the door several times, thinking she had heard footsteps outside, but there was never anyone there.

Every hour seemed to take a year to pass by and every hour brought despair closer. Where was Ragwulf? Always in the past it had been her own plight, her own pain and she had fought every threat with a fiery rage but now, there was no rage, just a cold fear in her breast.

Before she realised it she found she was lying on the bed sobbing like a child, her knees hunched up to her chest with her arms wrapped tightly around them. She had lost Ned's son and betrayed Amelie a second time.

As the hours crawled by, she stopped her weeping and paced around the room, her frustration building. It felt as if she was caged like some bear - confined for the amusement of others. She gazed around the cottage a thousand times but there was little to see. Ragwulf seemed to possess nothing: where were his weapons: his bow, axe and sword? Where was his cloak, his other clothes? She began to ransack the room and found not a morsel of bread or cheese or any other food in the house. No food, no clothes, no weapons.

He need only walk a few hundred yards to Goodwife

Harding so why take food if he was coming back to wait for her? If he had the child, why would he weigh himself down with bow, axe and great sword? If not, then where had he taken the child? What had he done with the boy?

The more she thought about it, the more she doubted him; he had volunteered to have the child - what self-respecting man at arms would have done that? She should have seen it at once; Becky had called her foolish - and she was. Then a worse thought crept into her head: what if he had killed the child? Henry would have paid him a great deal for such a service. Yet, Ragwulf had seemed so loyal; he had helped her at every step - had all that simply been to gain her trust? Surely it could not have been just that; after all, she liked him.

Good Christ! That was it - that was how he had done it. He had realised that she would fight like a she-wolf to protect the child, so he had charmed her into just handing the boy over to him. And she had been charmed - she had even flashed her scarred dugs at him. He must have thought her the most stupid woman in Christendom.

Stupid bitch! She kicked out at the wattle walls of the cottage and banged her head in anger against the oak beams. She shredded Ragwulf's mattress, tearing out great lumps of straw. She pulled at her hair and scratched her face before she fell quivering onto the bed's savaged carcass. As she lay there, her anger was forged into a cold determination. She sat up and looked through the small window opening. The sun was high now; she had waited all morning and he had not come.

She knew she could never face Ned again; she could not even face herself. She slid out one of Will's swords and touched the blade with her finger tips; the edge was rough but it was sharp and drew blood at once. A shadow passed the window opening; she gasped and sprang off the bed, the sword still in her hands. If the child was not with him, she would rip out his heart as he had ripped out hers.

The door swung inwards and Ragwulf stood in the

doorway; his face was grim and haggard and the child was not with him. So it must be, she thought. She threw herself at him, swinging her blade wildly as hot anger coursed through her veins once more. Only his fighter's instinct saved him as he ducked under the first slicing arc of her sword. Her blade bit into the door frame sending a large splinter flying back at her. It caught her on the cheek and lodged there but she scratched it away and raised her weapon to strike again. Ragwulf drew out his sword. Shit! She had hoped to avoid that. Well, she could still take him. He was taller; she must turn that to her advantage.

"Lady!" he shouted at her but she would not listen to him - he would charm her again.

She held her sword with both hands and aimed lower, cutting at his thigh, but he managed to drop his sword in time to meet hers.

"Hold!" he cried but his words meant nothing to her. She must finish him fast before his strength could tell.

She took a step back and then lunged forward swiftly. "Liar!" she screamed. He parried her blade once more; her arms shuddered from wrist to shoulder but she saw she had cut him a little at the waist.

"Are you mad, woman?" he shouted at her. He must be feeling the wound then. Now he took a pace towards her and she had to retreat. A sudden blow from his heavy sword tore her blade away and it clattered to the floor.

"Now! Enough," he said. But if he thought she was finished, he was very wide of his mark. She drew out the second of Will's blades and hacked at his thighs again. This time he barely managed to block her.

"You're getting slower," she snarled, though she was getting out of breath herself.

As their swords met again, he pressed her back towards the wall.

"Why are you doing this, lady?" he demanded.

Good, she thought, he's angry: he'll make a mistake. But he didn't; he pressed her backwards until their weapons were locked together and her shoulders rested against the wall. She thought of drawing out a knife but she needed both hands on her sword hilt. She felt her strength ebbing away and his growing. Words were her last hope.

Their faces were only a foot apart now as he held her against the wall. She spat in his eye and saw the horror on his face.

"You betrayed me," she breathed, "you killed the child and you betrayed my brother, your sworn lord!"

"No!" he cried. She felt the pressure of his sword against hers ease a little and tried to push him back. He only needed one hand on his sword and he now put the other around her throat.

"Listen!" he said, "the boy's not hurt!"

She tried to throw his words back, to tell him he lied but his hand was tightening around her neck. There was blood running down her face; she had not noticed it before. He was going to kill her now, she realised.

Then she saw beyond him, in the doorway, a girl - a girl who looked terrified but a girl who held a child in her arms. She stared wide-eyed at the girl; Ragwulf looked to the door and shook his head. Then he lifted Eleanor up by the throat and tossed her onto the remains of his bed.

No-one said a word. The girl stood in the doorway still - transfixed by what she had seen. Ragwulf pulled her inside and slammed the door. Eleanor threw her blade onto the floor and began to rub at her sore neck. Ned's son began to cry and she watched as the girl calmly sat down and put the child to her breast.

"Wet-nurse," croaked Eleanor.

Ragwulf said nothing but stalked around the small room, darting occasional glances at her and each one struck her like a slap on the face.

"When you didn't come…" her voice tailed off. She could not even explain it to herself, let alone him.

He stopped pacing about and stared at her. "Did you think so little of me?" he asked.

"I thought …"

"No, my lady, that's one thing you didn't do. I've done all I could to keep that boy alive in the past hours and you repay me like this. And what do you think young Bess here makes of you? She's unwed, lost her bastard child - a disgrace to her family; why, her father more or less paid me to take her away." Ragwulf laughed bitterly. "Some knight he is…and some lady you are!"

"I'm -" began Eleanor.

"So, I bring her from her home and she willingly suckles the boy at the midwife's. But I must meet you here and I'm very late, so I must take her from there where she felt safe. She was scared, lady: scared of me, scared of handling the baby, scared of what would become of her, scared of every soul that scowled at us as we walked here. And when she gets here, what greets her? A fucking mad woman - that's what."

He turned from her and went outside. She felt many things then: but most of all, she felt shame. She brushed aside the blood from her cheek and winced as she felt the tip of the splinter still there. She got up gingerly from the bed; the girl, Bess, shrank away from her and crushed the baby to her breast.

"I'm sorry," Eleanor said softly and stumbled outside after Ragwulf.

She found him leaning against the wall. She stood next to him.

"I was …wrong," she said, "I know."

He did not look at her but stared straight ahead across the fields. "Wrong? You were a lot more than just wrong," he said.

"I know; I can be …rash, sometimes."

"You were a lot more than rash," Ragwulf snapped at her.

"Aye; but when I get worried…"

"You try to kill the first man you see?" he said.

She shook her head. "I make mistakes. I beg your forgiveness," she said.

"Ladies don't need to beg from common men at arms,"

he said. "Ladies do what they will and men at arms die for them."

He left her and went back inside; she did not dare follow him. Soon he came out with Bess and the child.

"You'd best pick up your swords, my lady," he said. "Then you can tell us where you'd have us go." His voice was quiet, distant. If there had once been any bond between them, it was not there now.

She nodded, relieved that he had not taken her head off her shoulders for, in his place, she would have done. "The castle," she replied and went to retrieve her weapons.

44

28th May early afternoon, in the bake-house at Yoredale Castle

Everyone was speaking at once; well, everyone except Agnes. She listened to their arguing as she bathed Ned's face and head. They had brought him from the yard into the nearby bake-house and laid him on a long table. There she examined his head carefully: as she had done once before, in a different place. It seemed a long time ago now but she guessed it was probably no more than a week. Had her father truly been dead for just a week?

Her slender fingers probed Ned's skull; she knew a bit about skulls and she did not like the look of Ned's. She explored the wound more closely, while the argument drifted on around her. The poleaxe had struck him in much the same place as before; that could not be a good thing, she decided. The recent puncture had just begun to heal over but now, beside it, there was a mighty dent. The flesh around it was already discoloured and swollen. It was soft to her touch and at its centre there was an ugly split which still oozed a little blood. He stirred a little; was that good or perhaps it was just a sign that she had hurt him? She had a gentle touch, or at least so her father had often told her.

If she had been at home she would have applied poultices and given him herbal mixes to ease the pain, some yarrow perhaps. She used such remedies every day in the forest, but in the castle... Yet the forest of Yoredale was only a few yards away - surely she could find what she needed there. She stood up, gave Ned's hand a squeeze and then she hurried outside into the courtyard. At once she came to a halt. Of course, they had shut the gates. She returned to the bake-house; no-one had even noticed her leave - not only dumb but invisible, it seemed.

They were still discussing what to do: the tall black man was insisting that they must take Ned away, far away. He was most insistent but so was Spearbold. She was surprised how determined he could be and he was adamant that his lord should not be moved yet. He was right as far as she was concerned but they would not be asking her opinion. She tugged at Hal's arm.

"Wait, Agnes, we're talking," he said. It was said with kindness as if speaking to a small child; but she was not a small child, just a girl who could not be heard.

She pulled him harder, dragging him away from the others. Perhaps he remembered other times when he had ignored her but for whatever reason he finally let her lead him away. She took him by the hand to the gates and pointed to them. She dropped his hand and made as if to lift the great beam which barred the gateway

"Do you want to leave, Agnes?" he asked. "Your lord would not want you to."

She felt like slapping his face...hard; but she knew she was confusing him. Then an idea occurred to her and she put her hands on his chest, willing him to stay there. She ran back to the bake house then into the brew house next to it but could not find what she wanted. When she went out of the yard again Hal was already on his way in. She screamed at him, a long but silent scream and took his hand once more, dragging him across the yard to the Hall.

"Agnes?"

It was all he said; all he could say. He said it quite a lot as she led him through the butteries and from there into the kitchen. There she found what she wanted. She picked up the pestle and mortar and mimed grinding some herbs. Then she took him out to that gates once more and pointed to them.

Finally he understood. "You want to help our lord?" he said. She nodded eagerly and hugged him. He held her for a moment before she broke away and stood by the gates.

"No, it's too dangerous, Agnes," he said. "You must stay here."

She leant against the stone of the gatehouse, crushed; was this how every conversation would be? She turned away from him in disgust; she might as well throw herself off one of the towers. They all saw her the same way, even Hal: a girl who could not speak and therefore could do nothing useful. But Ned Elder knew different; he knew that she was worth something and she did not want him to die. She stalked away from Hal across the yard and returned to the bake-house where to her astonishment she found the argument still going on.

She threw up her hands and left them there, walking through the ground floor store rooms, past the armoury and into the stables. It was a shock; she had forgotten that Hal and Black had put all the bodies there; friend and foe alike. The tall stable doors were a little open otherwise she would have fallen over the bodies. She paused for a moment, reminded of her last sight of her father as Ned and the others had lowered him into a shallow grave. She had lain on that grave for a long time before Ned had picked her up and taken her away. He had promised he would be a father to her, that he would look after her and that she would not need to fear again. She had believed him, except that now he was dying and fear was all she had left.

She walked on through the near empty feed store for the horses and reached an archway and there, before her, was another gate, but this one was smaller. At once she tried to lift the bar across and just managed to move it: first one end, then the other. It made a loud crash as it fell onto the stone flags but she quickly heaved the door open and ran out.

§§§§

"I can't find her anywhere now," said Hal, "and the postern gate was open."

"Good. It'll be easier without her," said Black, "she held us up all the way - we'd have gained another day if it hadn't been for her."

Hal wanted to argue, to defend her; but she had delayed them. Perhaps Black was right; it might have made all the difference.

"Go and find her," ordered Spearbold, "Lord Elder is her protector and he'll want her kept safe."

Black grunted and looked at Hal.

"Alright," sighed Hal, "I'll get her. Have you decided what to do yet?"

"We have," said Felix, "there's a small cart in the yard. We'll put Ned in that and I'll take him north to the coast. I've a ship waiting for him at Hartlepool but it won't wait much longer."

"You can't just throw him onto a ship - he's near dead already!" argued Hal.

But it was Spearbold who answered him. "Hal, you've heard us go back and forth over this until we're not sure what we're about. But, in the end, Felix has persuaded me that it is certain death for Ned if he stays."

"Hah! What's different," said Black. "It's been that way for weeks."

"Well and good whilst Lord Elder could defend himself," Felix pointed out, "but he can't now. Taking him is a risk but leaving him is a death sentence. We have three more days of safe passage left. Then Ned Elder becomes a legal target once more."

"You'll not get him there in five days - let alone three," said Hal, "not in a cart!"

"What about the rest of us?" asked Black.

"You may stay or go as you please," said Spearbold, "Someone must go with Lord Elder."

"I'll be going with him," said Hal at once.

"Well, Lord Elder charged me to look after the girl," said

478

Spearbold "which reminds me, Hal…"

"God's Blood! I should be looking for her," said Hal. "I'll find her - just don't go without me, Felix!"

He ran to the stable and saddled his horse then he hurried out of the postern gate and rode out towards the forest to the west. Now, where had the blessed girl gone?

§§§§

For the first time in a long while Agnes was enjoying herself; she wandered east through the open woodland on the forest's edge, searching out the plants she wanted and when she actually found one she beamed with delight. She collected some yarrow - soldier's woundwort was what her father called it. He had been a soldier once but he had told her little about that. She took both the leaves and the roots and soon she also had an armful of broad-leaved comfrey. She had to go deeper into the forest to find wild garlic but her keen sense of smell led her to some soon enough. She would have liked some sage but accepted that she could not find everything.

Her calm was interrupted by the sound of horses coming through the trees towards her. She ran further into a thicker part of the forest to avoid them, clutching to her breast the herbs she had gathered. She hid herself in the undergrowth until the sound of the horses had faded away. She took a deep breath and then grimaced when she was nearly knocked over by the powerful odour of the garlic.

She got up and started to make her way back to the castle - except that, having taken a hasty detour, she was not too sure exactly which way it was. The castle was west, that much she could tell; but if she headed west and missed the castle then she would only lose herself in the forest. If she did not get back to Ned soon then she would have wasted her time gathering the herbs. Then she heard more horses - was it the same ones or different? She listened carefully: one horse this time; but still a threat to her. She continued west as swiftly and silently as she could - she was good at silence.

When she stopped to rest, she thought from the sun it was about mid-afternoon; she was lost. She still carried the plants but they were crushed and bent now - though still usable, if she ever found the castle again. She would have to head north out of the forest and see if the castle was visible. Her quick errand was becoming more of an ordeal and she began to realise that whilst the forest had been her home, she was not at home in this forest. She would be safer with Hal and the others - at least they knew she could not speak.

Too late she realised there were yet more horses approaching. She tried to flit back into the trees out of sight but skidded on a muddy patch of earth and slipped, scattering her plants far and wide. She got to her knees and tried to recover the leaves but the horsemen were already there. They surrounded her, their mounts jostling her. She tried to push them away but one of the men cuffed her around the head with his hand. Then he hoisted her up onto his saddle and she noticed the badge on his breast - an animal and a branch. She stared at it and then shrank away for this was a badge she would always remember. The man they called Shard wore it and some of those with him - those who had struck down her father.

The rider spoke to her; he sounded a little gruff, but not unkind.

"Now, lass; we're looking for a man called Ned Elder - Lord Elder perhaps to you. Do you know where he is?"

She shook her head vigorously. It was hard to lie when you couldn't speak and she was not use to dissembling.

"If you know you haven't seen him then you must know him. Can you tell us where Lord Elder is?" her captor asked.

When she did not answer, he gave her a sharp slap on her cheek. "Speak up, lass; no harm will come to you if you do."

She believed him too; but of course she said nothing and he hit her again harder. She began to weep.

One of the other men pulled her across onto his horse. "She's too shit-scared to tell us anything - still she might as well make herself useful," he said. "You lads go on; I'll join you in a bit."

He chuckled as the other men shook their heads and rode on. When they had gone he dropped her off the horse and jumped down beside her, seizing her arm before she could flee.

"Come on then; you're a quiet one, aren't you. Let's see if I can make you moan a little; I don't suppose you're a maid are you? I'm never that lucky."

"You're even less lucky than you thought," a voice called to him from the trees.

He spun around to see the speaker. Agnes could see no-one but she recognised Hal's voice.

"Come forward, friend," said the man at arms. Agnes felt his grip on her shoulder tighten as he guided her in front of him. "Do you know this lass?" he shouted.

"Aye," called Hal, "I do. So let her walk unharmed towards me; then mount up and ride away. Or,... I can put a yard of arrow in you."

"Very well; very well," said the rider, "no harm's been done. There she stands, free as a bird."

Agnes hurried towards Hal's voice as the man at arms made a hasty retreat.

She found Hal, mounted with his bow in his hand. Agnes wanted to warn him in case he did not know about the others but he seemed so pleased to see her, she gave up trying. Instead she went back to rescue some of her scattered herbs. He shook his head.

"Come on, Agnes; time is short."

She smiled up at him and he lifted her easily up onto his saddle behind him. She put one arm round his waist and the other gripped the remaining yarrow and garlic tightly.

He turned to look at her. "You stink of garlic!" he complained. She grinned and so did he; but their good humour lasted only a moment. They could both hear the horsemen returning.

"I was afraid of that," said Hal. He swung his mount

around to the south; Agnes noticed at once and glanced at him asking the question with her eyes.

"They're Warwick's men," said Hal, "and we can't risk leading them back to Ned. They're probably doing a sweep around on their way to the castle…but we can lead them off - perhaps scatter them a little before we make our way back?"

She gave him a solemn nod. He looked at the few remaining strands of green in her hand.

"Leave them now, Agnes; we'll make better speed if you hold on with both hands. You can always get some more." She dropped them and he dug his heels into the horse's flanks. Agnes thought Hal was an excellent horseman. In fact she thought Hal was pretty impressive in most ways. He rode fast and she needed to hang on at times, but it felt good. Riding with her young breasts tight against his back made her feel…different… and excited in a new way. Words would not have helped her to describe it, she decided.

After a few miles they slowed a little and Hal turned to explore the forest paths behind them. There was no sign of their pursuers.

"You can hold on a little less tight now, Agnes," he said breathlessly.

She pretended she had not heard him until he gently prised her hands from around his waist. Then she reddened and he looked at her in a way he had not done before. She smiled and felt her face flush; she felt suddenly very hot and turned away from him.

"How old are you?" he asked. "And why are you smiling so much?"

She was finding it hard to stop smiling though she wasn't sure why. She shrugged and held up all her fingers; then she held up four more.

"Fourteen?" he asked. She was not sure herself, so she just shrugged again and pointed at him.

"Oh, I'm a bit older than that," he said quietly. Well, she knew that much already.

"We'll follow the northern edge of the forest," he said,

"until we're near Yoredale but we must keep a sharp look out and keep quiet."

She dug him in the ribs and stared at him putting her hand across her mouth.

"I'm sorry Agnes; of course you can be nothing other than quiet; I'm the one who prattles on to little purpose."

She grinned and then her eyes noticed a familiar plant and she slid off the back of the horse. He pulled up as she rolled over and stumbled to her feet. She reached out to pull up some of the soldier's woundwort.

He shook his head at her. "Agnes," he said, "Please let me know if you want to do that again."

§§§§

"Damn me!" exploded Felix. "Where in God's name are they?"

"It's probably taking him a while to find her," said Spearbold, though his grey face betrayed his own concern.

Black chuckled to himself. "Of course, he might have found her some time ago…"

Felix frowned. "Am I the only one who is taking this seriously?" he asked. He was weary; he had been in the saddle for days, begged a favour of the King and fought without sleep - all to save a friend. Ned was still clinging to life but if they did not leave Yoredale today it was all over. Ned was too well known to tarry here too long and Felix had no doubt that Warwick would have men combing the area. They were only a dozen or so miles from Middleham; the Earl could put out the whole damned castle garrison to search if he chose to.

"Did you close the postern gate?" he asked Black.

"No, merchant, I left it wide open for any bastard to wander in! Of course I did."

"Well go back up on watch," retorted Felix.

"I'm the only one left who can manage the steps then, am I?" asked Black as he went out.

Felix looked at Ned. They had wrapped a woollen blanket

around him though it was not cold. Black had prepared the cart, though they had no farm horse or ox to pull it so they would have to improvise. If needs be Felix would pull it along himself - it wouldn't be the first time.

Black reappeared in the doorway.

"I thought you'd gone up to the ramparts," said Felix.

"I did - and now I've come back all the way down again to tell you they're on their way," he said breathlessly.

Felix nodded. "Thank the Lord!"

"Don't get too grateful," added Black, "because the Lord has sent a few others too: a dozen or more riders coming our way from the east."

Felix sighed.

"Warwick's," said Spearbold.

"Hal and the girl are only a hundred yards away," said Black, "they'll be here in no time but the riders won't be long either."

"We can't stay bottled up here!" said Felix. "Warwick has only to wait for a few days and Ned becomes an outlaw once more."

"With the cart we'll not get five yards," said Black.

"What then?" asked Spearbold.

45

28th May early afternoon, on the road
to Coverham Abbey

The ride, uncomfortable though it was, did Joan good: it gave her time to recover from the crushing disappointment of failure. She needed time to plan, time to think through a new design. She might be running now but she still intended to prevail. The three men who remained with her were not the bravest, or they would have been more inclined to fight on at the castle. One was Warwick's man; the other two had been Henry's and were now, at least for the time being, hers. They believed they were heading for the dubious safety of Middleham Castle. Joan, however, had no intention of going there yet. She knew that Warwick was almost certainly still at York and she doubted she would get a warm welcome from the Earl in any case. After all, she had surrendered the castle and lost most of his men.

The only good news she could give him was that Ned Elder was almost certainly dead. On the other hand, she no longer had anything left with which to negotiate with Warwick; but she had an idea about that. It was strange, she thought, how matters fell out: Henry, dead and gone, Ned, dead or dying. Yet here she was, little Joan, still alive and still able to win because of a few words she had overheard. She studied the horizon carefully; she could just make out the towers of Middleham in the distance. It was time to put her men to work; she pulled up.

The men at arms with her also stopped but looked at each

other, not her. She knew they did not trust her but they did fear her, just a little - hopefully just enough.

"How far is it to Coverham Abbey?" she asked Warwick's man.

The question clearly took him by surprise. "Coverham, my lady?"

"You've heard of it?" she asked.

"Aye, Coverham, aye but -"

"Are we not making for Middleham, my lady?" asked John - one of Henry's own.

"No," Joan's reply was curt and she was in no mood to encourage questions. She turned to Warwick's man. "Well?"

"Coverham's but a few miles south, my lady," he said, "if that."

"Good," she said, "come then; take me there."

But none of the riders seemed keen to change course.

"What is there at the Abbey for us, my lady?" asked John.

"You would question your lady's command?"

John did not answer but glanced again at the others. She could see they would need some encouragement to go to the Abbey when Middleham was already in sight.

"Very well," she said. "At the Abbey we'll find those who fled from the castle. The Earl of Warwick wants Lady Radcliffe's son and heir. If I can bring the boy to him, he'll show his gratitude - to us all. And of course, it may be that you'll find some trinkets there of interest to you..."

"Why would they let us in?" asked John. "Their walls are strong and we're but three."

"I'll get us in," said Joan, "you needn't worry about that. Lead on."

There was a brief moment of hesitation then. She felt humiliated when the others looked to John and only when he gave a nod did they move off. She would make him pay for that later but not now; for now, she needed them all. So they rode the few miles to the Abbey but Joan stopped some distance from its walls.

She turned to Warwick's man. "Tear my cloak," she

ordered.

"My lady?"

"Take out your knife and rip my cloak." The man shook his head but began to cut some long gashes in her clothes.

"Now, John, strike me on the cheek - not too hard!"

"My lady?"

"Go on; it needs to look convincing."

John gave a little smirk and slapped her across the face with his gauntlet. She rocked back on her horse.

"Sorry, my lady," he said, "was that too hard?"

Her cheek burned from the blow and she could taste blood on her lips. She took several deep breaths - sweet Jesus, he would pay dearly for that too.

"Wait under the wall beside the gate," she said, her voice trembling, "then come in smartly. We've one crossbow - how many bolts have you left?"

"Two, my lady," said Warwick's man.

"Well mind you use them well," she said, "now be quiet and be ready!"

She led them at a slow walk along by the wall until they neared the round arch of the gateway. There she left them and dismounted at the gate.

"Sanctuary!" she cried, "I pray you grant me sanctuary. I am Lady Joan Elder and I've been attacked! My cousins are already here. Let me in for the Lord's sake - I'm in fear of my life!"

She thought she sounded very convincing and expected the gate to be flung open to admit her. It was not; instead the gatekeeper's hatch was drawn slowly back and a dour face appeared. He stared at her for a moment, mumbling to himself.

She had to stand on tip toe to see his face.

"Can you not see what state I'm in?" she said. "I need your help!"

The gatekeeper peered down at her. "That's for the Lord Abbot to decide," he said, "and he's not here."

She pressed her face up against the small opening and

displayed her wounded cheek. "Look at me! I've been beaten."

"I'm not letting you in till he comes back," he replied.

"But I'm just a poor woman!"

She saw the flicker of doubt in his eyes.

"I'm weak; what harm can I do you?" A few well-judged tears reinforced her plight.

"Alright," he conceded, "but I warn you the Abbot might turn you out later."

"I shall throw myself upon the Abbot's mercy," she cried.

The gate rattled as he struggled to open it. "I doubt that'll do you much good," he said.

"Nor you, you wretch," she said as she thrust her dagger through his neck, spilling his blood all over the pair of them.

In a moment the men followed her in and dismounted.

"Now," she ordered, "Be swift! The guest house first and remember, the boy must not be hurt - I don't care about the rest."

She followed them at a safe distance. The guest quarters were easy enough to find since they were set apart from the rest of the buildings, along with the Abbot's House. She hoped they could snatch the boy quickly; then she might exchange a few words with her dear cousins, Emma and Eleanor. After that she must escape quickly to Middleham just in case. She had not seen Ned Elder dead and there was always a chance... but he would surely be in no state to pursue them. Then she heard a scream and gave a little smile; her men were at work.

§§§§

Emma lay on her bed; she was content - no, more than content, she was glowing. Garth, poor boy, was fast asleep after his exertions. He lay on his front with his arm resting carelessly across her bare waist. She wondered wickedly if he had any energy left - it must be many hours since dawn. She ruffled gently the curls of his dark hair; then she started to stroke his back with her hand and he stirred at her soft touch. She did not regret for an instant keeping him with her; she felt safe with him there.

He was supposed to be there to keep Richard safe but he was not really needed - Gruffydd and the girls were there too. It pleased her that Eleanor's girls, Becky and Jane, looked after her son so well. It went some way towards assuaging her guilt. She grinned; Garth's hand had wandered up from her waist. After this, she really must rise and show her face in the Hall, brave the knowing looks from Becky, the sniggers from Jane and the frown from Gruffydd. Then Garth kissed her and she closed her eyes, forgetting all else. All her worries were banished by that one kiss.

Then there was a loud crash from the Hall and a girl screamed; Jane! Garth was already half dressed by the time Emma had found her shift to put on. He pulled on his boots and picked up his sword; he was still bare-chested when he threw open the door and rushed out. Emma ran after him, out into the Hall and flinched at what she saw.

Jane had got almost to her chamber door with Richard in her arms. Now she lay with her body shielding the boy as an armed man beat her and tried to take the child. Near the Hall doorway, Gruffydd was grappling with another man armed with a large poleaxe whilst Becky shielded young Will and backed away from them.

Jane was screaming and squirming as each blow landed; her face was battered and bleeding but she still clung on to Richard. Emma saw with horror that there was a growing patch of blood on her back where a quarrel had passed almost through her thin body. Garth's sword almost took her attacker's head off and he collapsed to the floor in a bleeding heap.

"Take Richard and Jane into your chamber," Garth told her.

She lifted Jane up with her son and pushed them before her into the chamber.

"Come!" she said, seizing Garth's hand but he shook his

head.

"Stay in there! I'll help Gruffydd see off the others." He forced her inside and shut the door behind her. At once she opened it again.

"Stay in there!" he shouted. She nodded but left the door ajar and looked on as he went to Gruffydd's aid. The Welshman was trying to stop his opponent getting a clear strike at him with his heavy battlefield weapon, whilst he attempted to fumble out his dagger. Garth took a step towards them but a third figure appeared in the doorway, a loaded crossbow in his hands.

"Garth!" screamed Emma.

Garth rushed forward to close the distance and put the man off his aim. Emma ran out of her chamber but the bolt was already on its way and Garth was thrown back into her by the force of it. His sword clattered onto the stone flags as he stumbled backwards into Emma. She wrapped her arms around him and together they fell. Emma cracked her head on the floor. Blurred figures danced before her eyes and hands seem to beat up and down on Garth's body. She could feel the dull impact of every blow, then she felt a cut on her arm and her vision sharpened for a moment. There was blood all over her arms; it must be a bad cut she thought, for so much blood. Garth's body was crushing her chest. She cried out and her lungs ached; then a boot struck her head.

§§§§

Gruffydd saw Garth fall but could do nothing to help him. His opponent was strong and wore a thick padded jack. Though Gruffydd might hold him for a while, he could do nothing to hurt him so long as they were locked together. His adversary had been steadily pounding him on the shoulder with his poleaxe - they were weak blows but in no time they would punch through his own jacket. His sword lay propped against the wall in the far corner of the Hall - even if he broke free, he would never get to it.

Once the other man was finished with Garth he would be at their mercy. A gamble was needed but he was conscious that he was gambling with more than just his own life: with Garth down, there was only him left. Then a grim smile crossed his face: Becky had shoved Will into Lady Emma's chamber and thrown herself onto the man bent over Garth and Lady Emma.

Gruffydd knew this was the only chance there would be. He butted his opponent on the forehead and wrested the poleaxe from him, then he delivered a fierce blow to the stunned man's head. He dropped like a stone and Gruffydd stooped to finish him.

"Gruffydd!" cried Becky. He looked round to see her retreating with blood across her breast. The other man at arms dropped his bloody dagger and drew out his sword. Now he was coming at Gruffydd. The Welshman cursed and turned to face him. The poleaxe was unfamiliar in his hands - it had been years and this man would be too quick for him.

"Get my sword!" he shouted to Becky and watched her stagger towards it. She would be too late, he realised bitterly.

He parried a slicing sword blow with the axe but missed the lunge that followed it and felt the steel cut through his jack and into the flesh below his ribs. He reeled backwards but he got a bit of axe on the next strike glancing it aside. His opponent's eyes were fixed upon him as he forced him back towards the door. Becky tried to lift Gruffydd's sword and gave up. The big man watched her cross the floor unsteadily and reach down to pick up the discarded dagger from the floor. The swordsman never saw her coming and she swept his own knife across his throat from behind. Gruffydd snatched the man's sword from his dying hand and threw him to the floor.

He stuffed the axe handle through his belt. "Get the others!" he told Becky but only when she dropped to her knees did he realise how badly she was hurt. He took a step towards her and then felt a heavy blow in the back - a knife thrust. Shit! He hadn't finished off the first man. He turned awkwardly for his stomach was already on fire from the sword wound.

Blood dripped down the man's head but he was in better shape than Gruffydd and stabbed again. Gruffydd tried to block it with his sword but the long knife slid along it and sliced open his arm to the bone. Gruffydd let fall the sword and leant into the man trying to use his weight to press him back. In his belt he still had the poleaxe and he wrenched it out with his other hand. He used his last ounce of strength to bring it down upon the man's head. The blow landed with a crack and he knew it would be fatal. He left the weapon buried in the dead man's skull and moved away from the door. He glanced around the room: all three men were dead. Thank God and St. Michael! But the cost had been heavy.

He went into Lady Emma's chamber where Becky had crawled to be with her cousin Jane and the two frightened boys.

Becky looked up at him. "Are they…"

"Dead as dead," he said, "are you…"

"We're near dead as well," said Becky. "Will and Dickon are alright; Jane…she's bad but we need to get away. They know we're here - more will come!"

"Help your coz out; I'll bring the boys."

"Lady Emma? Garth?" asked Becky.

"I think they're both gone but I'll look at them a last time. Can you two walk? You look dreadful," said Gruffydd.

"Take a look at yourself," mumbled Becky as she half carried Jane out, "We Standlakes are tough bitches, aren't we Jane?"

Jane forced a ragged smile and blood dribbled from her mouth.

Gruffydd tore some linen from the bed and bound it tight around his bleeding arm. Then he walked through the Hall with the two lads behind him so that they did not see Garth and Emma on the floor. Then he pushed the boys on past.

"Go to Becky," he ordered them and his gruff voice forced them through the door. He bent down and gently lifted Garth aside: there was no doubt he was dead.

"Good Christ; it took a score of wounds to kill you, lad." He shook his head sadly as he examined Lady Emma. There was blood all over her too, yet her breast stirred with shallow breaths.

§§§§

Joan waited outside the guest hall for several minutes hoping the task would be accomplished swiftly. When several of the canons were drawn to the commotion inside, she brandished her knife and they backed away from her in bewilderment. She continued to wait impatiently but soon it became clear that her men had encountered some trouble. This was confirmed when the two servant girls stumbled out of the Hall door dragging the two boys with them. Only when they passed her did they recognise who she was; by then it was too late. Joan stabbed the younger girl, Jane and took Richard from her grasp. She put the knife to his throat.

"Go, while you can!" she ordered Becky. "But leave the other boy." He would have a bastard claim and since she was shedding so much blood, it was not worth the risk to leave him alive. But Becky did not move. She was clearly already hurt, but she looked strong. Richard squirmed in her grasp; perhaps it was better to keep what she already had.

"Get out or I'll kill this boy, Richard!" she growled. She took a pace forward and moved her knife as if to cut the boy's throat.

"No, don't!" cried Becky. "I'll go, but you're not having Will." She backed away towards the gate with Will ahead of her. Joan watched her go and then took the child into the guest hall.

The large Welshman was kneeling on the floor examining Emma.

"She's still alive!" he cried when he heard the door.

"Oh, good; she is my cousin after all," said Joan.

He looked up and tried to get up from the floor but by then she had picked up John's long knife and plunged it into his neck. Richard bawled at her and tugged to get free. She left the blade in Gruffydd's throat as he fell and slapped the boy with a bloodied hand.

"Be glad it's not you, boy!" she said fiercely.

She surveyed the carnage in the Hal with disdain; how could her three men at arms make such a mess of so simple a task against one youth, an old man and a few women. It truly beggared belief! There was no sign of Eleanor - that was a small worry; other than that, all was done.

Emma stirred nearby. Joan dragged Richard across to his mother. She sat him down on the floor. Emma rolled on to her side and caressed Garth's corpse, whimpering like a child. She looked briefly at her son and then threw herself upon Garth.

"Strange," said Joan, "you seem more upset to see the pretty youth dead than your own son about to be killed. I wonder why…"

Emma said nothing.

"Just teasing," said Joan, "I shan't hurt him; he's too valuable to me. My husband and your brother are dead and this little boy is the only male heir left to either the Radcliffes or the Elders. I'm going to take him to the Earl of Warwick who will keep him as a ward at Middleham. He'll have a good life, and sooner or later a good marriage, I dare say. In the meantime, I'll have all the estates."

Emma was still staring at Garth's blood-stained corpse.

Joan took out the document that set out Warwick's terms and laid it on the floor.

"When you can tear your eyes away from your lover, you'd better read this; it tells you what you must all do next - if you still want to live, that is."

She took Richard's hand and pulled him away. He stood his ground, eyes focussed on his mother, but Emma was looking elsewhere.

"Your mother's love is busy at the moment," said Joan and dragged him out. He continued to look back at Emma and said not a word. It surprised Joan at first but then she decided that she too would have been lost for words if her own mother had just let her be taken away without any attempt to prevent it.

Outside once more she paused. The other boy had gone - a pity, for she knew how much trouble a bastard could cause, if he really tried. Still, any further delay could prove fatal; even the canons were starting to look threatening though she doubted they would actually do anything to stop her.

At the gate she found only two horses; the girl Becky must have taken the others. She lifted the white-faced boy onto her saddle; then she struggled up on to it, standing on the dead gatekeeper to make it easier. She rode carefully out of the gates; it would be an uncomfortable ride but it was only a short distance to Middleham and sweet victory - so much for the value of sanctuary.

46

28th May afternoon, in the forest near Yoredale Castle

It was early afternoon when they reached the castle and Eleanor's heart sank when she saw it. Of Felix and the others there was no sign.

"The Radcliffe banners still fly from the walls and towers," said Ragwulf. "What do you want to do, my lady?"

It was the first time he had spoken to her since they had left his cottage.

"I don't know," she said, "what do you think?"

"It's for you to say, my lady," he replied tersely. He was clearly going to give her nothing but she couldn't blame him. In a way he was right: whatever had happened to Ned, she had his son and the fate of the Elders lay in her hands.

"We daren't risk the boy," she said. "We'll take him to the abbey."

"Is that wise?" he asked.

"I thought it was for me to say," she replied. She could be curt too.

"The boy will be seen there by many," said Ragwulf.

"We'll go to the Abbey," she said, "and the boy will belong to Bess whilst we're there."

He nodded and they both looked at Bess. She still looked terrified and Eleanor began to wonder if she always did. It was all the poor girl could do to blurt out: "yes, my lady."

The journey to the abbey was necessarily slow for the baby's sake and there were difficult moments: especially crossing the river and avoiding patrols of Warwick's men at arms - they encountered several. It was near dusk by the time they reached the abbey and as they approached the gate, Eleanor became wary.

Ragwulf must have sensed her disquiet. "Something wrong?" he asked.

"It sounds quiet enough," she said.

"Aye, and we can't stay out here all night," said Ragwulf.

She gave a long sigh and pounded on the gate but she made little sound and Ragwulf banged upon it with his mailed fist. Soon one of the canons came and, seeing it was her, pulled the gate open. She could tell from his face that something had happened.

"What?" she said, dismounting swiftly, "what is it?"

But she did not wait for him to answer; instead she ran to the guest hall. The door was wide open but the Hall was empty. There was blood everywhere, but no bodies. She rushed into Emma's chamber and stopped dead. Her sister lay on her bed, pale and drawn; two of the canons were in attendance - one she knew was Reedman who her sister had known years before.

"My lady," he said, "your sister sleeps now but Hell has come to our holy abbey."

"Don't talk in riddles!" she snapped at him. "What happened? Where's my son?"

"Your son lives, my lady; but others God has taken."

"Take me to my son!"

Reedman took her to the infirmary where Will lay peacefully asleep. On the bed next to him was Becky; she by contrast, looked dreadful.

Eleanor turned to Reedman. "Is she?"

"She has taken some wounds but we have poulticed them and given her some relief for the pain, my lady."

"Thank you, and... the others?" she asked.

"I was not there," said Reedman, "but only Lady Emma remains of the rest. I'm sorry, my lady. We...we laid out their bodies." He pointed to the far end of the room.

"Only Emma…" It was a bitter blow, all the more so because she had imagined that the Abbey would be safe.

"Leave me please, canon. At the gate you will find Lord Elder's man, Ragwulf, with a girl and her child; they are under our protection. I would be grateful if you would tell Ragwulf what you know."

He nodded and left her.

She touched Will's cheek, as if to reassure herself that he was still alive and cried when she felt the warmth of him. Then she sat on Becky's bed and stroked her forehead. She lifted up the woollen blanket and gasped to see the extent of the wounds and her breasts bound up. Becky woke up at once and the pair embraced like lovers who had long been apart.

"My dear," said Eleanor softly, "what have they done to you?"

Becky shook her head. "It all came upon us so quick…" she murmured.

"Tell me, please - if you can."

"Lady Joan came here with her men …and their crossbows and swords. I fought hard. I remembered my mother - she was a fighter at the last - so Bagot told me. We all fought hard…and Jane…" The words tumbled out quickly then, but words were not enough.

"I can't believe it: Gruffydd, Garth and your Jane…" said Eleanor.

"She took young Richard with her," said Becky, "He'll be at Middleham by now." She turned away.

"You need to rest now," said Eleanor, kissing her hair. "Thank you for saving my boy."

She walked slowly to the other end of the infirmary where the corpses lay, each covered with a linen shroud. One was larger than all the rest; she lifted the cover from Gruffydd's huge frame and gazed down upon his grizzled face. Few would have found it beautiful but she did: the face of the man who had saved her. He had told her often that he would retreat to the Welsh hills before he died; he should be buried there, she thought. She threw the linen aside to see the extent of his wounds but then covered him up again; he would not want her to remember him like that, torn and bloody. She left him and trudged to the door.

Becky called softly after her: "Without Gruffydd, she would have killed us all."

Eleanor nodded and walked out of the infirmary without another word; she wandered into the cloister. She doubted the canons would want her there but she did not care - it was a place for quiet contemplation, was it not?

Ragwulf moved quietly for a large man and she was not aware of him until he stood next to her.

"Grieve for the man, my lady," he said, "but not the manner of his death. Gruffydd was a great warrior in his day and this is how he would've wanted to die - saving your son."

She said nothing but she rested her head on his shoulder and then the moment passed.

"You can't stay here," he said, "it's no longer safe."

She nodded. "I know. I must speak to my sister; we have to decide what to do."

"If you can believe Reedman, she's not going to be much help," he said.

§§§§

She returned to Emma's chamber and sent away one of the canons, leaving only Reedman.

"How badly is she hurt?" she asked him.

"If you mean her wounds, they are slight; some cuts and bruises only."

"Then why's she lying there looking half-dead?" asked Eleanor.

"The attack... was a shock; the loss of her son to that woman...and the boy Garth's death - a brave lad."

"Very well. Leave us please, canon."

"If you would like me to stay..."

Eleanor fixed him with a cold stare. "If I wanted you to

stay... oh never mind, just get out!"

When he had left she shook her sister roughly by the shoulder. "Emma!" she said sharply.

Emma opened her eyes and looked at her. "Go away," she said.

"Emma, there are matters to discuss; there are things you don't know."

"I don't want to know." Eleanor heard the anger and weariness in her voice.

"Sister, you've lost Garth and that'll hurt - you may grieve for him all your days - but your son is taken. Ned's not here and we must do something to get him back."

Emma stared at her as if she was deranged. "Get him back? I don't want him back!"

"But he's your son!"

"A son forced into me by Edmund Radcliffe! What sort of a son could that be? He's better off where he is - and so am I." She turned away and closed her eyes.

Eleanor leapt onto the bed and knelt over her, forcing her to face her.

"I need you to help me!"

"You've never needed me," she said, "even when mother died and you were small; you were always stronger. You'll endure, Ellie, you always do. I am going to take holy orders and go to a nunnery. I've talked about it with Reedman."

Eleanor held Emma's face in her hands and stared into her dark eyes. "You'd become a nun because your lover died?"

"I wouldn't be the first, would I? You know it's not just that - in your heart, you know. If you'd just stop being so angry for a moment, you'd see."

"Reedman! He's put this foolish idea in your head!"

"No, he has not. I've been thinking about it for a long time. Why do you think I was visiting the abbey so often? Then Garth came along... and I had doubts, but I don't have any more doubts."

Eleanor got off the bed and Emma reached under her bed

cover and brought out a small document. "Read this," she said, "Joan kindly left it for us; it tells us what Warwick is prepared to allow us to do if… if Ned is dead."

"We don't know he is dead!" replied Eleanor, but she took the paper and read it nonetheless.

Then she tossed it onto the bed. "Ned would laugh in Warwick's face," she said.

"Ned's not here."

"No, but I'm not going to some God forsaken hole in the far north just because high and mighty Warwick wills it!"

"What choice have you got? Go to a nunnery?"

"No I've tried that. But it says you can have Corve near Ludlow, if you wish."

"And what would I do there? Sew? A nunnery will be less of a prison, I think."

"Well, I've been in one and I wouldn't agree," said Eleanor. "And I don't see why Henry should get all we have."

"Henry won't. Joan said he's dead."

"And you believe her. But even so why should our cousin have our estates?"

"I don't care if she has them. I don't care who has them - though Warwick will have them really."

"So says the woman heading for a nunnery - what about the tenants?"

"One lord is much the same as another. Warwick is not like the Radcliffes."

"I'm not going north! They're all savages in the borders!"

"You should fit in very well, sister."

"I'm not going north; I'm going to stay here and fight!"

"When you leave here, we'll probably not meet again," said Emma, "I want us to part as friends."

"We were never friends, Em, just sisters and whether you take holy orders or not, we'll still be sisters - and we'll see each other again. I don't have any doubt of that."

She kissed Emma on the cheek and went out. Canon Reedman was in the Hall outside.

"She's told you," he said with a nervous smile.

"Aye," said Eleanor coldly.

"It wasn't my doing," he said.

"Aye, so she said."

"I tried to dissuade her."

"I don't doubt." Eleanor gave him a bleak look.

"The abbot hasn't yet returned," he said. "Until he does, we will give you whatever aid we can. I fear though, his disposition may be different…"

"We'll not be here for long," she said, then regretted it for she had no idea what she would do next. She had intended to tell Emma about the child, to plan together what they would do. Now she was on her own.

47

28th May evening, at Yoredale Castle

It must have been hours since Agnes had applied a poultice to Ned's head wound and given him some warm liquid to ease the pain.

"He looks a little better," said Hal.

"That's because it's a little darker," replied Felix, "and you can't see him so well!"

"No, I swear he has more colour." Hal wanted to believe so.

"The torchlight gives him some colour," said Felix. "Still, let us not go over the same ground again; we must take him tonight whether he's any fitter or not."

"Better he dies with us than on the block in Middleham or York," said Hal.

"I'm sure," agreed Spearbold.

"The cart's out of the question at night - and it's just going to be too slow," said Black.

"But he can't ride!" said Spearbold.

"It can be done," said Felix, "I've seen it - he can ride with another. It will take its toll on the horse, but it can be done."

"We've enough trouble with the girl falling off her horse let alone him," said Black.

"How many horses do we have?" Felix asked him.

"Six."

"Very well. Agnes can ride with Spearbold; Ned will ride with me - I ride better than either of you two! Black leads the two spare horses and we hope they're enough to get us to Hartlepool. If we ride slowly but don't stop; we might just make it."

"Haven't you forgotten our friends outside?" asked Spearbold.

"No. That's where Hal comes in."

"Here it comes," muttered Black, "here comes your bag of shit, Hal boy."

Felix gave him a wry smile. "Leave us," he said, "Black, get the horses saddled; Spearbold help Agnes to prepare whatever salves she can take with her."

"I'm sure she can manage," said Spearbold.

"And I'm sure I want you with her," insisted Felix.

When they had gone, Hal was impatient to know just how large a bag of shit was coming his way. "Come on, Felix - out with it!"

"I need you to lead them in the wrong direction for us - you know the forest better than anyone."

"That doesn't sound so hard," said Hal. "But how will I find you later?"

Felix looked at him but said nothing.

"I won't, will I?" said Hal.

"No, you won't," said Felix. "You're not going to Hartlepool with us."

Hal felt his heart beat faster. "I can't leave Lord Elder," he said firmly. "The only way I'll leave him is if I'm dead! I don't see how Spearbold goes and I don't! He's only been with Ned for a month - not even that! And Black? Why Lord Elder released him from his oaths? Why take him?"

Felix put a hand on Hal's shoulder but he shrugged it off. How could Felix push him away like this? It was unfair; Ned had been a father to him and Felix knew that.

"Hal, there's more to be done here than a simple diversion. I need someone I can trust - and that others can trust."

"What? What more is to be done?" demanded Hal, still bristling at the whole idea of abandoning his lord.

Felix took him by the hand. "Hal, I think you know me well enough; there are matters which cannot be ignored. When you've shaken off Warwick's men, you need to go to Ned's sisters at the Abbey; tell them what we're doing. They'll need your help. They may need to flee - and if Warwick allows them to stay, they'll still need you."

"So, I'm to serve Ned's sisters?"

"I've not finished yet. Spearbold's told me about the men who stayed with Sir Stephen at Crag Tower. Many are your friends, I know. They'll have had no news; they need to be told and... Sir Stephen must then decide what to do. Crag Tower still belongs to your lord."

Hal shook his head. "Bag of shit is about right," he muttered.

Felix sighed. "There's more, Hal, I'm afraid. There are also the men who came south with you from Crag Tower."

"All dead, or near enough - all save me and Black "

"Indeed," said Felix, "and do you know the names of all those who were killed?"

Hal stared at the Frenchman in surprise. "I suppose - if I sat down to think about it...which I try not to do. Why?"

"Others will be thinking about them, Hal: mothers, wives, children..."

"Aye, I dare say they will." It chilled him to think of it; there would be many a widow in the valley.

"Before you leave the abbey, get one of the monks there to write a list and get his solemn assurance that he will tell the families - it's not right that they are left not knowing. Your lord would have done it himself - you know that - so it's fitting that you do this for him. That is the last of your burdens, Hal and, if it be the last service you do for your lord, let it be done well."

Hal looked down at Ned. He knew Felix was right, knew that he must do it; but hated the thought of leaving Ned. Nevertheless, he nodded and walked out.

He found Agnes and Spearbold in the great kitchen; Spearbold found a reason to leave them alone and Hal stood for a time watching her crush the yarrow root and grind it into a paste. He did not know quite what to think about Agnes, but he knew he had thoughts about her.

She stopped and looked up at him.

"I'm not going with you," he said.

She nodded. She already knew - perhaps Spearbold had told her. She smiled at him and when her glistening eyes met his, he smiled back.

"Look after our lord, Agnes," he mumbled. She nodded and came to give him a hug, pressing her whole body against him. She was trembling, perhaps with fear. She pulled away and returned to her pestle and mortar.

"I'll see you again," he said, though he doubted he ever would and the look on her face told him she doubted it too.

§§§§

Hal left the castle first by the postern gate and then walked his horse carefully around its walls. It was a cloudy night, no moon - which was good, Hal thought, except at this point he actually wanted to be seen. Warwick's soldiers, having hailed the castle in vain when they first arrived, had set up their camp in the forest about a bowshot from the main gate. It would look ridiculous if he passed too close to them yet he must attract the attention of as many men as possible. It was a delicate path he was treading as he skirted the forest to the south of the watchers.

He pulled up and waited. He needed to stir them up, make at least most of them follow him. They were noisy for they wanted those in the castle to know they were there; but that allowed Hal to ride close to them. He could see a group clustered around their fire but he knew others would be posted nearby and it was one of those he wanted. He dismounted then strung his bow, flexed it a little and selected an arrow from his bag. Not so many left again - he could ill afford to waste them. He trod carefully, peering into the darkness; he could not leave too great a distance to his mount or he'd be caught. Somewhere to his left, a word or two was said; he couldn't make it out but it told him which way to look. After a moment or two he saw them, crouched in the undergrowth - they must be very uncomfortable there, he thought.

He aimed to injure not kill; he didn't want to make them too mad, just interested enough to follow him. He breathed gently and drew his arm back in a steady unhurried draw as he had done a thousand times before. He loosed the arrow and moved back to his horse at once as the cry of pain came and the men around the campfire were alerted. Even then, Hal did not rush. He told himself to keep calm, to wait for them to move. He rode noisily back and forth through some heavy leaved branches; and waited. Every fibre of his body screamed at him to ride away but if he went too soon all his care would be wasted.

He unstrung his bow for it would only hamper him as he rode. He could hear them in the camp: shouts, horses snorting and whinnying. He'd been there himself often enough - a surprise attack by a half-hidden enemy. You might take a knife in the gut and bleed to death or a swift carve across your throat might end your troubles before you were even awake. He rode close to the camp making as much noise as he could, taking a greater risk even in the darkness. The key was the fire; he could still see it and that was a bad sign - then suddenly the bright glow disappeared.

He could smell the smoke as they kicked it out and then he heard them coming - and he turned and fled, crashing through the forest before them. How many had he drawn off? He was sorely tempted to look back but he would see nothing - best to keep going. If he seemed to be too far ahead, he slowed and made more noise to keep their attention. Once he was caught out, thinking they were far off when one burst through the trees towards him like a bolt from a crossbow. Hal remained where he was, holding his horse still; the animal was tired and so was he. After a few moments the rider disappeared but Hal did not dare move for some time afterwards.

He looked at the sky, trying to estimate how long he had until dawn - not long he thought. He should make for the abbey and just pray he had done enough to let the others get away.

§§§§

Felix and Spearbold lifted Ned into the saddle and then Felix leapt up behind him but when Spearbold let go Ned nearly fell off. This is not good, thought Felix, we've not taken a step yet and already I can't hold him. It was hard, he found, to hold the reins to guide the horse and also to keep Ned balanced. Spearbold had the slight Agnes behind him and they seemed to have sorted themselves out. He glanced at Black.

"Whatever you do, don't let those spare horses loose. Our weight is too much for this animal to carry at more than a walk. In the darkness we'll walk but tomorrow we'll need to go faster and we'll need those fresh horses."

They had decided to open the main gates; after all, if Hal's diversion had not worked, there would be men watching both gates. They rode out leaving the gates wide and headed east. There was no time to take a longer quieter route. They must head for the coast and hope the Lord was with them.

Spearbold led the way. His local knowledge allowed him to pick a gentle path. Felix would like to have followed the river some way but that would take them far too close to Middleham. Better to keep going north. Through the hours of darkness they hoped they were clear but when dawn came they realised at once that they were being followed.

The three men picked up speed and thundered after them. Felix knew there was no hope of flight. "Make for the trees!" he cried, pointing to a stand about fifty yards to their left.

He urged his horse forward but the beast was having none of it and almost stopped. No point in killing the animal, he thought: it was spent. He dismounted awkwardly and Ned fell on top of him. He carried him on his shoulder the remaining few yards to the trees - not that the trees would help them much. He set Ned against one of the thicker trunks.

"Look after him, Agnes," he ordered, but what he expected the girl to do he had no idea. She took out her knife and crouched by Ned.

By the time Felix had retrieved his staff from one of the spare horses, the men were upon them. Speed was vital; Spearbold barely knew which end of his sword to hold and the girl was plucky but doomed - it was up to him and Black. The latter had already dismounted and stood in front of the others as their attackers spread out, swords drawn. They looked confident, thought Felix, and why wouldn't they?

48

29th May morning, at Coverham Abbey near Middleham

Eleanor awoke with a start, forgetting at that moment that she was in the infirmary with Will clutched to her breast. She had elected to stay there with Becky rather than go to the guest hall. She stretched her limbs and Will stirred in protest; so she laid him back on the bed and got up. The canons could be heard at prayer; the bell to summon them to worship was probably what had woken her.

Becky slept, her breathing was soft and even; that was good. The bodies at the far end of the room had begun to smell, not a great deal just enough to remind her of their presence. Reedman had told her they would be buried today. And what would she do today? Should she tell her sister who the baby with Bess was? She had agonised over it but last night, in the abbey's bleak darkness, she had decided not to. Now, in the pale dawn, she had not changed her mind.

She walked towards the guest house but noticed Ragwulf was up and prowling by the abbey gate.

"Are you so anxious to go somewhere?" she asked, leaning against the gate.

"You have a reason to tally here longer, my lady?" he countered. Clearly, he had not yet forgiven her - perhaps he never would.

"There are dead to bury…"

"Aye, and if you delay too long, there'll be more dead to bury!" he retorted. He went to move off but she caught his arm.

"I need your advice," she said. Words she had never spoken to anyone in her life before.

His face softened. "I'll not desert you and the child," he said.

A hammering on the gate at her back made her jump forward and she gave a little cry of surprise. He caught her and held her for an instant before she regained her balance and turned to the gate.

Almost immediately there was a further hammering. "In the name of good Christ, will you stop that banging!" she yelled. "We hear you!"

"Sorry, my lady," a small voice replied from the other side.

"Hal?" She wondered for a moment if her ears had betrayed her.

"Yes, it's me, Lady Eleanor!"

"Open the gate!" she said excitedly to Ragwulf. "Open it! Open it!"

"I am opening it," replied Ragwulf

Where Hal was, you were sure to find his lord; he would have news of Ned.

"Hal!" She greeted the youth like a long lost son and crushed him to her so close he flushed and pulled himself away in embarrassment. Then she looked him up and down.

"You're thinner," she said, "now, tell me: how fares your lord - and where is he?"

"As for where he is, my lady, he's somewhere on the road to safety, I hope; but in faith, your brother's far from well."

Eleanor frowned. "He's hurt?"

Hal nodded.

"Grievously?"

"Aye, my lady."

"Come, you'd better tell us all," she said and dragged him along to the Guest Hall and there she gathered all of them. She insisted that her sister left her chamber, with Reedman to witness what was said. Ragwulf, Bess, the baby and young

Will; all were there. Even Becky walked unaided from the infirmary despite several offers of help.

"Now, Hal, tell us what has happened," said Eleanor.

The telling took Hal some time for Eleanor kept interrupting him but when he had finished there was only silence. Eleanor could feel it - the room had somehow become a chasm of doubt for all of them. They did not know if Ned would escape - or, if even he did, whether he would live.

"Thank you, Hal," said Ragwulf. "You've done well, lad."

"Aye," said Eleanor, "even if we are no closer to knowing our fate."

"That's hardly the lad's fault," said Ragwulf.

"No," said Eleanor.

"I shall certainly bear the news to the bereaved families, Hal," said Reedman, "we could begin the list now if you wish."

"Give the boy some respite, canon," said Eleanor, "I doubt he's slept or eaten much."

"In faith, my lady," said Hal, "if the canon is willing, I'd sooner get it done now. I've thought of little else these past few hours. I want it to be right."

Reedman smiled at him. "Worry not, my lady, he shall eat as we prepare the list."

Soon after Hal had finished, the Lord Abbot returned and summoned Emma and Eleanor to his house.

"You've missed all the excitement, my Lord Abbot," began Eleanor but Emma silenced her with a desperate look and proceeded to tell him what had happened in his absence. It was one of those rare moments when Eleanor was proud of her sister. Going over Garth's death must have been hard. The violent story did not seem to shock the Abbot as much as she had expected and instead it prompted him to lead the pair in a series of prayers of peace and reconciliation. Eleanor was seething but she remembered her experience in the nunnery accurately enough to know that it was best to let the Abbot's prayers wash over her before she tried to get his attention.

When he did stop for breath, Emma then stepped in first to inform him of her decision to take holy orders. He found this a good enough reason to enter into a general discussion of the decline in faith he had noticed in recent years. After a while, it dawned on Eleanor that the old goat was stalling them - he must be, but why? Then he began to speak of other matters, matters relating more specifically to the Elder family. He had said only a few words before she interrupted him.

"You've seen her, haven't you?" she said. "You've been to Middleham and she's there!"

"If you mean Lady Joan Elder, "he replied easily, "then yes, I have."

"So you already knew what happened before you even came through the gate!" said Emma. Even her sister was angered by that, it seemed.

"I had Lady Joan's view," he said.

"I can guess what that was!" Eleanor spat at him.

"Did you see Richard, my son?" asked Emma.

"I did indeed, "replied the Abbot, "and he seemed in good health and in good heart."

"Good men died when he was taken," Eleanor ground the words out at him. "Better men than you!"

The Abbot eyed her warily. "Good men? What good men? A drunken Welsh sot and a callow youth who fornicated in a holy place of sanctuary?"

Emma gasped but Eleanor's knife appeared in her hand with a speed which surprised even her. She held it at the Abbot's throat as she tried to quell the tears she had yet to shed for Gruffydd.

The Abbot was no coward for he continued to speak even with the blade against his neck. "I take it you do not want to claim sanctuary any longer within these walls," he said evenly. "Perhaps you should go to Lady Joan - she's taken up residence this morning in your abandoned castle?"

"Sister, put up your knife," said Emma. "This gains us nothing." But Eleanor was just getting into her stride. She kept the blade where it was and growled at the Abbot.

"I shit upon your sanctuary, I piss upon your walls and I curse your false piety. I think your abbey could do with a martyr, Lord Abbot; and I'm just the woman to do it."

"No, Eleanor!" screamed Emma, "No!"

Eleanor pressed her blade against the Abbot's neck and the sweat ran down his face as he began to take her seriously.

"Lady Eleanor," he stammered, "perhaps I've misjudged you…"

"You've judged me very well, Abbot: I consort with fornicators, drunks and… cutthroats!" She increased the pressure of the knife against his skin. In her heart, she had already decided to do it - it would bring the wrath of God down upon her, but it would be worth it! God had deserted her long ago.

The Abbot had commenced a low intonation - if anything was likely to encourage her that was! "God be with you, Abbot," she said softly and drew the knife across his throat - except his throat escaped as a powerful hand snatched the knife from her grasp and threw it aside. She fell upon him scratching and snarling.

"Not again, my lady," moaned Ragwulf wearily and punched her on the chin.

§§§§

When she came to she found herself sitting on the floor of the infirmary in Ragwulf's arms. She felt drops of cool water dripping onto her face. The first thing she saw was the flagon which held the water. The droplets ran into her eyes and mouth and nose; she coughed and spluttered, pushing the flagon away.

"What are you doing?" she bawled at him.

"Your face is bleeding," he said, "I was just bathing the blood off to see how bad the cut was."

"If it's bleeding, it's because you hit me," she grumbled, but her head was sore and she did not raise her voice.

"You needed hitting… my lady," he said.

"Alright, alright. How bad is it?"

"I don't know; I've not got very far yet."

"Never mind," she snapped and got to her feet. She swayed back and he caught her as she fell.

"I'm fine," she muttered.

"You're not!" insisted Ragwulf. "That's why I was holding onto you!"

Eleanor struggled free and gingerly got to her feet. "Well, don't ever hold me again," she said, "for any reason. And don't ever hit me again - and don't stop me killing people either."

It was then she realised how stupid she sounded.

"What did you hit me with anyway - a stone?"

He shook his head, showed her his fist and walked out.

"I wasn't prepared for it!" she shouted after him. Then regretted it; her head hurt.

"Better get yourself ready to go, my lady!" he shouted back.

"Who says that I'm going anywhere?"

"I do."

She tramped after him, feeling small, feeling disconcerted and feeling far from herself. Gruffydd was dead; her rock was gone. Why did men always die when you needed them most?"

In the guest hall she found only Emma and almost turned around to go back out.

"Ellie, wait."

"Not another sermon, sister; strangely, I've about had my fill of those."

"No, not a sermon. You've Ragwulf to thank that the Abbot hasn't put you in one of his cells awaiting his judgement."

"Yes, I noticed - the bastard hit me!"

"Yes, he did; you needed hitting."

"Don't you start, please! My head hurts."

"He may have hit you but he also told the Lord Abbot

that if he harmed one hair of your head he would have certain of his body parts removed in the most painful manner possible and boiled in oil."

Eleanor's acid reply was already forming on her lips when her sister's words sank in and she remained silent and then, before a clever reply occurred to her, she began to weep.

Emma embraced her.

"All we ever seem to do together is cry," said Eleanor.

"Go with Ragwulf; Hal will take you to Crag Tower where the rest of Ned's men await him. Make a life far from here, with your son. Forget about me and Joan and Warwick and Yoredale. Find some peace Ellie, while you can."

49

29th May, on the road to Hartlepool

How good, were these men, Felix wondered? Could they be discouraged by a wound or two, a cracked head or broken bone? Perhaps they could another time, but not this time. Killing Ned Elder was unlawful and they knew it. They would also know that Warwick did not want any prisoners - or witnesses. Oh, for his warm bed in Ludlow with his warm woman in it!

Outnumbered three to two - for he did not count Spearbold. Yet their attackers looked wary and their eyes were fixed upon his long staff. Then it began. Two men came at him and the other made for Black. He prayed he could occupy both of them until Black had dealt with his own opponent.

Felix swung his staff in a wide arc just clipping one man's shoulder.

"Lord Elder is reprieved till tomorrow morn!" he shouted at them. "You're law breakers, all of you!"

He glanced to his right and saw that Black was only holding his own. He would have no aid from that quarter for a while. The pair came at him again and he prodded at them both with the full length of the staff. They took a pace back.

"The Earl has men watching every port on the east coast!" taunted one. "You'll never get him out. Give it up now." As he talked his companion edged round to Felix's left side. They would soon get him in between them and then he'd be in trouble. He punched the iron tip of the staff at the man to the left, discouraging him at least but the other came at him

521

at once and he only just parried the sword with his staff, losing a great splinter from it in the process. Then one man struck high and the other low at his shins; he twisted awkwardly and survived but one end of his staff was chopped off in the swift exchange of blows.

He glanced towards Ned. Spearbold had drawn his sword and Agnes held her knife out with a grim expression on her pale, young face. Again the two men attacked him and this time they forced him back. Spearbold moved to Felix's left to try to distract one of the men at arms. Thus when the next assault came only one carried it through with purpose and Felix used the broken point of the staff as a lance against him, driving him back with sharp thrusts.

A gasp from behind him made him turn. Spearbold was on his back with his opponent standing over him. God! If you value this sinner, he prayed silently, please wake up Ned Elder now!

But Ned was not waking up. Instead, as the man at arms lifted his sword to plunge it down into Spearbold's quivering body, Agnes ran forward and brought her knife up under his jack and into his belly. Felix marvelled at the girl's strength - yet there seemed to be nothing to her. Spearbold rolled over onto his knees and got to his feet to help her as the wounded man roared at her and tried to slash at her with his sword. Agnes clung close to her victim so that he could not hit her with the blade. Clever girl, thought Felix, as he turned back to face his own adversary and pushed him back again with the point of his staff. To his surprise, he found Black retreating towards him - these fellows must be amongst Warwick's best men, he mused. Black was no novice.

"Look to Spearbold!" said Black, drawing out his long knife. "I'll hold these two."

Felix was horrified to find that somehow Agnes was laid out on the grass and Spearbold was sprawled on all fours. The wounded man was bending down to pick up his fallen sword. Felix reversed his hold on the staff and swung the iron shod end with as much force as he could muster. It struck the man on the head as he was half way back up. All heard the crack as his neck shattered and he dropped like a sack of corn.

"Oh, shit!" cried Black. Felix turned back to help him; he had been hit in the ribs by a sword thrust. It was madness, madness. A sword sliced along Felix's shoulder and he whirled around to deliver a swift blow to the man's chin. Black launched himself angrily at the last man, bludgeoning him back mercilessly, pounding his sword until his opponent could no longer parry it.

"I yield!" he cried, "I yield!"

"Too late," Black's words growled back at him and he brought his sword down onto shoulder and into chest. Then with disdain he put his foot on the dead man's heart and wrenched out the blade.

"Are you alright?" Felix asked him.

"Better than him," murmured Black, kicking the corpse at his feet. "Look to the others." He sat down and leant against a tree.

Felix insisted on examining Spearbold and Agnes but found they had sustained only cuts and bruises.

"They're fine," he said, returning to Black. The grizzled warrior was still sitting upright but he had laid his sword down beside him. Felix sighed long and hard. "Lord, bless us all," he muttered, for Black lay still. His wound had been mortal and he must have known it too, thought Felix.

Just then Ned stirred and tried to lift himself up.

Felix looked up at the heavens and shook his head. "Thank you, Lord," he said, "but a little earlier would have been kinder."

Within a few moments, however, Spearbold already had Ned sitting up and Agnes gave him some of the liquid she had made up for the pain. He stared about him, confused and hurting.

"I was by the stables..." he mumbled. "Where am I now?"

"We'll answer your questions by and by, my lord," replied

Spearbold, "but you must take it very carefully at first."

"Never mind carefully," said Felix. "Get him on a horse."

§§§§

30th May dawn, Hartlepool

Ned sat looking at the wharves and dilapidated warehouses of the small port of Hartlepool, still partly shrouded in mist. He could remember little of the ride but he knew that much had been sacrificed to get him there. As the ship edged out towards the harbour entrance, he could still make out the tall figure on the dockside saluting him with a final lazy wave of his arm.

He turned to Spearbold beside him. "Did ever a man have such a friend?" he asked.

"Indeed my lord, you have many friends but none greater than Felix of Bordeaux."

The motion of the vessel was already beginning to churn his stomach and they had only travelled a hundred yards, if that. It did not augur well. Agnes wrapped a woollen blanket around his shoulders and he smiled at her. She hugged him and stayed next to him with her arm in his.

"Spearbold," said Ned, "I have so many questions, I fear it will take the whole journey to answer them; but first tell me: have I left others in danger? Is there aught more I should have done?"

"You have left some in difficulty, my lord; but they will cope. You've left your sisters and Sir Stephen and young men such as Hal; but they will survive. You must look to your own future now - and I mean your immediate future. You're lucky to be here at all - thank loyal men and a sea mist for that. You're a free man as long as you do not return to England for five years. But you're attainted, so you have no lands, nothing. You must think what you will do in those years, how you will live - and ...there's Agnes to think of too."

"But what will I do, Spearbold?" he asked. "All I've ever known is left behind."

§§§§ §§§§ §§§§ §§§§

Author's Note: Rebels & Brothers

This is the second story in the Wars of the Roses series entitled Rebels & Brothers. Readers of the first book, Feud, will recall that it ended with many "loose ends." This was intentional as the series should be treated as an ongoing story. At the end of both books the central storyline has been brought to a conclusion but other, as yet minor, storylines remain in the air. The story will continue in book three. Where will Ned go? Will Eleanor go to Crag Tower? Will Emma take holy orders? Will Hal ever see Agnes again? Well, for the moment, you'll have to wait and see.

To find out more about the series and future developments as they occur, or to contact me, you can go to my website: www.derekbirks.com.

I also have a blog: www.dodgingarrows.wordpress.com.

Or you can follow me on Twitter as @Feud_writer.

My Facebook page is: www.facebook.com/feudwriter.

DEREK BIRKS

Historical Notes

The Wars of the Roses

Everyone knows about the Wars of the Roses – or do they? The range of historical opinion is so broad and varied on this whole period that I could not hope to do more than follow a consistent thread of narrative through it. Besides adhering to an accurate chronology of the events, I have also tried to set the events between the Elders and Warwick within a recognisable late fifteenth century context. Within that context, the rivalry between the Nevilles and Percies was very important.

Whenever the story encounters an actual person I have attempted to create a character who would at least be recognisable to students of the period. Since this story uses Richard Neville, Earl of Warwick and William Hastings as important named characters I have endeavoured to make them as believable as possible. For example, Warwick was in York during the period described in the book, though of course his actions in this story are completely fictitious.

The Lancastrian Rebellion in the North

For the first three years of his reign, the young Yorkist King, Edward IV, faced opposition from adherents of the deposed Lancastrian King, Henry VI. The major instigator of this opposition was the Queen, Margaret of Anjou, who was tireless in her efforts to help her husband recover his throne. Chief amongst the rebel lords were Ralph Percy and Henry Beaufort, Duke of Somerset. Both had been pardoned by King Edward and he was especially annoyed by their return to the old King. Both, it seems, did so out of conscience, regretting their earlier compliance.

The events of Somerset's campaign in the north, including the battle of Hedgeley Moor, are faithfully adhered to, aside from Ned's involvement, though I have given Ralph Percy a fictional conversation with Ned at the end which seeks to show a possible meaning of his alleged enigmatic last words: "I have saved the bird in my bosom."

The King's Secret Marriage in 1464

It is accepted that Edward IV married Elizabeth Woodville in secret, most likely on 1st May. The marriage was unpopular, which is why Edward kept it a secret, because the court expected a foreign marriage and Elizabeth was a widow from a Lancastrian family of middling birth. No-one is too sure whether Hastings knew about the marriage or not. I don't believe that he saw it coming but I think he was so close to the king that he must have known about it and could have been involved in bringing it about, as I have implied in the story. My representation of the actual marriage is based on what is known and surmised from what little evidence refers to it.

When the marriage was announced at Reading in October 1464, the Earl of Warwick and others were most put out. One of the main reasons for their concern was that Elizabeth brought with her a large family, most of whom would need to be provided with appropriate marriages. The result, many suspected, would be poorer prospects for other nobles and Warwick had two marriageable daughters of his own.

Coverham Abbey and the Praemonstratensian Monks - the White Canons

The order took a more pragmatic approach to their worship than some other orders and believed in going out into the community to fulfil pastoral roles in parish churches. There seems to be some doubt about who the abbot was in 1464 and my abbot is therefore entirely fictional as is Canon Reedman. Coverham Abbey remains now only in a few ruined fragments.

The Cliffords of Skipton

There is a reference in the story to the Clifford family taking back their castle at Skipton in 1464. The Cliffords had been staunch supporters of the old king, Henry VI of Lancaster and Lord Clifford was killed in the skirmishes that took place before the battle of Towton in 1461. In Feud, my account of his death cannot be far wide of the mark though of course Ned Elder was not actually there! Clifford's widow and young son took back Skipton Castle against a backcloth of the Lancastrian revival in the north and some feared that the unrest was spreading to North Yorkshire. It wasn't - at least not in 1464.

Other Place References

Yoredale is the old name for the valley of the river Ure, now called Wensleydale, an area once much more heavily forested than it is now. Ned's home, Elder Hall, if it existed would lie near the river Ure and the Radcliffes' Yoredale Castle would be further east and higher up the northern slope of Wensleydale. Nearby is the giant Neville stronghold at Middleham; it is a ruin now but it is still possible to get a measure of the majesty of this palatial residence.

Yoredale Castle is fictional but bears some resemblance to one or two castles in the Yorkshire Dales. Crag Tower is also fictional but is typical of the kind of small fortified castle in the border regions. Castles referred to at Newcastle and Morpeth are as accurate as I could make them. Regarding Bamburgh Castle, anyone who stands in the sand dunes below it will get much the same view as Ned Elder did.

Regarding North and South Shields, it was the case that the Newcastle authorities tried to limit the trade there as they saw it as a potential threat to their own revenues from customs duties for example. Hence the fictional Ship's Master, James Finch, was reluctant to stop there.

The scene which takes place on a section of what is referred to as "the ancient's wall" - or Hadrian's Wall to us - is set in a real place: the ruins of Brunton Turret. Brunton Turret would have been less ruined in 1464, as would much of the wall. Stone has been robbed out over the centuries but even today you can see the remains of the turret and can perhaps imagine Ned's stand there.

Derek Birks
October 2013

CPSIA information can be obtained at www.ICGtesting.com
Printed in the USA
LVOW06s1956131115

462480LV00009B/791/P